Mr Splitfoot

Samantha Hunt

corsair

CORSAIR

First published in the US by Houghton Mifflin Harcourt in 2016
First published in Great Britain by Corsair in 2016

1 3 5 7 9 10 8 6 4 2

All characters and events in this publication, other than those clearly in the public domain, are fictitious and any resemblance to real persons, living or dead, is purely coincidental.

A CIP catalogue record for this book
is available from the British Library.

ISBN: 978-1-472151-59-9 (hardback)
ISBN: 978-1-472151-58-2 (paperback)
ISBN: 978-1-472151-60-5 (ebook)

Printed and bound in Great Britain by CPI Group (UK) Ltd., Croydon, CR0 4YY

Papers used by Corsair are from well-managed forests and
other responsible sources

MIX
Paper from
responsible sources
FSC® C104740

Corsair
An imprint of
Little, Brown Book Group
Carmelite House
50 Victoria Embankment
London EC4Y 0DZ

An Hachette UK Company
www.hachette.co.uk

www.littlebrown.co.uk

Once again there are more
dead things than ever before.

— MARTHA ZWEIG

1 We are approaching the greatest of mysteries.
We float like a mote of dust in the morning sky.
We know that this is impossible.

2 We the people.
We believe all the words which thou hast spoken.
We cannot understand the words.
We fled all that day into the wilderness, even until it was dark.
We commanded the rocks and the mountains to fall upon us to hide us.
We will, we will rock you.

3 We cross this great water in darkness.
We lost a great number of our choice men.
We will change them into cedars.
We see there was no chance they should live forever.
We will change them into cedars.

4 We have spoken, which is the end.
We should call the name.
We should call the name.
We know that this is impossible.

FAR FROM HERE, THERE'S A CHURCH. Inside the church, there's a box. Inside the box is Judas's hand." Nat is slight and striking as a birch branch.

"Who cut it off?" Ruth asks. "How?"

But Nat's a preacher in a fever. His lesson continues with a new topic. "Baby deer have no scent when they are born." Nat conducts the air. "Keeps those babies safe as long as their stinking mothers stay far away." This is how Nat loves Ruth. He fills her head with his wisdom.

"My mom doesn't stink."

"You don't even know who your mom is, Ru."

"Of course I do. She's a veterinarian. She already had too many animals when I was born."

"I don't believe you."

Ruth looks left, then right. "OK. She's a bank robber. When you're asleep, she brings me money."

"Where's all the cash, then? Are you hiding it in some big cardboard box?"

So Ruth swerves again, returning to the version of a mother she uses most often. "I mean my mom's a bird, a red cardinal."

"A male? Your mom's a boy?"

"Yeah."

"No, she isn't. She's a stone. Bones. I spit on her." Nat steals confidence from thin air.

Ruth pulls her long dress tight across bent knees. She doesn't even know enough about mothers to fabricate a good one. Her idea of a mother is like a non-dead person's idea of heaven. It must be great. It must be huge. It must be better than what she's got now. "I'm just saying, wherever she is, she doesn't stink."

Nat flips the feathers of his hair. "Wherever she is. Exactly." He holds his hand in a ray of sunlight. "I'm here now." He lifts the hand that touched light up to her ear, squeezing the lobe, an odd, familiar affection between their bodies. Nat touches the scar on her face, tangled knots of tissue, keloid dots on her nose and cheeks. "Do you know how they deliver mail to the bottom of the Grand Canyon?"

"No."

"I taught you this before. Please." Nat is cruel or Nat is gentle. Nat hates/loves Ruth as much as he hates/loves himself. He'll say, "Sleep on the floor tonight" or "I'm taking your blue coat. I like it" or "Stop crying right now." But he'll also say, "Eat this" and "You can dance, girl" and "Stay the fuck away from Ruth, or I'll slice your ear cartilage off and give it to a dog to chew on." When the Father raises a switch, Nat gives his back. "Are you just someone who wants to stay stupid?"

"No. Tell me."

"Mules."

She wrinkles her nose.

"Don't believe me? You're welcome to shop elsewhere."

"I believe you. You're the only shop in town."

They are alone in Love of Christ!'s bright living room. They are happiest when they are alone together. "Tell me what you know about light."

"Not much."

"It's the fastest thing in the world."

"Faster than Jesus?"

"Way faster than Jesus."

Dust turns before her eyes. "OK. I believe you."

Nat looks right at her, smiles. "What killed Uncle Sam?"

She imagines a forgotten relative, an inheritance, a home. "Who's that?"

"Samuel Wilson, the meatpacking man once called Uncle Sam. Symbol of our nation? He's buried just down the road apiece. You didn't even know Uncle Sam was dead."

"I didn't know Uncle Sam was a real person. What killed him?"

"Stupidity, girl. Stupidity."

His, she wonders, or mine?

Nothing is near here, upstate New York. The scope of the galaxy seems reasonable. Light, traveling ten thousand years to reach Earth, makes sense because from here even the city of Troy, three miles away, is as distant as Venus. What difference could ten thousand light years make? Nat and Ruth have never been to Manhattan.

The Love of Christ! Foster Home, Farm, and Mission is a brick bear spotted with mange. Handiwork from days past—ledge and brace doors, finger-joint chair rails, and hardwood floors—is being terrorized by state-provided, institutional, indestructible furniture common to dormitories and religious organizations. The house's wooden floors are smooth as a gun butt. In summer *Drosophila melanogaster* breed in the compost pile. Each snaggletooth of a homestead constructed during the Civil War pleases Father Arthur, lord of the domain, founder of Love of Christ! "Hand of the creator," he says. Clapboards that keep out only some of the wind; sills that have slipped off square; splinters as long as fingers. The house is always cold with a useless hearth since the State frowns on foster home fireplaces. "Meddlers!" Father Arthur unleashed his rage against bureaucracy, using a sledge on the innocent, elderly chimney. Now once a day when the sun reaches alignment, a sliver of light shines into the house through the busted-up flue, a precise astronomical calendar if anyone knew how to read it.

At Love of Christ! children feel the Lord, and the Lord is often furious and unpredictable, so Father Arthur cowers from corrupting influences. No Walt Disney, soda pop, or women's slacks pass his threshold. The children milk goats, candle and collect eggs, preserve produce, and make yogurt from cultures they've kept alive for years. Blessed be the bacteria. The children remain ignorant of the bountiful mysteries filling the nearby Price Chopper.

Boys at Love of Christ! wear black cotton pants and solid tops from a limited palette of white, tan, or brown. The girls wear plain dresses last seen on *Little House on the Prairie* reruns. Simple fabric, a few pale flowers, a modest length for working. Fingernails are clean and rounded. Teeth are scrubbed with baking soda. The old ways survive, and seasonal orders dictate.

But—like the olivine-bronzite chondrite meteor that surprised a Tomhannock Creek farmer back in 1863—corruption has a way of breaking through. New charges arrive with words from the outside: mad cow disease, La-Z-Boy recliner, Barbie doll.

"You know what Myst is?" Ruth asks Nat.

"M.I.S.T. Yes. A secretive branch of the Marines. Surprised you've heard of it." He works with more confidence than facts.

"I thought it was a video game."

"Video game? What's that?"

When they had mothers, Nat's read him books and fed him vitamins until a bad man bit off the tip of her right breast and told her he'd be back for the left one. She didn't stop driving until she reached New York State. She left Nat at a babysitter's house, disappearing with a hero from the personal ads, a man who appreciated firm thighs more than tiny kids and perfect breasts. Nat set fire to his first group home. No one died.

Ruth never knew her mom, but when she was young, her sister, Eleanor, lived at Love of Christ! El was like a mom. She petted Ruth at night, told Ruth she was beautiful despite the messed-up scar on her face. "When you were a baby," El said, "you used to point at birds." Then Eleanor turned eighteen.

"Real sorry." The Father woke them with a fist on the door. "Time to go." El jumped up. Ruth froze cold. She was only five. El stalled her departure in the driveway, but Ruth didn't appear. "Bye," El spoke to the house. No sign of Ruth. No blood vow to find one another once El got settled. It would be a long time before El would be able to come for her, if El, an unemployed eighteen-year-old, would ever be able to come for her five-year-old sister. Ruth breathed into the window upstairs, looked down on the driveway scene, a surgery in some anatomy theater removing the only familiar thing she'd ever known. El was leaving in the truck. Ruth had no idea where it would take her. A bus station? The YWCA? Some mall parking lot in the capital with eighty bucks and a crucifix from the Father in her bag? Ruth pushed harder into the pane. A black thread, lashed around the chrome bumper, yanked an organ from Ruth's chest, dragged it in the dirt behind the Father's truck like a couple of gory beer cans.

Ruth said nothing for two weeks. No one noticed. Eventually the

State brought the Father a replacement, a boy named Nat who'd had trouble with matches and kerosene.

The Word became flesh and lived among them. The Word became flesh and lived among them. "You can be my sister now," Ruth told him. That was the Word.

Nat was also five, small enough to stuff inside the tall white garbage bag of clothes he carried. "All right," he agreed. "Sisters." Nat moved into the room Ruth had shared with El — didn't even change the sheets. One twin bed. They slept foot to face. Two heads on one body, joined like a knave card. Sisters.

Ruth grew. Nat grew. The bed stayed small. Her hair got longer. His beauty sharpened like a vampire's, and while the Father was distracted by meditations on his messiah-hood, fantasizing his interview with *Rolling Stone* magazine and Oprah, some dewy bridge, a bundled corpus callosum, metastasized between the person of Nat and the person of Ruth. Their intimacy was obscene. The Father tried to separate them. It was ungodly, he said, the way Nat and Ruth clung to one another, shared a toothbrush. But Nat didn't want to be separated. He drafted a report, accounts of drunken nights, corporal punishment, food shortages, and the possibility that state funds might have been used kitting out a black-and-orange monster truck the Father calls the Holy Roller. Nat showed his report to the Father. The Father never tried to split them up again.

Nat's T-shirt DIESEL FUMES MAKE ME HORNY defies the dress code. His pants are slung under his pelvis bones. A channel of dark hair points toward his fly because at seventeen — save in the eyes of the State — Nat and Ruth aren't really children anymore.

She curls her spine over bent legs. She holds the folds of her belly. On all fours, Nat rests his head in her lap. "All we need is a room somewhere. We can fix it up." He plays the part of the man.

"And a pair of jeans for me," Ruth says, playing the part of the woman.

"We'll see." Being a man is scary.

"Children! Come unload the van," the Mother calls from the bottom of the stairs. The Mother is a part-time parishioner, part-time wife, part-time drug addict. She's most visible in the residue she leaves after preparing midnight snacks or sneaking a shower. Her infrequent appearances allow the children to believe there is something holy about her, though she looks like the singer in a hair metal cocaine band. Purple velvet pants, high black boots. She's got a homemade permanent wave, and her face is soft, as if termites have had their way with the undercarriage.

"Supplies! Children!"

When the Mother's around and right in the head, she cares for some of the home's daily needs: shopping, cooking, math, science, the mission's tax-free status, state inspections, and a Christmas light display so involved, planning begins in mid-August. She does not follow the Father's partiality for olden times.

"Children! Supplies!" Or, for those who don't cotton to an approaching Armageddon, groceries.

Nat and Ruth join the ranks outside. The Love of Christ! children are a rainbow of deformities.

- Roberta, eleven, and her weird tiny body. She has an old face on a kid's body. She raises stray kittens in the barn, relying on coyotes to cull her pack.
- Tonya, sixteen, sold pencils and blowjobs when she lived in Worcester, Massachusetts, with her aunt. She compares the honeyed days of Worcester to "living on Capri," the Tyrrhenian Sea island she once glimpsed as a photo in an Italian restaurant downtown on Ida Street.
- Colly, fifteen, brown as a mummy, is a boy who thinks he's a girl.
- Vladimir, fifteen, the albino is Colly's bunkmate. He once described to Ruth the pleasures of masturbating in a jar of mayonnaise. She's not touched the condiment since.
- Shauna, twelve, and Lisa, thirteen, are actual sisters. Their mother, another addict, sold them to their uncle when they were nine and ten. He turned them out and made a pretty penny until Shauna was picked up by the cops. They speak in their own language, spare and coded.

- Raffaella, ten, has claw hands from arthritis.
- Sarge, sixteen. Her real name is Sarah. She was a gutter punk who arrived at Love of Christ! with dark insects skittering beneath the skin of her forearms. In the race to be the most messed up, competition is steep between Sarge and
- Tika, fifteen, a big girl who jig-tattooed the word "fuck" across her cheek and spelled it wrong, and
- Ceph, seventeen, whose body seems broad as Niagara and disturbs thinking in the same way. He resembles a scoop of lard. Ceph is angry enough to deform DNA.
- Then there's Nat, seventeen.
- Then there's Ruth, seventeen, and her wormy mess of a scar.

The Father requests damaged wards, parents who are dead, retarded, in jail, all of the above. The more desperate the case, the more money the State gives him. "Got any ugly ones?" The Father doesn't want reunions or adoptions. He doesn't even want scheduled visitations. He wants converts. He wants Jesus Warriors, foster kids for indoctrination, labor, and money to fund his mission.

Still it is not all bad at Love of Christ! The Father takes each child's face in his hands and reminds him or her, "You are the light of the world. You are the light." Most of these children have never heard that before.

Still, the adjustment's not smooth. New arrivals carve filthy words into their dry skin, aching for their absent mothers.

"You know who my mom is?" Colly asks one night. Four boys, two bunk beds. "Barbra Streisand. 'People,'" Colly sings. "'People who need people.'"

Ceph doesn't get the joke. Ceph doesn't know how white Barbra is.

Vladimir on the bunk below calls Ceph a dumbass, so Ceph pins Vladimir to the bed, strikes a lighter, and sets his hair on fire. The room fills with a sticky stench, caramelized and runny. Colly throws a blanket over both boys. Vladimir with scorched hair says nothing. No one tells the Father because the Father fetishizes obedience, developing creative punishments when he should be sleeping.

He withholds food until a child becomes docile. He locks children in the downstairs bathroom. He strikes the soles of their feet with a wooden dowel or sprays a child with a frigid garden hose, then screams at the child to cover his or her immodest, naked body. He issues shunnings, forbidding anyone in the house from speaking to a particularly willful child. The Father practices holding therapy, which sounds tender but entails sitting on a child, pinning the arms and legs to humble and break the will.

And *still* Love of Christ! is better than some of the other options the State has for hard cases. The Father says, "Come with me and you won't have to go back to public school, where just now a gang of sixteen-year-old thugs with nunchucks are anxious to sprinkle your teeth across the linoleum of F Wing. I have clothing, beds, food, and clean lavatories. I have a purpose for you, labor and the Lord. I have farm animals." Other foster kids bounce from home to home and school to school, but the Father never lets a child go. He deposits checks from the State and makes up a list of chores. "Stay," he says, imagining he's a savior performing rescues — and, in some rank way, he is.

The children make a human chain from van to kitchen, hefting bags of groceries into the house. It's hard to be the light of the world.

The Mother calmly praises their work. "Such strength. Such cooperation." She sings, "'Ride on, ride on, in Majesty!'" clapping the rhythm. She sings, "'Mama, Mama, I'm coming home,'" an insensitive choice from Ozzy Osbourne but one of her favorites. The children unpack supplies into the pantry, so happy to have food in the house again. Not many American children get to know how lucky they are on such a regular basis.

The Father supervises from the doorjamb, nodding, praising the Mother in turn. "The very spirit of love, sister." They'll be getting it on later.

Raffaella hefts a twenty-pound bag of rice. Her arthritis is not bad today. "The Father and I prayed hard last night. God took away the pain." Sometimes God takes away the pain, sometimes God sticks it back in, twisting the knife tang.

The Mother points at the kitchen crucifix, an emaciated thing. "Magnificent."

Ruth takes a long peek down her nose. "Yeah. Jesus is a hottie." Ruth does love Jesus, same way she loves Lincoln, Robin Hood, Martin Luther King, and Nat. Handsome men who fight for justice.

After morning chores comes school. The Father walks with the children out to the barn, a pied piper fantasy of the little children coming unto the Lord—if the Lord looked like a pale electronics department clerk. The Father wears natural-fiber clothing that he scrubs and starches before re-ruffling in an approximation of ancient Jerusalem chic. Every morning the Father braids his long hair, smoothing the split ends with beeswax. He coats his skin with a homebrewed sunscreen. He takes a spoonful of ground flaxseed and a spoonful of turmeric powder in his nightly goat's milk. He self-administers a coffee colonic on the fifteenth of each month. On the sixteenth, he reports any visions experienced during the purge. And every now and then, he loses control, drinking nothing but Canadian whiskey for three days. The visions he receives when drunk are a different sort of sight.

On a steely cherry tree, Ruth keeps a feeder she made from a pie tin. Birds hop in the grass below, eating rejected seeds. A couple of sparrows, a few starlings, but every now and again a goldfinch or cardinal in his brilliant red coat. Hello, Mom.

Sarge opens the barn door, a huge thing on wheels and runners. There's no heat inside. A number of plain benches rule the wooden floor. The goats are penned in the northern corner. The rafters reach high as a cathedral. Cobwebs too dusty for spiders drape the gables. The loft is filled with onion racks, devices of torture, traces of hay, urine, and hide. "Cold in here."

"And Christ suffered." The Father smiles. They enter the sanctuary, where he thrills his small congregation with vitriolic sermons each Saturday, the real Sabbath, so says the Father, so says the mission. The Father nods at the cross. "Yes, indeed. The Lord is reigning from the tree." Ruth hears, The Lord is raining, leaving her with a kindly, catholic idea of God. God is the tree. God is the light. God is the rain that falls on everyone, even girls with ugly scars.

If you ask the Father what denomination, his answer is, "I follow the Bible. Heard of it?" Father Arthur takes from the Baptists, the Episcopalians, and the Evangelists. Ruth trusts Nat's assessment of their caretaker best: "Part hippie, part psychopath."

Public schools, zoning boards, and outsiders terrify him. They hide the devil and a bottle of booze. Before he was the Father, he was a drunk in Buffalo on the jam band circuit. That's where he met the Mother. They'd drink and drug until the Lord saw fit to save their souls again. The hill is steep, but the Lord is full of forgiveness.

The Father rests one butt cheek on a stool set beside the lectern, like a folksinger in a coffeehouse. "Now. Where were we? The Jews? Yes, the Jews."

Ruth speaks out of turn. "Jews invented eyeglasses."

The Father is astonished. "Children, do we speak without being called on?"

No one answers.

"We do not. And where in God's glorious kingdom did you get that idea?"

She's not sure. It was just there in her head. She's never even met a Jew, but she wanted to give them something, a weapon, eyeglasses, before the Father tears them down. Ruth shrugs.

"Let me ask again, the Jews?"

A number of hands shoot into the air; the children are anxious to placate the Father, to keep him at simmer.

"Yes, Tonya."

The girl contorts her face in thought. She stands, hands clasped in front of her womb, the way the Father told her ladies stand. "Umm."

"Begin again. No hesitation."

"Right." Tonya steadies her eyes. "Jews murder their children through abortion and Christ rejection."

"Good."

Tonya blushes in the blessing of correctness.

"And let's not forget—slayers of Christ. Now, the Catholics?" The Father scans for volunteers, *Price Is Right* style. "Colly?"

Colly stands, the only black kid at Love of Christ! The Father keeps Colly around to defend against charges of racism. Or to have a whipping post.

"Posture."

Colly fluffs his sternum. "Mary was a sinner who masturbated in public."

"Indeed. And what does God have in store for brothers and sisters who are selfish with their pleasures?"

"Fires of hell." Like a platter of toothpicked cold cuts.

The Father steers the children from eternal death. "Undeniably. Watch for the cloven toe." He eyes Colly. "I've told you of my profligate uncle and the night we dragged his drunken body from a charred mobile home up in Mooers?"

"Yes, sir. Last week. And the week before."

"Flesh bubbled, burnt blacker than you even." The Father looks up thoughtfully. "And oddly yellow in places where the pus fat had boiled to bursting. I can't help but think of him when I see you, son."

"Yes. You've told me, sir."

"Burnt," the Father repeats. "Slave to intoxicants."

"So you've said."

"Just checking. Because it's important to Christ. He wants to forgive you. He wants to forgive all of us."

"Yes, sir."

The Father nods, smiles, moves on. "Good. So, Nat. Mormons."

"Mormons are just like you and me."

The other children hold their breath.

The Father sounds a dull buzz. "Just like us?" Slowly, chuckling. "We kidnap blond children and sodomize them while wearing magic underpants?" A number of the students snicker. The Father joins them in this laugh. Ruth looks to Nat. Ruth's hair is brown. "I've always appreciated your vivid imagination, Nat, but this is our history, and history asks us for facts, not fiction. Take a seat, son."

The Father mopes, staring at his shoes. "Ruth? How can I sleep at night when your soul will roast in perdition?" He's overcome by his sorrow. "Tell me how you love Jesus. Tell me how you adore his flesh and spirit." When the Father speaks of Jesus, it's so intimate it embarrasses Ruth, like he's talking about his penis or a case of hemorrhoids. Other days, better days, the Father mentions grace, mercy, and the majestic beauty of God's promised kingdom. Once Ruth even heard him say, "Christians glory in the well-being of others." But not today.

"I don't know, Father Arthur. I don't know what you want me to say."

"Correct." He blooms into a smile. "Tomorrow," he announces, "Muslims!"

Ruth takes a seat, and the Father begins the day's lesson on the chalkboard, geometric proofs detailing how the three branches of American government — executive, legislative, and judicial — are a false trinity. The lesson is long. The Father includes stops along the way at the Declaration of Independence, the Emancipation Proclamation (big smiles to Colly) and *Roe v. Wade.* The Father knows the story of history and manages to actually educate the children by teaching them to think and ask questions, to not accept the rubbish they hear, especially his rubbish.

Every day the lesson winds up at the Apocalypse. Total financial collapse, hurricane, earthquake, or nuclear war — it makes no difference to him. The Father used to prepare to survive the Apocalypse, spending the State's money on rations and rifles. He taught the children skills to live through the devastation: farming, engineering, dowsing, husbandry, canning, intermediate nursing, and marksmanship to destroy the hungry hordes moving north from the city. Then one morning, coming off a binge, John 2:15 came to him. "If any man love the world, the love of the Father is not in him." At breakfast he told the children, "I don't want us to survive." He looked around the room. "What was I thinking, children? Trying to forestall the time when we will dwell with Heavenly Father in paradise? I must have been nuts." Which, of course, he was.

When the Father's done, he asks, "Ruth? You ready?" Once a

week, as a senior student in his school, she's allowed to teach the other children about birds.

Ruth straightens her dress. "Thank you." In a quiet voice she tells the others, "This week, you might be interested in the Red-Eyed Vireo." She flips through her *Peterson Field Guide*, a present from the Father last Christmas, her only present and a generous one, as most books are not allowed at Love of Christ! "These birds build cup-shaped nests in the forks of trees and fall victim to brood parasitism at the hands of the cowbird. Does anyone know what that means?"

No volunteers.

"That's when cowbirds slip their eggs into the vireo's nest so they won't have to raise their own babies." Ruth moves through mating habits, habitat, diet, and migration patterns. "The good news is vireos spend their winters in South America."

After class, more chores. The Father retires to his private quarters, bolting his door. Rumors say he's got his liquor, an Internet connection, and the only phone in the house in there.

Outside the barn there's a plastic playhouse partially melted by vandals with a roofing torch. The Father keeps it around as a metaphor. Ruth thinks of her melted face, her endangered soul.

Nat and Ruth wash clothes in the laundry room. She handles undershirts; he pairs the piles of socks. Alone with Nat, a perfect place can exist, their own terrarium. "Nat." She lifts a clean shirt. He smiles. Her nose detects the alkylbenzene sulfonate surfactant in the laundry soap. She twitches. A sneeze mounts in her lower meatus. She swallows it.

They carry the damp bedclothes out to the drying line, the light of the long afternoon sun. In the yard behind the house, they hang blankets and sheets to dry. Nat makes a hidden place for them in the linens, away from the other kids. Ruth sweeps some dried leaves into a nest. He grabs her arm. "Pretend you're my wife. Lie underneath me."

She lies down. He takes his place on top of her. Two flat, straight, clothed bodies. Nat pins her to the earth, and Ruth doesn't flinch, doesn't even brush a hard stem or stick from her neck. They feel one another through their clothes, all the systems of their bodies—circulatory, respiratory, others whose names they can't remember just then. They don't kiss or grope. They're sisters. Some time passes, some birds overhead. Nat stands, dust his knees, and returns to hanging laundry.

"Wait," Ruth says. "Pretend I'm your wife still, but pretend I cheated on you with your boss. You have to punish me."

"All right."

Nat lashes her to the clothing line with imagined ropes. He lifts her dress over her head. He beats her bare back with a real stripped branch, gently at first. "Jezebel. Judas." When he strikes, rainbows are released from her skin. Three, four, five. She feels it. He lets in the air. Nine, ten lashes until finally she says, "That's good. Thanks."

Six damp sheets make a house. The afternoon sun warms the small room. If this were a Father-approved Christian teen movie, *Chastity and Adam* or *In the Sheaves,* this would be the moment where the young sweethearts feel God's love burning into them and the righteousness of their lives, imagining their wedding day. But Nat and Ruth—having just finished a tidy whipping—are not a Christian movie. "Sinners," he says.

"Jesus doesn't mind. He's like us. He is us."

"You're Jesus?"

"Sure. And you. Your mom. Telephone poles, flowers."

"Fried chicken?"

"Sure."

They return to the house more twisted into one another than they'd been the day before.

After chores, the Mother, and thus dinner, cannot be found. This is not unusual.

The Father doles out three dollars and sixty-five cents per child. They pile into the pickup. He drives to town. The Father says, "Heavenly Deity, we are grateful for these gifts we are about to receive." The Father waits while the children get supper at Hook's Diner. Hamburgers cost two twenty-five. The waitresses scowl at the non-tipping orphans. The other diners stare at the children's clothing, wondering if they are involved with a historical reenactment museum.

Nat and Ruth pool their funds for an open-faced roast turkey sandwich with gravy. Roberta eats a slice of apple pie, pocketing the rest of her cash so she's got some savings. It's risky. Things get stolen in the home. Underwear, food, toothbrushes, money, of course, photos of strangers. Many of these stolen items end up in Nat's dresser drawers.

The Father storms through room check. "I will plow your fallow ground! I will plant the seeds of understanding! I will cut off the ugly head of self-centeredness in you like a venomous viper in a baby's crib. Draw into a quiet shell and obey!" Spit flies. The Father crushes his fists together, wondering what Trojan den of iniquity his wife disappeared into today. He imagines her dancing on tabletops. He falls down to his knees and back up again, amazing feats of strength powered by jealousy. "Now let me hear you sing praises to God!" which confuses a number of the children. Draw into a quiet shell or sing? The Father passes out state-mandated anti-psychotics to some, Adderall to most. The Father starts a hymn. "And if the devil doesn't like it, he can sit on a tack!" He claps his hands while Ruth, Nat, and the other children join in. A blessed day at Love of Christ! comes to an end.

INDEMNITY IS A SUM PAID from A to B by way of compensation for a particular loss suffered by B. From eight-thirty until nine in the morning, I skim through claims. Three house fires. Seven no-fault car accidents. A flood. One act of vandalism. Who is responsible? That depends. I gulp cooling coffee. I don't handle business claims or life insurance. I make phone calls. After lunch I have an inspection in the field. I check the battery on my camera. By nine-thirty I need a break. I fire up my computer and run a search on Lord's wife, Janine. Nothing new. No obituary or anything. A couple of old records she broke in high school track and a picture from when she worked in real estate. Two eyes, a nose, and a mouth. Hair on her head. There's nothing special about Lord's wife.

I click a link to a house in Budapest where the carpeting cost four hundred seven dollars a square foot. My coworker Monique comes by. I show her the carpeting. "What's the big deal?" she asks, squeezing the bridge of her nose. Monique settles into her cubicle, sniffling mucus down her throat. "I'm oozing like a slug." From a blister pack, Monique pops a capsule brewed with such lovely stuff as guaifenesin, hydroxypropyl methylcellulose, sodium carboxymethyl, and magnesium stearate. A little something to get the chemical day started.

I compare prices on a couple pair of shoes, break off the corner of a nut-'n'-strawberry-flavored fruit breakfast bar. Overhead a fluorescent flickers. I order the more expensive pair and experience a feeling of euphoria. Having made the correct shoe choice, I now understand the nature of mystery in the universe. I now belong to a tribe of shod people. Waves of enthusiasm and moral righteousness inflate me straight up to heaven.

I click to check the weather. I read some news about Hollywood. The actor we thought was gay is gay, and this warms me, being part of a human crisis, tucked in with the rest of you who also knew he was gay, and Look! We were right. I search for a rice pudding recipe, my favorite. I cultivate a public persona based on my love of rice pudding. The girls in my college dormitory knew me as such, and now the people I work with share the same truth. I no longer wrestle with the challenges of identity. I am the woman who likes rice pudding, who wears fantastic shoes.

At ten I visit the ladies' room, hoping it will be empty. It's not. Denise is there. Denise handles life insurance, all the fraud and fun. Denise self-tans. She dabs her lipstick and glares at me. "Cora. Kind of rhymes with whore." She smiles at herself in the mirror, tossing the brown paper towel with her purple lip impression into the trash before leaving. The door shuts.

"Denise," I mutter. "Kind of rhymes with fucking twat."

Back at my computer, I e-mail Kendra in sales: "Denise eats donkey dick." I e-mail Joe in security: "Just saw Denise Clint stealing toilet paper from the ladies' room. Again."

Her boyfriend, Mike the claims inspector, flirts with me. B.F.D. We had lunch once, and he spent the whole time talking about her. He told me Denise likes it rough, as if that were something really special, as if she's an angel come down from heaven because she likes her heinie paddled. Mike went starry-eyed thinking about slapping her orange thighs. "She likes it rough? Who doesn't?" I asked. "Who, for Pete's sake, doesn't?"

I do a search for my name. Same as yesterday. Some flight attendant who got fired for throwing hot tea on a passenger; the mug shot of a woman arrested for obstructing justice; some teenage Mormon girl's blog; an adjunct professor of environmental science; then me, insurance adjuster, one-time Daisy girl, one-time honor student, dean's list, et cetera. I live far from the top of the search engine results. This is my cross to bear.

If I plotted a map of every person named Cora Sykes on planet Earth, what would the map look like? What secret history would be revealed? Maybe better not to know.

I check the headlines. I check the traffic. I check on Lord's wife, Janine, again. No change, she's still not dead according to the Internet. I leave for lunch.

Outside a bunch of starlings sit on a wire above the parking lot. I italicize them with my eyes. Copy and paste them right down the phone line. My computer and I spend a lot of time together. Like a dog and its master, I'm starting to look like it, act like it. I ask Google, "Why do I suck?" or "Should I break up with Lord?" I think I can edit/undo things with my mind, say, a cup of spilled coffee or an unintended pregnancy.

Lord is my boyfriend. Weird name, I know. Lord is married to Janine. Lord has romantic delusions about things like girls, hunting, marriage, honor, poetry, the ocean, America, facial hair. He used to be a Marine. Janine, Marine. I could write a poem. He once left a wild turkey on my doorstep, imagining I'd truss it up and serve it to him for dinner. I covered it with a black garbage bag and dragged it out to the curb. Lord grew a mustache to fool me into thinking he's actually a man. Like a real, real man, as in a human male who takes care of someone besides himself. I am the child of a single mom. I don't believe in real men. I also don't believe in the lottery or God. They are stories we tell ourselves at night when we're scared. I'm not scared of anything anymore. I know no one else is going to take care of me.

Lord's in my driveway when I get home from work.

"You want to go camping tonight?"

"Is your wife coming?" I regret that I cannot stop myself from asking these types of questions.

He grips the wheel. "You want to go or not?"

I check with the sky. "All right," I tell him. "All right."

We drive over to the Finger Lakes. We fill his packs with food, clothes, beers, and start our hike as the sun sets. All the while Lord quizzes me about birdcalls, bird species.

"What's that?"

"I don't know, Lord. I just don't know."

"Pileated." His disappointment reeks. "Who doesn't know the pileated woodpecker? Mercy. Were you raised by wolves?"

I shrug.

"No," he says. "Even a wolf would know the pileated woodpecker."

I was raised by Eleanor, my mom. She's not a wolf, but she was pregnant, homeless, and alone at eighteen, so almost a wolf. She still works at least two jobs. She never trusted babysitters so I raised myself. Maybe I'm the wolf.

We hike a mile. It gets dark. Lord's wearing a headlight. I follow along behind, stumbling some. I use the screen of my smartphone to see until the battery goes dead. We build a fire in the woods and eat stew dinner from a can with hunks of cheddar cheese melted on top. Then a few bites from a chocolate bar. Lord belches. "'Let me not to the marriage of true minds admit impediments. Love is not love which alters when it alteration finds, or bends with the remover to remove. O no. It is an ever-fixed—'"

"How'd you learn that?" I've got to tamp him down sometimes.

He coughs. Spits. "I read books. Ever heard of 'em?" Lord's got a hateful streak here in the forest. At home too. But I'm trying to improve myself so I listen to him.

"Some."

"What's that mean, computer girl? What kind of books do you read?"

It takes me a second to say it. Not because I don't know who I am but because Lord throws off a lot of interference. "I like ghost stories."

"Ghost stories suck."

"Why?"

"They aren't real."

"Oh yeah?"

"Yeah." He drinks his beer.

"All stories are ghost stories," I tell him.

"Is that right?"

"Yup." He's making fun of me. I don't care. "You want to hear one?"

"A ghost story?"

"Yeah."

"Fine."

"OK. Ready?"

"Sure."

"Sure. Here we go." But then I don't start yet. I want it quiet, real scary and silent, before I say anything. Let Lord listen to the woods. OK. OK. OK. "You know West Lane, the twisty road that heads out to the highway?"

"Sure."

"Well, it was dark out there one night. It's always dark out there, right? Raining. You know. A dark road. Wet road. No one around." I put plenty of space between each small description. Slowly, slowly. "A man, fella around your age, was driving home on that road, squinting through the raindrops on his windshield when all the sudden there's a pretty girl standing in the street, eight years old, wearing a summer dress, wrong for the weather. Think she was in my cousin's class at school, but I don't remember her name. Maybe you knew her. Anyway, guy slams on the brakes. Right?"

"Right."

I look into the woods. I look at my hands in the firelight. "He tells her to get in. It's freezing, wet, cold. 'Climb in,' he says. 'I'll take you home.' Right?"

Lord nods. "Right," like I'm wasting his time.

"'Thank you,' she says, and I know," I tell Lord, "if you're like me, you think that's the scary part, right? Young girl, bad dude? That's not the scary part. Just hold on. Girl says, 'My mother will be worried.'"

I'm doing my best with the voices, girl's voice high, man's voice low. And both voices slowly, slowly. Scary.

"Then he asks her, 'What are you doing out here alone at night?' The girl was so young and brave, acting like she had no reason in the world to be scared, like she'd never even imagined the bad things men do to girls every moment of every day." I am required to apply guilt to Lord, remind him how much he and, really, all men suck. "'There was a party,' the girl tells the man, or a recital, something like that. I can't remember where she was coming from. But she climbs in his car. 'What address?' he asks. 'Just up over the ridge. You know Horseshoe Hill? Half a mile past that.'

"The two drive on, and it's quiet in the car. He notices she's shivering. 'Take my coat.' He wraps it over her shoulders, a tan windbreaker, a real gentleman or maybe not. Maybe that's what a total creep would do, hard to say because, you know, it could have been a bad situation.

"The rain picked up, lashing the windshield, and he had to concentrate again just to keep the car on the road. It's dark out that way. Finally the girl stops him. 'Here it is. Just there.' And you're like, phew. The little girl made it home safely. A small white cape. Very tidy. You know it? I've looked for it, but I'm not totally sure which one it is. You know it?"

"No."

I watch the fire for a bit, saying nothing. I rub my thighs, pushing them open just the slightest bit to remind Lord what's between them. I look off again into the dark woods beyond our fire. I know Lord's horny because he's always horny, old guy, young girl. But I can't tell if he's scared. I want him to be scared. I watch the woods. I let the story percolate.

"So. The guy pulls over, and the little girl dashes out of the car, darting across the road into the darkness and rain. He can't see where she went or if she made it safely inside because of the rain. For a minute he thinks, 'Forget it. I did my job.' Turns out the guy's not a creep, turns out he's OK. He had parents who loved him. But he's *so* OK that he can't help it. He's worried about the girl. Plus, she has his coat, so he gets out. It's late but the lights are on downstairs in the little house. He rings the bell, and almost immediately an older woman answers the door like she'd been waiting for him. 'Don't say anything,' she tells him, which seems pretty weird. 'Come in.' Still he tries, 'Ma'am,' he says. 'Ma'am, did a young—' She doesn't let him finish. 'My daughter. Yes. Thank you. Please.' She hurries him in. 'Follow me.' The guy is starting to freak out. Everyone's acting weird and all that rain. Still, he follows her. The old woman leads the man upstairs and into a bedroom, a girl's bedroom. He stumbles in and there's a photo of his hitchhiker there on the bureau. 'My daughter,' the old woman says again, but it's impossible that such an old woman could be the mother to such a young girl. He starts to question, 'But—' Again she interrupts. 'Twenty years ago, on a night like this one,' she says, and the hairs on his neck rise. The storm blows. He doesn't want her to go on. Fear's making, you know, static in his head. 'My daughter was killed,' she says. 'Struck down by a car as she walked home. The driver never even stopped to see if she was all right. Now, when it rains, she returns. She comes back, finding a ride with some kind driver. She's home,' the woman said. 'She's home. She's come back again.'

"'No,' he says. 'No. No!' The guy, he runs down the stairs, out the back door. The rain's blinding him and he's lost his bearings. 'I don't believe in ghosts,' the guy keeps telling himself — just like you — clenching his fists. He's terrified, stumbling, trying not to see that right there in front of him, what he thought was a garden is a small graveyard, and in the graveyard is a tombstone and a low rusted wrought-iron fence. 'No. No.' He shakes his head, crazy because there, on top of the grave, is a tan windbreaker, his tan windbreaker, half buried in the muddy churned-up dirt."

Then I get real quiet, watching the fire, nodding my head. Finally, I add the clincher. "Ghosts don't care if we believe in them or —"

"Cora."

"Yeah?" I smile. I scared Lord.

"That's the oldest story in the world."

"What?"

"It's been told a million times. We used to tell it when we were kids. Different location and all, different item of clothing hanging out of the grave, but same story. It's not real."

I straighten my spine. Fucking jerk. "Doesn't mean it's not scary."

"Yup." Lord gives me a wink. "Pretty scary. Pretty, scar — BOO!" He pounces on me and bites into my cheek. Lord smells like boiled pasta. He digs his face into my chest, toggling between my boobs.

"You weren't scared?"

Lord walks away from our campsite as if he's going to take a pee. I shout into the woods. "It's not real?" But Lord doesn't answer and then Lord doesn't come back, so I think it's something a little more involved than pee, but he still doesn't come back. A really, really long time passes, so I know what he's trying to do. He wants me to think the bogeyman got him, think I'm all alone in the woods with a psycho on the loose.

I'm not going to let him do that to me. I put away the dinner dishes, strum his guitar, and later when I can't think of anything else, I just sit there by the fire perfectly still with a fucked-up-looking clown smile on my face. I'm good at that. Lord's too big a jerk to scare me. Orange light flickers on the underside of the tree branches. I think about the little girl who can't stop coming back. I wonder what would make her come back. Love for her mother? Anger at the driver who killed her? Why keep coming back? Why not just stay dead?

Lord doesn't explain anything when he returns. We do it like wild beasts for an hour right there in the dirt, like I'm the innocent little girl and he's the big bad man with the car come to run me down.

Afterward he asks, "Do you want to shoot the gun?"

"Sure." I'm still naked except for my hiking boots. The kick of his gun throws me three feet back. He thinks that's the funniest thing ever. Lord opens more beers. I rub my arm. My shoulder will be bruised yellow for days.

"Janine was nineteen when I met her."

His wife. Every freaking time the man comes, he starts feeling guilty. Every freaking orgasm.

"She was giving haircuts at a house party. Had no idea what she was doing, but the men lined up. Hatchet jobs. Including mine. Janine's so beautiful, like a model almost. I'd let her do anything. She's just so beautiful."

He means: She is; you're not. I want to tell him that she's just normal-looking, nothing too special, but I've never met her and I don't want him to know I stalk her on the Internet. He already thinks he's better than me because he doesn't use the Internet.

"We fell in love in a bloody way, thorns and hooks."

Lord's wiry and strong. "You must have been something at nineteen." I hope that hurts. Lord's old now. Forty-five, at least.

"Yeah. We got hitched and tangled together."

This never stops him from sleeping with me.

"Well," I say. "I can't wait to meet her!"

He keeps a hand on his mustache. "We'd been married a year

when she started screaming about men from the K.C.G. controlling people with solar panels and jet trails."

"What's the K.C.G.?"

"Kancer Containment Guard. Usually they're harmless old men, bumbling and sweet, but sometimes they're evil. They fill juice boxes with strychnine."

Lord looks at me, disappointed again. I put my clothes on. He makes me miss my faithful computer.

"I believed every word she said. I'd even make stuff up myself to confirm it for her. Wall vents, I'd tell her. Suspicious-looking cars. I created bullshit evidence. But then Janine told me my sister Emilia was the head of the K.C.G. and that we needed to kill her." Lord looks at me sideways. "You know my sister?"

I've never met his family.

"Emilia has spina bifida. She was twelve when Janine said that." Lord reaches for another branch for the fire. He pauses for drama. He does that a lot. "I kept Janine home until she brought scissors to bed and tried to use them on my neck. 'I'm cutting your hair!' That's what she was screaming." Lord wraps both hands around his neck, choking himself. "She's in the mental ward of the VA. Take your pill, watch TV, and sometime this afternoon an orderly will change your diaper."

No wonder the Internet doesn't have much to say about her. She's in the loony bin. Lord's wife is locked up like all the wives in a public television British miniseries. No wonder he's so in love with her.

Lord looks up into the dark trees. He's learned a lot from the movies. "Love of my life."

"Well," I say. "That's real nice you love someone, even if it's not me."

And he nods. Like I mean it. Like I actually mean it.

The next day Lord drops me off at the end of my driveway. "I've got to get to the hospital before visiting hours are over." I head up the drive. Purple loosestrife is beginning to bloom.

Eleanor and I live in the caretaker's house on a larger property. The cottage belonged to El's mother. She's dead now. I still live with

El. I pay rent. I buy food. I went to college. I cook and clean. I have a job. El and I get along fine.

She's always working, and work has made her large, strong. She gets mistaken for a dyke or a biker or a dyke biker. She never tells me that I am alive because of her, but I know I am and I'm grateful, since it turns out that getting born is the best thing that can happen for your life.

Sometimes my mom and I go to a bar together, and the man she has her eye on has his eye on me. Though this opens up an unnatural seam between us, El has never turned against me. She's had a couple boyfriends. She lets men visit, but they don't stay. She says, "I like men." But then she'll say, "I like dogs" or "I like toast." The truth is El likes me and not much else.

When I was a girl, there was so little to do around here. We lived with my grandma, a nasty woman. I avoided her, so before I was old enough for school, I was alone much of the time. I'd walk to the end of our driveway, a place of great opportunity where you could go one way or the other. Our street was quiet. Nothing much happened that I remember. No accidents or incidents of road rage. With the noise of other people gone, the sky could open up. The air, the grass, the asters, the stones on the road would take what they wanted, a little blood or breath, some nightmare or earwax. I didn't mind. Nature would nibble, thinning my body out like a piece of burnt film, light streaming through the holes of me. I was as much a part of the natural world as a shredded brown leaf gnawed on by a grub. I'd wait for El to get home from work. She'd join me out on the driveway. She didn't like my grandma either. I'd sit on her lap, and she'd sit on the gravel. She'd pat the skin of my hands, my arms. I'd tell her what I was thinking about holes and nature, and she'd say, "I know just what you mean."

On Monday I head back to Erie Indemnity. "Hello, computer." It never answers me. A girl I know from high school has posted new photos of her husband, her kid. Pictures of her drinking from the lip of a champagne bottle. Headlines say: STOCKS ARE DOWN. GOLD NAIL POLISH IS BEING WORN BY WOMEN IN THE KNOW.

A war is being fought. Another girl I know posted footage of her C-section. I watch the doctor slicing her abdomen open. Her fat looks like last month's ricotta. A guy I knew in college posts a photo of his kid bent over the toilet, vomiting. #puke #sickkid #dayoffwork. Another guy I know posts: "Not much to report here."

I call Lord from the stairwell. There's an elevator in my office building so only total freaks use the stairwell. I leave a message on his cell. "I'm pregnant."

I've known for three weeks, though I have no idea how far along I am. I wasn't paying attention, and I've never had regular periods anyway. Two months? Three months? Maybe even four. I was stuck with some stupid idea that Lord being married to someone else would stop me from getting pregnant. "I'm going to keep it," I tell his voicemail, and after I hang up, I sit alone in the stairwell. I put my hands on my stomach. Somewhere inside there is my baby. I don't care about Lord at all. I don't think I even like him, but this baby, even though it's barely here — some half-dead, half-alive thing — I feel it, and it's something big. To me at least, in all my smallness, this baby is really something very big.

A few days later, Lord calls me back at home. I can hear cars rushing by on his end of the line as if he's standing beside a highway. "You know anything about Safe Haven laws?" he asks.

"Homeland Security?"

"No. You drop a baby off at a hospital or police station. No questions."

"Oh," I tell him. "I'll be fine. I won't need that."

"You don't understand what I'm saying. Anyone can drop the kid off. It doesn't have to be you. You don't need ID. The baby just gets lost, becomes a ward of the state. Say someone were to take your baby. There'd be no way for you to find it again. It disappears into the system because it doesn't have a name. See what I'm saying?"

"You can't stop me from having it."

"And you can't stop me from getting rid of it."

Two weeks of nothing goes by. When Lord calls again, he says he wants to make me dinner.

"You kill something?" The only times he's made me dinner before is after he killed it. Venison with cranberry sauce, roasted duck, squirrel soup.

"No."

One good thing I can say about Lord — like if we were in couples counseling or something and I was required to provide one good quality about him — is that he isn't marked by the fever for documenting each chicken he roasts. He's old enough to have escaped social media. For people my age, including me, if we don't post it, it never happened. People's children will disappear if every ounce of magnificence is not made public and circulated widely. Lord's not like that. He kisses me without considering if we'd look better under a Lo-Fi or Kelvin filter.

"I don't know," I say.

"I've done some thinking, Cora. I've had a change of mind. OK?"

He shows up with a bag of groceries and some wine. I tell him no thanks to the wine. "Right," he says. "Right. You're pregnant." He goes back to the kitchen. He makes spaghetti and meatballs. It's just fine. Store-bought meat. I ask about his sister, and he says, "You ever seen *Rosemary's Baby*? The movie?"

"No. Why?"

"It was on the other night. Good movie."

He clears our plates and brings out two cups of tapioca pudding, one for him, one for me. "Your favorite, right?"

No, but he's trying.

Lord feeds me the first bite. This is strange. "I can feed myself." Tapioca is the unborn eggs of an alien fish species. Someone should design a video game called Tapioca Pudding. Still, he's trying, so I eat some of this disgusting stuff.

He does the dishes, puts everything away, and pulls on his coat, ready to go. "You're leaving?" I figured he was looking for some action. I figured that's why he'd called since I know there's no way Lord wants this baby. He couldn't be a father and keep his drama intact.

"Yeah."

"OK. Bye."

"You mind if I come back to see you again, say, tomorrow or the next day? El will be at work?"

"She's working every night this week." I queer my eyes at him. "Sure, Lord. That'd be fine." I have no idea what's going on in his head, but I think, OK, maybe everything is OK. He wants me, he wants this baby to be fed nutritious food. His wife is locked up in a psycho ward. Good. We say good night, and I go to sleep.

Lord doesn't come back the next night, and do I sit around waiting for him like an idiot? Yes, I do.

But the next, next night, he comes.

"Hi."

"Hi."

He has me undressed in minutes flat. He lays me down on the couch and drops down onto his knees. His tongue is like an infant thing, innocent and damp. I look up when he stops. Lord pulls something out of his pocket, unwraps it. "You don't need a condom. I can't get pregnant twice." He gives me a smile and pushes whatever it is inside me.

I sit up. "What are you doing?"

Lord leans back on his calves like a preschooler. He smiles, guffawing through bucked teeth.

"What'd you put inside me?" I reach down and stick one finger in. "What the fuck is that?" I pull out a slippery white bullet. "What is it, Lord?"

He starts to back away on his knees at first. Then up to his feet.

"Lord?"

He's smiling, laughing into his neck. "It's an abortion."

"What?"

"You took the first part the other night. In the pudding. This is just a follow-up. Probably unnecessary."

"You gave me an abortion?"

"Yeah," he says, and laughs into his shoulder again. "That's pretty fucked up, huh? Right?" he asks. "Right?"

The Internet tells me what's supposed to happen — cramping then bleeding, then no more baby. So I wait, one day, two days, three days. I wait a week. No change. No cramp, no blood. I still feel pregnant. Maybe Lord mixed up the puddings and gave himself an abortion.

I tell the doctor everything. He confirms that I'm still pregnant but can't say how far along. "Well," he tells me slowly. "Your baby will either live or die."

"Right." But what a stupid thing to say. Everyone will either live or die.

"It's wait-and-see or termination. If the fetus survives, there might be damage. The decision is yours." He finishes his exam. "Give it some thought and come see us in a week."

On the drive home, I check the back seat for bad guys so many times, I almost crash into an HVAC truck. I'm alone in the car, but this baby is so small, I cover it with my coat just in case. I wrap my arms around my middle before I dash from the car into our house.

El's not home yet. Tonight I'm going to tell her, just going to say, "Mom, I'm pregnant and Lord's a crazy M.F." The only reason I haven't told her yet is because I'm afraid she'll say, "Get rid of it," and even if that's really good advice, her saying it will mean that all these years she's been wishing she'd been able to get rid of me before it was too late. I don't want to know that.

The house is dark. I try to quiet my mind. I comb my fingers through my hair. It's nighttime in America. Here is a room, my room. There is a bed with a worn spread that has a small hole in it. I haven't any idea what made the hole. A cigarette. An errant spring. A gunshot. There is a shallow closet in the room, a chest of drawers, and a desk lamp with a pale blue glass shade. A framed print of a hunting party hangs on the wall.

The house is still.

What is the scariest thing that can happen? A child can disappear without a trace. A man could follow you at night. Someone could hide behind your bedroom door. There is a small throw rug in the room. There is a wooden chair by the darkening window. There is someone hiding behind my bedroom door.

Anything solid in my neck snaps, and I'm screaming, looking

into this hideous face, like some dark mold, a toxic messy thing. There is a person hiding behind my door. A monster. I cover the baby, backing myself away and into a corner, thinking, Please, Lord. No. I scream, but the monster doesn't grab me. She lets me scream. She stares into the hole of my mouth, and it is a long howl, so much terror, before I recognize her, before I know she won't eat my liver, drink my blood, kill my baby.

I haven't seen my aunt Ruth since I was a kid, but I know it's her because she's got a nasty scar on her face, brown dots and bubbles. My scream turns into a whimper, winding down, shaking off the shock. "Fuck! Fuck! Fuck! You scared me."

When Scout finds Boo Radley hiding behind her bedroom door, she says something that is scary because it is calm. Something like, "Why, there's the man right there, Mr. Tate." Or whatever his name is. Scout's not surprised to find a hollow-eyed monster in the form of Robert Duvall behind her door. She opens a line into magic, possibility. Or mystery, that's a better word than magic. Like an open hole in the ground no one noticed until Scout pointed it out, a place where men with dark secrets live behind every bedroom door. Scout's calm voice says, "The rest of you are blind."

Last time I saw Ruth she was seventeen. She was young then, and she seemed so powerful and tough because looking at her, I wondered how she'd survived her life. How was she there, hair glistening like it had been oiled with star shine, looking like she could box down a mountain?

Their car pulled into our driveway, and I stepped out to see who it was. Wintertime and awfully cold.

"Who are you?" she asked me. At my house. "El's girl?"

"Yeah."

"El had a baby."

"I'm not a baby. I'm eleven. I'm Cora. Who are you?"

"Cora, I'm your aunt Ruth. He's Nat."

El hadn't seen her sister in twelve years. That was a long time to grow apart, and the way my mom spoke of her sister, it was clear

El still thought of Ruth as a little girl. I was surprised when she showed up a woman with a beautiful man, a man I couldn't stop looking at.

El opened her arms. "Ruth? Ruth?" she kept saying, like it was impossible, like Ruth should be dead, not standing there looking like a teenage queen. Twelve years ago El left her sister behind in a group home. Ruth hugged El back. Ruth let a lot slide in that hug.

The first thing she did when she came inside was take off her coat and change the radio station in my mom's kitchen. She wore a tight T-shirt and a pair of new jeans. "Happy New Year," she said. She was amazing. It was January 1st. I remember that. Everything was new. Ruth asked me to dance, and her moves were as confident as a big American car. I was a kid. I flexed my knees to the beat. Ruth could really dance, not in a practiced way but as a person who genuinely felt the music and offered up her own interpretation. There was nothing fast in her actions, slow as a soul singer. She didn't even have to keep time to the music. It stuck to her. I was no match.

Nat, the guy she'd brought, started dancing too, and I thought I'd stop breathing. I was in love with them both. These were human beings, fresh and new, seventeen years old and different than anything I'd ever known. Like I'd never seen color before and then, suddenly, there's blue and green and purple standing in my kitchen on New Year's Day.

Ruth didn't want to dance with Nat. She shoved him when he got close, playing with him. She pulled me onto her lap and took cover behind my body when he tried to partner up with her. I was getting squished in between them and I loved it. Ruth was only six years older than me, but those six years were the difference between eleven and seventeen, a continent's worth of distance. Ruth knew stuff.

El watched from the kitchen table, nodding like the mother of us all, pretending she didn't feel bad doing nothing to look out for her little sister for twelve years. Nat danced and finally Ruth joined him on the linoleum. They started to move like this was the moment they'd practiced for since the dawn of time. I almost had to look away, look away or be ruined, wrecked, unsatisfied forever.

Nat cleaned out my mother's gutters even though it was freezing. I watched him do the whole thing. Ruth and my mom were in the hall. "It's not like that, El. It's not like that between us. He's my sister," Ruth said, which must have hurt El, even if she deserved it.

I went through the things in Ruth's bag, touching holy relics. Soft shirts and pajamas. I held them to my face. A silk purse with cheap gold jewelry inside and all of it brand-new. I stared at her comb, and my heart got seared by what she was. Her toothbrush and a small blue jar of hydrogen peroxide. I swallowed just the tiniest sip. It burned badly, but I knew I'd have her inside me now forever. Ruth was not my mother. I liked my mother fine, but Ruth was like being close to thunder. And then Nat. Lightning.

El cooked hamburgers that night as if we were a family. Things would be different with Ruth around. She'd be my auntie, and my life would be improved by her attentions. She would teach me how to do things El knew nothing about, enjoy music, attract boys. At dinner Ruth said, "So, El," and she giggled. "I got myself emancipated." Leaving unsaid that El never took custody of Ruth.

"How? You marry this guy?" — pointing to Nat.

"No. Nat's too young. Someone else."

El nodded, had a bite.

Ruth changed the subject. "I'll tell you something else funny."

"What?"

"Nat can talk to dead people."

I started to think maybe Ruth was on drugs. Maybe that was what made her shine.

"What?" El looked at Ruth.

"Just like I said. Nat talks to dead people."

El scowled. "How do you manage that?"

He smiled at me. Ruth buried her head in her arm on the table, lifting her eyes to El like she was flirting. El raised her burger to her mouth. "You talk to dead people? I've got an oceanfront lot in Missouri."

"I could probably sell it for you." Nat winked.

"Have you got any dead folks you want him to get in touch with?"

El pushed back from the table. "Sure. Sure." She wiped her lips with a cloth. "You ever try to talk to our mom?"

Ruth sobered, all the light extinguished. "Our mom?"

"Yeah."

"No." Ruth wrinkled. "She's dead?"

"She passed over a year back. I thought they would have told you."

"Nope."

"This is her house. Was her house."

Ruth thumbed her lips. "Is that right? You inherit it?" Ruth looked around with new eyes. "You saw her after you got out?"

El nodded yes, slowly. "I lived with her. Here."

"Then why'd she give us up in the first place?"

El dropped both her feet to the floor, exhaling hard. She shifted forward to stare at the ground. "She didn't give us up, honey. We got taken away." El raised her fingers to her lips as if she held a cigarette there.

"Why?"

Night chirped. Bodies digested.

"You weren't, uh" — she made twinkling fingers around Ruth's face — "born like that. Our mom did that to you."

"My face?"

El nodded. "She splashed you with bleach, then left you there for a couple hours. You were a baby, and she was a bad drunk. I called the ambulance, they called the cops, and the cops called the State."

Ruth lifted both hands to her face. "She gave me that?"

El nodded. "Barely missed your eyes."

"Why?"

El shakes her head. "I don't know."

"Come on," Nat says. "That's not true. Your mom was CIA, FBI, KGB."

But Ruth knows the truth when she finally hears it. "And you went back to her when you got out? You went to live with her? Guess that's why you never came for me."

El nods. "Where else was I supposed to go? I was eighteen and pregnant."

"Yeah, I guess you were," Ruth says. "But you haven't been eighteen for a long time now."

I crept downstairs that night to watch them sleep, hiding in the dark with the devotion of a zealot. They weren't asleep. Nat took a cigarette lighter and kept it burning for a long time. It made their skin glow gold. The flame went out, and he touched the metal part of the lighter to Ruth's back and arms. Her body tensed and shivered. She slurped as though drooling. He asked, "Is that better, Ru?"

"I feel it."

When he was done, she thanked him. The room smelled like barbeque, like they had a secret way inside each other down a path no one else would ever know.

Ruth and Nat were gone in the morning, and it took me a long time, a week or two, to get back into my dull life. Took me a month to forgive El for scaring off Ruth.

But now Ruth is here again, fourteen years later, and she's different. No Nat. No beauty. No power. No shine. Skinny as death and even older. Thirty-one years old around here usually means a mom with a dirty minivan and a bad job. Ruth's nowhere near that. She's hollowed out. Miles and miles of hard road. Someone sucked the life from her face and neck. It takes a minute to get my breath and understand that my aunt is back. "Ruth?"

She nods.

"God, you scared me." I put a hand on my heart to show her. "How've you been?" I've only met her once, but I've wondered where she is so often, picturing her on a map of America in Delaware, Texas, California, Alaska. Here she is. I step forward to hug her, and she hugs me back like she's forgotten how to and she's following an instruction manual: open arms, wrap arms around other person, squeeze.

Something I've noticed about being pregnant is that scents land differently. Everything smells like old meat or vinegar or blood. But Ruth hugs me and my face is so close to her, resting on her shoulder, in her hair, and immediately I notice it. Ruth has no scent at all. That's nice.

"El's going to be happy to see you. I'm so glad you came back. Last time," I start to explain. "I'm sorry. I know El has a lot of regrets, and I was so sad when you left. But here you are, and it'll be better this time." I smile.

She smiles back.

"El's really going to be happy," I say again.

But Ruth grabs my arm. She shakes her head no.

"Huh?"

She shakes her head no again.

"You don't want to see her?"

More nos.

"Why'd you come?"

She points at me, right at my sternum.

"For me?"

Nods of yes.

"What's going on?"

She points outside. She points to me. She points to her. She points outside. And it dawns on me that there's something wrong with my aunt Ruth.

"Can't you talk?"

No. Folds of skin around her eyes tighten like a person in pain, in labor.

"What happened to your voice?"

Ruth looks right at me, and there it is, the solid fact of silence.

She points outside again.

"You want us to leave?"

Yes.

"Where are we going?"

This time she points straight up.

I look up to the ceiling. "Up?"

No.

"North?"

Yes.

"Why?"

Ruth stares at me again because anything that cannot be explained with a pointing finger or a yes, no, will remain a mystery.

"I have a job."

More staring.

"Up north? Why? You left something there?"

Yes.

"Shoot. What'd you lose?" And then, "What's wrong, Ruth?"

Ruth moves in close. She takes my cheeks in her hands as if to kiss me but looks at me instead. She has the smallest smile on her face, and for a moment she's young Ruth again, all power and light. Like she knows I need to get out of here, away from Lord for a couple of days. I think of my job and feel very little, a dull gray fuzz. Summer's ending and the closest thing I've had to an adventure was a Google search of Baja California. I don't think of El, not just then. "OK," I tell Ruth. "I'll come."

She smiles wider.

"I'll come with you."

She looks down at her hands a moment, nodding yes, pleased even.

"Right now?"

Yes.

"Where are we going?"

No answer.

I suppose I don't really care where we're going. Away from here. "Now?"

She nods.

"Right now?"

She nods.

In those years of not seeing Ruth, my imagination had time to do a number on memory. I carved her into something perfect, and even though that's clearly not true, even though she looks like a dirty junkie, I want her. I want to know what she knows, even if it means following her into places unknown. "One second."

It's tough to pack because how long will we be gone? Where are we going exactly? "I need clothes?"

Yes.

"OK." Comfortable shoes, a soft sweater. I fill a small canvas bag. Some socks, a hair comb, an extra barrette, underwear, one hundred twenty-three dollars in cash from my bureau. I wear two shirts and a hoodie. I think of the baby, but right now the baby has everything it needs.

I consider leaving El a note, but I don't do it. I won't be gone long. Ruth opens the front door, and I feel the dark air out there. Lord, bears, all the terrors, and irresistible Ruth cutting through them, unaware of danger, braiding a lifetime of people's mean looks and cruelty into a smooth path that leads from my door to her waiting car.

The lights of Lackawanna are shutting down as we pass through town, a woman removing her jewels. Electric Avenue to Cazenovia Creek, past Holy Cross Cemetery and Red Jacket, to the outskirts of Buffalo.

"Are we heading to the Falls?" I ask, but Ruth doesn't look from the road. No answer. Fine. I'm tired and the car is warm. Shut up, I tell myself. Stop asking questions that don't have answers.

Twenty-five minutes later, the car breaks down north of Tonawanda in a place called Cambria. Not much has happened here since they found a meteorite back in 1818. Something snaps. Chain dragging. Rusting. Rattling. Twenty-seven miles away from El's house. My phone still has a charge. GPS even.

"What?" I ask. "No gas?"

The car coasts to an efficient end by the side of the road.

"Should I call someone?"

Ruth doesn't even look under the hood. She's as calm as if she'd seen the car breaking down in a dream, knew it was coming. She grabs a small backpack.

"What?"

Ruth starts to walk. Turns to see if I'm coming.

"Walking?"

Ruth doesn't answer.

"Back to El's?"

No.

My foot is up on the dashboard. "How far is it?" But like the car, Ruth is broken. She's got her reasons for being messed up. I'll give her that. Ruth has not had a good life, but what would make her stop talking? Maybe there's a reservoir of words we get, and hers is empty now. Maybe if we walk, some of her reservoir will fill back up. "What are we going to do?"

And there's that damn finger again, pointing, pointing. Ruth starts walking down the road away from me.

I spend a hard moment with the dashboard before collecting my things. I follow her. The road is blue as a vein under skin. Ruth and I begin our walk into the blueness, into the black of the coming night.

THERE'S MONEY TO BE MADE talking to the dead. Tonya brings her boyfriend, a kid who aged out a few years back. He lives in a shelter. No more Medicaid and the kid is sick, sick. At the periphery of the basement's coal bin, the boyfriend stands with his legs spread slightly, his arms crossed over his chest to display his muscles. He coughs like a buffalo every five minutes.

Tonya, Nat, and Ruth find seats on the cold ground. The basement creaks against the soil outside. Minerals grow. "Hello?" Ruth asks the dark basement. "Hello? Hello? Who is there?" But it's hard to get the dead's attention under the boyfriend's scowl. "Can you sit down?" Ruth offers her hand.

"No." He doesn't move.

Her arm remains extended.

"I said no."

Ruth buries her lips.

"This is bullshit," the boyfriend says. His posture is rigid, eyes straight ahead. "You're wasting your money, Ton."

"Uh-uh, babe. He's for real. He talks to our parents all the time."

"Oh yeah?" the boyfriend asks, though he doesn't mean it. "He's making it up."

"He knows their names, Trey. He knows things no one ever told him."

It's true. Children from the home pay five dollars, a fortune, and Nat talks to their parents. He knows their names. He says what they would say. I love you. I miss you. I'd be with you if I could.

"Bullshit."

"Well." Ruth lifts up to her knees, ready to adjourn. "If you don't believe it, let's skip it."

"No," Tonya says. "We've got nothing else to do."

That is true.

Nat looks to the boyfriend. "You don't have to believe it. It doesn't matter. I don't believe it, but that doesn't stop it from happening."

The boyfriend stays standing. "You don't believe your own shit?"

Ruth sits again, takes Tonya's hand.

"No."

"Well, I do." Ruth calls again into the dark to the ranks of dead people waiting to chat. "Who's there?"

Nat starts to shimmy. His shoulders twitch. Ruth sways slightly, a humming groupie. Nat feels Elvis, Jerry Lee Lewis, Chuck Berry. "Calamine. Calamine. Calamine. Mine." He moves his tongue and body, whispering, lashed from side to side. He borrows heavily from the Father's playbook. Rolling his eyes back, his jaw gets ready to deliver, huffing an exorcism of their boredom. Nat thumbs back and forth over a word that sounds like "prick." Nat tells Tonya that her mom would be with her if she could be. He tells her that her mom's name was Cleopatra.

"No. Her name was—"

"Eunice," Nat fills in.

"Yeah."

"Nah," he says. "That's just what the kids in school used to call her."

Tonya nods. "Is that right?" and lifts her chin like the daughter of a queen.

Even the prick's mom makes an appearance. Nat says her name. "Ursula." So the boyfriend drops to his knees and cries like a hungry calf until Ruth puts her arm across his shoulders and tells him that really, everything is going to be OK, everything's going to be just fine.

After Tonya, Shauna and Lisa take a turn, the sisters.

Nat's a bull ready to toss its rider, foaming like a terrifying moron.

"I see your mom roasting a chicken in her pajamas."

"That's her."

"She's brushing her teeth while talking on the phone."

"Oh my God. How do you know?"

"She says she'd be with you if she could."

Nat doesn't even say hello to some of these kids upstairs, but down in the cellar their mothers' words are in his mouth. "Miss you" and "Still" and "Soon, love," and "Remember when."

Ruth carries a box of tissues into the basement each time they go. She also works security when necessary. The first time Nat contacted Tika's mom, Tika went ballistic. "Dirty whore! Let me at her!" In his trance Nat kept saying, "I love you. I love you, honey. I'm sorry." Tika charged Nat, knocking his head back against the concrete floor, scratching at his cheeks. Ruth pulled her off, told her she wasn't allowed to come back to the basement anymore.

A few days after the sisters, the tiny, quiet Raffaella has her turn, and this is how they move through the months.

Ruth holds one of Raffaella's hands. It looks and feels like a flipper. Nat takes her other hand. "Yaawwchappa chappa chappa," Nat yammers in the murk.

Raffaella's flipper grips Ruth's hand tighter. It's the girl's first time. She thought Jesus wouldn't like her talking to dead people until Ruth pointed out that Jesus himself is a dead person who came back, talking.

"Choo chug choo chug." Nat's pupils are vacant. "Hello?"

Ruth opens her eyes a slit. Raffaella watches Nat, so hungry she'd eat him.

"Jumper. Juniper. Jennifer. Jennifer. Jennifer." Finding the right ghost is like selecting an entrée off a menu.

Raffaella's mouth opens. She straightens her spine. "That's her."

"Remember that lightning storm? We sat and watched it."

Raffaella nods, whispers, "I remember, Mommy."

"I'd be with you if I could." Every mother says that every time.

Raffaella asks, "What's stopping you?"

Ruth tilts her head. "The veil between the worlds is hard to pass over."

"Pardon?"

"It's hard to come back from the dead."

"My mom's not dead. She's in Miami."

Ruth's eyes open. "Miami?"

"It's *like* she's dead."

"Like she's dead?"

Nat comes to. He rubs his forehead and stretches.

"It's over," Ruth tells her.

"OK," the little girl says. "Well. Thanks." Raffaella releases their hands. She doesn't press it. She wants to believe. She pays them to not admit it's fake. Her footsteps are light on the stairs as she goes. The basement door shuts.

"Her mom's not dead."

Nat shrugs.

"I guess there are even more mysteries than I thought," Ruth says.

"I guess so." They climb out of the cellar. Nat lets Ruth hold the money.

Breakfast was seven hours ago. Ruth had a half bowl of Crispy Hexagons. Food supplies are low until the State makes its next payment. Ruth drinks water and a dandelion tea the Father brews when food runs out. Hunger's slowing her down, eating her brain. Hunger darkens her eyes on a young man speaking with the Father on the front porch. His hair's long as a gypsy's. His fingers are covered with thick metal rings, stones and skulls, some sort of fancy pirate. There's a suitcase beside the man, but he's too old to be a new charge. His pinkie nails are painted black. The Father won't like that one bit. Homosexual, he will say. The Father doesn't know anything. Ruth sucks her thumb, wondering if her hunger invented the man.

Nat and three of the other children watch a Father-approved television program in the living room, something about a boy and his monkey. TV is a luxury allowed during the lean times. Ruth tries to glean a word from the porch. The Father keeps his voice low, but the young man, a bright penny, can be heard plainly.

"My own household has been kindly increased in the arms of this product, sir. My solemn word." A salesman in graveyard boots. He's young to be a salesman. "I'll have you know, this product is held in surplus by not only the residents of the White House but their cabinet members as well."

"I don't much care for the government."

"No. I'm only saying—"

"What is it? Let me see what you're hawking."

"Indeed." The man eyes his case. "But is there perhaps a lady of the house I might converse with? A mother to these lovely children? She might better understand what I have to offer."

From just inside a living room window, Ruth buries her eyes in the young man's burgundy suit. He could be snapping baby photos at Sears in that suit. He could be pumping formaldehyde at a funeral parlor or even heading off to prom. Ruth falls away from the sway of Nat to a place of swords and sticks where it's every man for herself.

"Let me ask you something. Have you invited our Lord and Savior Jesus Christ into your heart?" That old saw. The Father tries it on everyone.

The man eyes the Father, his soft hands. "Invited him in, sir. He didn't care for the decor."

"A wise-ass, huh?"

The man blinks.

"What is it you believe, son?"

"You really want to know?"

"I'm curious."

The young man clears his throat, surrenders his sale. "Heaven is a dream of Disneyland for those unable to act here on Earth."

"That so?"

Ruth is surprised by the Father's calm.

"That's what I believe." The young man winks.

"Then I have one question left. How many orphaned children have you sheltered, fed, and educated? Two questions. How are you helping your fellow humans?"

The young man lifts a hand to his chin to think, which is unlike most people the Father engages. Most can't listen because they're already certain they're right. The man chews his top lip. "I beg pardon, sir. You're absolutely correct. I have done next to nothing to better my fellow man. That's the truth. God's honest."

But the Father's not done with this soul. "Christ forbid you should ever become guardian of a child who uses feces as paint; drools for his mother; screams profanities in your face for hours; refuses to bathe, speak, eat; kicks you in the kidneys at bedtime; breaks your nose at breakfast — because in those situations, if you've got no God to ask, 'Why Lord, why?' you're going to have take all your questions out on that child's flesh." The Father concludes business. "We don't want whatever you're selling." He shuts the front door, leaving the young man alone on the porch, hands open and empty.

Ruth's nearly proud of the Father, nearly buying his bull, until he breezes past her and she smells food coming from the Father's pores: scrambled eggs, meat, cheese. The Father's been eating bacon and not sharing it. Ruth is starving.

The young man palms his suitcase. Ruth steps into sight, clears her throat. "Hello, little sister," he says. Something new in town after so long living with old things. "That's some gorgeous explosion on your face, huh?" Ruth lifts a hand to her cheek. "Yes, it is," he answers for her. The young man takes his leave, throwing an arm up in farewell, whistling as he walks away. Ruth can't tell if he's a boy or a man. Closer to a man, she thinks. The shadow of a bird crosses his back. He doesn't even see it, doesn't know how lucky he is, free as that bird. Or maybe good things just happen to him all the time.

Her hunger burns worse when the young man is gone. "Apples?" she asks Nat. The farm has a number of hoary trees. Each fruit is good for two bites before a hard blue spot crops up. There are tons of them because the other kids won't eat what the worms left behind.

"Not today."

Troy is a tipsy municipality built on top of three powerful confluences: Panhooseck and Paanpack, the old peoples; shirt collars and steel, the old industries; Hudson and Erie, the old waterways.

People with cars pass Nat and Ruth on their walk into the city. The drivers pretend to focus really hard on their driving so that they won't have to, all Christian-like, stop to offer them a ride.

But as previously reported, he isn't a Christian. The young salesman's car is stopped up the road, a quarter mile from the home. He's attempting to turn the engine over again and again, but the engine won't fire. Nat slides past the car, but Ruth stops at his window. She touches the pane. The man turns the key one last time and the engine engages.

"Look at that." He rolls the window down. "You fixed my car."

Ruth smiles.

"My name's Mr. Bell. You're in need of transportation? Perhaps I could be of assistance. If you can trust a vehicle as wobbly as mine."

"Mister?" Ruth asks. She hears his funny way of talking, using more words than necessary as if he enjoys them. Maybe he went to college. Maybe he's Canadian. Ruth nods. He's too young to be a mister. Twenty-four tops. His car and clothes are clean. He wears his seat belt. There's no sign of his case. "Nat." Ruth calls Nat back quickly like a well-trained dog.

They press their faces against the back window to see what such an unusual young man has inside his car: a seasonally premature ice scraper, a well-used road map. They climb in the back as if riding in a taxi.

"Where to?"

"Downtown."

"Downtown." Mr. Bell laughs. Something about town is funny. They drive in silence, stealing glimpses. They pass the Roxy Laundromat. Ruth can see the side of the man's shaven neck, his suit and collar, the sloppy cut of his long hair, the length of his sideburns. She sees his hands on the wheel and the chunky skull rings. His fingers have sprouted dark down on each knuckle.

"Suppose you all heard about Pluto?" The man makes conversation.

Of course, they've heard of Pluto. They nod slowly, and he catches the nod in the rearview mirror.

"Glad old Tombaugh was already dead when they announced it."

More slow nodding.

Mr. Bell looks at them quickly. "They decided it's no longer a planet?"

"Right."

"Right."

Nat and Ruth begin to wonder whether or not they will be getting out of this car alive. Pluto not a planet? This man is clearly deranged.

"Pistachio?" Mr. Bell offers, raising a bag over into the back seat.

"No, thank you," Nat says, but Ruth decides to try one. She's starving.

The city of Troy, New York—after a brief shining role at the center of the steel industry—fell off the map of the modern world. Head of the now more-or-less dead Erie Canal, a number of buildings still display versions of Troy's once-bright future. Frear's Troy Cash Bazaar. Marty Burke's South End Tavern, with its separate entrance for ladies. The Castle, the Gurley, the Rice, and the Ilium. Burden Iron Works and Proctor's Theater. Some of the buildings have been emptied, some just collapsed. There are a number of 99¢ Shops and opportunities for mugging RPI students after dark. There's Pfeil Hardware and DeFazio's. There are quiet people making things in secret. And the mighty Hudson.

Fulton Street arrives quickly. Mr. Bell pulls to the curb. Nat and Ruth step to the sidewalk in front of the Jamaican Restaurant. They want to ask the question that will reveal why this young man is so unlike other people. Nat holds the car door open for a moment, but a person like Mr. Bell has places to go. "Be seeing you," he says, and his car pulls away past the Uncle Sam Parking Garage. Mr. Bell, who is not really yet a mister, is gone. After one truck carrying bananas and another carrying dry-cleaning supplies have passed, what's regular and dusty creeps back in.

A Jamaican couple waiting for take-out go haywire at their Love of Christ! clothes.

"Ku pon dis. A fuckery frock." The critics use high dialect to speak freely, coded, in front of Nat and Ruth.

"Dos dutty jackets dem from up de hill yaad. Tall hairs. Dem get salt. No madda, no fambly. Zeen."

"A pyur suffereation."

At the Stewart's Shop, Nat shoves two sodas, a tin of Pringles, and a chocolate bar down his pants. No one suspects a boy from the nineteenth century of shoplifting. They eat the loot on the library steps, enjoying each toxic bite.

"What's up with that?" There is no peace for Nat and Ruth in Troy. A trio of curious men from the Italian ranks of South Central approach. One Mets fan, one Buffalo Bills enthusiast, and one whose T-shirt boasts a mysterious message: WHISKEY TANGO FOXTROT.

"You got a costume party?" one man asks Nat.

"No. No. They're, what's it? Hamish people."

"Amish?" Ruth asks slowly.

"Aww, shit! She talk!" Two of the men high-five.

"No." Not Amish. "Yes." She talks.

People in their Corollas slow for a moment to observe Ruth in her long dress, Nat in his plain clothes. There's no recognition of fellowship or shared humanity. The people shudder or chuckle in their cars. They make a nervous radio adjustment, relieved that they have not been raised by religious weirdoes.

The walk back uphill is hot. Ruth has parceled out her soda to make it last. Nat asks for a sip, having polished off his own. By the time they reach Frear Park, he's finished hers as well.

That night, Ruth wakes. She pinches the fold of Nat's underarm. Artificial yellow light flows through the transom of their room. Where is her mom? Where is her other sister? On a map of the world, on a map of New York State, where are they? It wakes Ruth. If Nat can talk to Raffaella's living mother, why doesn't he tell her where her mom is?

She puts her hand on his calf.

"What?"

The room is silent.

"What about my mom?"

He pretends he's still asleep. Ruth cuffs her fingers with his. She digs her nails into his proximal phalanges.

"It's the middle of the night."

"Why don't you ever talk to my mom?" Ruth forces her tongue up against the roof of her mouth, making garbled, devil sounds. "Cooowla trappa waneenee."

"The dead speak English."

"Well, what does my mom say? In English?"

"She says she'd be with you, you know, if she could."

"Same thing the rest of the moms say?"

Nat wakes up fully. "No. Sorry. Come on."

The basement is dark as fur. Ruth scratches her fingers across the *Stachybotrys chartarum* mold growing on the stone walls, raising bits of the fungal growth under her nails.

She walks behind Nat; his bottom touches her belly. One bare bulb back at the staircase is the only light. The air smells of bad breath. Nat pats the darkness, arms outstretched, until he finds the corner coal bin. "You first." He pushes her in. They sit cross-legged. She sees bursts of color behind shut eyes.

"Want a bite?" Nat holds something under her nose.

"No."

He takes a bite. A sweet odor spreads thicker than it would in the light of day. Candy, taffy from Troy. He puts the rest of it in his mouth. "Call him." Nat chews. "He likes girls."

"Who?"

"Mr. Splitfoot."

She leans in. "But I want to talk to my mom."

"You've got to go through him first."

"Oh." So she tries, "Mr. Splitfoot? Hello?"

Doesn't take Nat but a moment to make contact with the dead. "Konk."

"Are you talking to me?"

"No. Shh." He bobs his head from side to side, clearing the air of her question. Mid-bob, he freezes. Their grip tightens. The house groans. A disturbed and breathy voice comes from Nat's mouth. "Got any more candy?" Mr. Splitfoot sounds sexy.

"Who are you?"

Nat leans into her, inhaling like an animal. She feels the brush of his soft stubble on her cheek. Then quickly, in her ear, "Who do you think, you filthy?"

She can just make Nat out in the dark. "That's my mother?" His chin is twisted, his neck hard-cranked to the left. His eyes bob in their sockets. "Nat?" She tilts her chin up.

Dirty water rushes through a pipe overhead.

Like an electric shock, his arms go rigid. His chin tracks right before resetting as an electronic typewriter might. A bit of drool forms in the corner of his mouth and dribbles out. “Say. Say.” The voice does not fit in Nat’s mouth.

“Who are you?”

“Let me check.” Nat’s eyes dip back into his head, white with fine strands of blood.

Ruth pokes Nat in the chest.

“Tirzah. Kateri Tekakwitha. Yaaa-deee!” He lifts up to his knees, a man begging his wife for one more chance. “Ruthie. Ruthie. Ru. The mangled and the mauled.” And a whisper, “Starlight. Star bright. First pair of shoes we’ve seen tonight. Ha.”

Nat’s head sways. His eyes are glazed. There are the sounds of the house. Then, “Kateri.” Then, “Claustrophobia. A little slice can feel so nice.” The room is charged with a fresh dampness. Nat wheezes, air passing through the stretched lips of a balloon. “Sorry, Ruth.” The voice is an old record in a deep well. “Oh, Ruth. Oh, Ruth.”

“Nat?”

The voice grows softer, kittenish. “She wish she may, I wish I might, get those lungs back, bitch, tonight.”

“My lungs?”

“Uh-huh. And heart.”

“Nat?”

“No. Not Nat.”

“Mom?”

“Yeah.”

“Go to hell.”

“It’s lovely down here.”

When it’s over, he reaches for Ruth’s hand, squeezing her fingertips separately, like release valves. “That was her?” she asks.

But it’s not Nat who answers. Another voice, positioned behind Ruth’s head, cuts in. “Bravo. Bravo. Good style, young ones.”

Ruth screams.

A hand swiftly covers her mouth and nose.

“Shh. Shh. Shh. Quiet there, girl. I beg you.” His words are so close, they move her hair.

“Who’s that?” Nat asks as Nat again.

"Hold your tongue. Tranquility."

They know his way of speaking. Mr. Bell draws the rest of himself up behind her. "Remember me?"

She nods yes.

"Can I uncover your mouth?"

Yes, again.

He releases her. He fumbles in his pocket for a match, a needle to prick the iris. She looks away from the light, sees his pants, his knees. He squats on the coal bin floor beside them.

"Very well done."

"What are you doing here?" Nat stands.

"Forgive my intrusion. I'm a traveler, trying to earn a living best I can, and you see this month I've come up a hair short. These are not the dwellings I'm accustomed to, but, we, I, make do."

Nat and Ruth wait for a further explanation.

"An opportunity presented itself. You folks have this large basement, and I needed a place to sleep. I'll ask you please not to reveal my pallet to your father. In the morning I will be gone."

"He's not our father."

"Forgive me. I misunderstood the nature of your relationship. Is there a mother? I haven't seen a mother."

"You snuck down here?"

"Sneaked. Yes. A mother?"

"Hiding?" Nat wants to know.

"Only to secure a night's rest. The air outside had a chill, and the good city of Troy impounded my chariot until she's made more homogenously legal."

The match burns out. Ruth hears him breathe. "What?"

"Car got towed." He lights another match and extends it into the back of the coal bin. The tight space resembles a coffin. His sleeping bag is a sack of orange nylon. Cowboys and Indians whoop across its flannel lining. "I was asleep until you two scared the fleas off me."

One good scream would wake someone overhead. "What's in that case? What do you sell?" Nat asks.

The man rubs his hands together. "I'd like to tell you, I would, but I'm wondering who you were talking to five minutes back." He stops the hand rub, chuckling as if he's got Nat trapped.

He doesn't have Nat. "Dead people. What's in your case?"

"Ah, the dead. Just as I thought, but you're doing it wrong. Too much gibberish. People like their supernatural to make a little more sense."

"What do you know?"

"Some things. I know some things about talking to the dead. And one of the things I know is that if you're going to con people, a little gibberish goes a long, long way."

"He's not conning anyone."

"Beg pardon?"

"He can really talk to the dead."

Mr. Bell draws his chin back. "Then he's even more clever than I thought."

"What's in the case?" Nat asks.

"What's in the case." The match goes out. "I'll show you and perhaps you'll allow me to teach you something about talking to dead people. Tomorrow? I haven't got the case here with me. Trapped in my transport. But tomorrow. You know Van Schaick Island, in the river? A place between, yes? Start of the Erie Canal. Or its end. Meet me there? Follow Park Avenue along the shores of the Mohawk. Sometime after four. Yes?"

Ruth doesn't wait for Nat's answer. "Yes."

She wakes before dawn. Their bedroom is a narrow closet at the top of the stairs, where the house's heart would be if it had one. They have one yellow blanket and a door that's so old, so glommed up with paint, it sticks in the summer and makes Ruth wonder about all those painters, about the people who were here before her. There's a stubby pencil on the bedside table sharpened so the letters embossed on the side now spell MERICAN. Ruth hasn't slept much. All night she imagined Mr. Bell in the basement, a strange person in an ordinary sleeping bag. Though probably he'd fled after being discovered.

Nat's still asleep. Their hips touch. Ruth turns to Nat's feet, acrid pale fishes. A few hairs sprout from his insteps. "Sleep is to ready us for death," the Father says, but that doesn't seem true of the way she sleeps with Nat.

A door slams down the hall. The Mother taking a predawn shower. Soon the house will wake but not yet. Ruth can lie with Nat under their yellow blanket, stewing and melting together.

Morning comes on slowly through the transom. "It's real, right?"

He stretches, his toes reaching past her head, pressing flat feet against the wall. Nat jumps out of bed and stretches again. He rattles off a dry report of farts, neither answer nor confirmation.

Ruth and Nat walk to Van Schaick. It's not easy to get there. Industry has kept access to the Hudson restricted, Homeland Security. The banks are often lined with trash. There are fuel tanks where Haymakers Field, a major league baseball diamond, used to be. The cars on the bridges overhead zoom like spaceships lifting off. Rushes growing by the river sound like snakes when the wind is in them. Ruth is wary of snakes. Fourteen or fifteen snow geese have landed on the bank. She calculates the omens. Spaceships plus snakes minus snow geese. She moves forward. "It's real, right?" she asks again.

Nat spits to one side.

In a forgotten part of the floodplain, between the Mohawk and the Hudson Rivers, Mr. Bell sits on his case still wearing his burgundy suit. Yellow weeds are flattened and dried by the tides. He's tossing rocks into the river. "Amigos." He stands to greet them. "A powerful confluence here." He jerks his chin out to the water. "Though the power isn't necessarily visible to the naked eye, this land looks forgotten, but I assure you, we're standing at a most important place. You know the history of this great canal?"

Ruth shakes her head no.

"This is where north and south meet east and west. From here" — he points one way — "New York City and the Atlantic. And there" — his finger follows the curve of the river up — "the rest of the country. A passage through antiquity: Utica, Rome, and Syracuse. Tonawanda by way of Crescent, Tribes Hill, Canajoharie, May's Point, Lyons, Palmyra, Macedon, to Buffalo. Each lock is a miracle of engineering built with nary an engineer. The excavated dirt formed a towpath beside the canal beaten flat by the mules who built New York State. These days, though, the canal doesn't get much use."

Ruth, Nat, and Mr. Bell stare down the Mohawk. "'Low bridge,'" Mr. Bell sings out, but he is met with blank looks. He has to explain. "That's where you sing, 'Everybody down.' Don't you know that song?"

"No," Ruth says. "Sorry."

"'Fifteen Miles on the Erie Canal'?"

"Sorry."

Nat jerks his chin. "What's in the case?" He's almost rude. Perhaps he's worried that Ruth likes Mr. Bell too much. The three of them stand around the suitcase, hands clasped like farmers admiring a prized pumpkin. Finally Mr. Bell flops the case open.

"There's nothing in there," Ruth says. It is empty save for its soiled pink taffeta lining.

"No, there's not."

"What was in there? What were you selling?"

"There's never been anything in there. I carry an empty case."

"Why?"

"It gives me a reason to knock on people's doors, ask them questions. You already understand the potential in empty space and curious customers. Empty space made you two agree to meet me, a strange man in an abandoned location. Why would you do that?"

No one, besides an outraged bird, makes a sound.

"Empty space lures your customers into a dark and dreary basement. Why?"

"What kind of questions do you ask?"

"Whatever I need to know." Mr. Bell claps his hands, smiles.

"Like?"

Mr. Bell squats as a catcher. He rubs his hands over his face, preparing his snake oil for presentation. "Do you have life insurance? Do you have a son? Do you own any property in Florida?" He straightens. "Just as examples."

"Why do you want to know those things?"

"Information enables me to shape my con, to make something from nothing."

"Pardon?"

"I am a con man." He offers himself to them without a filter, opening arms. "This is how I make my living, separating fools from their money."

"But we don't have any money."

"And I am not conning you."

"Did you con Father Arthur?"

Mr. Bell snickers. "As a man of faith, he's already familiar with my tricks."

"So why'd you want to talk to us?"

"For you, in my suitcase, I have a proposition."

Nat and Ruth bend closer to the empty case, peering inside again.

"No," Mr. Bell says. "I'm speaking metaphorically."

They stand.

"I should like to become your manager."

"That's what's in the case?"

Ruth sees a small path to the river, a muddy slide down to the water. "What will you manage?"

"Your careers as seers, mediums, psychics. I'll collect an audience. I'll be a barker of sorts. You're familiar with the term?"

No. "Yes."

"I meet a lot of people." Mr. Bell doesn't have to convince them. Up close, in the light of day, he's pocked with experience and some rough-looking tattoos. Mr. Bell still hasn't told them his first name. "Many of these people would be interested in your services."

"What are those?"

"Contacting the dead. Or putting on a good show."

"You don't believe in ghosts?" she asks.

"No."

"You will once you sit with him."

"I doubt it."

"Why would we let you manage us after you've admitted to being a con man?"

"Like likes like." When he smiles, his teeth are strong.

"You mean we're con men also?"

"Yes."

"Nat's for real."

"To you."

"So you don't believe in anything?"

Mr. Bell grins. "My beliefs are of a fossilized nature. Petrified. Luckily, my beliefs matter little. I'm a businessman, and if you say so, we're in business."

The river currents churn like something thicker: oil, booze, or blood.

"You must be rich."

"No."

"You went to college?" She's looking for any advantage he might have over her.

"No. Why?"

"There are no atheists in foxholes."

He smiles at her turn of phrase. "Not so, young lady. I can see the stars from this trench. Regardless of its extraordinary depths. Why? What do you believe?"

"Birds. Jesus." She leaves Nat's name off the list for now.

"A Christian."

"No. I just like the man."

"The man Jesus?"

"That's the one."

Mr. Bell smiles as if she's a cute kid, as if he's far older than he is. "Do we have a deal?" he asks Nat, but Nat looks to Ruth.

She studies the river. It's hard to read. "OK," she tells them. "A manager. Why not? We've got nothing to lose."

Mr. Bell lets loose a small whoop. He swings the empty case, orbiting himself before letting go of its handle. It lands in the river with a sucking splash, floating downstream on its way to a new life in the big city.

Mr. Bell buys milk at a pharmacy in Colonie. Nat and Ruth wait in the car. His strength already lifts them. He drives them to a fish fry. He leaves the milk in the warm car. The restaurant is decorated in a horseracing theme. The booths are made to look like paddocks, each one crowned with a portrait, a thoroughbred in his prime: Black Susan, King's Ransom, Secretariat. The restaurant is dark. A person could take his lunch here and avoid the sunshine.

"On this spot"—Mr. Bell drives a fingertip onto the table—"Mother Ann shook her thing."

"What are you talking about?" Ruth intends the question in the broadest sense, like, Where did you come from? Why do you talk so funny? How did you find us?

"Mother Ann, aka Ann Lee, led the United Society of Believers in Christ's Second Appearing. You know them by their nickname, the Shakers?"

"Shakers?"

"Christians like yourself."

"I told you, we're not Christians. Father Arthur is."

"Right. So the Shakers were into ecstatic dancing, hand-built furniture, gender equality, round barns, celibacy in preparation for the kingdom. 'Tis a gift to be simple."

"You're a Shaker?"

"No." The waitress appears. "Three orders of cod. Tartar sauce." Mr. Bell orders for all of them. "My treat."

"Fries?" the waitress asks.

"Fries"—Mr. Bell rolls the word back to her—"are for kids." And because they are not kids, except in the eyes of the state, Nat and Ruth quickly refuse similar offers of French fries.

A man enters the restaurant. He brushes off the hostess, scanning the room for the choicest table. He takes a seat at the counter, slowly spinning his stool. On each revolution, he stares at Ruth. Her clothes, her scar. She's used to it.

"You need some instruction," Mr. Bell says.

"In what?"

"Deceit. I can provide this. You lovelies do your basement reckoning for an audience. Top dollar for a sit with you and your spooks. And let's bring it out of the basement."

"Interesting." Nat steals a word from Mr. Bell.

"It's not deceit," Ruth reminds him.

The man on the stool has stopped spinning. He now stares at Ruth openly, directly, smiling bright. She notices his sideburns.

Mr. Bell winks at her quickly. "Doesn't matter, dear. People are desperate for their dead. Even they don't have to believe in it."

She likes being called dear.

The man on the stool strolls past their table on his way to the restroom. His attention is still caught on Ruth. He twists his neck as an owl might, nearly all the way around to not break his gaze. He passes so close, she can see the hairs on his hands, feel his stare. She hides her face with her palm, making a blinder.

"What do we do?" Nat asks.

"I'm glad you asked." Mr. Bell waits for the man to pass out of earshot. "First of all, just listen." Mr. Bell cups his ear. "They'll tell you what they want you to say. Listen, then feed it back to them. You've heard of psychoanalysis? Maybe you haven't, but it's like that. And if you have nothing to go on, keep it general. Keep it far in the past. No one's going to recognize their great-great-grandfather." Mr. Bell shakes a small pile of salt onto his fingertip and rubs it on his gums. "When all else fails, memorize a few old movies. Those'll do in a pinch."

"Someone's going to think we're criminals and lock us up."

Mr. Bell hunkers in close, protecting a featherless newborn bird. He looks Ruth up and down. "But you already are locked up. Aren't you, dear?"

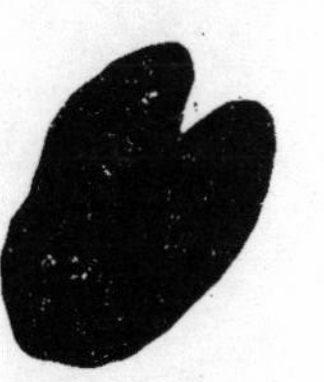

SHE AND I FOLLOW A PATH through a field single file. We are trespassing. Yellow grass reaches as high as my waist. If someone came along, we could duck into this grass and be hidden. So far this morning we've seen no one.

The path gives way onto the road. Ruth turns left as if she knows where she's going. Mostly it seems we're following the Erie Canal. We'll lose it for an afternoon sometimes but wind up not too far from the canal later on. We step over a garter snake hard-packed back to two dimensions. She walks and I follow. She hangs a left down someone's driveway so I think we've arrived, but she passes behind the house and out into another empty field. I tuck my neck into my clothes in case someone's home. Trespassing in upstate New York where gun shops litter the back roads. I pick freeloading burrs from my jeans as if they are spies.

Ruth bobs her head in time to the music playing on her Walkman. I didn't know they still made Walkmans. "No one's got cassettes anymore, Ruth." But cassettes are what she has, three or four homemade ones, flip and repeat, flip and repeat. We see a sign for a sauerkraut festival. We pass a man mowing a lawn that doesn't need it.

"When are we going to get there?"

But Ruth doesn't answer because Ruth doesn't talk.

That afternoon, when we don't arrive wherever we're going, we check into an awful motel. I dial El on my cell. She's called me five times already in two days. I haven't answered yet. The insurance company has called only twice. But I've walked far enough now. I've had a good adventure, and it's time to go home. When I'm back home, I'll post something about the crazy walk I took with my strange aunt. That will be cool. I snap a selfie in the motel. Ruth is sitting on the curb outside, bobbing her head to the music on her earphones. I snap a picture of her too, but the sunlight reflecting off the window turns her into a blur of light.

The motel room stinks of mildew as if it's under water. There's something wrong with Ruth. Where are we going? Nothing. How long will it take us to get there? Not a word.

I lift my phone to my ear.

El answers, "Cora? Thank God. I was so worried."

When I was little, El would hold me, curl my body over one breast, a crescent light around the moon. We'd shower together, and before diving under the spray, she'd yell, "Don't let go!" I'd claw into her, pretending we were Annie Edson Taylor, who, at sixty-three, became the first person to survive a trip over Niagara Falls in a barrel. El knows everything about Niagara Falls. She's worked as a groundskeeper there since I was little, using skills she picked up at the terrible group home where she once lived. The man who ran the home taught them to farm and to fear anyone outside the home. He was deranged. He named the home Love of Christ! — exclamation mark included like screaming a curse every time you say it.

The short history of El is she lived with my grandma until a few months after Ruth was born, then five years at Love of Christ!, then a short stint on the streets of Troy, where she picked me up.

"Who's my dad?" I asked her once.

"Well." She thought on it. "You know how girl dogs can accommodate more than one father per litter?"

"No. I didn't know that."

"It's true. So you could get siblings who are, say, half collie, half chow."

"I don't have any siblings."

"No. You don't."

"You don't know who my dad is."

"Not really."

"Someone in Troy?"

"Yeah."

"Who?"

El shakes her head. "I was eighteen and homeless. I slept around to find beds. Until no one wanted a pregnant girl in bed."

"Then what?"

"Then you were born, and I went to the library, started with Albany, Allegany. I checked the phone books until I found my mom in Erie. I had nowhere else to go."

"I'm sorry."

"Well, I'm not."

El saw a man attempt Niagara Falls in a kayak. She saw him coming from above, though no one else had yet noticed. She started up a whoop. "Look!" She whipped her arms over her head like a cowgirl, drawing attention to his ride. A few tourists saw it happen, and El was filled by the excitement, the slim chance she'd see such an attempt, but then the man went over the Falls, got pinned underwater, and died. El was pissed. "Goddamn waste." She couldn't forgive such carelessness when she'd worked so hard, waded through so much shit, just to stay alive.

"Cora?" El says again. She gave me such a nice name. But then Ruth turns, looking at me through the glass, frozen eyes.

"Hello?" El says. "Are you there?"

I am here, listening to my poor mother worry, twisting up inside because the last thing I want is to hurt El. But I'm also here still stuck with all the ways I've always wanted to be like Ruth—wise, cool, and tough. Even if I imagined her, even if I don't really know Ruth, there are things I still want to be, want to see. There's a courageous way of living I want my own baby to know about.

"Cora?"

So it comes down to this, stop asking questions and walk with Ruth, or stay home, be an ass for Lord, get rid of this thing, hold on to my insurance job for dear life, surf the awful Internet forever.

"Hello? Cora?"

"I'm fine, Mom. Please, don't worry. I'm fine." Then I hang up.

Early the next morning, I leave a message for my boss. "I'm sick," I say. "Really, really sick." Ruth and I start walking again, another day, me following her, Ruth saying nothing at all. On a road beside a cornfield, my mom calls again, the fourth time since I hung up last night. I hold my phone out for Ruth. "El. Again." Ruth takes the phone, looking at the device sideways, a species of glowing insect she's just now discovering. After a number of rings, the phone quiets. Ruth passes it back to me just as the voicemail signal vibrates, a hiss that startles her. Ruth drops the phone onto the pavement. It lands with a celebratory smack. That's how that world slips away. We inspect the ruined phone. Its dark and cracked screen displays nothing except the tiniest bit of reflected blue sky. I pick up the carcass and shove it into my bag. We keep walking.

The first two days without a phone, my insides are jumpy and nauseated, a true withdrawal. My veins ache for information from the Internet, distractions from thought. I'm lonely. My neck, lungs, blood hurt like I'm getting a cold. The world happens without me because I'm exiled with no Wi-Fi. I wonder if my shoes have arrived yet. Maybe Lord is trying to reach me with news of his divorce. I have a parade of grotesque urges. I want to push little buttons quickly. I want information immediately. I want to post pictures of Ruth and me smiling into the sun. I want people to like me, like me, like me. I want to buy things without trying them on. I want to look at photos of drunk kids I knew back in high school. And I want it all in my hand. But my cyborg parts have been ripped out. What's the temperature? I don't know. What's the capital of Hawaii? I don't know anything. I don't even know the automated systems in my body anymore. I don't know how to be hungry, how to sleep, to breathe.

We keep walking. "Talk to me, Ruth." I'm fraying.

Ruth says nothing.

What's her problem? "What's your problem, Ruth? If you don't tell me, I'm going to think something awful. I'm going think you got gang-raped or something."

Ruth keeps walking.

Another day goes by. I'm losing count. Does that make five days? I never imagined we'd walk this far, but Ruth is a strong magnet, a used-car-lot magnet pulling me behind her as she goes. "Please talk." She looks like a concerned relative at a hospital bedside, pained by my pain but not pained enough to make the pain stop. She says nothing.

I pick berries growing at the side of the road. They look like blackberries, but I don't really know about stuff like that. I eat them anyway. They might not be blackberries at all. Maybe they are poisonous. Ruth watches me chew. She doesn't say anything. The berries don't kill me. We keep walking.

I hear *swoosh* and *whoosh.* Words like "burlap" get stuck in my head on the road. Burlap. Burlap. Burlap, the sound of our footsteps. Songs stick in my head too. "White Christmas." "Sentimental Lady." "Star-Spangled Banner." I hear TV shows and greasy burps, things that were once inside me coming back through on their way out. After only a week on the road, I am changed. It's hard for me to stay too long at a diner or coffee shop. I hear so much now. The air conditioners, dishwashers, coffee machines, and restroom hand dryers rage like an angry electric army. We eat quickly. I steal foil packets of butter to rub on my aching feet.

I should go home and I would, except that I keep thinking we are bound to get there soon. We have to.

People stare at us while we walk, human females traveling alone. We must want to die or else we must be criminals, because we are two full-grown women walking together, single file, not talking, on busy roads, on back roads. No one would mistake us for exercising housewives. Certainly not any of the men who leer and jeer and ask creepy questions like, "Where you heading tonight?" Ruth's scar could creep out the creepiest creeps, so she leads, bearing her mark ahead of us as a shield of protection.

We walk through places no one ever walks. Places with piles of trash at the side of the road. I read a few words from yellowed newspapers. There are plastic water bottles full of pee. Road salts and Styrofoam to-go containers whose insides are coated with the remnants of sloppy joe.

U-Pick signs dot the landscape. Modular homes are for sale. Billboards advertise cluster fly spraying services and "The Power of Cheese." Outside an Oneida casino, a handmade signs says NO SOVEREIGN NATION. NO RESERVATION and then KARAOKE WITH ROGER AND ARLENE. Silos, flags, tractor sales, and cabins. Aging Christmas decorations, yard sales, summer camps, rifle ranges, meth heads in trucks, and gray people behind screen doors who look out as we pass. A large bird, Lord would know what kind, perches on one foot in an irrigation ditch. Cloud shadows on fields and a father, smoking a cigarette, hauling his kids down the road's shoulder in a trailer hitched to his lawn mower. Thunder and lightning. Up and down. Up and down. Sometimes I think about sex.

We never travel far in one day. We might spend two hours walking. We might go as long as four. "Where are we going?" I ask. Then, "Are we even here?"

My feet ache, my whole body. In one small town, there are no motels, so we find an abandoned car behind a service station. We lock the doors. When I wake in the night to pee, one streetlight casts long shadows. Stones look like fierce animals; trees look like dangerous men in leather jackets. I get back in the car and lock the doors.

When I wake, Ruth is looking at me because my shirt's ridden up in the night. She sees my belly. The bump is becoming obvious. I hadn't told her. I scratch blood to my scalp. "I'm going to have a baby."

Her face is hard. She lifts my shirt again, resting her dry hand on my stomach, lump of dough. Ruth palpates a few spots until she finds one she likes. She keeps it there. The conspiracy of cells dividing underneath my skin makes Ruth smile. I like it when Ruth smiles. It's almost like speaking.

I buy a cup of coffee at a gas station. A nurse in turquoise scrubs coming off a night shift tells the cashier, "I'm heading home to eat hot wings with blue cheese." For the first time since we started, I don't miss the comforts of home.

A large group of walking women dressed in bright pink pass us by. Some are in crazy costumes, pink wigs and tutus. Some carry stuffed flamingos. Some carry pictures of dead women. I stop one. "What's going on?"

She's pretty, healthy. Her cheeks are cherried with exertion. "We're on a walk," she says.

I nod.

"For breast cancer. A five-K."

She catches up with her buddies, switching her tush as she passes.

"Five-K?" I say to Ruth. "Amateurs."

Ruth smiles again.

"Man, we should have found a sponsor. We'd be raking it in."

Men honk. Teenagers play chicken with our bodies and their cars. A nasty dog charges. I pick up a stone aiming for its flank, but — *crack* — it lands in a soft spot on his forehead. The dog stops. I raise my arms overhead. It's a small victory for the pedestrian. I don't even feel bad. It's really hard to be a walker these days, a pregnant walker. Drivers scream from their windows like we're the selfish ones, decadently traveling on foot. Time moving luxuriously slow for us alone.

Well, take that right between the eyes.

The first time I feel the baby move, I think it's my phone on vibrate until I remember I don't have a phone anymore.

Someone's left a plush gray sofa and a busted recliner on the shoulder of a side road, curb furniture. We sit in them for a rest. They smell like pond scum and air freshener. Birds make a fuss in the tree behind us.

We come to a lake with a beach. There's a small wooden walkway and an empty lifeguard's chair. The day's warm. There's a dock and a line of red floats in the water marking a safe boundary. It's late afternoon. Children are splashing. Families are gathered on the beach. The fathers wear white shirts and black pants. The mothers wear thick hose and long dresses. Their heads are covered with scarves. Orthodox Jews. A group of teenagers wears matching sweatshirts and black jersey skirts so long, they swipe the ground.

I remove my shoes to feel the sand. "Hello." But we're intruders here. Ruth and I find a spot on the beach and shrug off our bags. When I sit, bent in the middle, my already-unbuttoned jeans cut into my belly. The beach gets quiet but eventually the boys return to splashing, ignoring us. Some wear prayer shawls. All of them, even those deep enough to breaststroke, cover their heads with yarmulkes. There are no girls swimming.

The children shriek. The mothers scold. The teenage campers are watchful.

Ruth loses her pants first, then her tops. People are not going to like this. She stands in her modest bra and underwear — a plain white brassiere and pale blue briefs that rise to her navel — loud as a siren, but the boys keep swimming. Her body is ghastly white and trim. She has the physique of an elementary school gym coach, not cut, but strong, flat, fit, just fine. Everyone ignores her. Maybe they think she's a boy.

She walks to the water's edge. "Ruth?" But she keeps going, looking to the low green foothills on the other side. The cold water doesn't stop her. She walks straight in, out past the boys to where she can begin to swim. Her arms paddle through the brown, cool lake.

I stand to wiggle out of my jeans, disrobing down to my T-shirt and undies. Immediately people take notice. The other beachgoers freeze, stunned. One father realizes what's about to occur. Pregnant female flesh is set to corrupt the oasis where his son has come to bathe. The father sets off an alarm, panic flushes his forehead. He stands, arms waving. Sweat pastes his silver hair to his doughy skin. "Boys! Boys!" he yells. "Everyone out of the water!"

The boys stop their frolic. Ruth's long brown hair floats on the surface. She waves to me to join her. More panic at the shoreline, arms paddle swiftly, rushed with surprise and embarrassment. The boys sprint to dry land as if pursued by a great white.

If Ruth notices their revulsion, she doesn't show it.

Spits of "Feh!" as I make my way to the shoreline. I've never caused such a reaction. But Ruth's arms swish, gentle as wings. I borrow her courage. The coolness of the lake, our buoyancy. Underwater I lift my shirt for my messed-up baby without sin.

We float for a long time. Fireflies appear, stars beaming their light all the way from far-off outer space. Ruth is walking me away from the world I know into one I don't.

We spend a day in a motel waiting out hard rain, watching daytime TV under the covers of a double bed. Ruth wields the remote. We spend the next morning walking through the drizzle to escape the horror of daytime TV.

After lunch the sun comes back out. Ruth smiles. I pinch her rear and shuffle my feet, a boxer in the fresh air. She opens her arms, steps to one side, then the other, some old Latin dance move. Ruth can still dance. She laughs. It's not talking, but it's sound coming out of her. She kicks some pebbles in our path. In one hour I'll forget what her laugh sounded like, but right now I play it on rewind over and over again.

I don't know anything. Lord's wife might be dead. Nuclear bombs might have destroyed New York City. It could be Tuesday, the day I go to the gym after work. I don't know when the equinox will come or if it already came. I don't know a thing about the bones in my feet. I don't even really know skin. Parts of my feet resemble corned beef hash, a mash of chunky pulp smelling just as foul. Blisters lanced and drained, swollen ankles.

We fall asleep like corpses, end of the film, but Ruth really is a horror movie villain. You think she's dead, done, conquered. The audience, including me, breathes easy for a moment. Phew. I can go home now, have a snack, take a bath, but then Ruth bolts upright, her head rigid, ready to walk again. Unkillable. Unstoppable. Undead all over again. It's alive. It's alive.

"Where are we heading?"

She points down the road, someplace I can't see, but each morning I say to myself, Today we'll arrive. We have to. We've been walking so long. And each night we don't. "Where?" I yell at her, dedicated drama queen. "Talk to me!"

I smell burning plastic and Chinese food. We walk past the entrance to a Walmart. "Can we go in?" It's not home, but it's familiar. Ruth rolls her eyes but allows the excursion.

Across the huge expanse of parking lot, the magic doors sense our presence. An empty cube of frigid air escapes as we enter. We are greeted by an older woman in a smock. HELLO, her badge says, I'M RITA. "Can I help you find something?" Rita, full of welcome, smiles at filthy, undeserving me, aware that most likely we'll buy absolutely nothing. We might even leave some grease behind or shoplift. Rita keeps on smiling. People do that near Ruth's scar, like kissing the ring of an evil queen or keeping a mad dog calm. "No thanks. Come on." I lead Ruth first through the accessory division. Here, I am the guide. Watches, wallets, and leather driving gloves bleed into a scented bounty, rows of body lotions, bubble baths, multivitamins, and cream rinses. I move slowly through these items. The jewel-toned surplus reaches up to the ceiling. People select their identity from hundreds of shampoos, supplements, and suppositories. Dove + Garnier Fructis + Finesse + Crest + Secret. We head into homewares. Shams and sheets. I stop to feel a comforter, testing its thickness. I relax in the linen department. Ruth and I test a model bed, resting in the calm pleasure of things. We wash up in Walmart's bathroom. I let the warm water rush over my hands, wrists, elbows. Ruth scrubs her hairy pits. No one cares.

I find a pair of jeans with a flexible panel. I need these. But I also want to buy something I don't need for the luxury of spending money. After trips through sporting goods, craft supplies, stationery, and lingerie, I choose a bracket of wooden beads. Looks like an abacus. Supposed to be used as a foot massager. Ruth shrugs. "I'll carry it." She selects a blue tarp. The tarp worries me.

"What's that for?"

Ruth doesn't answer.

"To sleep on?"

She nods back at me while she's walking away and winds up banging straight into an older man neither of us saw.

"Well, look at you," the man says to Ruth, smiling, standing from a crouch. He'd been comparing a couple of empty plastic storage containers, huge Tupperware. "How's it going for you?" he asks Ruth.

She nods, doesn't answer him, of course.

"I see," he says. "Cat got your tongue. Yup. That happens sometimes." But he's indifferent to her silence, keeps right on talking. "How are you finding the canal?"

"What?" I step in.

"The Erie," he says. "That's why you're here, right? I love it but find it requires something a bit more waterproof." He gestures toward the plastic containers, looks at Ruth. "You need one of these?" he asks her.

She crouches to examine the containers better. Pats the plastic lid of one, then shakes her head no.

She moves into the shoe department.

"How much farther is it, Ruth?" She chooses new sneakers for me, so there's my answer. Ruth doesn't need replacement shoes yet, a further embarrassment of pregnancy.

Along this strip mall street, a forgotten, unclaimed house remains. A family that held out against the inevitable and was surrounded before they could sell out. Target, Home Depot, Barnes & Noble, Jo-Ann Fabric, Stop & Shop, Staples, and their family home. A real estate sign large as a living room advertises the parcel. The house is white. Honeysuckle unhitches its jaw over the front porch. In a car it would be easy to miss. On foot it is impossible. Ruth jerks her chin toward the house.

My bag is heavier, rubbing a new spot raw on my shoulder. I already regret the stupid wooden beads.

Inside, the noise from the road is buffered a bit. It looks like someone's still living here, someone who hates to dust. Every surface is coated with greasy grit from vehicle emissions, but besides the dust, there's little sign that the humans ever moved out. The kitchen table is still draped with a cherry-printed tablecloth. There are some drippy brown spots on the fabric. There's a bowl, a glass, and spoon in the sink as if someone ate breakfast and disappeared. The Rapture happened after orange juice. Or like the way I left home without telling my mom I was going.

I don't dare look in the refrigerator.

On one wall there's a collection of phone numbers scrawled in lead, four digits each. The phone has a rotary dial. I lift the receiver. Nothing.

"You want to stay here tonight?"

Ruth nods. She fingers a kitchen counter covered with forget-me-not contact paper as if it's human.

"Cool."

There's a couch in the living room. On a low coffee table, there's an old *TV Guide* with Loni Anderson on the cover. Her hair preserved forever. Beside it there's a handwritten note. "Ezra, Don't forget to water my damn ficus. — P." The TV is gone. The ficus is dead. What happened to Ezra and P.?

Ruth runs out to the gas station mini-mart for some bottled water, potato chips, and sandwiches that we unseal from triangular wedges of packaging. I rest my feet on the coffee table the way P. & Ezra probably did before. Without electricity I watch the lights of the cars pass by. The traffic never stops, waves on an eroding beach, creeping closer to the house each night, eating the quiet fields, the neighbors, stars in the night sky.

Upstairs there are two bedrooms. We split up because we can. Before sleep, the smallness of the house, the tidy afghans on the beds, the dormer windows, make me think of El. She's probably watching TV. She's probably thinking about me, same way I think about her, same way I think about the baby every night, wondering and wondering and worrying across the distance.

In the morning the sunlight in the room makes me wish we could stay here and play house. Buy a broom for the kitchen. Clear out the dust and cook dinner. Get that phone working again and call El.

The house is so still, for a minute I worry that Ruth went on without me, but just as I think it, she appears at my door. Time to go. I remove the foot massager from my bag. I use it once before stowing it underneath the bed so that whoever lands here next can give it a try before falling off to sleep.

We pass a field of electric monsters, high-voltage transformers marching across a marshland. Each day some things beautiful and some things ugly. We pass a house held up by the pure junk hoarded inside and out. Tractors, cars, refrigerators, old metal beds. We come to a town where the men wear camo. Two teenage boys have tattoos on their necks, instantly halving the alienation they'd hoped to achieve. A sign outside a church speaks to God. LORD, it asks, GRANT US G —, but the last letters are gone. I fill in: groceries, gumballs, gorillas, good, clean fun. We pass a trailer park called Presidential Estates, an unbuilt development that exists only as a sign: MADISON FARMS. There's another basement gun shop, ugly new homes, falling-down old ones, and a street called No Lake Avenue.

That night we eat dinner at a dairy bar. We sleep in an apple orchard and wake to find the honeybees hard at work above us.

A pickup truck pulls over. The truck is just a shell of a vehicle, seems hard to believe it can still be used as transportation. A man with a blue baseball cap waves. He looks friendly. He wears his hair in a long braid down his back. I like that. You'd have to have done some thinking to be a man in braids. We haven't yet hitchhiked. What kind of maniacs hitchhike? Those who want to get chopped to bits. But here's a man offering us a ride. He doesn't even look scary. I'm tired and Ruth is scarier than anyone.

"Yes. Thank you."

He steps around to the passenger side door and opens it for us. There's a plastic tab on the back of his jeans fake-branded to read PABLO CORTEZ, AUTHENTIC LEGWEAR.

Ruth climbs in first. He helps me into the cab. "Thank you." His radio choices, wrappers from snacks his body got rid of weeks ago, years ago — it's weird stepping into the intimate space of a stranger. Ruth removes her earphones. She wants to hear the conversation, or maybe she thinks it's rude to listen to music other people can't hear. Other people besides me.

The truck's been used harshly. The door panels and console are gone. It's like we are riding inside the old bones of a horse, the old empty bones of a dinosaur.

"Where are you headed?"

Ruth studies him, looking like a wild animal ready to bite. So far she's not done anything like that.

"I'm Sequoya," the man says. "You know what I'm named for?"

"No."

"You know those trees out in California? The tall ones."

"Redwoods."

"Kind of. Sequoias. Like redwoods."

"You're named after a tree."

"Nope. I'm named after the man they named the trees for, Chief Sequoya. He invented the Cherokee alphabet."

That's not his name, and he's got a thimbleful of native blood in his left toe. Same as me, same as everyone in North America. I say nothing, but he seems to intuit exactly what I'm thinking.

"You don't believe me?"

"You're Cherokee?" I ask.

"Muh-heck Heek Ing."

"What's that?"

"Mahican."

Last of, I can't help but think it. They must hate that book. "A full-blooded Indian?"

"No."

I knew it.

"Mbuy, wtayaatamun ndah."

"Pardon?"

"He requires my heart."

"Who?"

"The water."

I shift, uncomfortable a moment.

The man smiles. "What are your names?"

"I'm Cora and she's Ruth."

He draws his chin back to get a look at us. "Yes," he says. "She don't talk much."

"No. She doesn't." I smile as if Ruth's silence is just the friendliest thing.

"She forgot how?"

The engine chugs and an old cassette player suited to this dried-up truck chews through the end of a tape, then clicks and spits, flipping over. Classic rock. Pine trees line one side of the road. The Erie, looking just like a river, skirts the other side.

"Forty thousand men and women every day. Forty thousand men and women every day," the old radio sings.

Sequoya peps up. "You've been traveling awhile?"

I think he means we stink. "Yes, bu—"

Suddenly the other side of the road in the windshield. Squealing, a crunch of bone and metal. Two minutes into this drive and we nearly wrecked. Sequoya lifts his foot off the clutch. The truck jerks and stalls. "Mother! Did you see that?" A buck with four points had jumped up out of the canal and in front of the truck. It looks around, making sure he's got all his parts. His back left leg dangles from the halfway mark. The deer takes off into the woods, even with a bum leg. Sequoya reaches behind the seat for a rifle. "Excuse me." He leaves us parked, sprawled across both lanes, key in the ignition. The buck runs as fast as he can. The fake-Indian boy gives chase into the pines at the edge of the road. The woods are thick, and in a few steps he's disappeared into them.

Ruth moves slowly. She rubs the spot where her head hit the rearview, then closes his door. Together we ratchet the bench seat forward. She turns the key, and the music switches back on. "Come on, baby."

We don't get more than a mile away before she stops the truck. She opens the glove box. Ruth find his registration card. Clifford Sequoya Shue. It's out-of-date but, still, that's his real name. She finds a bottle of water and a small box of tissues that seem the most tender thing a man could have in his glove box. What awful job did Clifford Sequoya hold down in order to purchase this sorry vehicle? How long has he been driving it? Ruth turns the truck around, and in another mile he'll never know we almost stole it. She parks on the shoulder. She clears a couple of pieces of hard plastic—what was once Clifford's headlight—from the road as penance for our attempted larceny. I use one of his tissues to wipe spit from the corners of my lips.

Eventually Sequoya reappears, lugging the deer over his back. The beast is taller than he is. Its hooves drag a wake of forest debris. Ruth opens the truck's bed and lifts the hind legs from Sequoya's back like lifting a bridal veil off a bloody bride. The deer's chin hangs over his neck. He uses the antlers as handles. Blood spots the ground. The body trembles the bed when it lands. I see its brown eyes, its loose, lifeless tongue. Sequoya fetches the water from the glove box. He pours a drink of it over the dead deer's tongue. "There," he tells the deer. "You won't remember any of that." He turns to Ruth. "I'm out of season." She produces our blue tarp, and he hides the animal underneath it. A bit of my stomach brew burns the back of my throat. I don't feel so good. I hold on to the baby. Ruth squeezes me into the middle of the bench. Blood has dripped down Clifford's authentic legwear.

"You all need a place to sleep tonight?"

"Yes."

So Sequoya drives us back to his trailer. It's on his grandparents' property, a small plot with access to the canal. "Good boy," his grandfather says. Together they string the deer up by its hind legs, binding it to a tree limb behind the house. Split open from chin to tail, the deer drips blood into a rusted pan. I've never been so close to a dead thing, at least not that I know of.

Sequoya invites us in. His trailer is covered with posters of metal bands, their names lifted from mythology: Karybdis. Clotho. Lethe. "These are old." As if he's embarrassed by the posters. He's got a record player in his small living room, and he selects some music presumed more appealing to females.

"You ladies like a glass of water?" He sets two glasses of water on the table before us. He takes a seat. Then jumps up quickly again, thinking to wash the deer off his hands. Ruth looks down into her water. Neither of us drinks it.

"You still got a long ways to go?"

I nod my head though I don't know.

"How come you decided to walk?"

"Well." I pretend to think hard, as if I can't remember. We sit there awhile listening to the music. When side A reaches its end, Sequoya doesn't get up to flip the record. He just lets the automatic arm reset itself. Side A plays again.

Later he makes a bed on the floor of his living room. A couple sheets and a blanket. Ruth climbs in, but I decide to follow Sequoya back to his room.

"You want me to take off my clothes?" I ask.

"Yes," he says. "I'd like that."

I would too, someone to scrub away the traces of Lord. I take the band out of his hair and smooth it over his shoulders. I get myself undressed. Sequoya does the same, leaving his shirt for last. When he finally lifts it, his torso is covered with pockmarks, old scars like gray polka dots on his brown skin.

"What's that about?" I ask, touching a few of them.

"I had smallpox a long time ago. Don't worry." He laughs. "You can't catch it." He reaches out to touch the curve of my belly. He stares into my navel, a lighthouse in the night. "I've never seen anything quite like that."

When I kiss him, his mouth tastes like carrots or potatoes or maybe it's just dirt. Sex with Sequoya is a bit awkward at first. I suppose it is always a bit awkward with a stranger. Sequoya's inside me and usually that's a warm thing, but he feels cooler inside than out, an empty box. Maybe the box used to hold ice and the ice has melted. Or maybe the box has always been empty. A box that's forgotten how to hold things. Sequoya, I think while we're doing it, and how I haven't considered any names yet and how, unlike him, I have no idea what Cora even means. I don't know if my baby's a boy or a girl or something else entirely, a messed-up conch-shell sort of deformity that won't live long enough to hear me speak its name.

Sequoya's body goes rigid, but I pull myself off him quickly before he comes inside me, still thinking about that empty box, still thinking about my baby. Sequoya tries to make me come with his hand, but it doesn't work because his neck and hair smell like the paraffin wax my mom uses for canning jelly. I can't come when I'm thinking about my mom.

Sequoya falls asleep just fine, and I'm left alone, thinking of El, parsing through the confusion of motherhood and sex and wondering what shape she's in right now.

When Ruth wakes me in the morning, I'm confused for only a moment. Then I remember the road, and I'm happy to leave like I have the best job ever, walking across the state of New York with my mute aunt. We slip away before the sun's up. Sequoya's grandfather watches us go. Inside his kitchen he's listening to a religious broadcast. The man on the radio is reminding listeners how years ago a 7.0 earthquake struck an island nation because the island had made a pact with the devil. Sequoya's grandfather, while surprised by this news, believes it because people will believe just about anything.

We see mountains in the distance. "'The hills are alive,'" I sing with some idea that Ruth won't be able to resist joining in the song. She resists.

That night I find a pay phone that still works.

"Momma."

"Cora?"

"Hi."

"Oh," like a heart attack.

"You OK? What are you doing?"

"Watching a movie."

"Do you want me to call back?"

"No! I'm just telling you what I'm doing. Where are you?"

"With Ruth."

"Ruth? Ruth who?"

"Your sister."

"What? How'd you find her?"

"She found me. She came to our house."

"What? Cora, what does she want with you? Let me talk to her."

"Mom, it's fine."

"Where are you? You're OK? What's Ruth up to? When are you coming home?"

"Eventually."

"Eventually. Eventually." She says it twice because she's trying not to yell. "Cora, I need— Can I talk to her? Honey, I was so worried."

"I'm sorry."

"Let me talk to Ruth."

"She's not talking."

"What?"

"She doesn't talk."

"Where are you? What's she telling you? Don't listen. What has she said about me?"

"She really doesn't talk. Not a word."

"What? Where are you?"

"I don't know."

"I'm coming. Where are you?"

"I really don't know where we are exactly. New York."

"The city?"

"No. Farmland."

"Where?"

"Mom, I'm OK. I'm OK on my own."

"Where are you?" She screams it this time, and it's going so badly that I decide it would be best to just hang up. I don't want to hear her this upset.

Ruth sits on the curb waiting for me.

"I called El."

She lifts her face to hear more.

"She's pretty mad. That makes sense. Probably more scared than mad."

Ruth nods.

"You're not doing this to get back at her? Right?"

Ruth bites her lip. She hadn't considered that. No, she shakes her head.

"Because you don't have to. It wasn't ever easy for El either."

Ruth nods again.

We start walking and after an hour she motions, don't I want to stop?

"Not yet." We walk farther than we've ever gone in one day, following the course of the old canal, unknotting knots, untying a belly button. Every tree we see reminds me of El. There's sacrifice, antagonism, rebellion, obsession, and adoration, but no properly complex word for what's between a mother and a daughter, roots so twisted, a relationship so deep, people suffocated it in kitsch and comfort words to pretend it's easy. I look to the trees. I hold my stomach tightly but I'm not strong enough to stop mothers and daughters from splitting apart.

I see forests and subdivisions. Rednecks slow as they pass, their tongues darting between their pointer and middle fingers. Packs of wild teenage girls and flat, open places where UFOs could land. "Livin' on a Prayer" becomes "Hello Mary Lou (Goodbye Heart)." We see more men, more lawn mowers mowing lawns that don't need it. We see a brother and sister tearing around in their grandpa's electric wheelchair up and down their driveway as if it were a go-kart. Ahead of me, Ruth flips the cassette in her Walkman, and the song she's listening to, whatever it might be, starts playing again from the start.

RUTH SCREAMS LIKE A DONKEY. Her entire middle is on fire. Everything hurts.

"I will break you to the saddle! Lord Jesus enter in!" The Father prays over her. Nat crouches by the bed. The Father's been praying for a day and a half to no effect. God will not ease her symptoms. The Father's begun to curse. Ruth sweats through the night, biting Nat's fingers when it hurts too much.

Finally the Father drives Ruth to a hospital forty minutes down the road instead of the closest one. A lower price had been negotiated for emergency room services. The Father says he was waiting for the state to call him back with instructions, as if she were a broken DVD player. He comforts her on the drive. "You'd be dead by now if the Lord thought you were ready."

"Guess we'll all be here a long time."

The Father drops her off and leaves. The hospital keeps Ruth for a week. Her appendix had ruptured. She's put in the children's ward. The place is filled with parents taking care of their sick kids. All day Ruth hears the children call, "Mom" or "Dad." And the reply, "Yes, dear? What do you need?"

Still. Ruth's fingers come unclenched in the hospital. If someone wants the sheets or the poly gown she's wearing, they can come and take them — indeed, an orderly does exactly that once a day. She's never been so long without Nat, and it is interesting to feel the places where she expands, the places she contracts, without him.

She receives visits from candy stripers, nurses, doctors, and chaplains. A lady with art supplies shows up every other day so that Ruth doesn't question a visit from a tall man who comes and sits beside her. He has damp blue eyes and long sideburns. For a moment he's familiar. "Are you from CPS?"

"No." He's brought her a bouquet of wildflowers including the lowly, lovely dandelion among the stems.

"Thank you," Ruth says.

"My pleasure." He claps his hands the way a pediatrician might. "So. Where are you from?"

Ruth drinks up his attention. She tells him about Love of Christ!

She tells him about Nat and the other children. She tells him about the Mother, the Father, the goats, the homemade yogurt.

"All of you are living there together?" He takes his time with her as if he doesn't have other children to meet with in the pediatric wing.

"Yes."

"How brotherly," he says.

And that's a new way of thinking about the home for Ruth. "What about you?" Ruth's happy to have someone to talk to. "Where do you live?"

"Me?" he asks. "I own a self-storage center in Troy. I'm by myself now but hope to meet a nice woman, start a family, and settle down soon. That's my plan."

"Hmm," says Ruth.

"I've had some trouble meeting women in the past."

"Hmm," she repeats again, unsure what to make of his revelations.

"Can I bring you something from the cafeteria?" he asks. "Jell-O? Ice cream?"

"Sure. I'd love that. Thank you."

"No trouble at all."

He returns a few minutes later with peach gelatin. "Here we are. That'll do you good." His pale eyes match his blue shirt. His hands look strong as a firefighter's or someone's dad.

"What's your name?"

"Zeke." The man steps up to the edge of her bed.

"Do you work at the hospital?"

"No," he says. "The storage center. I told you."

Ruth puts the Jell-O down on her bedside table, suddenly scared. "I've seen you somewhere before," she says, but she can't remember where.

"Yes. I get around."

"What are you doing here?"

His cheekbones are high, leaving the area below sunk in shadow. His nose is long, comes to a definite balled point. "Visiting."

"Who?"

"You." He extends his hand to her. He lifts her wrist, and for a moment she thinks he's going to kiss her palm. He reads her admission bracelet. "Ruth Sykes. Beautiful."

"Thank you," she whispers.

"Can I take a look at that?" he asks.

"What?" He moves his hands up to her face. Maybe he really is a doctor.

He doesn't touch the skin but hovers over it. The man stares at her scar as if it is a glowing geode. Then he does touch her, tracing the lines of her scar with an index finger. He cups Ruth's cheek. The curve of his palm is damp, hot as breath. "Yes." He eyes her scar the way others might a sunset. "An entire cosmos." He nods. "Do you feel it, child?"

Ruth feels something.

"There's home between you and me."

A nurse bangs through the door. The man steps away.

"Good news," the nurse says. "Discharge day." She stops. "Is this your father?" the nurse asks.

"No." The man steps back from the bed. The nurse is fussing with a chart, checking levels. Ruth touches her scar as the man backs out the door and is gone.

Ruth lifts her dress to show the kids where she's been stitched back up.

Ceph says, "Nothing special in you." The pits of his eyes are vicious.

"What's a Ceph?" Ruth asks. "Ceph? That's nothing."

Nat smiles to watch her spar, relieved to have her back. A week in the home without her felt like death. He and Ceph had gotten into trouble, hanging the crosses in the barn upside down.

"Fine with me," the Father had said in a voice calm and chilly. "Since them hogs need castrating." He sent Ceph and Nat to the pen with one pair of snips and two flat rocks so the meat wouldn't give off boar odor when cooked. Five boy piglets. Nat and Ceph took turns in the easier job of leg restraint at first until Ceph developed a passion for smashing pig scrotum.

“Have you seen Mr. Bell?” Ruth asks.

“Yeah. I told him you were in the hospital. He says we need practice, get the jitters out.” Nat turns to Ceph. “You want to play Mr. Splitfoot?”

“What, a game? Like with a knife?”

Ceph is the opposite of Mr. Bell. No charm, no intrigue. “Not Ceph,” she says. “And it’s not a game.”

“He’s perfect. Tough customer.” Nat turns. “No, Ceph. There’s no knives involved.”

Ceph’s presence brings out the actor in Ruth. She draws a creepy circle with charcoal in the basement. She makes him sit inside it as punishment. “Shh,” she spits. “Total silence,” though he’d said nothing. “What,” she asks him, “are the rules? What makes the dead come back?”

“How the fu—”

“I’m not asking you. I’m telling. First. No perfume ever. The dead don’t go in for unnatural scents.”

“I don’t wear—”

“Second and most important, you have to pay attention. You have to notice them. Be quiet. Listen. Try to learn their names. If you don’t know their names, you probably won’t be able to see them.”

Ceph laughs like he knows better.

“And the last rule.” Ruth looks at Ceph. “Comb your damn hair. The dead hate your messy hair. So do I.”

“That it?”

“That’s it.”

Nat’s head begins to loll, sweeping across his chest from left to right. He draws in one very loud breath that alters his voice like a gulp of helium. When Nat opens his eyes, there are no eyes to be seen, only the whites. Ceph’s bottom lip cranks into a posture of disgust.

“Butter. Butter.” Nat sounds ditzy, far away. The original owner of his ribbed undershirt sweated yellow crescents. Nat sniffs the air tilting in toward Ceph. “Black walnut. Yeast scum.”

Ruth rocks forward and back, forward and back.

Ceph hollows out his chest. "Hell—"

She sinks her nails into the bulge of muscle above his bent knee to shut him up.

Nat's head, caught again in a loop, moves from side to side.

"Please, Mr. Splitfoot," she says. "Continue." She keeps her nails buried in Ceph's skin, rubbing the smallest patch of his thigh with her thumb.

Coal shifts in the bin but not enough for any of them to actually believe that a dead thing's in there. Nat's silent.

"Dammit," Ruth says. "You messed it up, Ceph."

But her words are a trigger. Nat lifts his head. "Hi." Pure Lana Turner. "How are you? Name's Tina."

"Tina?" Ceph asks.

"Tell him," Nat goes on. "No! No! No! That's an old song, Teenie Weenie." He snaps his left hand, keeping time to music Ruth and Ceph can't hear. "Tell him, bye-bye. Tell him, bye-bye, Tina. Tell him."

Ceph's mouth opens.

"I'd be with you if I could."

Ceph swallows hard. "Where're you going?" he asks the voice. "Don't leave me."

Upstairs there's a knock loud as a wake-up call. The air changes and Nat's eyes open. More pounding. Someone's at the front door. "Anybody home?" The faraway question leaks through the basement windows.

"Huh?" Nat acts surprised to find himself coming to in the coal bin.

"Tina?" Ruth asks him.

Nat shrugs. "Tina?"

"You don't remember?"

Nat shakes his head. He pulls his legs into his chest. "Who?"

"Tina!" Ceph shouts.

"Who's Tina?" Nat scratches the back of his head.

"My mom."

Ruth lifts slowly. "Your mother's name is really Tina?"

Ceph nods.

Ruth grabs his wrist. The threat of her nails rears again. "Did you tell him that was her name?"

"No."

More pounding from above.

Nat stands. "He never said."

"Did you tell anyone your mom's name? I'll rip your teeth out if you lie."

"No."

So she turns against a cold front behind her, something buried a long time ago. Ruth heads for the stairs. Ceph and Nat follow swiftly. The wood of the banister feels less solid because when Nat delivers something beyond the miseries at Love of Christ!, Ruth's world gets pocked with holes, flooded with light, so much brightness and possibility.

Upstairs the sun makes them squint. The knocking continues. Ceph growls through his awful breath. Ceph's a mad dog, an exposed nerve without his mom.

The front door opens. "Anybody home?" the knocker asks.

Nat barely looks at the man standing there. Nat walks out, ignoring the visitor, trying to get some distance from Ceph, who is crying after Nat like it's his fault his mom is gone. "Where she at?" Ceph's vicious. "Bring her back!"

But Ruth is stopped by the visitor. "Hi," he says.

The guy from the hospital is standing on the doorstep. Did she forget something? She didn't have anything. "Zeke?"

"I'm happy to see you," he says.

"Me?"

"I missed you." He steps closer.

"It's only been one day." She looks down. She's not wearing any shoes. He brings his chin in line with her ear. His breath makes a humid patch Ruth feels in her stomach, lower. Her swallow's loud as a gulp. "What are you doing here?"

Zeke steps back. "I've come to talk to your foster father. Is he here?"

"Him?"

"Yes. Please."

"You know him?"

"Not yet." Zeke smiles.

Ruth sees more holes. She backs into the house as Nat disappears down the drive.

"The girl's not for sale." The Father squints at the strange offer.

"Not sale. No, but maybe there's some sort of trade we could make." Zeke chews his lips.

The Father wouldn't mind figuring out a way to strike a deal. He remembers how Ruth's sister, El, turned eighteen, crying, animal sounds, moaning and thrashing. Awful. She'd clung to his truck, grabbing onto the gearshift. He had to shove her off the seat with his boot, out the door, and quickly lock the truck. He'd tried not to look back as he pulled away from the mall parking lot, but couldn't stop himself, Lot's wife in the rearview. A child he'd cared for, now tiny and alone and frightened in the world. Awful, awful business.

Plus the Father likes for things to multiply. Once he even had a job working on an assembly line and it pleased him.

He stares out at the land, considers this man's offer. The bottoms behind the house run down to a tiny creek. If he could place Ruth in someone else's care before she ages out, he'd avoid the nastiness of moving her along at eighteen. Ruth's been with him for so many years. In the past he's made arrangements for the young women no longer in his care. A number of senior members from his congregation met their wives this way. Brother Warren. Brother Brett.

The Father looks out at the land, feels like Moses. He'll look for the virtue. This seems a decent fellow, has his own storage business. He'll take care of Ruth.

The Father balances the ball of his hand on top of the porch newel post. He strikes it once. "The girl earns me around eighty dollars a month, and she will until she turns eighteen." Practiced at husbandry.

"How old is she now?"

"Just seventeen. Not sure I can replace her. My thought is perhaps you make a small gift to me. Eight hundred dollars? In exchange, you'll get my blessing and consent to marry her. It's legal at fourteen when you've got parental consent."

"Eight hundred." Zeke considers the price.

"You and Ruth have discussed this?"

"Some. You'll take eight hundred dollars for the girl?"

Father Arthur shudders to deal so plainly in humans.

The man sees his unease and tries to demonstrate the righteousness of the plan. "The universe brought me here, brother. The universe is right."

The Father queers his eyebrows, unable to use the word "right" in conjunction with whatever this man has in mind for Ruth.

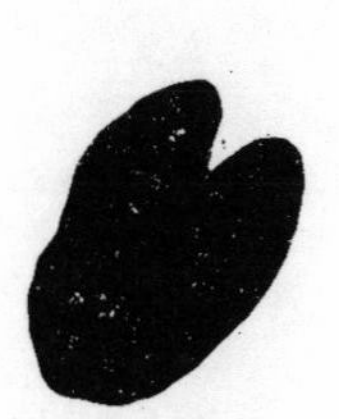

I'M SMARTER NOW that my smartphone is gone. I can pay attention in a different way. I know what strangers are thinking. I know when a town is coming before it comes because the pollution changes a half mile out. There's a thickness to the air like when you bring the palms of your hands toward one another. It's not magic. It's just attention and observation.

One store, one diner, one post office, and a heavy machinery rental center. The first humans we see in this town are a pack of kids on bikes, five or six of them. They ride past, pretending we're invisible. Ruth and I walk on, but in a few minutes the kids pass us again somehow traveling in the same direction as before. They've made a loop on the town's secret byways. I raise my hand and call out, "Hello." This greeting makes them pedal faster.

At the store I buy a loaf of bread, a quarter pound of Muenster, an eighth of salami, and yogurt. Ruth always eats yogurt.

The clerk says to me, "If you're pregnant, you shouldn't eat cold cuts." Now that my belly shows, I'm public property. Strangers speak to me all the time. They tell me how I should do everything. They want to know, boy or girl? What will I call it? Cloth or disposable diapers? Breast or bottle? Women either tell me that pregnancy hurts or that it is a miracle. Old men say some variation of "Whoa! Whoa! I'll boil the water and get some sheets."

Nothing stranger than pregnancy could happen to a body. Not drugs, not sex. An unknown that gets bigger every day. An unknown I feel stirring, growing, making me do things my body doesn't normally do. A program set to play. One day it will talk to me. It will die. How's that possible?

I pay for the food. I wish the clerk hadn't mentioned the cold cuts. Without a phone I can't even check to see if she's just coming up with random rules for her amusement. Making shit up.

We sit on the grass by the side of the store for a little picnic. There's a spigot to fill our water bottles. Ruth divvies up some cheese, some meat, and passes me a sandwich. I peel the salami off and hand it back. I haven't taken more than three bites before those kids show up again. The youngest screams out, "Howdy, yourself!" They deposit their rides outside the store.

"What's that?" the oldest girl asks. She's maybe eleven, boobs just starting to bud.

"Salami and cheese."

"Where are you from?" As if salami is such an exotic lunchmeat. Elizabeth, Katy, Drew, Alex, Amy, and Charley are brothers and sisters. They stand in a half circle around us. I offer them food. Charley tries a slice of salami. The other kids watch him chew it.

"Why are you walking?"

I look up. The girl who asks looks smart.

"Why don't you just ride a bus?" Questions flying from little mouths.

I take a bite. "Buses," I tell the kids, "are for going to school."

The children nod. Birds chirp.

"We don't go to school anymore," Drew, the oldest boy, says.

"That sounds like a bad idea."

"Not just us. None of the kids here do. They shut the school down."

"For good?"

"For a while. Our town couldn't afford it."

"That's not what happened," the smart one says. "The adults voted to cut the budget so the teachers walked out."

"So. No school? What do you do for fun?"

Most of the village is visible from here. There's one intersection. A notary sign hangs outside a ranch house. There's an oak dresser on a porch with a FOR SALE sign duct-taped to the front. There's a water tower with the town's name painted diagonally and, behind that, the school—a chain and a padlock around the front doors.

"Two things. Come on."

From hands and knees, I push up to standing. Ruth arranges the pack behind her shoulders and lies back, uninterested in fun or kids. She shuts her eyes in the circle of six unpeopled bikes. The kids stare at my belly as I stand. Charley, the little one, chuckles until Amy stops him. "Nothing funny about that."

The kids lead me away from the store, oldest first. I fall in line behind small Charley. Out of earshot from the others, I tell him, "Well, it is kind of funny."

Katy stops to pick up a stick, something to drag through the dirt. They tell me their mother had been born here, which is rare because there's no hospital or doctors. She was delivered by a neighbor who'd given birth three times herself and so knew something about it. I tell them I have no idea how to give birth. They tell me their mother has a loom. She makes rugs and sells them to an outfit in New York City that marks the price of the rugs up 700 percent. The kids tell me their mother loves a man more than their father, but she hasn't seen the man in twenty-five years and everything she loves about him has, at this point, been made up by their mother.

We stop in front of a small house with a concrete porch. "This is the first fun thing," Elizabeth says. The house is vinyl-sided. There's a discarded mini-fridge in the yard and a woman as large as I've ever seen, a cumulus cloud of yellowed flesh, cottage cheese in a polyester skin on a sagging double porch swing.

"What?"

"We look at the fat lady."

"For fun?"

"Yup."

I steal one glance. Her average-size soul hides behind her rib cage. Sounds of body processes bounce and rebound through the spiral galaxy of her middle. She's like a human whirlpool, pulling everything in toward her.

The children stare as if looking into an oracle. "You can say whatever you want to her. She just takes it. She can't really move, at least not fast enough to catch you."

"That's fun?"

The woman watches us.

"Yeah."

One of the children tries, "Fatty."

Charley attempts, "Toi-let!" — the dirtiest word he knows.

The woman doesn't flinch and doesn't take her eyes off me. I walk away quickly.

The children bombard the woman with insults and absurdities

before catching up with me. After the first fun thing, I'm not certain I want to see the second, but the children take the lead and I fall back in line. Eventually I think of something to say to the large woman, but "Hello" occurs too late.

We leave the road, cutting through an overgrown lot, a garden planted during the Reagan administration. There's a sage bush and some asparagus fronds. There's a fence still standing. The children find a hole. Each takes his turn ducking under the wire. Alex and Amy hold it up as I squeeze beneath.

We follow a path through yellow grass. Charley sings a song about a zebra. Amy sings with him. Elizabeth turns to reassure me. "Not much farther now." Mostly the afternoon is quiet. My eye catches some color up ahead, garbage caught in the grass, a cookie wrapper that has weathered nights and storms in this field. It was here last time I kissed Lord, last time I ate dinner at El's.

"Is that neighbor still around?"

"Neighbor?"

"The one who knew about babies?"

Elizabeth stops walking, which means we all stop walking. The path is narrow and she's in the lead. "No. She's gone." She turns to look at my middle. "Why? When's that going to come out?"

"Well." I scratch the sides of my stomach. "I'm not sure." I try to start us walking again, but Elizabeth doesn't move.

"No due date?"

"No."

"You forgot?"

I shake my chin no. All I see are the tips of my sneakers beyond my curved belly. "I never really knew."

Someone has dumped the front door to a house in the field. It has a small diamond-shaped window with smashed glass. Charley sings, "'He used to like to wear galoshes until a pair of oxen told him those were only for the rain. Now the zebra prefers his sneakers and wears them as often as he can.'" Big black squirrel nest in a leafless tree.

Some part of pregnancy is familiar. When I was a girl and it was quiet, I felt an enormous weight, a dentist's lead blanket across my body. My hands would get heavy, huge, impossible to lift. The world would go soft, metallic, and heavy. That's kind of what pregnancy feels like. That, plus the best present you ever felt coming. Mostly I'm surprised how little most people know about growing babies. No one tells you about all the weird things that will happen, like how your mouth will get full of spit. What's that about?

The kids don't have to tell me when we're there. We step out of the trees and into the open. The expanse could cover eight football fields. There's nothing there except a huge depression. We're standing at the edge where the ground falls away under our feet.

"What is it?" My voice dribbles down into the hole. The seven of us line up shoulder to shoulder along the edge. In the space and stillness, we wait for something to happen.

Charley sings a sudden, loud pitch. His siblings join in, striking alternate notes. Like a trained choir, one child drops out to breathe while the others keep up the chord. The noise is big as a church organ. I can see it disturb the emptiness. It travels out, down, up, across the depression over to the other side. I join them, quietly at first, then I really start to belt. Breathing, belting, breathing, belting. The sounds lift us, like we could step off the edge and not fall. One noise, an awkward, ugly chord, until we are empty. Each noisemaker drops out, and when the quiet returns, it's equally impressive. The quiet focuses everything. I run my hands over my hair, straightening it, calming something electric, and once I have, across the hole, as if we yelled him into existence, I see a man. "Who's that?" I hit Charley's shoulder and point. "You know him?" The man watches me. He's huge, solid as a wall, Sasquatch in a brown jacket and dark sunglasses like a character from a cop show plopped down here by accident. He walks with a cane though he's young. When he sees me see him, he steps back from the edge and disappears.

"Who's who?" Elizabeth asks. The man is gone.

"There was a guy. Nothing. Forget it." In a moment I'm easily convinced I imagined him.

"So, this is it," Amy tells me.

"What is it?"

"It's a hole."

"This is fun." Especially compared to the last thing. "Singing into an old mine."

"It's not a mine," Drew sneers. "It's a crater from outer space. Meteor strike."

I look into the woods. "A meteor made this?"

"Not a meteor," says Alex. "It's a sinkhole." He's matter-of-fact. "Our town is getting swallowed because the gas company's sucking everything out from underneath us. That's the real reason they closed our school. They're getting ready to kick everyone out of town so they can get the gas."

"That's not it," Charley says.

"Then, what is it?"

"I don't know. I'm just a kid." Charley starts up the sound again, and the rest of us join in. There isn't any point to it. I'm not getting anywhere. No start, middle, or end. The children scream and I scream, and the noise we make goes out and down and round and round and round.

That night it starts to rain, drenching. My bones ache. They are damp. Hot baths march across my mind, warm beds. Ruth and I break into a basement window of the school. It hasn't been closed up for long. Artwork hanging in the hallway still has its color. The freezer in the cafeteria's kitchen is plugged in, stocked with small square pizzas and garbage bags of frozen corn.

There are two vinyl chaises in the infirmary. We stretch out, but it's creepy sleeping in the sickroom. "Come on."

The library is like a dollhouse. Everything built for half-size people. The books are still on the shelves. We settle into Story Corner. It says so in construction paper cutouts above our heads. A pile of pillows, soft pads, and blankets. In the streetlight I read *The Owl and the Pussycat.* I read *In the Night Kitchen,* holding the pages open so Ruth can see each illustration. She hands me the next book. I crack its spine and begin. "'We were tired of living in a house.'"

That night I dream I'm a pack mule.

When we wake, I make pretend at the librarian's desk, surrounded by office supplies. Stamp pads, pencil sharpeners, envelopes in all sizes, string, and a rubber thimble for turning pages, accessories of usefulness. I set the due date stamp, giving myself a little bit longer than I think I actually have. I press its blue ink onto my belly.

Ruth reorganizes her backpack, dumping all its contents out onto a child-size table. She folds and sniffs things. She pulls out a simple-looking book she's been carrying. "What's that?"

She turns the cover toward me. It's primitive looking, like some early American religious text. *The Book of Ether,* it says, stamped in gold.

"What's it about?"

She passes me the book, and I carry it over to the window to see better.

298 Hide up the records in the earth,
hide up the records which were sacred, the
    records played only if there are advanced
    spacefaring civilizations in interstellar space
hide up the records,
hide in the wilderness,
hide in the dust
and hidden things shall come to light.

When I see him outside the school in his leather coat and sunglasses, I welcome the experience of familiarity. But then I see Ruth's face. Her eyes follow every step he takes. I close the book. She watches him rattle the chains of the padlock, bang his cane against the doors, as if we are the last nuts in a jar he'll shake until we fall into his hardened hand.

This whole time we've been walking, I thought we were heading somewhere, but just now, seeing her scared face, I know that we're also running away.

Ruth shoves me back from the window. She takes my arm roughly. Still clutching her book in my hand, I grab my things. We exit through the boiler room transom. We run through the playground, through the soccer fields. We run into the town where people live and people buy groceries and people do many normal, regular things, but even then, among these normal people, Ruth does not want to stop running.

THE FOOD IN THE KITCHEN belongs to old people: saltines, sherbet, cling peaches. The chrome canisters for flour, sugar, and coffee are pocked by rust.

"Hello?"

Mr. Bell had asked them to meet here, had given them the address and apologized. "I've an appointment and won't be able to fetch you."

Ruth had spent the night wondering what sort of appointment Mr. Bell might have to keep. Who are his friends, his associates? What are they associating over? She'd thought Mr. Bell was theirs alone, that she and Nat had conjured him, had asked for him to appear one night in a dark basement. Now it seems that's not true. Other girls can see Mr. Bell, talk to him, eat food with him, lie naked beside him in bed, say, should anyone want to do something like that.

Nat and Ruth set out after dinner. The Father has already disappeared behind his locked door. The air outside is perfectly cool. Some leaves have fallen. They walk to the address Mr. Bell provided, a small house in a solid block of other wooden homes, one in a line of aged identical sisters, each clothed in a different shade of chipped paint. Ruth knocks. There's no answer. Muslin curtains obscure the first floor. She opens the door a sliver, letting it hang that way. "Hello?" She sends the question through the narrow opening. A car engine turns over across the street. She pushes the door open a bit more. "Mr. Bell? Are you here?" Nat steps inside.

From the foyer they see a living room wallpapered in gold. Two straight-backed yellow couches, a low table, two Windsor chairs, one empty bookshelf. The hallway, papered in red flowers above the wainscoting, leads to the kitchen behind the stairs.

"Mr. Bell?" Nat heads to the back of the house, leaving the second floor for Ruth to search. A painted glass pendulum lamp hangs overhead. "Mr. Bell?" She climbs three-quarters of the way up, her head above the second-story landing. She moves slowly. "Hello?" The railing, the floors, the dark wood trim work. Each of the four doors off the upstairs hall bears an etched brass door plate. Each door is closed. A framed print hangs in the hall, Irishmen and Africans building the Erie Canal. Someone's once-tidy home.

"Mr. Bell." She gains the landing. "Are you here?"

Ruth walks with hands in front of her body, palms turned sideways prepared to karate chop whatever may strike. She opens the first door. A plain bathroom. Small white hex tiles on the floor. A basin stained blue by the metallic drip. There's a clawfoot tub with a white plastic curtain. Ruth backs out of the room.

She tries the next door, no longer calling for Mr. Bell. Her throat's gone dry. The room is empty but for a set of mauve polyester curtains and a crank-operated hospital bed dressed in a filthy sheet. Ruth retreats swiftly, her breath coming faster.

The next room is slightly less empty. There's a single bed with a painted pine headboard, no sheets, no blankets. There's a night table, and on the table there's a lamp whose stem is a ceramic ballerina in a blue tutu. The ballerina holds a bare bulb in her lifted hand. A large round mirror hangs on one wall, and on the floor below the mirror there's a packed canvas army surplus duffle.

Ruth kneels to inspect the luggage. Her knees pop as she bends. The sound alarms her. She holds her breath and digs carefully, making as little noise as possible. A number of white tank-top undershirts. A wrinkled overcoat. She covers the trove with both hands. It's Mr. Bell's stuff. She's found his lair. Ruth continues to dig. She unpacks a stack of three books, one mystery, one field guide to North American trees, and a novel, *Delta of Venus*. Ruth opens to a bookmarked page and begins to read. Two naked ladies and a horsewhip. It's a dirty book. "They reached the full effulgence of their pleasure." Even Mr. Bell's pornography uses funny words. Ruth keeps digging, touching his things. Mr. Bell's toiletry sack. A Bustelo coffee canister half filled with grounds and a red plastic scoop. Each thing she touches makes him more real. Ruth looks behind her. No one there.

She reaches deeper into the duffle, anticipating a cobra strike, a severed arm, Mr. Bell's dark and throbbing soul. Instead she pulls out a broken watch and a jar of black nail polish. She pulls out a plastic yellow comb and a box of waterproof matches.

There's a sigh from the house.

She looks behind her again. "Nat?" Nat does not answer.

She returns to the dark cavern of the duffle. The violation is as clear as if she were digging not through his luggage but into his mouth and throat, touching his lungs and liver. Ruth finds a tiny, precise, portable set of tools. The hammer is no bigger than her foot. She examines the screwdriver and wrench, handling each item carefully, delicately. There are undershorts. There are oxfords and socks. There is a spiral-bound sketchbook. The cover is worn, and there's an old photo taped to its back side. An image of a woman, a hippie whose long brown, beaded hair obscures her face. Ruth opens the book. On the first page, there's a pencil illustration. It's a series of points linked by a network of lines. Same thing on the next page, delicate lines moving out from ten or twelve heavier nodes, like flight patterns out of twelve different cities, only there's no map or picture to explain what connections are made between the dots. A chaotic spider web. Ruth flips through the book. The same illustration has been drawn on every single page.

"What're you doing?"

The book falls to the floor with a brutal slap. "Jesus." But it's just Nat. "You scared me to death."

"What are you doing?"

"Snooping through Mr. Bell's stuff."

"What'd you find?"

"Check this out." She stoops to pick the sketchbook up again, opening it for Nat. "Same picture on every single page."

Nat fingers the pencil lines. "What is it?" He takes the book in hand, studies it. He looks up to Ruth with the skewed mouth of a stroke victim, looks back to the book, then up to Ruth's face, eyes troubled on her.

"What?"

Nat turns her so that they are shoulder to shoulder in front of the large mirror. He holds the open sketchbook in front of his own face.

Ruth meets her eyes in the mirror. Side by side with Mr. Bell's drawing, the pattern locks into familiarity. Dots, lines, paths. Mr. Bell has obsessively replicated and drawn the explosions that scar Ruth's face. She's twinned with the illustration on the page.

A door slams shut downstairs. They move with the quiet swiftness of children trained in self-preservation. They collect the spilled items and jam them back into the duffle, threading the rivets, locking the clamp.

"Hello?" he calls from the staircase.

"Mr. Bell," Ruth says flatly, no trace of her terror. "We were just looking for the bathroom. Hope that's OK." Nat and Ruth take up casual posts in the hallway outside his door.

"Of course." He smiles to see them.

Ruth does not smile. "Whose house is this?" Her voice is flat.

"Yes. Umm. My mom's?"

"So where's the bathroom?"

Mr. Bell opens the last door. It's a closet. Then the next. The hospital bed. Then the next. "Right here. Of course. Always has been."

"Where's your mom at?" Ruth asks.

He sticks a hip out, resting one hand on it. He thinks a long while. "Uh, Jersey. She retired to Jersey." Big smile.

And left her sherbet behind.

Nat changes into an outfit selected by Mr. Bell. A pale blue button-up shirt with just a glimpse of a black lanyard cord showing around his neck. His pants are woven to a silver sheen. He wears his own work boots. Mr. Bell hadn't thought to purchase shoes. Nat's hair is brushed.

For Ruth, Mr. Bell selected a celery cover-up. The tag inside says MADE IN INDIA and another one GOODWILL STORE $4. Her bra shows through the fabric. The gown drags on the floor. It smells like wet wool. She sits next to Nat on the couch. They look like seven-year-olds impersonating Floridian retirees. Neither of them leans back. Even Mr. Bell is nervous; even he seems young. "I'll wait in the foyer."

Finally there's a knock. "Please. Let me take your coats," and then, "What a lovely kerchief. Welcome." Mr. Bell leads an older married couple into the living room. Perhaps they're here to contact someone before they themselves pass on. They sit opposite Nat and Ruth. The man rubs his palms on his thighs. It's embarrassing to admit one believes the dead can speak. His wife twists his wrist like the accelerator on a motorcycle, and the whole premise suddenly strikes Ruth as bizarre. Why do the living assume the dead know better than we do? Like they gained some knowledge by dying, but why wouldn't they just be the same confused people they were before they died?

Nat and Ruth quickly realize they should have waited in the kitchen until the audience was assembled. Next time.

Another knock. Two more couples, same as the first: white and nervous. No one speaks. The people steal glances at Nat and Ruth, glowing, toxic child brides. One of the couples seems to have arrived straight from a punk concert. Her skin is gray from cigarettes. His hairdo is as big as hers. In opposition, the next couple looks like health nuts, comfortable shoes, thin as marathoners, people who vote. Everyone has dead people.

Mr. Bell comes in last. His movements belong to a man who doesn't need sleep. He takes a long time pulling the nylon curtain across a bay window. He then raises one brow, meaning, I have done my part to separate these people from their money. Now it is up to you, partner.

Nat looks like a fine blue thing. Ruth gets to work before thought can catch up. She raises her hands, holding the sun. "Great unseen force, remove all obstructions between this world and theirs. Lift the veil so that we might receive guidance and the gift of spirit here with us tonight." She holds her pose for just a moment. Such antics come naturally after life with the Father. Mr. Bell nods. And she's practiced. "Close your eyes." Their movements are swift, each of the six obey her readily. She takes Nat's hands. "Ready?" His chin is already lolling, saliva gathering between his lips. But what's the point of Nat's rabies routine if everyone's eyes are closed? A misstep. "Open your eyes, please." She focuses her gaze, pinning down the air between them, urging it to become charged. "Hello?" she asks gently, politely. She doesn't name it Mr. Splitfoot in front of strangers who might imagine the devil. That's not what Ruth thinks. For her, Mr. Splitfoot is a two that is sometimes a one, mothers and their children, Nat and Ruth, life and death. "Are you there?" Ruth thinks of El, like a photographer's flash firing. There then gone. Again she whispers, "Hello?"

"Craw" is the first word from Nat as not-Nat. The rough voice. Eyes rolled back.

"Sorry? Crawl?"

"Crack."

The marathoners sit upright.

"Crack?" Ruth asks to confirm.

"Crack. Crack. Who's there?"

"Is there a name?"

Nat shakes his head as if water is lodged in one ear. "Car."

The marathoner wife is perched on the edge of her chair, ready to pounce on a bingo.

"Car?" Ruth verifies the message.

"Kar?" the wife poses.

"Crack!" Nat repeats, a bullwhip. His hips begin to stir, winding up.

"That's her." The wife reaches out to touch whatever's there. "Our daughter," she explains to the others. "Karolina."

"Drugs," the father says. "But we hadn't imagined crack. We don't know anything." He stares at the carpeting. He looks intelligent. Ruth wonders if he'll suspect a con, but he lifts his gaze to the top of his wife's head, so depleted by grief, he's divorced from reality. "Karolina," he calls out. "Sweetheart."

"Karolina?" Ruth tries to confirm.

"Kar," Nat says low, slow.

"Mommy and Daddy are here." The mother's eyes roam, tracing the air near the ceiling.

"Cree-ack," Nat says.

"We have a contact." Ruth, as some sort of ghost traffic controller, confirms. She adjusts her body on the brown plaid couch. "Would you like to deliver a message, Karolina?"

"DB-D-DD." Nat dribbles like a baby, lurching over the low, pressed wood coffee table.

Ruth feels suddenly sick. Their dead child's been reduced to grunts from a boy in slick polyester clothing.

A smile crosses Nat's face. He speaks clearly, precisely, dramatically. "I'll tell you a story. A lovely story. You must hear it. I shall tell it to you. There, now, you sit there."

Mr. Bell smiles from up on tiptoes.

All six paying clients lean in. The marathoners are particularly eager — every ache they've felt since their girl's been gone.

Nat's eyes flutter, revealing a bit of white each time. His mouth resembles a sea creature's. "On the dark nights, stormy nights, you can hear him, the wind, and the fluttering of his great cloak, beating wings. The thunder is loud and louder." Nat raises his voice. His best Vincent Price. "At the midnight hour, he gallops. Always searching, always seeking. And if you stand on the bridge at the wrong hour, his great cloak sweeps around you, his cold arms clasp you to his bony chest, and forever you must ride and ride and ride." Nat's head tumbles to his chest, wasted after his performance.

"Oh," the mother says.

"The very story of addiction." Karolina's father shakes his head. Tears are forming. He holds his daughter's name in his mouth.

"Is there something you'd like to say to Karolina?" Ruth asks.

The mother turns to her husband, the destruction of the past years evident on her skin. "Mommy and Daddy are here," the mother whispers. "Mommy and Daddy," she begins again. Every failure she served her daughter ruffles her face. How she forgot to pack one hundred Cheerios on the one hundredth day of kindergarten. How she was late to high school graduation because the parking lot was congested. Nights that teeth went unflossed.

Nat moves. He braces his arms on his knees. He shakes a little bit from the shoulders, some sort of boogie-woogie. "Donald!" he calls out loud and sunny.

The marathoners twist their noses. They don't know anyone named Donald.

"Donald and Karolina." Nat finally says the dead girl's name. "Together forever. And that's a looooonngg time." Nat giggles, does the Elvis shake again, then it's over. He grabs the back of his neck, looks at those gathered, and disappears into the back of the house.

The father, having waited for a sign to break down, does, a whining moan. Tears shake his chest. He balls his hands in front of his eyes. But the mother's sorrow is most sickening. "Karolina." She stands. "Karolina." She swings her hands through the air searching for her daughter's body. "Karolina, don't go." But there's nothing there.

Mr. Bell offers the mother a box of tissues. She holds on to the box with two hands, as if it's someone's head. She sobs. No one knows how to comfort her, so they don't. They listen to her cry until eventually the punk guy interrupts. "Sorry, but that's it? Where's our dead person? Where's theirs?" He points to the older couple.

Ruth collects her gown around her.

"Communication with the spirit world can be utterly exhausting for the medium," Mr. Bell says. "I'll remind you, there's no guarantee with the dead. It's not AT&T."

"'Scuse me? The freaking kid tells one crazy-ass story? For a hundred bucks? You got to be freaking kidding me." He throws his shoulders back, getting in Mr. Bell's face. "My wife lost her dad last year, so you go get that little faggot back out here."

"A hundred? We paid more than that," the old guy says.

Mr. Bell sours. Things are about to go very badly, indeed. "Sir, please."

"Bullshit!" Barrel Chest turns to the others.

Karolina's mom huffs. "Just because your dead person didn't show up doesn't mean —"

"My dead person?" He's shouting like a drunken uncle. Ruth pulls her legs onto the couch, under the cover of her gown. "You think your dead kid's better than my father-in-law?" Black curls and a red face. He beats one hand into the other. "I bet you do. Think 'cause you paid more that your dead person's going to show while we get nothing? Fuck you and fuck your dead kid!"

"Please. Please!" Mr. Bell moves between the two like a jumping spider.

“What did you say?” Karolina’s mother asks. “What did you say!” But it is Karolina’s father who responds. He’s still crying, but he uses all that grief to land a punch on Barrel Chest’s left ear. The guy ducks but not enough, and the punch throws him back into his chair.

“Please!” Mr. Bell shouts. “Please!”

“What the fuck?” Barrel Chest goes ape shit. “He punched me!” He tells his wife, “The freaking stiff punched me.” He flexes his arms, an overweight gorilla about to charge, when Ruth has a moment of inspiration.

She rolls her eyes back and, mustering a clear, crowd-dousing voice, asks, “Sweetheart?,” loud enough to draw the heated room to immediate attention. “Peanut?” she continues. Everyone’s watching her now. “Sugar? Little girl? Baby doll? Princess?”

The punk wife grips her husband’s flexed arm. “Holy shit, Mike. It’s him.”

“Princess.” Ruth repeats the key word.

“Daddy?” The woman draws one whiny breath before cracking into sobs. She collapses into a chair, hauling up sorrow like a sloppy, wet bucket. She lifts her eyes, face already running with boogers and black mascara. “Why, Daddy?”

“Forgive me, Princess.” Ruth keeps her voice low, her eyes twitching. She shakes her arms and shoulders. “I’m so sorry.” She flutters her lashes. The woman is bent forward, convulsing with coughs, some thick stream is working its way out her mouth.

“Know that I love you. That I’d be with you if I could.” Ruth breathes through her mouth.

“Daddy?”

Ruth hesitates only a minute. “Maybe I cheated.” She pulls bits of a stranger’s imagined life together. “Yeah, I, uh, cheated.” The room is silent. Ruth makes sure to twitch and convulse.

“Daddy?”

“It wasn’t true.”

“OK. We forgive you. Whatever it was.”

“Thanks,” Ruth says, a terrible, terrible impersonation. It doesn’t matter. Then one last time, “Princess.” Keep it rare. The woman sobs, and suddenly Ruth doesn't feel bad anymore. She feels like a bitter orphan taking aim at a town filled with parents, dead and alive. Ruth opens her eyes in time to see Mr. Bell's surprise melt into smiling conspiracy. She's been accepted into his con man's union. He nods with a tiny tick in his cheek, a meter counting the dollars they're going to earn.

Nat and Ruth buy a box of Frosted Mini-Wheats and two pairs of jeans for her, the first pants she's ever owned. She hides them in her closet. They buy a used Ping-Pong table for the kids at the home. The Father doesn't like that. He smolders. He doesn't know how to play Ping-Pong. He doesn't know how they got the money, but he knows it's sinful. "God placed the law in men and you shall yield!" He locks Ruth in the downstairs bathroom. He goes at Nat's backside with a length of plastic tubing right outside the bathroom door. Ruth sings any song she can think of, something for Nat to hold on to, "Here You Come Again," "Old Dan Tucker" loud as she can.

Eventually Ruth falls asleep on the tile floor. When the Father unlocks the bathroom, he hits her in the head with the door. "Forgive me," the Father says. He's weepy. She passes him by. She does not offer forgiveness. Upstairs she applies a beeswax salve to the welts on Nat's back.

The Father damns the Ping-Pong table. He packs it up and sells it for twenty-five dollars at a flea market held in town on Saturdays. He uses the money to purchase flannel sheets for his bed in order to purify the funds.

But still there is no yielding. Ruth tries on her new jeans when they are alone in their room. She bends over, strokes her thighs. No wonder the Father never lets her have them.

"How do you feel?" Nat asks.

She squats, stretching the fabric. "In these pants, I could do things I've never done before."

"How do you feel about those drawings we saw in Mr. Bell's stuff?"

She straightens up. "It's not my scar. The drawings were old. He didn't even know me yet."

"Then let's ask him what they are."

"It's none of our business. We were digging through his bag." Ruth changes back into her dress before going downstairs. "Don't scare him off. Please."

At breakfast the Father calls her name. He's leaning against the countertop in a bright white T-shirt with a red cross, like a lifeguard, except it's a crucifix and the shirt says MY LIFEGUARD WALKS ON WATER. Maybe that's why the Father never taught them to swim.

Nat looks up at her name.

"You know a man named Zeke?" the Father asks her.

"Not really."

"Owns that self-storage down by the river?"

"I guess so."

"Well, he knows you. Come on." He pulls out her chair. "We need to talk."

Ruth follows the Father up to his room. She hasn't been inside in years. The Mother's stretched out on the bed reading a book called *Dawn of Dementia.* She looks up. "Ruth. How've you been, honey?"

On TV the news anchor helps some Chinese lady demonstrate a recipe for pickling cabbage. The newscaster wrinkles his nose. "Woo!" He shakes his telegenic hands. "That's a spicy meata-ball!"

There's lots Ruth would like to tell the Mother, but she's distracted by the room: laundry both ways; a pink starter kit from Mary Kay cosmetics, including twelve shades of lipstick, skin regimens for oily, normal, and dry, and seven eye shadows. None of it yet sold. On top of the kit there are several afghans, a few issues of *More* magazine, and two two-liter bottles filled with ocher pee. There's a stack of word puzzle magazines, a box of Almond Roca, two artificial flowers, a fringed leather jacket hanging below a poster of Stevie Nicks. The Mother's built a fortress from things purchased at the 24-hour pharmacy. An Easter basket with plastic green grass, a white teddy bear holding a red embroidered heart, a pillow with electronic massaging balls. Four pairs of Isotoner slippers. Padded envelopes. Acrylic yarn. Three jumbo boxes of Special K with freeze-dried strawberries. "I'm fine."

"So Zeke," the Father says. "Seems you've caught his eye. And we're proud of you, Ruth. Mother and I wish you the best. We hope your marriage will be a fruitful one."

The Mother belches loudly. "Pardon. IBS," she explains.

Ruth has no idea. IRS? "Marriage?"

"Yes. I didn't even know you two were friendly."

"We aren't."

"There's so much about your life these days I don't know," the Father says. "And I figure if you're already grown and gone, you might as well actually go." The Father waves something out of the air, enjoying his moment of cruelty less than he'd hoped. "You'll need our consent, seeing as you're only seventeen. But we're happy to give it."

"Consent to —"

"Get married."

Ruth's head tilts hard to the left. "You want me to marry a stranger?"

"Heavenly Father has led me to believe that this is exactly what you were made for. That's why your appendix ruptured. Now I understand why my prayers couldn't heal you that night." He moves slowly, taking her shoulders in his hands, squeezing hard enough to grind her bones. "Happy for you," he says. "I worked this out special. Zeke'll take care of you."

"How old is he?"

The Father shrugs. "My age?"

"Old."

"Not that old and, you know, there's never charges when you're married."

"Charges?"

"Rape."

The Mother experiences a further wave of cramps.

"If I get married, I'm allowed to move out of the home?"

"Of course."

Ruth focuses on the Father's fly. "What about Nat?"

"Once you're married to Zeke, you could probably start adoption proceedings. The state is more or less giving away dysfunctional seventeen-year-olds."

"Make me Nat's mother?"

"If your husband approves. Everybody wins. Most importantly"—and the Father, his chest puffed up, points an index finger up to the sky before deflating, acknowledging that not everything in his plan is lovely. "What am I supposed to do, Ruth? Turn you out on the street?"

She shakes her head no. "I won't end up on the streets. I'll find a job."

"I know it's scary, but it's less scary than aging out with nowhere to go and no one to take care of you."

"Nat'll take care of me."

"Nat can't take care of his shoelaces."

"That's not true. I'll take care of me. I always have." This pisses off the Father.

"You want to give me some more lip?" he asks.

"No."

"Now we need to discuss some things about your wedding night."

The Mother's sick gut pinches her mouth into a turnip. "Happy for you, honey, but I need to visit the commode." She takes that cue, exiting the bedroom quickly before more poison leaks out.

"You want me to get married?" Ruth asks.

The Father doesn't answer that question. "Let's see." Chin in his hand. "So. You've seen the rabbits, when they're in a fever?"

"Sick?"

"No, dear. When they cleave to one another. Inserted, bred—"

He's talking about fucking. "Yes."

"Well, it's nearly the same with humans, but I'd like to explain a few things. There is a loving way a husband treats his wife. Caresses and movements privy only to those wed in God's eyes. Certain actions and membranes."

"Pardon?"

"You don't know this yet, Ruth, but your body conceals private chambers open only to your husband's probing key." He lifts his hands, fingers splayed like a shining sun. "Secret cavities that belong to him alone."

Ruth feels sick. Is he kidding?

"And in the moment a husband and his wife's flesh are bonded as one, certain fluids will be exchanged. Do you understand what I'm saying?"

"I don't want to, Father Arthur. Please don't kick me out."

The Father shuts his eyes. He remembers El and the day she had to go. He'd heard she'd found nothing but trouble down in Troy. "You're scared, girl," the Father says, "and I understand, but a woman can't bow her knee to God until she bows her knee to her husband. Find Christ and lose your fear." He smiles. He takes her hand. "A blushing bride, my, you've grown. We'll work it out for you, dear. Happy for you."

Ruth looks up at the Stevie Nicks poster, meditating on this beautiful woman. Marriage would mean no more state. A kitchen, a refrigerator of her own. Zeke humping up on her front and back each night until she's eighteen, but if Nat could come with her, she'd be OK. I'll go see the man, she thinks. See what sort he is. What's coarse in her life will lift her up, carry her down past the industrial park and the anonymous block of buildings whose sign reads TOOL AND DIE. All the way to the self-storage office. Her fingertips will buzz, freedom in there, for Nat and her, lovely as the sun through a bottle of old pee.

Each séance takes place in a different home. "My cousin's boss is out of town." Mr. Bell picks Ruth and Nat up at the appointed time and takes them to a new address. The car windows are rolled down even though it's cold. The outside air smells of balsam and rain. In the back seat Ruth fingers a realty sign that'd been yanked from the ground. She watches Mr. Bell drive. He's a creature who makes his own tools. She admires that.

"What did Father Arthur want?"

"Some loose ends from the hospital."

Nat nods. Mr. Bell parks.

Some of the houses have books. Some have TVs that cover entire walls. One has a room given over to a collection of dull-looking rocks. One has no furniture in it at all. "My uncle's condo," Mr. Bell explains.

Nat and Ruth dress in clothes provided by Mr. Bell. He tells them that their clothes, the stuff from the Father, scare people. "*Children of the Corn,*" he says.

"What's that? Like we're farmers?"

"No. Sociopaths." He gives her a wink.

Nat and Ruth wait in the bedroom until he comes to fetch them. She sits in a windowsill. "You know I'm making my bit up?" she tells Nat.

"I'm fine with that."

"But you're really talking to dead people, right?"

"How many times are you going to ask me that?"

"Can you just tell me the truth?"

"I talk to dead people. Yes, yes, yes, I do." To the tune of "Skip to My Lou."

"Good because otherwise it would be stealing. I don't want to steal from people who are already so sad."

When Nat and Ruth are led into the living room, the guests are sitting cross-legged on the floor as if telling ghost stories around a campfire. Ruth and Nat join them there.

"But they're children." One man wrenches his spine to complain to Mr. Bell.

"Precisely." Mr. Bell pats the man's shoulder, a familiar gesture. The man smiles as if the teacher just praised his correct answer. "Children have not yet hardened the divide between life and realms of the undead. In India" — Mr. Bell lifts a curled finger to his temple — "the most attuned mediums are always children. India," he repeats, "and Brazil. And" — feeling inspired — "Morocco, of course."

"Brrrriiinnnng!" Nat's off. He twists his hands, tuning in. "I'm speaking with a man named Lester. Yes. Anyone have a Lester? Sorry Leroy. No Leonard."

"Yes!"

"Brrrinnnggg! Yes, sorry. Leonard. Now Leonard was your —"

"Grandfather."

"I was about to say that. Brrrrriiiinng! Served in World War II, yes?"

"How did you know?"

"He told me." Nat had practiced too.

"Grandpa."

"You're a hick, and nobody ever helped a hick but a hick himself!"

"Pardon?" the man asks.

"I'm standin' here on my hind legs. Even a dog can do that. Are you standin' on your hind legs?"

The man looks around himself. He remains sitting.

Nat foams, spits, rails, swinging his arms. "Here it is, ya hicks! Nail up anybody who stands in your way! Give me the hammer and I'll do it myself!"

Mr. Bell rubs his hands together. He's really not that much older than Ruth, but he works it with confidence, with his suit, and people believe it.

"Grandpa Leo?"

Later Ruth hits on a vein. "I see a toddler in a costume," she whispers in her trance. "Dressed as a lion." She pauses. "No, it's a bear. A dog."

One of the mothers explodes, grief on the walls of this foreclosed home. "That was her second Halloween. She was a poodle."

"Yes," Ruth says. "I see jack-o'-lanterns. Candy corn."

The mother rolls with sorrow, as if there is a button inside her Ruth can just keep pushing, flooding fresh tears from a never-empty well. At least the mother will sleep tonight.

Afterward, over chicken with cashew nuts, they count the money. Ruth gets quiet. "Sweetheart, sweetheart." Mr. Bell touches her hand. "It's not as if you're pretending the dead are alive. People want to be told what they already know—the dead were once here and they loved us. You should be happy to tell people that."

Ruth nods.

"Why do we split it three ways?" Nat wants to know.

Mr. Bell pushes his Adam's apple left then right in a samba beat. "Because there's no end to my generosity." He exhales with an open mouth, blowing breath and insult Nat's way. Mr. Bell looks to Ruth again. "Buck up, little flower."

She and Nat keep their money stuffed up the hollow leg of their metal bed frame. Eventually the bed can hold no more. Nat slices open the lining of his winter coat and fills it, like a transfusion re-fluffing the flat garment with cash. It's so much money, Nat doesn't bring up the three-way split ever again.

Word spreads. People line up to talk to the dead. Parents who have lost their children. Children who've lost their parents. A young woman who survived, in utero, the car crash that killed her mother sits beside the father of a boy who'd mixed a potion of Drano and grapefruit juice for his girlfriend and himself. The town alderman misses his mother. A high school history teacher whose nephew was caught in an undertow. Mr. Bell collects them. It's not hard. Dead people are everywhere.

Sometimes the same people return, though Ruth, in the spirit of egalitarianism, has each new person receive word from their dead before issuing repeat performances.

Mr. Bell counsels a skeptic in the hallway. "Sometimes it's two or three generations removed. You might not recognize a great-great-aunt. Don't worry. She knows you." He squeezes the man's arm. "Please leave your coats in here," Mr. Bell requests. "We've found it best to be unencumbered by material possessions when spirit is present."

And Ruth is quite like a spirit. "Mary?" her voice crackles, the warm static of an old radio. "Is someone here looking for Mary?" Silence. "I'm sorry. The name is Larry. Larry?"

And a woman whose cardigan is pulled tight as a tourniquet round her middle sucks in her breath. "Harry is my husband. Harry." Her cheeks spot with blood.

"Of course. Harry." Ruth walks like a ballet dancer on her toes. She touches the living, placing hands on their shoulders to calm them. Ruth laughs. "Harry just made a joke. He was quite funny, wasn't he?"

Afterward, over souvlaki this time, Mr. Bell asks, "What have you two been learning in school?"

"We don't go to regular school. The Father instructs us."

"What's he teaching you?"

"Sine. Cosine. Jesus," Ruth says.

Mr. Bell mulls it over. “Can’t say I remember that.” He looks above their heads. “How about Sherman’s charge on Atlanta? Did you cover that yet?”

“We’re still working on Herod’s expansion of the Second Temple.”

The storage center’s sign is big as a billboard. OUTER SPACE. The plastic veneer paneling of the trailer is made to resemble wood. A sign is taped to the wall. RENT ~~DO~~ ON FIRST OF MONTH. Someone had crossed out the misspelling. Zeke’s alone in the office, smiling like there’s no one he’d rather see.

There are a number of file cabinets, a gun locker, a plastic lunch box, and, behind the desk, a poster of the solar system with all the planets, including Pluto.

Zeke wears a country-western shirt with pointed pockets unsnapped to his sternum. He looks different today, sweatier, skinnier, more scruff on his chin. His eyes are red.

I can get divorced in ten months, Ruth thinks.

“You need some storage?” Zeke teases her, friendly as a man with something to sell.

She should’ve worn her new jeans. She feels like a child in her old dress and apron. “What kind of stuff do you store here?”

He leans into her. “All manner of celestial wonders.”

“Pardon?”

He huffs his shoulders in a fake chuckle. “Just getting started so at the moment I’m primarily storing space.”

There’s a newspaper on his desk, today’s paper. Upside down Ruth makes out a story about bodies in the Middle East and another piece speculating which movie will earn the biggest box office receipts this weekend. She’s been to a movie theater twice in her life. “Father Arthur told me you talked with him,” she says.

“Some big stuff is about to happen here. We need you. I do. I want to take care of you.”

“What sort of big stuff?”

“The cosmos aligning for the righteous.”

“Me?”

"Comets, collisions. One space rock is all it would take to send the whole of us into orbit."

"You're an astronaut?"

"No." On Zeke's desk there are a number of different rock specimens and a tiny souvenir, fake ruins molded out of plastic. He leans forward. "Have you ever been taken care of by a man?"

Ruth imagines the factory where they specialize in fabricating plastic ruins. "Nat," she says. "The Father."

"That's not what I mean. I'm asking are you intact?"

Zeke reaches for her wrist. He bows into her open hand so she sees the back of his head, the gold in each greasy brown strand. She feels a wet warmth. Zeke separates her fingers. Every filthy word she knows comes into her head. "Intact" seems the filthiest. Moving from thumb to pinkie, Zeke takes each digit in his mouth, licking her clean. She's unsteady. She's damp. She couldn't be intact. Each breath is a labor he can hear.

When Zeke finishes licking her fingers, he rolls back, dries his meaty lips on the side of his hand, done with his meal. Ruth canters forward.

"I need—" His voice is loud. Zeke stumbles for the right word.

"A wife," she gives him, still reading the upside-down paper. The Pope is angry at some nuns.

Zeke smiles. "Yes." He opens his top drawer. "But not just any wife. I need you." He passes Ruth a foam squeezie toy cratered to look like the moon. The number of the self-storage is printed on it. "I want you to think, Ruth. I want it to be right. Are you ready to go with me? I want you to cogitate and give me a call. Will you do that?"

"Cogitate."

"Come to me when you hear an answer."

Ruth squeezes the moon, letting it adsorb the sticky saliva Zeke left behind on her fingers.

When she gets back to the Father's house, Mr. Bell and Nat are waiting. While it was a short walk home, she's long done cogitating.

"Ready to go, love?" Mr. Bell asks.

"Yup." She climbs in back next to Nat. Mr. Bell adjusts his seat and the radio station before putting the car in drive. Ruth stares at his head. "Are you married, Mr. Bell?"

"Married? My. No."

"Want to marry me?"

His accent goes British. "What a deep honor."

Nat cuffs his fingernails in the palms of his hands.

"You and I get married, then we adopt Nat. No more foster home. No more Father Arthur."

"That"—Mr. Bell turns in his seat, twisting a bit of his hair—"is a good one, Ruth." He laughs but stops when he's laughing alone.

"You wouldn't, you know, really be my husband or anything. Nat and I would get an apartment by ourselves since we have enough money now. You wouldn't have to take care of us. We're fine on our own."

"A genuine proposal. My goodness."

"It's easy, half an hour at town hall. Soon as I'm eighteen, we can get a divorce."

"Ah, a romantic."

"Mr. Bell," Ruth says. "Please."

"My," he says. "Well." He thinks. "Does marriage require a birth certificate?"

"Weren't you ever born?" Nat asks.

Mr. Bell looks at him in the rearview. "I've been born again and again. They just keep forgetting to give me a certificate."

When Mr. Bell drops them off that night, the Father's outside on a metal folding chair. The chair leans to the left on buckling legs. The Father raises his hand to his brow, blocking the headlights' glare. He's been drinking. Nat and Ruth climb out of Mr. Bell's car. Their breath is visible. The Father snickers, imagining bestial actions.

Nat has eleven ten-dollar bills neatly folded in his front pocket. They raise opposite arms, a Rorschach blot saying goodbye to Mr. Bell. The car pulls away.

"Shackles!" the Father calls out, as if landing the answer to a crossword clue.

Nat and Ruth stick to the dark, creeping their way past him.

The Father allows the broken chair to dump him on the ground. Nat passes by, but Ruth hesitates. The Father's lying on his side, one cheek in the dirt. "Commit thy works unto the Lord, and thy thoughts shall be established. God's Grace. God's Grace."

Ruth goes to him. "Here." She gives him her hand to pull him up.

"I don't want your help."

"What's wrong?"

From the ground, drunk and spitting, he says, "No matter how much I pray for you Ruth, you're going to die."

She crouches beside him. "That's OK."

"No. It's not OK to die until you've been forgiven."

"For what?" She catches up with Nat. "I didn't do anything wrong."

The Father's laugh is scary, and when they reach the front door, they understand why. Nat tries the handle but the door is locked.

"Animals," Father Arthur tells them, "sleep in the animal barn."

Nat climbs into the boxwood hedge to bang on the living room window. Raffaella and Vladimir are watching TV. Raffaella shakes her head no. Vladimir switches off the set, and they disappear into the back of the house, scared sheep.

"Fuck," Nat says. "Come on." He takes Ruth's hand.

"You're really going to lock us out of the house, Father? It's freezing."

"Rejoice inasmuch as you participate in the sufferings of Christ so that you may be overjoyed when his glory is revealed."

Nat grabs Ruth. "Come on." The mud of the yard is crusted with ice. He leads her into the barn, a small improvement. Nat collects a burlap sheet and a saddle blanket. He pitches fresh hay into the largest of the stalls, leading all four of the goats into the pen. Ruth constructs pillows. "Wish we could call Mr. Bell."

"We're going to be fine. Same as always." Nat spreads the burlap then the blanket. He lifts one corner. "Come on," he says. "Get close." The goats sniff and nibble the new hay. Nat leans back, opening his arm so she can find a warm place beside him. Her breath is still visible, and the tops of her ears sting with blood, but in a few minutes beside him, she sees he is right. Ruth is warm enough. They are going to be OK.

Nat rests his chin on the top of her head. "Mrs. Bell."

"You're jealous."

"Yes." The stall smells of goat urine. "I don't like people besides you."

"And you don't even like me. I mean in that way. The marrying way."

His eyes are gray and shining, light leaking in from the flood. "No, I don't." Nat's voice is a low whisper. "Nothing's grown back since my mom." He puts a hand over his throat. "I don't feel anything. I love you, but I don't feel anything."

"Nothing?"

"No."

Ruth lifts her chin, looking up to the rafters. "I'm going to get us out of here."

"But Mr. Bell doesn't have a birth certificate."

"There are others."

"Other people who'll marry you? Who?"

"Is that so unbelievable? That a person would want to marry me?"

Nat shrugs. "Yeah. To me it is."

At breakfast the next morning, one of the kids asks, "Do you know how to multiply a fraction?"

After chores Ruth returns to their room alone. The door is already open. Ceph, in a sweatsuit, sits on their bed. He broke in during their exile. He's found some of the money and has it spread out on their blanket. "This you?"

Ruth nods. She approaches the bed and puts her hand on the crumpled bills.

"I need it," he says.

"For what?"

"I'm getting extradited."

"Emancipated?"

"Fuck."

"How?"

"I'm turning eighteen."

"When?"

"Soon."

"It's almost winter."

"I know. I need money."

She thinks a moment. "You'll be eighteen. What about a wife?"

"What about it?"

"You could take me with you. We could get married."

"You?"

"I need to get out of here. Then you won't be alone."

Ceph looks at the bills, considers his options. "You know how to do it?"

"Leave the Father?"

"No. Fuck."

She thinks of the question about fractions. She thinks about intact. "No."

Ceph winces. "Pay me, let me do it with you, and maybe I'll take you when I go."

She doesn't think long. It doesn't mean anything to her. It's her body and she'll use it. She grabs some of the money and puts it in Ceph's hand. "Fine." She shuts the door, trying to think of Ceph as an opportunity, like government-provided job training.

"Take off your panties," Ceph tells her.

She moves slowly, folding her underwear before depositing them in a laundry bag hung on the back of her door. Ruth keeps her dress on. Ceph lifts it up, uses it to cover her scar. He tucks his head into her neck, carefully opening her left leg and then her right. "Hold steady," as if he is performing a precise surgical maneuver.

With Ceph moving on top of her, one thought fully jams her mind. "This is it?" It's nothing. It's nothing. It's nothing, she says to herself, and moments later it's over. She can't reconstruct how it felt or what happened or what the big deal is. Words from the Father present themselves as still unsolved mysteries: membranes, fluids, cavities. "Can you do it again?" she asks, still under cover.

"Hold on." He kneads her boobs for a minute or two.

The gray world. From under her dress, Ceph could be almost anyone.

"OK."

This time Ruth pays attention. She peeks, watching Ceph's chest and hips. She sees the shadow of someone's feet arrive just outside the door, a person listening from the hall. She presses her lips to Ceph's ear. She lets her breath come heavy, and Ceph responds in kind, grunting loudly.

When Ceph's done, he sees three drops of blood on the blanket. He looks from the door to the blood, from the door to the blood. All the years Nat and Ruth slept in this bed not doing anything. Ceph feels strong as a criminal. "You're mine."

She tilts her head quickly, once. "You're eighteen soon?"

"Yeah."

"I'm yours if you get Nat and me out of here."

Ruth sits on the edge of the bed, her legs still open to the room. Ceph slides the lock back, opens the door. "Mine," Ceph says, marking his claim in front of Nat.

Nat looks in, past Ruth's dark hair.

This is a test. She keeps her legs open, asking, Do you really feel nothing?

No.

Thought so.

"Get your coat on," Nat tells her. "Mr. Bell's here."

THE OBESE WOMAN is no longer on her porch. I bang once on her door, but Ruth doesn't wait for permission to enter. We step into the foyer of the woman's house uninvited and out of breath.

All manner of thrift store furniture clutters the space, chintzes and striped velvets. It's as if the ocean rose and receded, rose and receded, a flood of unloved junk right here in this drowning woman's living room. The walls are crowded with paintings of children and animals, photos of the mountains at sunset, posters advertising California vineyards, international craft festivals, tulip parades in Holland. One couch is given over to an arc of stuffed animals arrayed for a tea party. A patio lounger is covered with pillows printed with dogs, pillows made from madras, pillows with cross-stitched Christmas wreaths on their fronts. There are shelves of jigsaw puzzles. The room's as fattened as her body.

Ruth's strange book is still in my hand. I lift it to my face, my only shield. I enter the parlor as though preparing to swat a fly. "Hello?" Our other option, being chased by a man with a cane who scares Ruth, seems a worse choice.

The woman's voice is high, squeaky. "I'm here," she says. Not the bassoon I anticipated from that rain barrel. She's crammed into a double-wide wheelchair. "What's your question today?" Like a tinkling bell. "Or more insults?"

"I'm sorry. Those children were very rude." The book is still raised. "I'm sorry to bust into your house, but there was a man," I explain.

The woman sees the book in my hand. Her eyes squint as if the book is a too bright light, shining in her eyes. "Oh. Him." She belches as if she's just gulped a large swallow of water.

I check behind us. Who?

"Are you with him?"

"Who? There's just us. Cora and Ruth."

She braces for battle. "Where'd you get that ugly little book?"

I lower the volume to read the cover again. "*The Book of Ether*?" I shake my head.

Upping the helium in her voice. "'127 Woe unto them which

are with child, for they shall be heavy and cannot flee.' Right?" She smiles, wicked. "Right? 'Therefore, they shall be trodden down and left to perish.' He wrote that one about me. I'm his real wife, the legal one, and when he's gone, that house'll be mine."

"What house? What?"

"You're one of the new wives? That his kid?"

I look to Ruth. "I'm nobody's wife."

"But you came to hear about Mardellion?"

"No." I'm ready to take our chances with the man and his cane, but there's Ruth beside me, nodding crazy, yes, yes, yes.

"She did." The woman's wheelchair engages, its engine chugging under the load. "I try not to think about him anymore."

"What's a Mardalon?"

"Mardellion is a man. A bad man. My husband. Head of the Etherists."

"What's that?"

"Cult." She gestures outside, swirling her hands, scissoring her sausage fingers, ticking off qualities. "Same old story. Charismatic leader collects damaged souls, tithes all their money, shares their kids, promises a better life." Her wrists twist like a flamenco dancer's. "But power poisons his mind. He isolates his followers, sticks it in as many holes as he can, then realizes he's collected a bunch of fuckups he can't take care of. His only way out is to distract them with an apocalypse while he scoots off with cash. The End. It's an old story."

"What?"

"Sit. Down," she tells us, equal emphasis on each word.

I inspect the stuffed-animal couch. Elephants, hedgehogs, zebras, bears. Ruth parts the front curtain a sliver, looking out to the street. She locks the door and joins me on the couch. The woman lowers her arms. Her chair cruises toward the hi-fi. Jan and Dean spin a song about a car crash. "Mardellion, or whatever his real name was, grew up in Utah. Mormon." The woman opens her hands on her lap, tuning a receiver in her palms for the whole story. "The twisted, back-desert, Fundamentalist kind of Mormon. Where one man, a prophet, controlled everything by sowing ignorance and fear. Right?" She powers her wheelchair closer to me, nearly running over an empty, unlatched box, made for storing 45s. "It's easy to be scared."

I look to the door.

"Once that baby's born, you're going to have a million more reasons to be terrified." She eyes my stomach, but Ruth pats the woman's knee with impatience. She doesn't want to talk about the baby just now. Ruth's never impatient.

"Mardellion. All right, girleen. Utah. So no contact with the outside world. No education. The prophet ran the place like a ranch. Only guess what animal they were breeding?"

I know by her look I won't like the answer.

"Adolescent girls. A steady crop of teen breeders to keep the old men flush with young pussy. Each old guy had twenty, thirty wives. So consider what happens to the boy babies on such a ranch. Take lambs as your example."

"Meat."

"Indeed, girleen. Indeed. Mardellion didn't get eaten, but he did get run off that place soon as he turned thirteen. Too handsome to keep around those fertile young things. He was taken out of his home, snatched from his seventeen moms, and dropped off in Provo. He had nothing except what his prophet told him. 'You,' the guy had said." She draws it out. "'Look like a young Joseph Smith.'"

"Who's that?"

"Smith started the Mormon church. He was a treasure hunter. Murdered by forty."

"A pirate?"

The room and all she says are starting to swirl, a flood of hoarded words along with the other junk. Open the floodgates.

"No. A real treasure hunter. He dug in the dirt, looking for buried stuff." The woman's face doesn't move much when she speaks, hidden in her jowls. "Smith's from around here. He found golden tablets in the ground in Palmyra. You know Palmyra?"

"No."

"Lock on the old canal, up by the holy land of Rochester. Kodachrome. Silver plates." She smiles. "But Smith's golden plates told a history of ancient American people. Smith couldn't read the language printed on the damn things, so he tossed a couple rocks in the bottom of a stovepipe hat." The woman pantomimes his actions with her chubby hands. "Put the hat over his face." She frames her cheeks. "That cleared things up just fine. He translated *The Book of Mormon* by staring into the bottom of a dark hat. Took thirty brides."

"I heard about that. Where are the golden plates now?"

"Oh." She smiles. "I think I have them somewhere." She looks around briefly, picking up a quilt, checking underneath it. "Oh, wait. No. Smith had to give them back to the angel Moroni. Shame." She slaps her hands on her mighty thighs, laughing. "But you want Mardellion, not his prophet, not Smith."

Ruth nods.

"Sometimes it's hard to tell the difference. A hundred-odd years after Smith, in the seventies, Mardellion's thirteen years old and on the streets. All he's got is this idea that he looks like Smith. He receives some social services back in Utah among actual Mormons. They help him enroll him in high school. He lives in a house with other boys who'd been cast off by Fundamentalist sects. He learns to play football. They even send him on a mission to Mexico, but then his twenties roll in and he's misfiring. He's got no family to steer him. He's working as a cashier in a pharmacy. He's unmarried. Not much of much and he wants it all. So again his prophet's words come to him, 'spitting image of Smith.' And Mardellion gets an idea.

"Every summer in Palmyra, the Mormons put on a big show up on the hill where Smith found those golden plates. People from all over the world travel to perform. Mardellion decides he's going to play Joseph Smith, a stop on his sure way to Hollywood. Riches, fame, power, et cetera, revenge on all his parents." She motors closer to our stuffed-animal couch. Ruth listens hard, a living room jam-packed with stories.

"His car makes it from Utah to Palmyra but barely. Mardellion's convinced that it's running on faith, so toward the end he tries not to blink or breathe too much. He's chugging with this idea of himself as Smith, imagining a steed, brushing back his hair, triumphant.

Despite other shortcomings, Mardellion's a fine-looking man." The woman levitates some thinking about his looks. From the stack of 45s piled high on the center post, the record player drops the next one, starts its spinning. "'I Want My Baby Back.' By Jimmy Cross. Know it?"

Never heard of it.

"Guy digs up the grave of his dead girl in doo-wop. One of my favorites."

Ruth pats the woman's leg.

"Right. So Mardellion's driving east, imagining everyone will love him." She brushes her broad belly. "Case in point. He cut my heart out. Cut it out, killed me dead."

"How?"

She freezes momentarily, a hand on her neck, a hand on her sternum. "I'm getting ahead of myself." She digs into a box of Nilla Wafers and pops one in her mouth. "Cookie?" she offers.

I grab a handful from the wax-lined box.

"So Mardellion gets to Palmyra and tells them he's going to play Smith in the pageant, and while the directors acknowledge a real likeness, they say the cast's been in place and practicing since December, and anyway it's a ten-story stage, so no one can see what your face looks like. Probably they sniff out the Fundamentalist on him. It sticks with a person, odor of death. You know that, right, dear? 'Please,' Mardellion begs. 'You can be a Lamanite,' they tell him. He's too late for greatness, and he can't even get that mad because he's dealing with Mormons. Christians." Words rushing out of her now, a heavy tide. "But he is mad." She smiles to say it. "He's never been so mad, and with all that blood in his head, he gets another idea. A better one. He never wanted to play Smith in some dumb show. He wants to be Smith, wants people to believe him, follow him to extreme lengths. He's going to start his own religion. Get the wives and worshippers."

"He starts a religion?"

"Just like that." She braces her chin with one hand. "Frankly, though, Mardellion's a little late again. Smith was brewing up his religion back when people thought solar eclipses were signs from an angry god. Back when people'd believe anything to stave off the grave. In Smith's time, in New York State alone, you had the Mormons, the Spiritualists, the United Society of Believers in Christ's Second Appearing. There were Bible Communists in the Oneida Community, post-menopausal women mixing it up with teenage boys and vice versa. There were Millerites, on and on. It was easy to find believers then because people were terrified. I heard of one religion based on wearing overalls. And Jemima Wilkinson, who woke up from a fever, announcing that her body was inhabited by something called the Publik Universal Friend." The woman tilts her head. "Hello, friend."

I'm having trouble following so many different names and stories swirling in an eddy.

"But in Mardellion's time? There're TVs and billboards advertising Fresca, babies born from test tubes, and Mardellion's thinking, I'm never going to get anyone to believe me, but he's driving around upstate. All those mountains and rivers and lakes. He's thinking, he's thinking, he's thinking. Mardellion the honeybee." The woman's eyes follow some unseen movement through the parlor. "He thinks, I need a book. Yes, I need a book, something to give people, teach them of my righteousness. He's not smart enough to write his own book, so he steals from Smith again. Takes a little bit of this, a little of that, adds some free love, some communal living, a little polygamy 'cause that felt right, home-like to him." She lifts her eyebrows. "Then some Jesus stuff, sandals. The Bible. He throws it together with some rock-and-roll songs he'd heard on his cross-country drive and comes up with the Etherists. That little book you've got there."

"People follow him?"

"The heart wants what the heart wants."

"What's that?"

"There's your real question. The heart wants someone to take away the fear. The heart wants answers even if they're made up. So here comes Mardellion with a whole bunch of answers. You don't even have to pay rent anymore with him. Mardellion will take care of you, love you always." The woman pushes back in her chair. "Yes, people follow him."

"How many?"

"Forty? Fifty? Something like that."

"You're an Etherist?"

The record drops again. She takes a peek. "'Two Hour Honeymoon.' Paul Hampton. I was an Etherist. It started with twelve of us, young people with energy, ready to work, happy to build something beautiful. I was gorgeous. You don't believe me but I was. Tan and healthy, a real beauty. We all were. We pooled our money and efforts, so there was time to spend reading or making things, gardening, taking advantage of the free-love principles. We were hippies living in a commune run by a beneficent dictator. It wasn't bad at the start. We'd eat meals together, snuggle, screw, hike in the woods. And Mardellion had a power. Knack, charisma. You know. He was all glue and charm. Slim and strong as an ox. We wanted to please him." She smooths a blanket across her knees. "Then September 28, 1980, *Cosmos,* Carl Sagan's TV program about the universe premiered. Mardellion knew nothing about outer space before that. All he knew was heaven. I don't think he even knew they'd landed people on the moon. So *Cosmos* comes along and he's hooked. He's crazy about Sagan and the *Voyager* missions. It was everything he'd been missing. Sagan and Smith. That night, watching TV, it clicked. Outer space is Heaven."

Ruth's hanging on every word.

The woman looks toward the kitchen as if she's got something cooking there. "The *Challenger* hadn't exploded yet, and the US was deep in the Cold War. So if outer space belonged to us, it meant we were safe from nukes. We could find a new planet if we destroyed this one. And that idea of safety was Heaven."

"How long did the Etherists last?"

"I was gone before the end. He started on worse delusions, drugs. He said the end was coming, but then it didn't come and it didn't come, and people, especially me, wondered why. So Mardellion decides the women are talking too much. He says women can only speak after the sun sets. I organized a coup against him. I stole what he'd stockpiled, what all his followers had given him, and I stashed it with the only person up there I could trust. But my coup failed, and Mardellion had me booted out in the dark of night. He put tape on my mouth and a trash bag over my head. I was blindfolded, spun 'round and 'round, and dropped off here." She waits for the next record to start, holding us there, a little lost in the vinyl's spin. "'Last Kiss.' The Cavaliers."

"When did he die?" I ask.

"I don't think he did, but you don't have to be dead to haunt. Parents, songs, exes."

"Are you making this up?" Babies.

She moves even slower. "No."

"It sounds crazy."

She thumbs her chin. "Years later Mardellion got arrested, some underage mess. I went to the trial hoping to see my son."

"You have a kid?"

Her voice loses its tinny ring. "He kicked me out and kept my boy."

"What?"

"I've tried to find him, but I have no proof. I gave birth up on that mountain, so there's no record. I don't even know where the mountain is."

"You don't know where you lived?"

"We never took trips into town. Mardellion had a car, but the women were not allowed to use it."

"You lost your son?"

"That's the right word. Lost."

Ruth goes to kneel in front of her, takes her hand.

"Aren't you sweet." The woman looks at Ruth. "You believe me?"

Ruth nods yes.

"So where'd you all find that book?"

"It's hers." I signal Ruth. "How'd you get it, Ruth?" We wait for a reply, but Ruth — quiet as the stars, sure as something — isn't going to tell us.

MR. BELL DRIVES to a new colonial. He doesn't have the keys and curses in a foreign language. "My friend forgot to leave them under the mat." He boosts Ruth on his knee, hoists her through the bathroom window.

It seems unlikely that Mr. Bell has friends.

Ruth moves quietly through the house. It's chilly inside. She lets them in the front door. Mr. Bell cranks the thermostat up to seventy-five. He has a new dress for Ruth. Less Florida retiree, more Atlantic City palm reader. "Perfect," he says. "Except, come here." Ruth sits on the coffee table. Mr. Bell pulls the table closer to his perch on the couch. He takes her chin in his hand. He pulls a wand of mascara, a round of dark eye shadow, and a lipstick called Raisin Hell from a plastic zip bag.

"Where'd you get that?"

"Found it in the bathroom."

"So your friend who lives here is a girl?"

He studies Ruth's face. "I respect your intelligence too much to construct a narrative that might convince you of a reality far from the truth." Mr. Bell applies makeup to Ruth's lips and eyes, dusting her cheeks with fine glitter. "So." With his work done, he asks, "You want to get married?"

She nods.

"And you want to marry me?"

She nods again.

"OK," he says. "We'll get married."

"What about the birth certificate problem?"

"They'll take a baptismal record plus a license. I checked."

Ceph had been a waste. "You were baptized?"

"Two or three times to be sure." He looks at her face from all angles, studying his work. "Get me some tissues, Nat."

Nat does.

"So you and I can get married?"

"Yes." Mr. Bell blots Ruth's lips, rubbing a bit of the excess color onto her cheekbones, across her scar. "Perfect."

She touches Mr. Bell's knee. "Thank you." She feels fire at the center of their triangle.

Mr. Bell shuts Nat and Ruth in the bedroom, whispering through the door, "Soon, lovelies." They watch an episode of *Hollywood Extra* and the end of an old movie, *The Swimmer.* Burt Lancaster in square trunks. She simmers, set to boil. "We're going to be free soon."

Nat squeezes her hands. The doorbell rings. In the mirrored closet, they check their clothes, noses, and teeth. They hear voices from the living room. The buzzer buzzes again and again and once again. Mr. Bell says, "I'm sorry for your loss." He makes the women blush, leaving his ringed hands on their waists a moment longer than a more timid person might. He has the confidence of youth. He touches their collarbones while removing their coats. The price goes up.

Finally he swings open the bedroom door. Ruth and Nat stand ready, charged to receive and inform. "Ladies!" Mr. Bell addresses those gathered, then whispers into the hollow between Nat's right ear and Ruth's left, "The one in the suit's the fickin' mayor's brother." His voice grows loud again. "And gentlemen! Your attention this minute, right here, forever." Nat and Ruth, glorious blossoms, step into a room full of sad people.

At City Hall Ruth removes her winter parka quickly so it won't spoil her outfit. Underneath she wears one of the gowns Mr. Bell bought her, sea-foam silk. Nat carries her bouquet and the signed forms from the Father. Nat takes her arm. Mr. Bell wears the same suit he wears every day, and when the clerk asks, "Do you, Carl Bell, take Ruth Sykes to be your lawfully wedded wife?" Ruth and Nat catch eyes, wondering why he never told them his name. Carl. It's so normal. "I pronounce you man and wife. You may kiss your bride." Mr. Bell, his pale skin against his dark hair, dark lips, kneels to kiss her hand, holding it as one would an injured moth.

"Thank you."

"Thank you, my dear." Mr. Bell might even be a gentleman.

Outside the leaves on the trees are red and orange and gold. This is Ruth's wedding day. They go to Hook's to celebrate. Nat sits next to the bride. He toasts the newlyweds with a cup of coffee. "Your name is Carl?"

"Shhh." Mr. Bell finds the sugar shaker empty and positions it at the edge of the table for a refill.

"What?" Nat looks behind him in the booth. "What's wrong with Carl?"

"Carl Bell sounds like fast food. Plus, I'm trying to forget where I come from."

"Where's that?"

He scratches his chin. "Hmm. I already forgot." Mr. Bell polishes off his coffee and smacks his lips. The three smile.

"Thank you," Ruth says again.

"It was no trouble."

Their place mats have a map of New York State printed in pale red ink. Niagara, Finger Lakes, Lady Liberty, the High Peaks, the racetrack at Saratoga, the Erie Canal.

"Never knew we had a state insect." The waitress appears. "Pancakes?" Mr. Bell asks them. "Belgian waffles?"

Ruth nods.

"Two orders of waffles, please. Whipped cream."

"I'll have an egg sandwich with cheese," Nat says.

The waitress takes note, sees the empty sugar shaker, and, leaving her pencil behind, disappears to refill the shaker.

Mr. Bell smiles again at Ruth. He uses the waitress's pencil to doodle on his place mat. Ruth half imagines he'll write R.S. + C.B. in a heart, the way he keeps smiling at her. Outside someone has potted decorative kale heads in Italianate concrete planters. Cars come and go in the parking lot.

"What's that about?" Nat asks.

On the map of New York State, Mr. Bell has reproduced the same pattern they found in his sketchbook, connected points.

"Old habit. Something I like to draw."

"But what is it?"

Mr. Bell lifts his brows twice. "Well." He spins the map right side up to Nat and Ruth. He circles each point as he names them.

"Scriba. Cambria. South Byron. Schenectady. Seneca Falls, go, Suffragettes. Bethlehem. Burlington. Mount Morris. Yorktown. Peekskill. And closer to home, Tomhannock and Lasher Creek. Meteorite landings in our fair state."

Ruth is slightly disappointed.

"What about the lines between?"

"Ley lines," Mr. Bell says. "That's me trying to make some sense."

"Of what?"

"Patterns, predictions."

"Predicting what?"

"Where my mom went."

They look at the map. "Where'd your mom go?"

"I don't know. I lost her."

"Why would your mom follow meteorites?"

"They used to be of interest to her."

Mr. Bell studies the lines, his face pinched with figuring. "But I checked all those places already and didn't find her." He exhales, shaking his head. "So what I once read as the handiwork of God, now looks like a random mess."

"I think it looks like Ruth's scar," Nat says.

Mr. Bell studies Ruth's face. "My, yes." He nods, smiles again. "Yes. I guess I can see that. Hmm. That's odd."

"Maybe Ruth is God."

Mr. Bell winks. "Wouldn't surprise me one bit."

The waitress appears. She deposits their food, dropping a plate of hot waffles on top of the map and meteorites, and when her hands are once again empty, she notices that Mr. Bell has her pencil. She scowls, underpaid, full of furor. She reappropriates her forgotten item with a *humph.*

A week after the wedding, Nat and Ruth find an apartment in Troy above a veterinary hospital. They pay cash for six months' rent. The first night there, they sleep half awake under coats. They have no sheets yet, just the mattress the last tenant left behind. Matthew 6:26: The birds of the air neither sow nor reap nor gather into barns, yet Heavenly Father feeds them.

Ruth curls her head into the crook of Nat's arm as one who's bloodthirsty, a truth of twisted love. Fangs, claws, a matted tail. "Son," she says into his elbow, pulling a hot wire through their hearts, though there's been no adoption. The Father let Nat go for five hundred dollars cash, saying he'd deal with the State. The Father is disgusted. He wouldn't even look at them. He wouldn't give them a lift to town. He was furious because he'd had to return the cash Zeke had given him for Ruth.

"What about 'Be fruitful and multiply'?" Ruth asked before she left.

"What about 'Honor your Father'? I gave my consent so you could marry an upstanding member of our community, and you sneak off and marry someone else?"

Ruth kept Mr. Bell's secret identity from the Father and the other kids. She didn't want her problems to become Mr. Bell's.

"I can find out who he is, Ruth. It would take me two seconds."

"I know." But she hoped he didn't really care where she'd gone as long as she was gone.

Mr. Bell honked the horn twice and helped load what they had into the trunk of his car. After seventeen years, what Nat and Ruth had turned out to be very little outside of three plastic bags full of cash. All the children except Ceph came out to tell them goodbye. Raffaella put her flipper on the hood of Mr. Bell's car. "Is he your husband?" she asked Ruth.

"Him?" Ruth acted shocked. "That would be weird." Which wasn't a lie.

Ruth slipped each child eighty dollars like a visiting grandma paying them off, expunging her guilt only slightly, the oldest girl walking away from the littler ones, as if being born a girl makes her responsible for everyone alive.

Nat and Ruth select new blankets and towels from the discount store. They shop as if they are the married couple. They even fill out a pharmacy-bought Last Will and Testament, leaving each other everything they own including a couple of shirts and a brand-new cheese grater. They buy groceries. It takes two hours to fill their cart the first time because so few things in the grocery store look like food. Ruth picks up a package of Twizzlers. "What is it?" she asks Nat. He shakes his head.

They tell people, "She is my sister, he is my brother," because if they told people they were sisters, Nat would probably get beaten up. Nights when they are not working, they go downtown to be among other people. Ruth wears her new jeans. They find a restaurant or a park bench. Ruth sits on Nat's lap, leaning into his chest, his hand between her thighs as a word wedged into the white space. Hard to read and not at all like a brother.

The other kids become phantoms. Love of Christ! is a bad dream Ruth had. Though at quiet times she misses things she'd never thought she'd miss: dipping candles, laundry, singing together, having something to do each day, Ceph, even Ceph.

Mr. Bell picks them up for work. He smiles at Ruth a bit longer, sometimes dazed as if watching fairies dance on a lily leaf. Ruth, his wife, is something he can't believe.

"He won't stop smiling at me," she tells Nat.

"Yeah. What a jerk." But he doesn't mean it. They study Mr. Bell's boots, his chin, his hair, as if these totems might explain where he came from, how he found them, and who he is.

The sun sets early now. Ruth does not enroll in public school as she was instructed to do. Instead she buys the newspaper every morning. She bakes a lot. Nat sometimes says, "I wish I were a poet," but a week passes and the urge does too. Ruth builds new bird feeders.

Life in the apartment is quiet after the home. They buy a used couch, a Chesterfield according to the man at the Salvation Army. At night, after the doctors and techs have gone home, the dogs downstairs howl at being left alone.

In the day Nat and Ruth find people on their doorstep, most often a mother without her kids. The mothers sit on the curb, slumped over a pile of matted fur: an overweight German shepherd, a cat who's lost its teeth, a mangy Newfoundland with flaking bald spots, a poodle with pus for eyes. The animals move in slow motion, looking off at something shiny beyond their owners' shoulders, unaware. The mothers say goodbye. The mothers sob, stroking their pitiful creatures. "I'm so sorry, baby. I'm so sorry," or "Mamma loves you. You know that, right?"

Nat and Ruth toast the recently departed. "To Nellie."

"To Blue. To Boo."

A song from the '80s comes on the radio and they dance. They think it is a new song, because to them it is.

It's hard to find homemade goat's milk yogurt in downtown Troy.

The landlord turns on the heat. That's never happened before either. They live on the top floor. They are unaccustomed to warmth. Nat's skin feels damp as if he's melting.

"It is hot as hell." Ruth opens a window and sticks her head outside. A man disappears into the dark on the sidewalk.

"Truly." Nat joins her.

"We need some food."

"Seven-Eleven?"

"Ten-four." They try their best to be disciples of Mr. Bell.

By the convenience store beer coolers, there are a few soldiers from the Forty-Second Infantry and an old man wearing a party sombrero. He's deposited an assortment of stuffed plastic bags by his side.

"Bud? Miller? Schlitz?" the soldiers want to know.

"Where's the goddamn antiperspirant?" the sombrero asked. "How much are the bananas?"

Nat buys a bag of pretzels, thin mints, a Fresca, and a six-pack of beer. The cashier asks to see ID. "Sure," Nat says, "sure," and passes him his ID that clearly states he's only seventeen years old. The cashier looks at it, hands it back, and sells Nat the beer anyway.

Outside they eat the pretzels on the curb. "What was up with that?"

"I erased his mind."

It starts to snow, just a little, first snow of the year. "Really?" Ruth asks.

A large kid, big as a Sasquatch, skulks across the parking lot wearing a lined canvas coat, hardly enough clothing for this weather, a sure signal to the world that he is deranged. His shoulders are up, his head down. He shakes his chin in disagreement. They watch him get closer. Ruth would be scared of him if it weren't Ceph.

"Ceph," she calls. She's not seen him since she left.

"Nuth. Rat." He doesn't stop.

"Where you headed?"

Ceph keeps going as if she hadn't said a thing.

"What are you so mad about?"

But Ceph won't stop and Ruth already knows what he's mad about.

They walk a circuit through town. They go to the high school, to the Texaco, down to the river. "What do you think Mr. Bell's doing tonight?"

"I don't know. He's your husband," Nat says.

Kids in sedans breeze by. Kids with parents. Kids whose parents taught them how to drive. Spoiled brats. Nat dribbles saliva onto the sidewalk. It'll be frozen by midnight. The moon rises, the moon sets. Ruth squeezes her hands into the back pockets of her blue jeans.

A few days later Ceph shows up underneath her window when Nat is out. Ceph yells, "Bring me down a cigarette!" The word "bitch" is silent but understood. Ceph scares the dogs with his yelling. They begin to howl.

Ruth doesn't even smoke. She meets him on the sidewalk but won't let him upstairs. He's mad she didn't take him with her. He is confusing her with his mother. "You're going to be fine. You'll find a job. Save your money and you can get an apartment. It's not that hard when you have a job."

"You think I could live by myself? Alone-like? I can't do that."

Ceph's wearing a pair of dark sunglasses and a brown leather jacket. He's carrying a cane.

"What's the costume about?" she asks.

Ceph burns. He's trying to look like a man, a tough man. He's terrified. He had parents for too long, and now he doesn't know how to take care of himself. "You said you were mine."

Ruth shuts her eyes. "I was wrong about that."

"Some meth-bitch gave me herps."

She wants to ask, Before or after me?, but she's scared it will make him angrier. Plus, she's pretty sure no one else would actually have sex with Ceph. No one besides her, that is.

When she doesn't respond, he quotes Scripture, slowly, fully. "'The devil that deceived them was cast into the lake of fire and brimstone, where the beast and the false prophet are, and shall be tormented day and night for ever and ever.'"

"I think you need some help," Ruth says.

"That's why I'm here."

So she lets him upstairs.

"Which kitchen knife is sharpest?" he asks.

"What is it, Ceph? What's wrong with you?"

His body is shaking slightly, a minor earthquake. "I'm eighteen soon."

"That's great. You're going to be free."

"Free to what?"

But Ruth has to think for so long that Ceph puts his head in her lap and falls asleep. Ruth lets him sleep. She thinks, It's the least I can do.

When he finally wakes, the room is almost dark. Ruth's thighs are hard with stillness. "You look like a Neanderthal when you sleep," she tells him.

"What's a Neanderthal?"

"One of our ancestors."

"Like George Washington?"

"No."

Ruth makes Ceph a mozzarella and tomato sandwich. Mr. Bell taught her how. Mr. Bell likes food from Little Italy. Capicola, sun-dried tomatoes, blood oranges. Mr. Bell showed her where to shop. Ruth offers Ceph a salad called arugula. "Can't eat that."

So Ceph takes her to Burger King in the Father's truck, an absurd vehicle. Its tires are so large, it's barely street legal. The Father has sunk a fortune into this truck. Its black paint has been detailed precisely with red and orange flames, a visor painted to read HOLY ROLLER, and JOHN 3:16 in white script over the gas tank.

"How come you have his truck?"

No answer.

"Does he know?"

"You think?"

Ceph orders from the drive-thru for both of them. "You pay," he says, and she does. Ceph thinks Ruth should pay for everything: his mom being dead, the world's cruelty, the stinky burgers and fries. When she cracks the window, Ceph tells her, "Roll up. Black people live here," and she's so glad she's not married to Ceph.

Like a stomach flu, word of Nat and Ruth's talents spreads. A librarian tells an aunt who tells a dentist who tells a lawyer. Nat and Ruth buy new clothes. They eat new foods. They have a stereo for playing new music. They have a hand-held beater for making cakes and muffins, a comforter filled with a down-like product. They have an electric yogurt maker and a scrub brush for cleaning the toilet when it's dirty. Each object enters their home as a holy totem, a relic from the world they never knew. They study it, learn it, and eventually grow used to it.

A few days later Ceph leaves her a message. "I put my head in an oven." Ruth walks through the snow to the Father's house to see if it's true. She doesn't want Ceph to die. She just wants him to leave her alone.

Ruth feels like a celebrity at Love of Christ! since she managed to escape. She brings a box of bakery cookies, fancy Italian ones, even if the Father will just throw them away untasted.

The congregation is gathered in the barn. Ruth looks for Ceph in there. The Father is standing on top of his stool up front. He's got the people on their feet. Fists are raised. A few congregants stomp, jumping as children in a tantrum. There's sweat in the Father's hair. He arches back with power. "God does not love everyone!" he screams. "God does not love everyone!" He gets the parish chanting, laying his own track on top, detailing a record of God's hatred. "Leviticus! 'And I will destroy your high places, and cut down your images, and cast your carcasses upon the carcasses of your idols, and my soul shall abhor you.' Psalms! 'The foolish shall not stand in thy sight: thou hatest all workers of iniquity.' Psalms again! 'Thou shalt destroy them that speak leasing: the Lord will abhor the bloody and deceitful man.' And Psalms again! 'The Lord trieth the righteous: but the wicked and him that loveth violence his soul hateth.'"

"Amen!" someone cries out. "Hatred!"

"Proverbs!" the Father keeps on, spit, furor flying. "'The mouth of strange women is a deep pit. He that is abhorred of the Lord shall fall therein.' Malachi! 'And I hated Esau, and laid his mountains and his heritage waste for the dragons of the wilderness.'" Must mean the Mother ran off again.

Ceph's not in the barn. Ruth shuts the door behind her. Her bird feeder is empty. She finds Ceph inside the house watching TV.

"How come you don't have to go to church anymore?" she asks.

Ceph just looks at her.

"You need a gas stove to kill yourself, Ceph. This one's electric."

"I don't need a stove."

"Good. I'm glad to hear —"

"'Cause I'm going to buy a gun."

"Did you call your caseworker?" Someone, anyone, besides her.

"On vacation till the new year."

"What's going on, Ceph?"

"*Friday the Thirteenth.*" Totally contraband.

"No. What's going on?" Ruth's voice is steady.

"Who's your husband, Ruth?"

"Who cares. It's not like I love him."

"That's good."

"Why?"

Ceph shuts off the tube remotely, still looking into the darkened set. He's wearing gray sweatpants, plastic flip-flops, and an undershirt with something like chocolate ice cream dribbled down the front. Pitiful. "Come on. Let's walk," she says, if only to prove the Father wrong. The hairs of Ceph's chest are visible through the fabric. "Put on a coat, please. And some damn boots," Ruth says.

Ceph points out local disasters on their walk downtown. "Bunny rabbits under the lawn mower there. I saw it." And "Gunther Wright was decapitated there. You know Gunther?"

"No." They pass Walgreens, Popeye's, and the Recovery Sports Bar, neon Budweiser sign in the window. "You're making it worse." The sun cuts a square of light through some trees. "You're choosing to make it worse." They pass another pharmacy. And then another. "Let's get coffee." She's freezing. Ruth takes one step into Hook's Diner and sees Mr. Bell at the counter. Her husband. She never just runs into him. She's *tried* to run into him before and never has, but now, the one time she doesn't want to see him, there he is, talking to someone, arguing maybe. A tall guy in a wool cap. Ruth can't see the guy's face because they're sitting at the counter. She tries to listen, but they are too far away because it sounds like Mr. Bell is saying, "ANFO? ANFO?" And that makes no sense. She wants to get Ceph away from Mr. Bell. She feels the panic worst in her lungs.

"Changed my mind." She backs Ceph out the door.

"What? Let's get coffee."

She's desperate. "Maybe you can stay with us until you figure out a place," she says as she walks out the door.

"Really?" he asks once they're outside, down the block, out of Mr. Bell's sight.

"No. On second thought, that wouldn't work."

They sneak into the Hilton's swimming pool. Tika told them about this trick. It's in the basement of the hotel. It's empty. Winter in Troy, New York. No one wants to swim. Ruth strips down to her underwear on the tiled deck. "Come in." Her voice bounces off the floor, ceiling, and mirrored wall. She clears a rainbow film from the surface before lowering her body into the water. It's warm enough to host a municipality of germs. Ruth thinks of the Hudson and Burt Lancaster. No one swims in the Hudson since GE ruined it.

"Your tits are hot." Ceph stands on the deck. "I'll miss your tits." He adjusts the waistband of his sweats. Looks into the mirror.

"Where are you going?"

"Far from here."

Ruth looks down at her simple, lumpen, soaking wet brassiere. "Good," she says. "That's the spirit, Ceph. Get out of here. Find a new town, a new life." She's relieved he'll be gone soon. "Come on in."

"Can't swim."

"I can't either." Swimming was not one of the skills Father Arthur thought important. Ruth falls forward in the shallow end. The water enters her ears. It's got her surrounded. Why does she feel responsible for Ceph? Why is he making her feel responsible for him?

Ceph is saying words back in the dry air, but it all sounds like bubbles underwater. She doesn't want to hear him talking his gorilla talk. She wants to believe that she can escape the life she's led so far, casualty-free. Bubble, bubble, bubble. Ruth holds her breath, floats on her belly. She tries to think of Nat, liquid, pitch blue. They're going to be OK. She imagines Nat swimming up to meet her out of the deep end. What took you so long? Nat pours them an underwater tea party, then knocks it out of the way. He slaps her hard across the face. Her neck falls back slowly, dramatically wounded like a matinee idol. Her lungs are empty. She stays underwater until her brain starts to pop, until Nat becomes Mr. Bell. You?

It doesn't have to hurt, dear.

It does if I want to feel it.

Mr. Bell sips his underwater tea. We forgot, Till death do us part. He lifts his hand to Ruth as water enters her lungs. She surfaces, sputtering, coughing. That hadn't been one of their vows.

"Did you hear what I said?" Ceph asks.

"No." She spits chlorine from her mouth.

"Nothing?"

"No."

"Good fucking friend."

"What'd you say?"

"You didn't hear nothing?"

"No."

"I said I would have married you. I would have taken care of you." He's standing by the edge of the pool still wearing his dirty, sad clothes. He's nothing to her, a blank or, worse, a blob. She doesn't even like Ceph.

"You can't take care of yourself."

"You were mine."

"Well."

"You lied?"

"Why do you want me?" Her head is at his foot level.

"I can't be alone."

"I'm sorry."

"So where do I go?" For a moment she thinks he will start to cry. She really hopes he won't because she knows if he cries in front of her, he'll only hate her more.

"You have no one? An aunt? A granny?"

"No. Just you."

"But, Ceph."

"What?"

"I don't even like you."

"Don't matter."

"It does to me."

"Who'd you marry, Ruth? Who is he?"

Ruth sinks under again. Hudson plus Erie. The river under the river, under the city. And the city under that. So many lonely people. Water moves around Ruth. The tides on the Hudson. What does one broken child mean to the world? Time passes, growing older, cut deeper and chilled by the current against her legs. Dirty water that circles in eddies on its way down to the next town.

Christmas comes. Ruth invites Ceph and Mr. Bell over for dinner. She warned Mr. Bell not to tell anyone he's her husband, especially Ceph.

"Lie?" Mr. Bell asked.

"Yes."

"No problem."

Ruth and Nat cook all manner of foods. A ham, brownies, potatoes, wild rice with butter, Brussels sprouts with chestnuts, cornbread. Mr. Bell brings a bottle of wine and some green apples.

In the kitchen Ceph is under foot at every turn like a real baby, getting in the way. "I'm trying to put a meal out, Ceph. Could you, please?"

"What?" he asks.

"It's like you're following me. Even in this tiny kitchen."

"I *am* following you. I've got nowhere else. I'm going to follow you wherever you go. Wherever."

Ruth shuts her eyes. Merry Christmas, she says it inside, ten times fast. She opens her eyes. "Ceph, sit down." And he finally does.

Ruth has presents for each of the three men, god's eyes she made from a couple of sticks and some yarn, a craft learned at the home. Nat and Ceph remember, but to Mr. Bell they are new. He calls his "a thing of beauty" and hangs it from his suit coat's button.

Ruth and Mr. Bell do dishes. Ceph continues to watch from his seat. He keeps his sunglasses on, but she's sure he's staring at Mr. Bell. Ceph looks awful. He barely says a word except when Mr. Bell steps into the other room to collect more dirty glasses. "I got myself a Christmas present," he tells Ruth.

"That's a good idea. What'd you get?"

"A thirty-two."

"Thirty-two what?"

"Caliber."

"A gun?"

He nods yes.

She turns back to the sink, scrubbing. "Sounds like a bad idea," she finally says. "A really sad, bad idea. Did you really or are you just trying to frighten me? On Christmas?"

"What do you think?"

Ruth dries her hands on her thighs. "I think there must be some law that says it's illegal to sell you a gun."

"You'd think so, right?"

"Yes."

"There is."

"Good. I don't want you to die, Ceph."

He looks down at her kitchen floor. "You don't want me to die, but you don't want me around either." She cannot argue with that.

They sing "Hark! The Herald Angels" and "Deck the Halls." Ruth pretends Christmas, forces good feelings. They sing "O Holy Night." Ceph doesn't really sing, but he listens without being nasty. Ruth takes a turn sitting on his knee and then Nat's and then, because the night is just so friendly, Mr. Bell's.

A week later Mr. Bell says, "Some people called me. They want a session tonight."

It's New Year's Eve. "Don't you have plans?" she asks Mr. Bell.

"No. No plans."

Nat sits on the windowsill in another guest bedroom where they've been sequestered. He wears royal blue. Mr. Bell always chooses jewel tones. "Ruth." He presents a beet-colored gown. "For you." She turns her back to the men and undresses, aware of the muscles in her shoulders. She asks for a zip. Mr. Bell beats Nat to her zipper. She shows them the outfit.

"I knew that would bring out your scar. Gorgeous," Mr. Bell says. No one—excepting cruel children—ever speaks of her scar. She raises her hand to her nose.

"When I tell you something's beautiful, don't cover it."

She lowers her hand.

Ruth decides she needs a glass of milk before she goes on. Mr. Bell is talking with the hostess, laughing. Mr. Bell with this woman. Mr. Bell with that woman. Why would Ruth care? They are in a private house. They've been invited here by wealthy people. "I need a glass of milk." The hostess is sent for and moments later returns with the milk. Ruth sips. "Is this skim?"

"That's all we have."

Ruth holds the glass out for the wife to take back. Nat does not flinch. They face each other, locked as some muscled viper winds its way between their mouths. The movement sours Ruth's stomach. "I need a glass of real milk."

"Many apologies," Mr. Bell offers. "I'll dart out to the store." He looks at Ruth like he's proud of her.

"No," the hostess says, sucking what she can from Ruth, absorbing an idea of power. "Don't be silly. I can send my husband."

The husband makes it to the store and back in twenty-five minutes. The wife pours a tall glass of whole milk and knocks on the bedroom door, her own bedroom door. Ruth drinks it down, missing the goats again.

As they enter the living room, the guests go quiet. Ruth squeezes deep into Nat's grip. She listens. On a large brown couch with simple beige pillows, an anxious bearded man with thick glasses wears a navy collar shirt. He's pale and chubby, plays too many video games. He's not here for nostalgia. He's here because someone died and didn't tell him which bank account the money's in. His wife sits beside him. She seems kind, has brown eyes that twinkle. Ruth thinks: Good cook, keeps secrets from her husband like that she's looking for a message from a boy she once knew who died young. Beside her is a young woman in a wool skirt and wool tights, twenty-five maybe. She went to college and doesn't believe any of this but misses her dead father regardless. And next to her is the Mother. "Ruth." The Mother smiles. Her teeth are melted gray bits. The Mother is a black hole in the living room, fully empty of care or compassion or qualities a real mother might have.

"Silence, please." Mr. Bell sways on his feet in the doorway like a Secret Service agent. He has no idea who the Mother is.

Any clarity or confidence Ruth felt is gone, sucked into the Mother. The people are waiting, eyebrows lifted in anticipation. Nat shrugs, So what. She's nothing to us anymore but a paying customer. Get started.

Ruth shuts her eyes. She changes her breath, and the people gathered know things have begun. She exhales forcibly three times before making her call. "Spirit?" she asks. "Spirit, are you here? Join with us tonight." Her body arches as if electrocuted or possessed. "There's an older gentleman here with me. Yes. I'm getting chills. Look. Yes. He's here. The first thing he wants to say is that in life he would never be here. He's not a believer."

The young college woman smiles before she cries.

"You lost your father?" Ruth asks. It's that easy. Why else would a college girl be here?

She nods and tears are falling steadily now. The kind wife rushes a tissue to her friend. Mr. Bell is right. People who don't believe in the dead are still affected by them.

"Well, he's here with us tonight. He's always with you. Is there something you'd like to say to him?"

She's racked with sobs. It's hard for her to speak. The Mother puts her hand on her shoulder. "I wish he knew so many things. He's missed so much."

"He's not missing it. He sees." Ruth listens a moment. "And he wants you to know he forgives you and he loves you."

The woman stops crying and looks at Ruth. "Forgives me?"

"Yes?" The question mark is a mistake. "Is there anything else you want to say to him?"

The college girl is no longer crying but has hardened. "No, thank you." Ruth went too far.

Nat times his entrance perfectly. "I'm speaking with a girl named Patricia."

The Mother's head cocks to the side, but the sign is not sure. Who is she here looking for?

Ruth reminds the guests. "Consider your dead. This could be an ancestor. Great-great-grandparent. You might not recognize your dead."

Nat turns to look directly at the Mother. He speaks to her. "Patricia had long hair, braided. She wore emerald rings. Arthritis, maybe. She watches out for you and is taking care of you. Loving you and following your life. She says not to worry about that itchy rash?"

The Mother nods.

Nat bows his head.

Ruth says, "There's a woman standing near me. She says her name is Willie?"

"Yes." The hostess is astonished but really it had been easy for Ruth to look on the back of a black-and-white photo displayed on the bedroom vanity, a child in a christening gown. *Wilhelmina, 1938.* Once she has the name, anything's possible. Ruth's mind opens. "She's saying she wants you to feed the birds."

"The birds?"

"Yeah. Like outside. A feeder, you know?"

"Sure." The wife nods. "I'll do it."

"She says she loves you and she misses you."

The wife begins to sob.

"Is there anything you'd like to ask Wilhelmina? Or tell her? She's here."

The hostess bites her lip. "Tell her we've had a child. We named the child after her."

Ruth looks down. She smiles without meaning it. "She already knows." And then, because she's feeling sheepish about the trouble with the milk, Ruth conjures a kitty cat dead since the '90s. "Meow?" Ruth asks in her trance state.

"Sheba?" a guest asks. "Is that you?"

"Meow! Meow!"

Ruth tries to escape down the hallway when it is over, but the Mother stops her. "Hi."

"Hi."

"How've you been?"

"What are you doing here?"

"I sell Mary Kay with the woman who lives here. She invited me."

"Oh."

"Ruth," she says, and grabs Ruth's hands, choking on a gurgle rising from her chest. "Please." Some sort of flood.

"What?" Ruth directs her into a bathroom that smells of damp towels. Maybe the Mother wants to apologize for not taking care of them.

The Mother calms her voice. She breathes in and out through her nose like an actress. "I need you to talk to him for me."

"Arthur?"

"No."

"Nat?"

"No. My son."

"You have a son?"

"Or daughter. I don't know." The Mother studies the tiling. Ruth sits on the rim of an enormous tub. The Mother kneels knee bones to tile. She lifts her hands to Ruth's thighs, like she's a beggar. "Please."

"How come you never told anyone you have a kid?"

The Mother claws Ruth's skin through the purple gown. "I had a miscarriage." The Mother grips. "That's why I need you to help me. No one's helping me." The Mother's thick foundation makes her look like a zombie. There are tear streaks through the face pancake, riverbeds revealing red skin below.

"There's nothing I can do." Ruth's dry, getting drier.

The Mother drops a cheek to Ruth's legs. She squeezes, claws. Her mouth is wide open with no sounds coming out. Ruth sees her scalp. The brown and silver, wires on a bomb. Ruth imagines a story she could tell, about how the child was reincarnated into a pony on a farm where they help war veterans. But she doesn't do it. The Mother doesn't deserve it. Ruth keeps her mouth closed. All these parents who want their children. A freaking miscarriage. Who cares? She didn't even know the kid. The Mother smells of oil. With her hands on either side of the Mother's face, Ruth prepares to toss her skull off her lap like a head of turned lettuce. "It's fake," Ruth says finally. "I make it up."

The Mother holds still in Ruth's lap for one moment.

"It's a lie," Ruth says again. "I'll give you your money back."

The Mother's face peels into disgust. "You make it up?"

"The dead are dead are dead. They don't talk to me."

"You're a liar?" The Mother sharpens.

"Yes."

The Mother wipes eyeliner expertly, using the edge of one finger as swab. "That's got nothing to do with my child. You're a cheat. That doesn't mean there's not a world greater than this. Just means you'll never see that world. You're not the gatekeeper, Ruth. You're not even invited."

Ruth nods. "I know."

The Mother has a miserly thin mouth. She picks dried spit from her lip like a boll of cotton. "Good luck. You've got nothing else." She arranges her clothing in the vanity's mirror, looking extraordinarily human, plain, and broken. The Mother sleepwalks from the room. Her grease and grief linger.

Ruth spends a few minutes counting the tiles in front of her eyes, each one lined up next to its neighbor, each identical. A freaking miscarriage. Why did Ruth's mother never look for her? Where did her sister go?

She swings her shod feet into the tub. Ruth closes the bath's drain and turns the hot water tap on high. Beside the tub there's a cylinder of Comet bleach scrub. Ruth shakes a generous quantity of the bluish powder into the water.

It's time to find her sister El, to find their mother. Ruth needs to get out of here too. She climbs into the tub, into the Comet, as if it is her space pod. She rings in the new year, making herself clean and ready for a new life. The water scalds and purple dye leaks from her dress, brightly colored as any suicide.

HIGHWAYS ARE BAD PLACES TO HIDE, but I didn't know we were hiding until Ruth started running. "Who is he?" Like a kind of torture, I keep asking her the same question. Ruth readjusts her headphones. I would think a person who doesn't know what's she's running from can't really be on the run, but that's not true. Here I am.

A cop car coasts to a stop a few feet behind us. We keep walking. They turn on their lights so we stop. They sit in their car. We wait for them to get out, but the cops don't get out, so I tell Ruth, "Fuck it. Let's keep walking." Then they hit us with the siren, which, that close, is a bolt of electricity from below, spine-clearing. It exits through my brain. They use their bullhorn. "Hold your position."

When I worked in an office, it was the same thing, people using phrases that made no sense. "Action item," they'd say, because our job was so dull we used mysterious phrases to make it seem more exciting, as if we were spies dealing with top-secret, pass-coded information. Only there was no way to break the code because none of the phrases meant anything: Bring it to the table. Deliverables. Go live. Leverage. With that said. Moving forward. Offline. Branded brain dump.

"What'd they say?" I ask Ruth. We lean against the guardrail and wait.

The cops finally climb out of their patrol car.

"Your car break down?" he asks me, as if Ruth's become invisible. That's fucked up but that's what happens to women. We grow up into ghosts. No one wants to screw Ruth anymore so she's invisible.

"Yeah. Her car."

"Whose?"

"My aunt Ruth's."

"ID, please."

"You want to see our driver's licenses?"

"Correct."

"But we're not driving."

"You're trespassing. There's no walking allowed on the highway."

I look at them blankly. "Walking is against the law?"

"Yes, ma'am."

The cops give us a lift to the next exit, another town where the houses have lights in each window. Homesickness raises questions like, Why don't I live in a house? Why am I punishing El? I don't know the answers, but walking can untangle knots, spread things out, so at least I can see the strands: walking, mothering.

We pass Walmart, Walgreens, Starbucks. Everything is new in this town, even the trash barrels. A man mowing his lawn watches us as if he's on patrol. The town playground has forts, tunnels, platforms, and a padded surface. A father and daughter are heading home for supper. The sun is sinking behind the trees. Three teenagers, a girl and two boys, are on the swings, pivoting on pointed toes. Each of them wears headphones. Each of their faces is illuminated by the glow of a smartphone.

El told me that she worries about kids today, about me. She said we're screwed because we've never known life without the Internet. And then she told me a story about the first time she heard Linda Thompson sing, "I hand you my ball and chain." "You know Linda Thompson?" she asked me. "Of course," I said, because I know everything now, that's my job, to know one drop of shallow information about every single thing. El told me how she was driving home from work years ago, before the Internet, and how the radio station broadcast that Linda Thompson song and, like a tractor beam, it took her over, prickled her skin, lifted her up. Her body felt every signal the Earth was issuing, every twitch of spring coming in the winter air was palpable on her forearms because that song's so good and it spoke to her. And Thompson's voice. El pulled over just to listen. She waited through three more songs, frozen with a shred of paper she'd picked up off the floor, the receipt from an oil change. She waited with a pen in hand, like her life was depending on hearing that fast moment when the DJ would rattle off the name of the lady who sang that song. Hear it now or lose that beauty forever. The DJ said the name. El wrote it down. She drove twenty miles to a record store, ordered a CD the guy working there had never heard of, waited two weeks for that guy to call, drove twenty minutes back to the store, and left with Richard and Linda Thompson's CD in her hands, holding it above her head like some Jesus cross umbrella, a relic of protection against death because she had found it and it had found her, and the chances of that encounter were so very slim.

El said that kids today never sit still long enough to see how the river changes. What, she wondered, was going to happen to people who think they know everything? What's going to happen without chance? Good question.

My back aches. I'd like to stretch out on my side on the bench, but a janitor is securing a padlock on the trash dumpster out back. They lock their garbage here. Even the teenagers eye us suspiciously. We stay upright until the janitor and the teenagers are gone. Ruth and I climb to the highest platform on the "Play Structure." We're hidden. Ruth takes everything out of our bags. She even pulls out my broken phone. I look at its dead screen but not for long. It's not like it's going to come back to life again. She distributes blankets and extra clothes around my body, tucking them behind my back, between my knees as needed. Ruth knows how to make a bed. She takes nothing soft for herself but lies flat on her back looking up at the sky. She rests one light hand on the baby.

I've come to think of Ruth as the father of my kid. She takes care of us in a way I'd hope a father would. Ruth will smile the day this child is born. No one will smile more because the baby is hers too now.

"You remember your mom, Ruth?"

She shakes her head no.

"I do."

She stares at me, wanting to hear more, but it takes a moment to think of anything nice about her mother. It's actually hard to come up with even one good thing. Finally I get, "She had long, pretty hair like yours."

Her eyes open wider, so ready for information her mouth gapes. Ruth is one big ear.

"I lived with her when I was a kid. It was a bad idea. Your mom was nasty. She'd tell El, 'You're fat. You're lazy. Should've burned your face instead. Would have improved your chances for finding a man.'" I'm giving shape to a dark room in Ruth's head. "Your mom was a drunk but we stayed. A house, a yard. I went to a good school, ate good clean food. El never left me alone with her, not when I was young."

Ruth plies a bit of hair from the corner of her mouth.

"Your mom seemed to think that being cruel to El equaled being nice to you. She was twisted by guilt, and I'm sorry she was your mom, but I'm glad you exist, Ruth. I'm glad she had you."

Ruth turns to keep me from saying anything too nice to her. But fuck it. I can be as nice as I want to Ruth. Why shouldn't I? Someone ought to. I can even say I love her if I want. What's she going to do? Tell me to shut up? "I love you, Ruth." I hope El gets the message too somehow. "Thanks for coming to get me. Whatever this turns out to be."

Night comes down and her breath deepens. Millions of stars overhead make the violence of the Big Bang clear. So much force that matter is still sprinting away from the center. I feel the velocity of space pinning me to this platform. I'm tiny but I'm going to be someone's mom, someone's everything. I touch the baby. None of this is easy to believe. The stars leave streaks, we're moving so fast. Ruth breathes heavily. One small scintillation above — a gossamer thread of light — gathers oceans, every word ever spoken on the radio, each calorie of sunlight ever captured and stored in a kernel of corn. You know. Things like that. And the star beside it: the tongues of every lizard, spider, leopard. If spiders have tongues. One day the sun will suck us in. I'm not too angry about that. Lying in these stars, despite them, somehow I can imagine my child seat-belted in a minivan while I stress the importance of sharing chocolate Easter eggs or stuffed toy pandas or bags of corn chips with the other children. And I'll mean that being alive matters, even being alive in the smallest, smallest way. And aren't you lucky to be here.

We've been walking forever. The weather is growing colder. The leaves are turning. Some ancient program is switching on in my hormonal body saying winter is nearer than it was yesterday. Take shelter. Wolves, coyotes, and bears will become hungry, and a child, to them, will taste so sweet.

Ruth could tell me so much. When we sleep like this, I imagine all she knows, flowing into me, into the baby, a transfusion of history, stories, and maybe even some simple sketch, a rough outline, of what the hell is going on.

THEY STOP UNDER AN OVERPASS. Mr. Bell does Ruth's makeup in the headlights of passing cars. "Short vacation?"

Things had not gone well at El's house. Ruth doesn't want to talk about it.

"I'm glad you're home." Mr. Bell pulls one side of Ruth's hair back and pins it there with a purple orchid as if he's escorting her to prom. Mr. Bell's breath is close. He paints her lips to match the flower. He touches them with a tissue.

"You stole that makeup from the other house."

"You make me sound like a thief."

"Thank you," she says when he's done.

He starts the car again. "What sort of job is this?"

Nat had arranged everything except transportation. "I don't know. They got in touch with me."

"Who are they?"

"I don't know."

Mr. Bell alters the angle of the rearview.

"They have a question for us," Nat says.

"What question?"

"Hold on. I love this song." Nat leans into the front, putting his arm in between them. He turns up the radio, hums along a little.

"Where'd you meet them?" Ruth asks.

Nat draws one hand up to his ear. "I didn't."

"You don't know them? Did you check them out at all?"

"They called me," Nat says again.

Mr. Bell looks put out. "Is this the place?"

Nat checks the address. "Yeah."

The house is a low ranch, lit, warm, glowing as if it's still Christmas. All three bend their necks to check it out from the safety of the car.

"I'll wait here in case you're not out in, what, an hour? I'll come get you."

"Why?"

"Because you didn't check these people out, and while I know you think I do nothing to earn my share, that isn't true. I always ensured your safety." Mr. Bell draws one thumb down his sideburn, smoothing it.

Nat looks at the door mechanism. "What could be dangerous about dead people?"

"Ruth?" Mr. Bell clears this with her. "Are you sure you want to go?"

He's making her feel more like a stripper. "It's a job."

"OK. But be out in an hour."

"Ready?" Nat asks.

The car door shuts. Ruth follows Nat to the house.

"So they're not looking for a person," Nat tells her. "They lost a box."

"Like a jewelry box?"

"No. Cardboard."

"Cardboard is going to talk to you tonight?"

"The box is filled with cash."

"How much?"

"I don't know."

"A box of cash?" Ruth stops ten feet from the house.

"Yeah." Nat knocks.

The door opens.

The woman who greets Nat has silver hair. Her skin is encased in powder; she has coral lipstick, brown smoker's teeth. She wears a tailored coat, a pencil skirt.

"Good evening."

"Evening." Nat steps inside.

The woman looks at Ruth, standing ten feet away in the darkness. "Hello."

"Hello."

"Cold out."

"Yes."

"Are you going to come inside?"

The living room is decorated in an American idea of Scandinavian simplicity: blond wood, graceful lighting, two prim couches upholstered in cream. The house smells of an Asian spice rack. Someone trying to improve herself by purchasing air fresheners.

There's a round man in the living room. He's wearing a long beige duster with taupe cowboy boots that are really just shoes, shorties. A counterfeit cowboy. "Nat," the cowboy says. "Right?"

"Yes."

The woman smiles quickly, limiting the glimpse of her teeth. "Please," inviting them in. "Have a seat."

A small tabletop fountain trickles in one corner. Ruth saw the same model for sale at a hardware store in town, had even considered a purchase.

"Make yourselves comfortable." The woman smiles.

Ruth sits on one couch with Nat beside her. The walls are brain-colored.

Nat clears his throat, his voice rigid. "What can we help you with?"

"Both of you are mediums?"

Nat nods.

The woman sits opposite them, arraying her limbs on the sofa as a Hollywood starlet might. "Both of you are touched with the sight? How unusual."

"It's less sight. More listening."

The woman turns toward the cowboy, throwing out an elbow. "I told you. Highly recommended. He knew there was something special about her."

"Who?"

"Are you alone?"

"We are together."

"Of course. We won't take much of your time. I understand you're in demand." The woman claps a call to order.

"Thank you." Nat drags his nails across the couch's fabric.

"Hold hands?" Ruth asks, unsteady. "We need to do that, right?" Her speech is slow.

"Of course we do," the woman says. "Of course."

The four of them scoot in close. Ruth holds the cowboy's hand while Nat begins to sizzle, saliva pooling at the top of his throat. His eyes shut and Ruth follows him, down or back or up, wherever it is he goes when he goes.

Ruth lifts her arms — and consequently one of the cowboy's and one of Nat's — to address the universe. She speaks like a hungry child reciting grace, rushed and reductive. "Great spirit, gather here with us today. Help these good people." She's hopeful. "Great spirit, finder of the lost, engage our souls in your work so that we may in turn serve the realm where you dwell."

Then the room is silent for a minute, two minutes.

"Please," she adds to her entreaty, a little late.

Nat grunts. His head rolls like a bowl ready to spill, swinging from four o'clock to seven, stopping at five. He opens his eyes.

"Ask your question," Ruth instructs.

Nat growls.

"Slowly," Ruth cautions as if they are approaching a wild creature.

The woman slides forward on the couch. She looks left and right. She closes her eyes, opens her sternum and arms. "Where is the vessel containing the trust?"

"Vessel?" Ruth looks for some clarity. "Trust?"

The woman lowers her arms, her chin. "What happened to the funds?"

"Money?" Ruth tries to confirm again.

"Yes. The trust."

Nat raises their clasped hands to his brow for a moment, then down to his mouth, inhaling, dribbling spit on Ruth's thumb. When he lets go, he gives a sour look. The room is still. Nat blinks, remains quiet until — Ruth hears it first — there's a sound like dice. Nat's jaws are shivering. His teeth click against each other, bones. "Unearth," Nat says. "Catechism. Cataclysm. Really now." Nat chuckles as if in response to an unheard dirty joke. His head swivels, lifting his left ear to the sky, then his right. His eyes are white. "What's the matter? I thought you were going to dive. You thought I was going to dive? There's no water in the pool."

They'd seen it a couple weeks ago. Burt Lancaster's navy-blue swim trunks in *The Swimmer.* Ruth allows a moment to wonder why the supernatural comes to Nat as old movies.

Nat shuts his eyes lightly, lowers his torso into his lap, draws his knees together, shaking. "You see, if you make-believe hard enough that something is true, then it's true for you."

The moment passes.

"I see an empty swimming pool," Nat says.

"The money is in an empty pool? Are you sure? It's been gone a long time." But the woman's words are lost as a rush of people file into the room from the back of the house. The trance is broken. Nat looks up, awake. Fifteen people, twenty, all of them dressed in the brightest colors like a rainbow choir. They move silently. They are all white. Many of them are young, in their twenties. Their smiles are cemented. Their eyes are as glazed as a drug addict's.

Ruth thinks this is not right.

The people find seats on the ground. None of them sit on furniture. They cram in together, unaware of borders and personal space, the way insects crawl over other insects. They say nothing. Once they're seated, a tall, slim man follows them in. The colorful people look to him, and their smiles take on a fresh electricity. He's the candy man.

Ruth's ribs fold in an act of protection.

The man enters mid-song. "'I'm not the man they think I am at home. Oh. No. No.'" His singing stops. "Oh"—suddenly aware of Nat, of Ruth. "You began without me."

It takes Ruth a moment to understand what she's looking at. The man's arms are open to receive, though Ruth wants to flee because the man's face has an awful flatness, ragged with dried blood. The man does not have a nose, but rather two cavities, two crusted holes. "Brothers," he says. "Sisters." He wears a magenta tunic and turquoise slacks like a hippie, a noseless hippie. He lights a stick of incense. Ruth thinks of a lion's sliced nostrils, a camel's open beak. It is horrible to see a man without a nose.

"Yes. Sorry. Just getting started." The woman stands. "May I introduce you to Nat."

Nat stands.

"And this is —"

"Ruth." The man provides her name. He extends both hands for a double shake. "Congratulations, Ruth. I hear you recently married. What happy news. To some."

The room unravels. Zeke. The carpeting becomes cold, damp sand. The rough stucco walls crest and trough, a cream-colored ocean. He used to have a nose. Ruth dips her chin into her neck, wonders if she might get sick. Where is his nose? Last time she saw Zeke he had a nose.

Zeke takes a seat on the arm of the couch across from them. He nods to Nat. He smiles again, but it is hard to see a smile on the face of a man who has lost his nose. "Happy to meet you finally, Nat. Ruth has spoken to me of your closeness."

"You know one another?"

Ruth stammers. "I met him at the hospital. My appendix."

"You never mentioned me to Nat?" Zeke asks her.

"No."

"You also never told me you could talk to the dead."

"It's more Nat than me. He's the one."

"Is that right?" Zeke smiles at her. "Is Nat also the lucky young man, your husband?"

"No," she says. "No. No. No." Ruth sickens.

"Come on," Zeke says. "I'm happy for you. We're friends, Ruth. I mean it was my idea, but we're friends. Right?"

A large dog, Saint Bernard, emerges out of the back room.

"Right. Friends."

"You like dogs?" he asks.

Ruth nods, noncommittally.

Zeke snuggles the dog in a particularly intimate way, allowing the holes of his nose to be licked. The dog finds a seat near Zeke's feet. "Yes," he says. "Dogs don't attempt to deceive. Who wouldn't like that?"

The woman smiles at Zeke, lifts a hand to her neck and further up to her freakishly white ear, cupping it, catching sound waves.

"Green tea?" the cowboy offers around. "It's no trouble. I'm making one for myself."

"Lovely," Zeke says, and the cowboy, after picking his way over the seated, silent people, disappears through the same doorway.

Ruth's horror is fully unveiled. Zeke leans into it, into her. "You can't look away, can you? I know. Neither could I at first. Go ahead. Take a good look." He leans in even closer, so close she can smell what a man with a rotten hole in his face smells like. He's right, she can't look away. He rocks forward as if he'll kiss her. Instead Zeke stands, singing again. "'And I'm going to be high as a kite by then.'"

The people watch him, anticipating a sermon or speech. He does a back bend, some dance move. Finally he delivers what they're waiting for. "In a town upstate — long time ago — there were three sisters, Kate, Margaret, and Leah. There are always three sisters, right? These three heard voices. Or at least Kate and Maggie did. Leah was older, wiser. Still, she went along for the ride. The sisters claimed the voices belonged to dead people. Much like yourselves, they could speak to the dead." Zeke twists, cognizant of his entire audience. "And thousands of people believed them. It's incredible how many people believe this, right? Incredible how much people will pay, right? If they're desperate enough, yeah? Say a mom who lost her kid. I bet you get a lot of those. I bet that's a real moneymaker for you."

Ruth stiffens.

"Or people don't even have to believe it. Doesn't affect your business. Everybody's got dead people. You probably even have nonbelievers lining up to pay you. Right? Genius! Wish I'd thought it." The more excited Zeke gets, the damper his nasal cavity becomes. "But these sisters heard rappings at night. How they knew it was dead people instead of, say, a tree branch or a squirrel or their own ankles cracking, I don't know. Same way you know, I guess."

Nat stays low to his lap.

"So the sisters decide that there'd been a murder." Zeke brushes the knuckles of one hand lightly. "They say the voices told them."

Ruth's back becomes brittle. "A murder."

"The rappings told the girls, and the girls told their parents. Said that there'd been a murder right in their house. And the parents believe the children, so the family digs out the whole basement looking for the bones. And they found them. Tibia, humerus, et cetera. Could have belonged to anything, cow, coyote. Or maybe there was a murder." Zeke bends low.

Ruth worries that he will bring his noseless wet hole of a face closer to her. His hair is shoulder length and greasy. He stretches back again, hands on his butt. His tunic lifts to show his hip girdle. He straightens, takes one step closer.

"The girls fingered a guy, a stranger, a traveling merchant. Three young girls accused a grown man on account of some late-night rappings and a cow bone. And still, the whole town believes them, whole town shunned this man, drove him away. Why?"

Zeke looks around to the group gathered. They smile and nod as if they already know the answer but will let him deliver the punch line. "Because belief is easier. Belief is fun, right? An entire religion was born from these girls, hundreds of people to this day, unshakable in their belief, even after the girls admitted making it all up." Zeke wraps his arms together like some sort of snake yogi, this way, then that. "Because it's not untrue to the people who believe it. That's what I think I hear you saying, Brother Nat? Yes. This bit about the pool?"

Zeke isn't really talking to Nat. He isn't talking to anyone besides Ruth. Zeke laughs. First just a heaving of the shoulders, then a hack. He cackles. He reaches up to the sky before wiping his eyes. "I love that story." Knee slapping. "I love that G.D. story!"

The people begin to twitter, colorful birds who forgot how to fly. They also love that story. Zeke claps his hands for silence.

"Faith is beautiful." Zeke smiles gently. "For example, what if I told you, Ruth, that you were meant for me? That you and I, together, were supposed to alter life as we know it on Earth? What would you think if I told you that?"

"I think you need help."

"I needed your help, but you went and married somebody else."

The twittering of the peanut gallery starts up again. "Who are these people?" Ruth asks.

Zeke turns to gather them. He smiles. "These," he says, "are the faithful. The believers. At least some of them. Am I right, Sister Sylvia?"

The woman in white nods.

The cowboy returns just then bearing a tray of steaming ceramic cups, the sort with no handles. And on the tray beside the tea set is a paper cylinder of Comet, the cleaning powder.

"Thank you, Confucius." Zeke again takes his seat. Confucius is not a cowboy nor is he Chinese. He looks Bronx Italian, stuffed into his clothes. He serves Zeke tea.

Zeke lifts his mug to his chin. He breathes like a horse, inhaling the fragrance from the brew. The caked darkness of his sinuses turns his entire face into a respiratory apparatus, fleshy nodules flare with each exhalation.

Confucius sprinkles a pile of the pale aquamarine powder on the low table. He claims a seat, rocks onto one hip in order to pull a small slim box from his coat pocket, a cigarette case. He pops the clasp and, using the hard edge of a credit card, cuts and divides the cleaning powder into rows and rows of fine lines. Zeke selects a small section of straw from the case and, inserting its plastic into one open flap of his sinus cavity, he uses his hand to close off any other opening. Zeke inhales deeply, snorting Comet, loud as a slurp.

Ruth has to, finally, look away.

He lifts his head, cracks into a broad smile. "Light of the world. Want to try it?" He extends the damp straw to Ruth. His nostrils are splattered-speckled blue now that the pale powder has dampened.

The Saint Bernard quite suddenly has a desperate itch, windmilling his leg to scratch the spot.

Ruth voices an obvious truth. "You are not supposed to snort that. It's toilet bowl cleaner."

"It" — Zeke lifts the canister up to his cheek — "has been a heavenly deliverance from the betrayal you dealt me."

"Me?"

He lifts his mug to his chin, breathes like a horse, inhaling the fragrance of the tea. He wipes his sinus cavities clean with a sleeve. "You were the catalyst, Ruth. You were going to lead these people where they are supposed to go. Now they've got no mother."

Cowboy has his chin in his palm.

"Why me?"

"It's printed clear as day across your face. You're a map. You were my wife, and I was your husband, your true husband!" He screams it loud enough for the neighbors to hear.

Nat and Ruth stare openly at each other. "What? No."

"You don't have to be scared of me," Zeke tells Ruth.

"I'm not scared. I'm leaving."

A faint trickle of creamy blue oozes from his non-nose. Again he wipes. "Hold on. Just hold on. I didn't mean to scare you. What about the box? That's why we're here, right? Sylvia, Confucius? That's our purpose tonight, right? Money?"

"Yes," the woman says. "Tonight that is our purpose."

"Sylvia wants proof I'm no thief. Right?"

The woman doesn't answer. Her chin ticks back and forth.

"See, years back, we lost a whole lot of money, and we really need that money just now. Sister Sylvia needs it so much she's starting to suspect that maybe I was the one who stole the money. Right?" he asks Sylvia.

"Right."

"So if we find the money, then all's well, right?"

"Right," Sylvia whispers again.

"But if we don't find the money, if bad things happen to good people, then why bother believing anything at all? Right again?" Zeke chuckles.

Sylvia takes her face into her hands. "Right."

He turns to Ruth. "I think we can kill two birds with one stone. Find the money and finish my story, the three sisters, OK? Because what I'm wondering, what I really want to ask you"—he puts both index fingers up to his temples like two guns—"is where's your third sister? You're missing one. Where is he, Ruth?"

"What?"

"Where's that guy you married? I've got a hunch he can solve this whole mystery."

"No. He's not like us."

"No? I've got a strong feeling Carl knows exactly where to find our money. And he doesn't even have to talk mumbo-jumbo to find it. No, ma'am." Zeke is laughing again but silently. His shirt gapes. Ruth can see the top of his chest. "Is he waiting outside, or did you sneak off without him tonight?"

Zeke looks to her for a reaction. Ruth says nothing. How does he know Mr. Bell?

"Thinking of cutting him out eventually? More profit for you two, right? Smart. I see you got your own apartment without him. Cute place above the vet clinic, right?" Zeke slaps his thighs. "But, woo-hoo! I'd be careful messing with Carl. He was trained by the best. He's ruthless, I tell you. Ruthless." Realizing his pun, Zeke queers his face. "Oh." He smiles. "Not you, dear." Zeke turns his back on her. "So, while we wait for Carl to show up"—he faces his congregation—"who wants to see some stars?"

Shouts of delight are raised. Confucius pours a huge pile of Comet onto his tea tray, a heaping mound. He empties the container. He plucks a fresh straw from his cigarette holder and, holding the tray with one hand like a cocktail waitress, offers the straw to the first of the colorful congregants. The man dives into the pile with relish, delivering himself from the mess of his life, from this moment in time with a toot of toilet bowl cleaner named for an astronomical uncertainty.

Zeke starts to sizzle. Confucius makes his way down the line of people. Zeke moves his hips, grooving. "Yeah!" he calls out. "That's it!" A coach on the sidelines. He claps. He moves over to the stereo, finds the song he's looking for, and lifts the volume to a deafening level. The song tells the story of a spaceman devoid of his earthly comforts, floating through the ether. He misses his wife and children. He misses home. The spaceman tries to play it cool, saying, "I don't understand" and "It's just my job," but the truth is something that holds him there in space, floating in the darkness, free from gravity.

Zeke falls into the song. His eyes close. His face twitches from smile to grimace and back. Comet coursing through his thoughts. Sky shot and soaring. His body rocks. His hands try to grip the song, hold it, and all the while, over the volume, the tray of powder gets passed from congregant to congregant, each individually going wild for his or her communion with the stuff, snuffing and huffing, star-nosed moles in a tunnel, smiling and rejoicing at the sacrament. It is sexual. It is scientific. Some see stars. Some start to sway and drool, modern flowing movements, snorting a bleach cleanser. They do not dance with each other. It is a singular journey. A rocket man. A rocket woman. Eyes more glazed, more drugged. Futures and furniture get hazy. Zeke claps his hands. He screams to be heard. "I love this song! Don't you love this song!" No one is listening. He dips and whirls, swirling. "'All this science, I don't understand.'" A storm drawn of chaos and chemicals, and no one is paying attention to Nat and Ruth. She takes his hand. Slowly, slowly, they stand. She does not breathe. Slowly, they slink from the table, from the couch, through the drugged dancers. Moving without motion, slowly, slowly, to stay invisible. The rear hallway shines bright, an escape pod back to planet Earth or at least a window set low enough for a jump. The music is so loud. Up here alone. Zeke's eyes are still shut, and Nat and Ruth move like plants. No one sees them grow toward their escape. The others dance, sway. The others stumble, smile, blissful in happy catatonia. Nat and Ruth are nearly there, nearly clear.

And then the record comes to a trance-breaking, drug-haze-shaking skip.

The plants sprout legs. Nat and Ruth sprint out the back hallway. Nat finds an exit for them, a porch door that leads back to the world. He pushes Ruth through the jamb. He pushes Ruth back out into the night. Darkness cracks, an explosion — or else it's just the sound of the screen door slamming shut behind them as they run for Mr. Bell's waiting car.

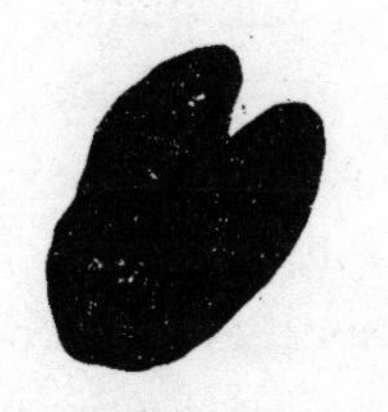

I'LL NEED NEW SNEAKERS AGAIN in the near future. The road is hell on soles. Before this walk, I've never before actually used up a pair of shoes. I've never even thought of shoes as a thing that can get used up.

SON SCREEN PREVENTS SIN BURN.

FREE TRIP TO HEAVEN. DETAILS INSIDE.

WHAT IS MISSING FROM CH CH? U R.

COME IN FOR A FAITH LIFT.

FREE COFFEE. EVERLASTING LIFE.

IF YOU WANT TO TALK TO JESUS, TRY A KNEE MAIL.

We pass many churches, many white light signs. The plainest one says GOD LOVES YOU. We pass an auto repair. God gave me a baby. We pass a bookstore. Then God gave me Lord. Then God gave me whatever Lord stuffed up my vaj.

We pass a place that looks like an old Elks Lodge or grange, only there are no windows, just a white clapboard box with a peaked roof. PLAYMATES INTERNATIONAL it says. The idea of international here demonstrates a lot of hope. Maybe "International" in this case means every now and then a French Canadian stops by. A flyer tacked up outside shows a tanned girl with a burlap bag over her head. "The Elephant Woman Takes It All Off."

God loves the Elephant Woman. The French Canadian.

"Where are we going? Where are we going? Where are we going?" I have a minor tantrum, stomping on the asphalt. "Who was that man?"

Ruth keeps walking.

Inside a broken Ford Taurus, I wake before her. That never happens. I hold a finger beneath her nostrils to make sure she's not dead or anything but get distracted by her Walkman instead. It's on her chest. Her eyes are still shut. I pull the tape player and headphones into the back seat with me. Feels like sharing Ruth's toothbrush. I lean back. I push play.

The sound I first hear is not recognizable. A machine. Static, clicking, zooming. But I don't have time to understand because Ruth, wild mountain cat, pounces over the seat, clawing for the headset. Her nails take a scrape out of my neck as the player is yanked from me. She withdraws into the front with her prey. She faces forward. I face forward. Both of us are breathing heavily. "Sorry. I didn't know it was such a big deal."

Her shoulders lift and lower.

"I just wanted to hear some music."

Still no reaction.

"But that's not really music, is it?"

Ruth pulls hair behind her ears. The great wall of nothing she is all day.

"No," I answer for her. "It's not." Maybe Ruth is a robot. Who else would listen to a machine clicking all day? Who else could walk like this? I try to get my finger under her nostrils again, check for life, but Ruth swats my hand away. She doesn't look like a robot. We start walking again.

"Your baby will either live or die," the doctor had said, like it's a half-alive creature. But Lord's trick didn't work. This baby didn't die and has now grown into something I feel move every day, its own independent thing. I still think of Lord's hands or neck, his chest pinning mine down. I stay in the flood of his body for as long as I can, imagining him in parts, using the good bits, since taken as a whole, Lord sucks. I don't know why his parents named him that. They had no way of knowing how he'd crawl into people's lives and sit there on his throne, ruining everything.

Sometimes the rain doesn't stop. There's a nuclear power plant down by the lake. Steam lifts from its core. We pass a club named Dominick's that advertises an event called "Caged, the Traveling Metal/Sex Circus." The town has changed a little bit since a meteorite landed here in 1834. This part of the state is haunted by businesses and marriages that didn't work. Not to mention all the regular old people underground in the cemeteries.

We pass a deer-crossing sign. The deer we've seen on this walk, and we've seen a lot of deer, are never standing near the deer-crossing signs.

"Hey, Ruth. You know how abducted people fall in love with their kidnappers?" The ends of Ruth's hair sway with her walk, sweep of a pendulum. "Well," I tell her. "Yup."

We buy lunch from the shelves of the Mount and Morris Grocery Store. It hasn't much to recommend it: a package of Ritz, some cheese, and a box of shelf milk. We sit out back on the curb beside a trash barrel that has leaked congealed yellow grease. There's a sign in the window. FREE WIFE. We eat in silence. I mean, FREE WIFI. We always eat in silence. The sun is setting, and a few cars pull into the lot during our meal, quick stop for beer or bread. The shoppers think we turn tricks and do drugs. They think they are not like us. My baby makes them shudder. Maybe I'll be the worst mother ever. Five of the shoppers won't meet my gaze. Four of them want to help. One with a tattoo, "Rocked in the Cradle of the Deep," pulls a five-dollar bill from his pocket and gives it to me.

We'd be able to travel a lot faster if all these mountains weren't in the way. Up we go. Down we go. Up to the sky again. This road follows a ridge through state land, and once we reach the top, the going is easier in the clouds. I expect bear or moose. I look for deer-crossing signs. There's a closed ranger's station and four or five shuttered hunting camps. No large mammals appear. Around one turn in the road, the sun is setting. It's cold and it looks like we'll be sleeping outside tonight. But then around the next turn, we see a large building up ahead, a series of stone shards cut into the cliff like the Wicked Witch's castle. Its lights are coming on. There are diamond-shaped windows, some with blue glass, some with gold. We hear singing inside. Hymns, I think, until I recognize *South Pacific*. "I'm Gonna to Wash That Man Right Out of My Hair" and, as we get closer, "Willkommen" from *Cabaret*. Ruth rings the bell.

"Yes?" A voice greets us over the intercom.

Ruth says nothing. "Hi. It's Cora."

"I'll send someone down."

Ruth exhales in measured, forced breaths.

A nun opens the door.

"Good evening." A squat toadstool in very comfortable shoes and suntan support hose. "I'm Sister Leah." Dressed in a habit. Every synthetic fiber is made to stretch and shape. "What brings you here so late?"

"We were walking by."

"You walked all the way up here? Hiking? A pregnant hiker? My."

"Yes."

"Come in." Sister Leah pokes a finger under her wimple. She has papery cheeks. "Come in." She takes the measure of my belly. The downy fur of her chin trembles. We have a seat on a bench in the foyer. It's draped with two acrylic afghans. The inside of the building is as plain as the exterior is magnificent. "One moment, please. I need to notify Sister Kate of your arrival." Leah disappears down a hallway.

I smell food and cooking gas. There's a crucifix made of yellow pine. There's beige paint, a vase of fake flowers on a wall pedestal, and a series of portraits, Mother after Mother. The song becomes unmistakable, "Somewhere Over the Rainbow." Two windows focus our attention on the dizzying view and its command, Look outside yourself, but I'm too tired to look anywhere. I lift my legs onto the bench, going back to back with Ruth. She stiffens so I can rest through "Happy Talk" and "How Do You Solve a Problem Like Maria?," a local favorite. "Some Enchanted Evening" gets interrupted. The convent falls silent except for the occasional door opening and closing down unseen hallways. Sister Leah does not return. No one shows up. It's warm and dry. I have a hundred one-second dreams in between the roll and jerk of my sleeping neck. I wipe drool from my lips. Ruth stands, walks the hall twice. I lie down. She studies a piece of framed calligraphy. "To set the mind on flesh is death." I roll my lumpy body to one hip. Ruth covers me with an afghan. She lies down on the bench across the hallway.

A bell tolls one, two, three times, followed by a rush of footsteps, people walking above. Then Sister Leah's head. "Are you coming?"

"Where?"

"The bells for Compline. Come."

"Compline?"

"Service." The bells keep ringing. "Come."

I can't serve anyone right now. I look out the windows, rub my face awake. The nun leads us down another beige hallway set with heavy wooden chairs. She totters, side to side. I totter behind. The hallway darkens up to a door. Nuns pass into a chapel. The crucifix over the altar is carved from dark wood showing Jesus's ribs and thick nails driven between the bones of his feet. On either side of the chapel, two pews are filled with robed monks. The nuns and a few laypeople find seats in the small nave facing the altar. It's dark, smells of wax. Sister Leah passes me a breviary for Ruth and me to share. "Don't try to sing along. And don't talk when it's done. Great Silence begins immediately afterward."

"'The Lord Almighty grant us a peaceful night and a perfect end.'" The monks sing in voices high as girls', even two who require oxygen tanks. The girls don't sing. The monks are round under their robes, minds clearly not set on flesh. They chant the Psalms in alternating voices, one team to the other, varying the amounts of silence between verses. The calculus of these sacraments could take a lifetime to decode back to twenty-six letters. "'Render evil to those who spy on me.'" Brown Jesus is almost naked, slender and long, tortured. The wound carved into his side looks like a vagina.

On the road a few days back, a woman stopped me. "Your first?"

"Yes."

"It's awful. They cut you open right up the middle." She gestured to her crotch. "You get what I'm saying?" Her finger points in my face. "They are going to use scissors on your twat. Got me?"

The monks sing, "'Do I eat the flesh of bulls and drink the blood of goats?'"

She was the fourth mother to tell me about her episiotomy. A collection of scars. Or maybe it's a hazing ritual. If Jesus is to move us beyond the flesh, why make him sexy? Because beyond the flesh is not the point.

The monks sing, "'When you see thieves, you make them your friends.'"

I'm shushed by Sister Leah as we file out of the chapel, though I hadn't said anything. No one speaks — the Great Silence — but I hear plenty: footsteps, clothing, carpeting, a cough. Upstairs the nun opens a door labeled ST. TITUS. One twin bed, a reading chair, a lamp, and a crucifix. Only one bed. Ruth doesn't seem to care and no talking allowed. So. She takes a seat in the chair and shuts her eyes. She's got no curiosity or cause for concern. I'm not like that. I can't sleep until I try the lamp's switch, look out the window, feel the weave of the blanket. I have to make sure I'm safe, make sure for the baby.

There are words in my throat like bits of gravel, questions about the monks and the strange songs they sing. Out of habit I almost loose these words on Ruth but stop myself. In the Great Silence, I hear my body like being underwater with the sounds of my heart, my breath, the baby's rhythm. Silence is anything but, at least at first. If Ruth does this every day, I can do it for one night. I switch off the light and lie down, but it's hard to sleep now that it would be easy. The baby moves a heel or elbow across my stomach.

Someone passes down the hallway. Night ticks by. Quiet as rocks that grow in layers and erode in too much sound. Does Ruth mind the silence? Is her brain still filled with words and thoughts that agitate her? Or did she give up all that when she gave up talking? In the air between us, her breath seems solid, a pill I can swallow and feel what it is to be Ruth, to be silent.

Eventually Linda Thompson got some of her voice back. I can wait around until the same thing happens to Ruth. I've got a lot of questions I need to ask her, like, How does she know herself without a mother? How does she know herself without sound? I guess she knows the shape of things that aren't there instead. Imagined or borrowed ideas like: mothers make food; mothers provide homes; mothers tell stories before sleep comes and remain steady when you are sick; mothers answer the phone when everyone else is asleep.

El was homeless when she went into labor with me, living on the streets of Troy, having contractions on the curb, and still she never hated me. She was alone through her whole labor. Nurses were few between in the welfare ward. She did the work herself, and at the very end an old man who'd specialized in podiatry in med school caught me. "You keeping this?" he asked her.

"That's my daughter." She held me close as she could, not alone anymore.

I've been a little shit, a spoiled, selfish brat. In this silence, when I close my eyes, I'm standing on stage and El's the only audience member, clapping her heart out. El made herself into a really good mom with nothing, rubbing dirty hands together. And then I slunk off. I had no idea how hard this was. All I've got is a loose plan: Tell the baby it's lucky to be here, then spend the rest of the time watching out for wolves. It's not much of a plan, only slightly more evolved than El's for me, which was something like: Don't throw bleach on the baby's face. That's a good plan too. I'll incorporate that into mine.

Even when I try to be silent, I can't because worry is like words, hard to stop them from getting in, messing up your house. I need to call El. And after we're done here, after I see what Ruth wants me to see, I will. I'll go back. I'll let El be a grandma. She deserves that. She deserves way more than that.

Ruth's hands are squished together under one cheek, a sleeping child from a Christmas card. One of the sisters shuts off the exterior floodlight and the window disappears, but I still feel it lurking somewhere out there — a clear idea of what being a mother means, and every day I'm getting closer.

When I wake in the night, there's a pair of knobby knees under thick brown hose in front of me. It's still dark. I look up from the knees. The nun smiles. Her headgear conceals all but a few silver-brown hairs, the thin ruddiness of blown-out pores. "I saw you at Compline." She tugs at a thread that's unraveled from her wimple.

Ruth sits up.

The nun continues. "So it's time to go."

"What?" I rub my face.

"Time to leave."

"You're kicking us out in the middle of the night?" Not very Christian.

"We're going together."

"We don't have a car, lady. Sister." I swing my legs to the ground. Dig fingernails into my scalp.

"No car?" She holds her chin. "OK. We'll walk."

"Can't we wait until morning?"

"No."

"Where? Why?"

"I'm leaving the convent."

"But we like it here."

"You wouldn't after a while."

"Why do you need us?" I whine. I'm tired.

"Because the Lord told me you'd come."

I look out the one small window. The Lord didn't tell me anything.

"I'm Sister Margaret. Just Margaret now. Come on."

"I'm Cora. She's Ruth."

"Ruth?"

"Yes."

"Come on."

It's hard to look tough while slipping on maternity jeans. I tie my hair into a ponytail. Ruth finds our bags. Why don't we resist? Why do I have the idea that I'm in training and must meet every challenge?

Sister Margaret heads downstairs and we follow. She hesitates by one door, holding its handle without opening it. She bows her head against the wood.

"Where's that go?"

"The enclosure. The cloister. Sisters only." Her wimple keeps much hidden.

"What's enclosed?"

"Exactly." She wags her finger, smiles. "Wouldn't you like to know."

"Yeah."

"I know you would."

"You're not going to tell me?"

"Why buy the cow when the milk's free?"

"But I was never even looking to buy this cow."

"Still."

"But what is it? What does that even mean? An enclosure?"

"It's space. Protected space, fenced in, walled off, boxed up."

"Why? What's in the space?"

"I can't tell you."

"Why not?"

"A girl's got to have her secrets."

The night air's cold. Ruth pulls on my hoodie, covering her head. It's filthy. We need a Laundromat. She adjusts the pack, hefting my bag up on one shoulder. The nun looks at the stars. Ruth starts walking and we follow. The nun switches on a flashlight beside me. "There," she says.

That's different, talking company. "Why are you leaving?"

"The Lord said someone would come when it was time to see my kid again."

"You have a kid?"

"Yes."

"How, like, how did the Lord tell you? In words?"

"Yes."

"How'd you know it was the Lord and not your own voice? I'd have trouble separating the two."

"Yes. You might."

I think that's an insult. "So. You have a kid?"

Ruth looks back at me.

"A daughter. From before."

"How long have you been at the convent?"

"Since she was eight months."

The mountains are moist before dawn. "You left an eight-month-old?"

The beam of her flashlight bobs. "I did."

"What'd you do all that time you were gone?"

"We support a brother monastery. I was a seamstress. Lots of silence." The nun uses her fingertips to tap her side, then her shoulders.

"What do the monks do while you're supporting them?"

"Pray." She rubs her hands together to stop the tapping. She moves faster.

"What'd your kid do?"

"Her father took care of her." When she looks at me now, the flashlight's under her chin, a horror show. "That's a cruel question," she tells me.

"Sorry. I haven't had anyone to talk to in a long while."

"Yes. Your friend's quiet."

"My aunt. She doesn't talk."

"She doesn't talk?"

"No."

"I'm pretty good at that too."

The damp air's medicinal. I like the privacy of walking at night and how it fuels dread and excitement. If something interesting's going to happen — say, aliens landing — it's going to happen in private. It's going to happen at night.

"To be in touch with our smallness," the nun says. "Closer to God up here."

"Feels that way."

"The world needs stillness."

"True."

"I wasn't always still. I sat with the dying. Cooked for the hungry. Once we visited prisoners. I made decisions. I helped pregnant women like yourself. I spun thread."

"Huh."

The nun sizes me up. "Why? What did you do back in reality that was so great?"

"Sold insurance."

"Wow. Real important stuff."

She's a mean nun. Even if she's right.

The sun blues the sky. We head down her mountain into the valley of the next peak. I have to lean way back to stay balanced. "What's with the show tunes?"

"Sister Kate. I'll miss that."

The road flattens eventually, and we head into town. We leave the berry briar and white pines. We pass through a forest of car dealerships, three on the left, two on the right. Despite their open, optimistic nature — broad plate-glass display windows, generous lots with wide drives — only one of the five dealerships remains in business. A battery of fast-food restaurants lures travelers off the cloverleafs. Sister Margaret sets her hands evenly on her hips. She stops walking. "What's that sound?"

I stop to listen. Water running. We must be back by the canal. "The Erie." We should have taken a canoe down the canal instead of all this walking.

"I haven't been off the mountain in a while."

"Why are you going to find your kid now?"

"Think she forgot about me?"

"No. But—"

"Listen." Margaret sharpens again. "Do you have any idea what's about to happen to your life?"

"Some."

"You won't ever know peace again."

I shrug.

"I was a terrible mom. I couldn't stop worrying. I thought about men with machetes, pedophiles, high staircases, electrical sockets. You name it. Once on the street, a stranger chucked my daughter under the chin. He thought she was cute. I went home and covered her with anti-bacterial gel. She was three months old." Her eyes roam the air behind me as she makes her list. "Redneck drunk drivers, brain damage from a fall off her changing table. I thought about her soft head all the time. I couldn't sleep and I couldn't let her sleep. Sleep looked like death. Eating looked like choking. Friends looked like murder.

"Hormones attack you," she says. "Hormones will try to kill you."

"You didn't let your baby sleep?"

"I imagined danger so well, I made it real."

"You didn't let your baby eat?"

"Her father took better care of her than I could." She looks up. "Motherhood," she says, "despite being immensely common, remains the greatest mystery, and all the language people use to describe it, kitschy words like 'comfort' and 'loving arms' and 'nursing,' is to convince women to stay put."

The sun lands on us awkwardly. I don't say it, but I think she's forgetting half. There's a lot about mothering that's good. I had a really good mom. We walk on in silence.

"Where are you going?"

"My aunt's taking me somewhere."

"Where?"

I hesitate. "I have no idea."

"Exactly. That's what I'm telling you." She looks at Ruth. "Maybe she's hardening you up into the warrior you'd better be before that baby arrives."

"Maybe."

Feels a little bit like more mother-hazing, so I prepare for another episiotomy story, the horrors of child birth, blah, blah, but one doesn't come.

"How old is your girl now?"

"Ten."

"Well, what are you going to do? What's the plan?"

"Catch a bus to Forked Lake. Find her. See if she'll forgive me. Let me in her life somehow."

"What if she won't?"

"Yeah," Margaret says. "Then there's that."

In town the nun points to the pharmacy where the buses stop. HALF GALLON OF MILK $1.50. The terminal's not open yet. The nun takes off her wimple and shakes out her hair. With the wimple removed, I can see her neck and it's a horrible thing. Thick brown, purple, and black lines, ligature marks, damaged and ghastly as if she'd been hanged then resuscitated or her wimple had been fastened so tightly it choked her. I worry her head will detach entirely without it now. She sees me staring and nods. "I'm telling you, it's not easy. Life and death are not clean, separate functions." She gently touches the marks on her neck.

I want to get away from her, but she keeps talking.

"Motherhood makes you a dealer in death. No one tells you this beforehand. You will become obsessed with all the ways a person can go because while it might be easy to deal with the fact that you will one day die, it's not at all easy — totally unacceptable — to deal with the fact that one day your child will die. Do you hear me?"

I nod. I hear her. I do. "What am I supposed to do? Just give up? Not even try to be a good mom?"

The nun exhales. “You’ve got yourself a real live one here,” she says to Ruth, smiling. “Are we done? We’re OK?”

Ruth gives her something, money maybe, like she’d hired the nun to teach me, though clearly that can’t be true.

Margaret tucks whatever it is into her bra. She has a seat, waiting for the bus with a drunk and a soldier on a bench out front, feet planted for battle, rubbing her neck.

“Good luck,” I mumble.

“Same to you.” Then the nun asks God to be with us. Then the drunk hums “O Night Divine” though Christmas is still a long way off.

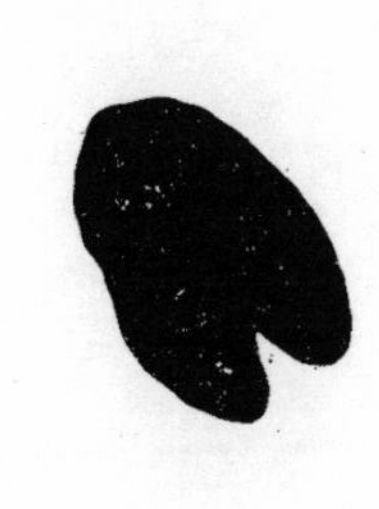

A WOMAN ON THE RADIO speaks with a French accent. "Brasserie Caribou. You cannot beat our meat." Nat and Ruth fly into the back seat. "Howdy, lovebugs," Mr. Bell says. "How'd it—?"

"Go!" Ruth need only say it once. Mr. Bell locks the doors, engages the engine, depresses the accelerator with everything he's got. They find their breath in the dark car. She leans forward as he speeds away from the house, and as they fly past, she sees a man running for the car. The man is not Zeke. It's Ceph, running out of the woods by the house. Ceph calling her name, "Ruth! Stop! Wait!"

"Don't stop," Nat says. "Don't."

Streetlamps ripple overhead, passing in sickening waves of darkness and light. None of them speak yet because Mr. Bell's I-told-you-so is loud enough for all to hear.

The vehicle moves away from the house at speeds ranging from thirty-five to forty-five miles per hour for a time period of twenty-three minutes. Once sufficient distance is gained, Nat can finally speak. "I need some water. Please."

"Of course."

At Andy's Discount Food and Dairy, Mr. Bell locks Nat and Ruth inside the car while making his purchases. As soon as Mr. Bell's gone, Nat starts to plead. "Don't tell him I fucked up so badly. OK?"

"But the man knows his name."

"The man knows your name too. Maybe it's your fault also. Did you think of that?"

She looks out the window.

"Don't tell him. Not everything. Please."

"If I have to, you can't be mad." She pushes a spot between her eyebrows. "What happened to his nose?"

Nat shakes his head. Ruth imagines the lonely appendage stashed in a cup, a mug, a gift box, blackened, crusted in parts, and all the smells it ever knew. Grass. Bacon. Seawater. Mildew. More likely though, it was eaten away slowly, crumbled and wasted in bits.

"And what the hell was Ceph doing there?"

"Poor Ceph," Ruth says.

"What's that supposed to mean?"

Mr. Bell passes Nat a bottle of water, juice, and a bag of snacks. He opens beers for each of them, using a quarter pinched as a pry bar. "You look like ghosts. What happened? Did the dead actually speak this time?" He smiles. The alcohol hits Ruth's blood, swiftly cooling hot metal. Mr. Bell catches Ruth in the rearview. "What is it?"

She shuts her eyes, so Mr. Bell drives. They pass three farms and one home-heating oil depot. Finally she answers him, "The man didn't have a nose."

"What?"

"He didn't have a nose. It had been eaten away. Just a hole in his face."

"Terrible."

Nat grabs her thigh, squeezes as if holding her reins.

"More snow in the forecast, Jim. The county's on alert. We're looking at accumulations of anywhere from thirteen inches to two feet. More than that up in the mountains."

"No nose?" Mr. Bell stretches his fingers, regripping the wheel. The streetlamps end. "What happened?"

Ruth turns to Nat. He's still looking out the window, though there's little to see besides the metallic flash of the passed mile markers. "They lost some money, and Nat told them it's in an empty pool."

"A man lost both his nose and his money? Seems a bad sign. How much?"

"They didn't say."

"Well, Nat? Is it in a pool?"

"Not that I know of. No."

"Maybe?" Mr. Bell asks.

"I don't think so."

Nat allows his half-drunk bottle of water to fall into the foot well. They drive a ways in silence.

"He knows you, Mr. Bell. He called you Carl."

Nat digs his nails into her leg.

Mr. Bell takes a moment to respond. "I've never met a man without a nose."

"Zeke. He knew you."

"He called me Carl? Did you tell him that was my name?"

"No."

"He called me Carl? And he lost some money?"

"Yes."

"Well, I've never met a Zeke." Mr. Bell shakes his head.

"It didn't go so well," Ruth says, but begins to worry that she's brought trouble to Mr. Bell. If Zeke knows his name, it's because he looked at her marriage record. She's endangered Mr. Bell. And Nat.

"Why? They thought you were lying?"

Ruth leans into the front. "Do you know a motel we can stay tonight? Outside of Troy?"

"We're not going home?" Nat asks.

"He knows where we live."

Mr. Bell finds Ruth's eyes in the rearview. "I'm sorry." He has to look back to the road in order to drive. "I'm so sorry."

"Why? What did you do?" The challenge between Nat and Mr. Bell is plain. Mr. Bell doesn't answer. They pass the paint factory's color test field. They pass a rotten dresser someone left on the edge of his property.

"I know a motel," he says finally, and drives toward Bethlehem, where on August 11, 1859, a meteor fell nearby. They pass Snake Hill. They pass Old Pond. They pass a street whose name remains unknown because a vandal stole the sign and stashed it in his basement years ago.

Ruth chews the dead skin of her thumb. Mr. Bell drives haltingly as if out practicing with a learner's permit or lost in thought. The road dips. There are a few houses, a mobile home, then nothing for a stretch. A sewage treatment plant lit up like a UFO crash site appears. He keeps driving. A sign says something about the Forestry Department. Nat curls up. Ruth irritates a hangnail. A few snowflakes start to fall. They pass through towns at night. They pass a prison. They pass a number of businesses with vague names: AmSure, Angiodynamics, Noss. The carton of grapefruit juice has warmed up between Ruth's legs.

An hour later, near Lasher Creek, meteorite found in 1948, Ruth sees a sign for a motor lodge. Underneath the words there's a depiction of a bosomy woman, dressed in a hula skirt, shaking it underneath a limbo bar, though there's nothing else Hawaiian about the place. It looks like a cinder block.

Mr. Bell rings the office buzzer twice. A young girl lets him in.

Nat is slumped against the car door, snoring.

Mr. Bell returns to the car with their room key attached to a wooden spoon bearing the number four on its bowl. Ruth squeezes Nat's wrist. "Come on." The three of them drag into the room.

"No one's to blame," Mr. Bell tells Nat. "Every town has a time limit. Our luck was running out in Troy and I knew it. In fact, I suspect that this is probably my—"

But Ruth doesn't want to hear them bicker. She locks the bathroom door behind her. She adds no cold to the mix, climbing into the shower, scalding her shoulders and chest. She unwraps a thin bar. The soap will make her skin tight. She lathers up anyway, standing under the water until the burn fades. She scrubs her armpits and crotch with the soap, plucking her curled hairs from the bar and dropping them into the tub. She dries off and gets dressed.

The room is dark. The men have already gone to sleep, two exhausted lumps under synthetic covers. Ruth climbs into Nat's bed. She rests her hand on his stomach. Her fingers brush the wires there. Nat's grown a tremendous amount of hair rather suddenly; even his belly button has changed, because she's in the wrong bed. She's in bed with her husband. Ruth holds her position a moment longer, a tailor making measurements, so close to what's inside Mr. Bell: blood, brains.

Ruth finds her shoes and the spoon key. She steps out into the night. There's a light on in the office. Maybe someone's making coffee or setting out plastic-wrapped Danish, that fake, sweet cheese. The door opens with a jangle. There are out-of-date magazines as in a doctor's waiting room or transfer station. Ruth takes a seat, opens a women's periodical. "Best Low-Fat Potato Chips." "Our Favorite Bras." "Tools to Organize Your Living Room." Essential female information.

Don't leave him there alone, Ruth tells herself. At the end.

The smell of coffee finally hits her nose, and there's a shuffling behind a set of saloon doors. Ruth sits up straight. The noises stop. Then a racket. The doors swing open. "What'd you say?"

"Me?" Ruth asks. "I didn't say anything."

"Don't leave who there alone?" The young woman steps up behind the registration desk. "Early riser, huh?" She's not a typically sullen kid, looks more like someone who relies on curiosity to survive.

Ruth nods.

"What brings you here?"

"Visiting a friend."

"A friend from here? What's her name?"

"Umm. Eleanor. Bell. Yeah. El Bell."

"Cool name. Never heard of her."

"You know everyone in town?" Ruth closes the magazine.

"Pretty much. It's a small place."

"What goes on around here?"

The woman shrugs. "Not much." She rests an elbow on the desk, chewing one finger to help her think. "Lots of waiting around, I suppose."

"For what?"

"Grow up, get married, divorced. Maybe a kid. You know, die. School to start. Coffee to brew."

Ruth takes a seat. "Mind if I wait with you?"

"Knock yourself out."

"What are you doing up so late?"

"I got a call to open the lock."

"The door?"

"No. The canal. Erie runs right behind this place. You're in a lock house, so whoever's on duty at the motel is also responsible for opening the locks when a boat's coming through."

"People still use the canal? In this weather? I thought it was decommissioned." The Father had told Ruth that.

"Mostly pleasure crafts but, yeah, people still use the canal."

"Doesn't it freeze in winter?"

"You'd think so, right? Doesn't stop some people."

"How do you open the gates?"

"I'd like to show you because it's amazing, a feat of engineering, and the people who built it weren't even engineers. But I'm not allowed to show you. Sorry."

"Why? What is it? Coast Guard? Homeland Security?"

"Something like that," she says.

Ruth curls her legs up on the bench. She falls asleep before the coffee's even had a chance to percolate.

Eventually morning comes on. The girl's gone. Ruth helps herself to three pastries, two coffees. Nat won't drink the stuff. She kicks their motel room door. "Mr. Bell. Nat. Wake—"

Mr. Bell opens the door. "I'm up."

"You want coffee?"

"More than a cake wants a hot oven."

She thinks that means yes.

"Nat's just washing up, then I think we can shuffle along." He heads toward the car. Ruth follows with the coffee and pastry. She has nothing to collect from their room. She left Troy with nothing. They wait for Nat. Mr. Bell turns the engine over. Though they're separated front seat to back, the quiet unnerves her. She wonders if he was awake last night when she felt him up.

He thumbs his chin. "You ever watch *Bacteria Workshop*? I saw one episode about thermophile microorganisms that defecate magnets. Honest to goodness. I could not make that up."

Ruth has nothing to say. She blows her coffee.

"You need sugar?"

"No, thank you."

Mr. Bell climbs out. "What's become of our young man?" Closing the door behind him. "Nat!" he calls, ducking into the office for sugar.

Ruth reaches into the front seat. The cushion where Mr. Bell had been sitting is warm. She carries that warmth to her face, leans back again.

Mr. Bell returns shaking two packets of sugar like maracas, like the limbo lady. Ruth is sitting directly behind him now so that she can hide. He faces forward, prepares his drink, takes a sip, issues a yum of approval for the watery, sugary brew. “I want to ask you something.”

She tightens.

He doesn’t turn. He pinches his nose quickly. “Are you familiar with the concept of *wabi-sabi*?”

Ruth watches the back of his head. “More bacteria?”

“Nah. It’s Japanese. It’s where a thing can’t be beautiful or perfect without an imperfection. Say, Nat’s teeth. The front two are crossed. Just the littlest bit wrong. Yes? They’re the snag that a person gets hung up on. Yes? Caught?”

“You mean my scar?”

“Yes. Perfection scribbled out or the imperfection that makes you, me, anyone perfect and complete because it includes the truth of our mortality. Get it?”

Ruth rests her head on the glass. She imagines Nat’s teeth tearing into raw meat, a bear in a cage. She imagines Nat’s teeth tearing into her scar. “Why?”

“I’m telling you I’m a faulted man who’s done bad things. Many bad things. But” — he turns — “I’m telling you with the hope that you might still be my friend.”

“Well,” she says. “That depends. What is it that you did?”

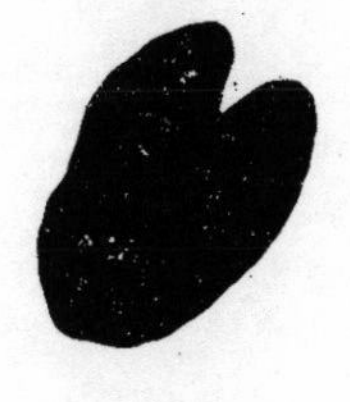

I WALK LIKE A COWBOY. Ruth waddles, making fun. "I need to sit down." My belly's more bomb than baby. I'm splitting in two. One way or another it's going to tear me up. We find a seat across the road from the canal. The ground's cold. "We should have gone someplace sunny." She tilts her face up to the sun, milking any warmth from the pale disk behind a flat cloud. A corner of Ruth's flannel blooms red. "What's that?" She touches the ground beneath her. Her palm opens, wet and red. "Blood."

We look up to see if it came from the sky. We look down and around. Ruth stands for a better view. I don't know how we missed him, five or six feet away in the grass, his face turned into the dirt, and behind him — down a small embankment, through a path of broken pines and laurels — is the car that spit him out. The vehicle rests on its back like an insect. A pair of feet in tube socks are stuck out the upside-down window.

"Jesus." I lift myself up.

Ruth runs to him, touches the man's foot, spine, neck. She rolls the body onto its back. He's an old man. His face lifts to the sun as well. His skin runs with blood and bits of road. Ruth touches his forehead.

The tube socks move. Someone's alive in the car wreck, whispering. Ruth points me down toward the vehicle.

"Hello?"

The whispering stops.

"Do you need help?"

The legs pull back inside the window like a turtle's neck. Whispering begins again as if this thing hiding inside the car isn't a victim of the crash but the demon that caused it. I crouch for a look inside. "Do you need help?"

The tube socks belong to a middle-aged woman, the man's daughter perhaps. "Yes." She's crouched on the ceiling beside the overhead light. She wears a man's windbreaker over a light summer dress. "I need a ride home. My mother will be worried."

She's my age, maybe even older. "We don't have a car."

"No car."

"No. We've been walking."

"OK." She climbs out the window feet first. "OK."

The woman has lost her shoes. I just say it. "Your father's dead."

The woman walks slowly over to the body. "He's not my father." She kneels carefully beside him in the blood. Like Ruth, she touches his forehead.

"Who is he?"

"Just a kind man who gave me a ride home." There's silence for as long as it would take a pot of water to boil. She touches his cheek, wipes blood from his chin. "OK. Let's go." The woman scrambles up the embankment to the road. "It's not far." She's oddly accustomed to death.

"To the hospital?"

She stares at my belly. "For you?"

"No. You."

She looks down at her arms and legs. All are still attached. "I don't need a hospital."

"But we should get some help for him."

"It's too late to help him." She sets off moving a good deal faster than Ruth's and my customary gait. "I need to get home. My mother will be worried," she says again. So we leave the guy there. We follow the woman.

I've never seen a dead body before.

After a mile or so, I ask, "Can we rest a moment?"

"Of course." The woman stands on the shoulder. Ruth helps me to the ground. "You're going to have a baby?"

I nod. In the gutter there's a running shoe that's sprouted some grass. The woman chews on her fingers. Ruth throws pebbles up in arcs. We watch them fall. "I'm sorry. About your friend."

"Yes. You said." Our rest doesn't last long. "It's not far." She lifts under my armpits. Ruth takes one of my elbows. My joints are rubbery, and at times it seems a thigh could slip from my hip. I'd teeter on one leg until my belly tipped me forward. Ruth waits without complaining. She'd have to speak to complain.

"There it is," the woman says after a bit.

"What?"

"End of the line."

It's a motor lodge. On the sign there's a bosomy woman dressed in a hula skirt, shaking it underneath a limbo bar, though there's nothing tropical about the place. It looks like one big plain cinder block.

"Thanks," she says. "I'm OK from here." The woman pulls a key from her pocket and lets herself in to one of the motel's rooms, turning once to wave goodbye. "The office is right over there," she says, directing us with her chin.

Ruth and I don't discuss other options. We check into the motor lodge.

When I tell the young woman at reception about the accident, she nods. She already knows. "It's happened before. It happens all the time."

"It does?"

"Yeah. That road can be bad in the rain. Dead Man's Curve. So. You guys staying the night?"

The paperwork is an old-fashioned index card. The young woman gives us a room key attached to a wooden spoon: #4. Ruth pays her, making exact change. I purchase a beer from her and drink it in our parking spot since we don't have a car to put there. I'm sorry, baby, for drinking, but I need a small something after seeing that man's face.

There are two double beds with polyester covers, darkly patterned and abstract in design. There are two metal luggage racks, a television, and a small table between the beds. There's a framed print on the wall of a woman walking beside a river. In the picture the banks are covered with red and orange flowers. In the picture the sun is shining.

I draw a warm bath and climb in. A few curly hairs skim the surface. They are not mine. Gross. Who do they belong to? I fish them out aboard the paper soap wrapper.

I hear Ruth flick through the TV channels, stopping on a music program. I dip both hand towels into the bathwater, draping one over the baby and one over my eyes.

I don't feel her. I don't hear her, but in a few minutes when I lift the towel from my eyes to wet it again, Ruth is sitting on the toilet tank staring at me.

"Damn, you sc—"

She shoves a rough hand over my mouth. She tucks her chin, shuts her eyes until I relax. Only then does she remove her hand, shaking her head no, no. And she listens. She points outside.

I listen too. An ad on the TV claims, "Grandma would be proud."

Ruth sits back on the toilet lid, wrapping her elbows around her middle.

"What?" I mouth. "The man?" But she turns her eyes into sharp death. We sit in silence listening hard.

It takes an hour for the water to lose every bit of its heat. We still don't move. I have pruned up in unimaginable places, my ankles, my knees. My rear end is turning into cement. I don't know what she imagines outside our door. There's one small frosted window in the room. Through it, the sun dies. Still Ruth doesn't move. We sit in the dark. The water's freezing. My bones ache, and hours—I think hours—pass this way. I'm shivering. I'm dissolving. The evening news gives way to a crime drama in the bedroom. I rest my head on a bathmat on the edge of the tub. I pee in the water. Eventually I fall asleep, and when I wake, it sounds like one of the late shows.

Ruth is gone.

My knees have little interest in holding me up. I'm wobbly. I turn on the hot shower full blast to burn away the cold.

Ruth isn't in the bedroom either. I dress, pull on my socks and sneakers, then climb into the far bed, pulling the covers up and over my head.

I wake twice in the night to pee. It's dark. Still no Ruth. It gets so quiet, I can hear the trickle of water outside, the canal.

A person just entering this situation, a person who hasn't been on the road for weeks, would call the police or at least call El. But I'm not just entering this situation. Calling the police to find Ruth is like using a bulldozer to needlepoint.

When the sun rises, there's still no Ruth, and I'm not sure what to do. Some eggs, I guess. A cup of coffee. There's a diner a short hike from the motel. There's a squished squirrel on the shoulder, its furry tail lifts with the wind of every passing car. Maybe this is the end. Maybe we've arrived wherever it is we're heading. I don't know though. This doesn't feel like the end.

My place mat is a state map marking presidential birth sites, national monuments, the state flower. Rose. Bluebird. Before my eggs arrive, I fold the map and tuck it into my pocket in case I'm alone now. At least I'll be able to find my way to Martin Van Buren's house.

Back in the room, I lie stiffly on the bed, a pillow between my legs. I don't know how to get where we're heading. I don't know how to get back to where we came from. I don't know why or if there's danger. I lie on the motel bed, a pregnant nothing, having no idea what is going to happen to me.

Before I was pregnant, I thought carrying a baby meant knowing a baby. That's not true. I don't know anything about this child. Pregnancy is a locked door in my stomach, all the weight of life and death and still no way to know it. The baby gives me a small kick, taking what's delicate—lung tissue, tiny see-through fingers, hair fine enough to spin webs—and hardens it into a tough thing, a thing that likes it rough. It'll grow and I will be the only one who remembers when it was unmarked and delicate as a moth.

Ruth left her bag behind, pinning me here. What if she came back and I was gone? Do I take the bag or leave it? What if something happened to her, if she's hurt, fallen into a hole? What about bad guys? The bad guy? Then I realize that it's not just me following Ruth blindly. She needs me. She can't talk.

The TV feels like heart cancer and homesickness. I switch it off. I poke through Ruth's things. I find her hairbrush and use it to brush out the knots the road has given me. When I'm done, hair combed, I pull out that *Book of Ether.*

16 The universe is revealed by science.
The universe or nothing.

The universe is rich in mystery.

No shit.

Someone knocks at the door. I'm still for a moment, but loneliness overrides fear. I open the lock.

The young woman from reception is there. She's small. Her dark hair is loose and curly, parts have been streaked blue. She wears a tight swath of muslin around her hips and, underneath that, layers and layers of burlap like a down-and-out pioneer. She wears red pantyhose, and she's painted a line across the bridge of her nose joining together the eyeliner on either side. She's chronologically messed up, some sort of time traveler. She's only as high as my chin. Her motorcycle boots appear to be hand-me-downs from an older brother. "You've got a phone call." She flicks her hairstyle in the direction of the office.

The motor lodge is L-shaped with an office at the far end. The canal runs along the backside of the motel, though nowadays the canal's so still, running isn't the right word. The office awning is scaffolded by spider webs. There's no neon or kitsch, none of the good stuff one looks for in old motels. It more closely resembles a publicly funded housing unit. Plain, sturdy, and functional. Its plainness explains the extraordinary efforts the young woman has gone through to look different.

A bell tied to the office door handle rings as the girl throws it open. I follow her in. Five old desk phones, each with a heavy handset, are lined up on a low shelf. That's four more phones than a motel this broken down requires. One phone rests off the hook. I lift the receiver. "Ruth?" No damn answer. Of course. "Ruth. Quit it. Tell me where you are."

And then the person on the other line does make a sound. He clears his throat. He.

"Hello?" I try, quietly. The young woman tilts her head.

"You're mine?" he asks.

"What?"

"You're mine." And the line goes dead.

The woman licks and seals an envelope; her tongue makes a timid point.

I'm so scared, I start to lie. "You're breaking up," I say into the dial tone. "I'm sorry," I pretend, too unnerved to admit I'd been careless, that I might have put us in more danger. "I can't hear you," I say, replacing the handset and taking a shaky seat on an outdoor bench that's been moved inside. "I lost whoever it was," I tell the girl. "Maybe they'll call back." I can't return to the room by myself. I'm too scared. You're mine? Maybe Lord found me. It didn't sound like Lord. Plus Lord would never call me his.

I sit with a magazine, and the words there — some new theory for building safer tunnels — crumble. I don't want to understand Ruth's life. There might be a really good reason she doesn't talk.

A small transistor radio is up on a high shelf above the woman, set to a station that's not seen much change in stock or personnel since 1943. "Midnight blue was the color of her eyes, the sorrow of her sighs."

I bite one thumb. It's hard to stop walking once you start because stopping gives the bad things a chance to catch up.

The woman checks her makeup and hair. She taps the eraser of her pencil. "So," she says. My feet swing just above the ground. "Will you be staying another night?"

"What's the name of this town again? Byron? Scriba?"

Dead boredom lifts from the woman's face. She perks up. "St. Eugene. After Gene Boniface, not a saint at all. During the Civil War, he sold parcels of land that never existed. This land was gold then, back in the glory days of the canal. Can you imagine? The canal cut transportation costs by ninety, ninety-five percent. Anything was possible. You want to move that there? Fine. I want to move these things over here. No problem. Transportation is human. Transportation is life, and Gene was a master con man back when it was easier to work a con, back when nobody knew anything. Information was polite. No newscasters' colonoscopies. No satellite images of the North Pole melting. Anything was possible. Know what I mean? Gene swindled soldiers, sold fake land to men who thought they'd be dead soon. It's so easy to roll the fearful. Right? Piece of cake. After Gene, this place became a sort of haven for con men."

"Are you related to him?"

"I wish."

"You know a lot about him."

"I'm old-fashioned. I read books." She swoops her lopsided hair from her face. "I can't help myself. I love books. Even though I get enraged at the tyranny of text."

"What's that?"

"You know. Left to right. Punctuation. Page 1, page 2, page 3. Text has a lot of rules. Kind of like getting born, living your life, dying. You know. Text only has one direction. Frustrates me."

"I see."

"Plus, I talk to a lot of people. Still."

Considering the company I've been keeping, this does seem a banner of marked difference. "What about the tyranny of talking?" I ask.

"Don't even get me started."

"My aunt doesn't talk."

"Really?"

"Uh-huh. I mean she can. I think. She just chooses not to."

"Wow. Why?"

"I don't know. She won't say."

"Right. Exactly. Cool. And you're just left with this pounding hammer: Why? Why? Why? There's truth for you. Where's she at? I'd like to not-talk with her."

"She should be back soon." Changing the topic. "So are you a con man?"

"I'm more like a con man's assistant. Or nurse. Or Gal Friday."

"Do you live at the motel?"

"Lord Jesus, no, and no offense if you're planning on moving in, but only dead people live here."

"Huh?"

"This place is like a waiting room for dead people. You know, people with unfinished business."

"I kind of like motels."

"They're great for a short visit."

"Why would the dead come here?"

"Why come back at all is a better question."

"Yeah. Why?"

"From what I understand, there's three kinds who come back. All of them are people who get stuck, like some bad pop song, when you were a kid, that track you couldn't stop listening to over and over and over? Of the three, mothers are the worst. They never let go. Especially, say, a mother who lost her kid. Forget it. She's going to stick around forever 'cause first she's got to find her kid, then she's got to make it right. Not always easy. What if the kid's dead himself, right? How are you going to find him?"

I squint at her, wondering if she might have been somehow sent by El. Or is on drugs.

"Next there's the angry dead," she says. "You know, looking for revenge. I don't care for them one bit. They always seem desperate. Mouth breathers, I call them."

"Huh?"

"You know." She makes a Darth Vader sound. "Desperate. And last, you've got the lovers. Here it gets even stickier. Say someone's hanging around to take care of his little sister. Then his wife ends up hanging around to take care of him. Then the wife's daughter is worried about the mom. On and on, right? Pretty soon this place is filled up with people who didn't get quite enough love in while they were alive, and—shudder to think—what if a living person ends up falling in love with a dead one? Love gets messy when you're dead." She nods at me. "I've got plenty of messes around here just keeping the sheets and towels clean."

"How would a living person fall in love with a dead one?"

"Please. James Dean? Come on."

"No, I mean, how would a living person see a dead person?"

"Thankfully most can't, but sometimes a situation arises, say, a person who's alive but maybe also not totally alive, right? Like a halfway-alive thing. You know?"

"I mean how would you know they're dead?"

"The dead tend to carry around some sort of empty box."

"Like a coffin."

"Could be. Could be. But really any size. Sometimes tiny, say, a jewelry box. Sometimes huge, maybe a whole mansion. All that matters is the emptiness."

"You're speaking metaphorically, right?"

"Oh, sure. Of course. Metaphorically. Transubstantially. Cryogenically. Whatever you need. Whatever gets you through the night."

I have no idea what she's talking about. "How'd you end up here?"

"I'll tell you." She runs her tongue hard against her front teeth. "I'll tell you. It's like this. In college everyone chose a niche, a microscopic subset of the human race they wanted to fight for, lay down on the tracks for. You know, poets with AIDS, Ethiopians with cholera. Remember this? We'd organize a conference, and my friends would ask, 'OK, did we invite a Lithuanian butch communist? Or have we represented the voice of African American cowboy storytellers who believe in UFOs?'" She twists her lips. "All interesting demographics to hear from, for sure, but it started to seem like so much rooting for the home team, and the home team only. I didn't want to choose one small group. I wanted to understand real diversity, so I turned my scholarly attentions to the greatest population."

"The poor?"

"Not even close. Dead people."

"Right."

"A totally underrepresented population. The people underground. No one's looking out for dead people's rights. Right?" She slams her fist on the counter. "No one's making sure dead people are invited to speak at conferences on semiotics or the effect of polar vortexes on the Gulf of Mexico. I became a ghost activist. I'd start arguments with my classmates and professors as to why they always privilege being over non-being. Why they behave as if the only words people hear are spoken ones. Makes my blood boil. What about the unsaid? Right? What about the dead?"

A man with well-greased trousers enters the lobby. "How's it hanging, Sherry darling? Loose?"

"Sure. Loose." Then she turns back to me. "Ask Carl. He can tell you."

"What?" He blushes. "And, please, don't call me that."

"Sorry. I was just telling her only dead people live here. Right?"

"Not exclusively." The guy definitely looks like someone who lives in an upstate motel, a sexy bandito with a messed-up past. Lots of silver loot on his hands, bracelets on wrists. The man smiles and shakes one ringed finger at the young woman, scolding with a smile. "You're a funny one, Sherry. Any caffeinated beverages at the ready?" he asks. "I can't seem to stay conscious."

She looks at the brewing coffeepot. "Almost."

"Right. I'll be back in a jiff."

"Sure. Hey, Carl, you have that money you owe me?" she asks him.

"I'm working on it. Working on it." He swings out through the door. "My great pleasure to make your acquaintance," he says, though we barely met.

The woman lifts a brow after he's gone. "So you guys staying another night?"

I look toward the phone, nearly believing my own fabrication of moments earlier. That it had been Ruth, that she'd said something to explain why the plan had changed. Why I was stopped here, waiting for her, holding the knapsack. "Yeah. Another night."

"Got any plans?"

"Nope."

"Cool. I get off at eight. I'll be round to get you. If you're interested."

I don't ask in what. I'm interested. "I'll look for you then."

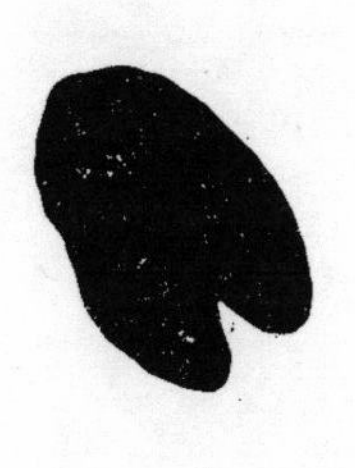

MR. BELL PULLS his greased hair behind his ears. "Back to Troy?"

Nat joins them in the car.

Ruth imagines Zeke's non-nose. "I don't think that's a good idea." They pass a dairy farm, an abandoned paint ball area, and a house whose yard is dominated by whirligigs and birdbaths.

"I know a spot. At least for a night," Mr. Bell says.

"Far from here?"

"Far from any place really."

Ruth nods a slight yes like a mafia boss. They pass a field of three transmission towers. In the field there's an abandoned lightweight truck. Nat taps his nails against the window.

The radio speaks of nothing but the coming storm. "It's going to be a doozy!" DJs ratchet up fear. "No end to this nastiness in sight, folks!" They are bullies taunting winter into bad behavior.

Seventh Lake, Eighth Lake. There are so many lakes in the Adirondacks, some are numbered rather than named. Homes swarm by the lakeshores, leaving huge areas of unpeopled land. Mr. Bell's car heads up into the mountains. Ruth has her forehead flattened against the window. "A bear." She sits up. The bear is not alone. There are three, four, and another one across the street standing in front of a trailer. The giant bears have been chain-sawed from trees and painted black as fur.

A highway turns to a county road to a back road. The car climbs higher. Many of the homes look like chalets with carved wooden shutters. Cheaply built vacation condos collapse under the weight of winter and neglect. There's a plague of empty tourist businesses, restaurants that catered to the summer crowds until the summer crowds found something chicer than a week in the high peaks. Small flakes fall, covering their tracks.

They travel slowly through the morning, higher and higher, up where the snow berms are as tall as a child. No one is here.

Mr. Bell spins the tuning on the radio. Even the weather forecasts have petered out at this higher altitude. There's one country station and one for Jesus. Mr. Bell switches it off, and they are left with the sound of slush rushing under the tires. He says, "Ah, yes," or "Of course" every mile or two as if he's just remembering how to get there. He hurries. "Sorry to rush but there's one stretch of the road that becomes impassable very quickly in snow. I'd like to get there before that happens."

Ruth's breath fogs the window. She wipes it clean in time to catch a momentary view. The trees drop away, the hills open into a vista. Huge ancient mountains disappear into clouds and snow. The road switches back. The view tightens and trees close back in on either side. Ruth fogs her window again. Oxygen thins. The road twists. They drive on.

The next town has an oversize highway department and a bar whose parking lot's filled with snowmobiles. There's a gas station and a general store rolled into one. Mr. Bell parks. A community bulletin board on the porch advertises clean fill, chainsaw repair, and a double mattress for sale. The door makes an electronic *ding* as the three enter. Mr. Bell extends his hand toward an uninterested mutt curled on the cashier's wooden counter. "Bonjour, pooch." He passes shopping baskets to Nat and Ruth with the instruction, "Fill 'em up."

"How long are we planning to stay up here?" Ruth asks.

"Depends on the storm."

Five or six people have gathered by the coffee counter—some seated, some rubbing their hands near a wood stove. They stare. Mr. Bell smiles to his audience. "Could one of you remind me where I'd find the lamp oil?"

No responses but wide eyes drink in Mr. Bell's shine. He twinkles his fingertips above his head releasing them from his spell. "Hello?"

The clerk jumps to attention. "Follow me." Mr. Bell disappears down one creaky wooden aisle into the back of the store. Nat and Ruth stand in the gaze of the townspeople before shuffling off to their shopping.

The store specializes in canned, frozen, and cured provisions. Ruth finds whatever is fresh, or once was: eggs, milk, bananas, iceberg, and onions. There's penny candy and a mounted moose head as large as the ice cream cooler. There's beer and a wall of movie rentals. There's a post office, presently closed. There's a rack of magazines, locally made jams, and a tray of fudge. Road salts, shovels, winter boots, emergency flares, motor oil, and lug nuts. Ruth selects three tins of Vienna sausages, some creamed corn, maple candy, cheddar, yogurt, biscuit mix, fruit cocktail in syrup. She puts her full basket up on the counter beside Nat's and Mr. Bell's.

The big ears at the wood stove watch them. There are three older gentlemen individuated only by the messages on their baseball caps. CAT says one. STIHL says the second. HOW CAN I MISS YOU IF YOU WON'T GO AWAY? asks the third. There are two women—one old, one younger. Both with short, styled hair, diamond-chip wedding rings, and winter parkas. All five people stare, prompting Mr. Bell to shuffle his feet, Bojangles style.

"Where you kids headed in this weather?" one of the old-timers finally asks.

Mr. Bell stops dancing. "Up the mountain a stretch. Over the river. Through the woods."

The man lifts his lip and squints trying to see what Mr. Bell is talking about. He blows a raspberry and turns back to his circle of familiars. "Heard about them city hikers?"

The circle nods, studying boots and cracks on the wooden floor.

"Yup. Two weeks to thaw out their bodies. Though I heard it wasn't the cold that got them."

Mr. Bell's interest in the old guy has now been piqued.

The man nods to his friends. "Yup." And then the bastard doesn't say what killed the city hikers.

The cashier rings up their purchases. Nat adds some trucker speed. Mr. Bell pays and their supplies are loaded into three cardboard boxes as Ruth imagines starving to death, falling off a cliff, being hacked to bits by some old-timer in a baseball cap.

With the car loaded, Nat takes a moment to piss over the snow berm in the rear of the lot. A group of young men have parked their trucks and snowmobiles by the propane tank refill center. They practice machismo in front of the strangers. They imagine the fearsome cluster of manhood they present. One boy spits an ugly if expected word in reference to Ruth. She doesn't hear it. One boy scratches his, as of yet, untested testicles. Ruth notices one of the boys because he's dressed crazy for the cold weather, in shorts and a concert T-shirt. His hair is as dark as his shirt. She leans back into the seat, making eye contact with this boy as Mr. Bell finds reverse and Nat slams the door shut.

A mile or two away from the store, the town disappears. They take a right onto a road where the plow hasn't tried very hard at all. The notion of trouble is immediately upon them when two pickup trucks and a snowmobile follow them onto the off road.

"It's not far now." Mr. Bell speaks to cancel any alarm.

Ruth monitors activity out the rear window. "The boys from the store are following us."

Mr. Bell tucks his chin, wraps a hank of hair behind his ear. "Nothing but ignorant rednecks."

"Ignorant rednecks getting closer." The first truck races up to their bumper. Ruth ducks. "They're here," she says, seconds before the truck lurches. Bumper meets bumper. The second truck pulls up alongside, overtaking Mr. Bell's average sedan. The truck comes to a dead halt across the road. Mr. Bell uses two feet to brake, sliding toward a small river, one that washes through these mountains timidly, a forgettable stream that collects water from all these lakes, rolling down the mountains until it reaches the magnificent Hudson. The car comes to a stop, leaving just enough space for a minor paperback mystery to slide between the two vehicles.

A number of crows sitting in a spruce wisely decide it's time to leave.

Mr. Bell steps from the car. Hands on hips, he approaches the lead truck. "What is this? Some sort of pickle sandwich?"

Four boys from the store climb out of the trucks, another arrives on snowmobile.

"Pickle sandwich?" Nat shakes his head and gets out as well. Ruth follows.

The dark-haired boy is there. "Which one's your boyfriend?" he asks Ruth. She looks down at the truck's hubcap. "And which one is a mother-fucking faggot?"

She doesn't understand the question entirely. All she'd done was look at him for a moment. Is it good or bad to be her boyfriend?

Does that carry some sort of immunity? Or does boyfriend = head beaten with a crowbar? More likely faggot = crowbar with these boys. Even more likely, nobody's safe because they don't even understand what it is that's making them angry. Chunks of muddy slush cling to the flap behind the tire, hanging on for life.

"Generally." Mr. Bell draws them off her. "Male homosexuals don't go in for mothers." Raw meat to maggots, they turn toward him.

"What'd you say?" asks a slow one.

"Oh, dear." Mr. Bell sizes him up, hand on chin. "You, presumably, own one of the trucks?"

"Why?"

"Strapping young lads such as your friends here only socialize with the hideously obese who can afford fancy cars."

"Cocksucker." The guy begins his waddle toward Mr. Bell's neck, arms raised zombie style.

"Yes, well, Fatso. The truth do hurt." Mr. Bell takes a seat on the hood of his car, arresting Fatso's advance with indifference. Mr. Bell dusts a few snowflakes off his knees.

"I think you three are in trouble now," says the black-haired boy, closing in on Nat, who suddenly looks tiny in the big world. Ruth churns with nausea, a wave of blind sickness to see Nat made unstrong and scared.

"Is that right?" Mr. Bell asks.

Ruth tries to count. Five of them. Again. No six.

"Yay, boy. We're the Destructo-Crew." The black-haired boy's voice makes a high screech, striving for the amped-up insanity of a metal band but sounding more like a happy dinosaur on a children's cartoon. "And we like to blow shit up!"

Threats met with silence sound absurd. "Like what?" Mr. Bell finally asks. "Balloons? Bubble gum?" Again he draws the bullies off Nat and Ruth. "I don't imagine we're meeting here by coincidence?" He shifts gears, begins his attack. "So I wonder why we've been selected for this honor. Is it because one of your lot . . ." He looks around. "I'm guessing you." He points to the dark hair. "Longs to pound your pale, pitiful worm against the dewed and virtuous flesh of my bride? Yet due to some malformation in your person, you lack the refinement to pursue her eye in the more traditionally charming ways — flowers, phone calls, candlelit dinners? You follow instead the caveman paradigm, the old club and hair drag?" The boys are stunned dumb. "Grunt once for yes, twice for no."

Brown slush drops from their mud flaps down to the road. Mr. Bell stands, dusts off more snow.

"You're one of those religious weirdoes from Tahawus. Ether?" The statement comes from a boy who has not yet fully climbed out of his cab. "Yeah. He's one of them," the boy says to his friends. "I can tell by his pants."

Mr. Bell puffs up his chest and regards the pants he has on. "Hmm." He rubs the fibers of the fabric between his fingers, puzzled.

"Is she?"

"Am I what?"

"A weirdo."

Ruth considers this.

Mr. Bell pinches his chin. His silence is a bit frightening, brewing something. The boys wake from a fantasy of manhood.

Ruth re-asks them their question. "Am I a weirdo?" She's ignored.

Mr. Bell does not blink but ever so slightly nods assent. Yes.

"I knew it," Fatso says. "Let's go." His cronies do not disagree.

"Sorry about that," one utters.

Mr. Bell nods.

The boys beat a retreat, executing two rapid three-point turns, radios blaring. The black-haired boy strikes a hand gesture most certainly intended to be devil horns but which is, in actuality, the American Sign Language manual expression of the phrase "I love you."

Nat, Ruth, and Mr. Bell return to the car, shaking snowflakes from their shoulders and crowns.

"Morons." Mr. Bell tries to wash away the incident with one word. He keeps the speedometer steady at twenty-five miles per hour, breathing in practiced labor, calmly, firmly, but it is not so easy for Nat and Ruth to carry on. While they are accustomed to measured doses of violence, their force fields are weak.

"What were they talking about?"

Mr. Bell takes a right onto a smaller road through pine trees and then a left onto an even smaller road. LOWER WORKS says one sign. MT. MARCY says another. SLEEPING GIANT. Ruth can't read all the signs before they pass — something about private property, something about the DEC, something about a missing boy. Their rear end fishtails slightly. The road is not cleared.

"I'm sure I have no idea." Mr. Bell looks once again at his completely average pants.

The snow continues to fall. The deeper they move into the forest, Ruth feels calmer. Mr. Bell is a weapon so secret, he doesn't even know the secret.

The road goes higher still, and after a mile or two it straightens, allowing a view that tightens every nerve in Ruth. "Mr. Bell." She leans forward.

"This is the stretch I spoke of."

"We have to cross that?"

"I'm afraid so."

Nat leans forward as well, and through the front windshield the three of them study what's ahead. The view is sickening. The road narrows to an extended, one-lane wooden bridge with railings constructed of rough branches no thicker than a woman's arms. The bridge curves in a crescent over a chasm whose bottom is deep enough to be unknowable, a slice carved through the mountain's stone since before time began.

"Are you sure?"

Rather than respond, Mr. Bell starts out across the pass in a crawl. All three hold their breath as if the slightest change in air flow might send the vehicle plummeting over the edge.

Safe on the far side, they travel a few miles in grateful silence. Finally, Mr. Bell speaks. "It's really more dangerous on the descent. One wants to slow to allow for the curve, but braking on a frozen one-lane bridge is the worst idea a driver could ever have."

Through the trees and snow, there's an enormous structure

built of stone beside the road. It's dark and towering, nothing like a house, closer to an ancient jungle temple, built by people who believe in human sacrifice. She hopes they won't be staying there.

"Blast furnace."

This triggers no response from Nat or Ruth.

"There was a mine here a long time ago." Ruth cannot see the top third of the furnace from inside the car. They pass it by. "Some of the pits are down there." Mr. Bell points through the woods. "They're filled with water now. Deepest lakes in the Adirondacks. During the mine's high years, almost a thousand people lived up here. Tahawus."

"What?"

"Someone told me it means Cloud-Splitter, though I can't finger the language. Something native perhaps. It was a company town with all the attendant alienations and snug circumstances that suggests. There was one YMCA. People fished or hunted. People mined until the eighties, when it became cheaper to bring ore in from South America."

"You have a summer home here?"

"No."

"This is where you grew up?"

"The mine was closed by the time I was born."

The car slows again. "Then what were you doing?"

"Here." Mr. Bell turns down an unplowed drive. The wheels spin and, less than a few yards down the path, the vehicle lurches into a shallow ditch. He spins the tires a few times before announcing, "All right. We are firmly stuck." As though he'd intended it. "We can hoof it in from here."

Each carries a box of food, and as long as they are careful, they can walk gently on top of the snow like cats trying to not break through the crusted surface. When they are less careful, the surface breaks. Mr. Bell goes under first, plunging in up to his mid-thigh, dipping into a world that is cold, bright, and without oxygen. He extracts himself on all fours, and they set off again, stepping lightly, mastering the slow art of walking on top of snow.

None of them speak. It's work enough to bear the supplies, but after a quarter mile, Ruth sees the house: tall, gray, enormous, and proper, like a stone woman kneeling by the side of a lake, gazing into the water for something she lost there. The house is utterly grand, a mansion in the mountains, totally unaffordable. “This is your house?”

“Sort of.”

Mr. Bell is a rich kid. Though once again he has no key.

“One moment, please.” He disappears round back, leaving Nat and Ruth alone. They wait on the covered landing. There’s a rusted bell on a cord. Nat jangles it, but the bell makes no sound, the clapper’s frozen in place. Overhead there are more crows.

Ruth cups her hand to the glass of the door. She can’t see much. Most of the windows are shaded with green canvas, giving the inside a swampy feel as if the house is not beside the lake but under it. There’s another moose in the foyer with a rack the size of a loveseat. Someone has hung a number of umbrellas on his antlers. The moose looks large and dumbstruck. The moose reminds Ruth of Ceph.

The wind blows snow and ice against the house, a tiny tinkling sound. Cloud-Splitter, falling back to Earth. Mr. Bell reappears, spinning a ring of keys on his index finger. He tries each one in the lock, raising his eyebrows, pleased when the tumblers finally fall. “Welcome.” He steps back to allow Ruth and Nat entrance.

The house is built for giants. “What is this place?” The furniture is fashioned from felled trees and worn leather. “This is your house?” Ruth walks through the living room. A wall of old photos mark glorious times here on the lake.

“Sort of.”

“You grew up here?” The same question she’d already asked.

“I haven’t been back for a long time.”

“Can I ask you something?”

“Why am I sleeping in basements when my family’s loaded?”

“Yes.”

“It’s more complicated than that. Please,” he says. “Come in and be comfortable.” Mr. Bell leads them through the enormous living room. A grand piano is under a canvas dust cover. There’s a hearth tall enough for a man to stand inside. It's freezing. Mr. Bell draws back a heavy set of curtains. Seven deer cross the lake ice in single file like the gang of rednecks.

"Is that a lake or a pit?"

"Started as a pit. Now it's the deepest lake of them all."

The mustiness of the house smells like swimsuits and the yellow odor of board games.

"How deep?"

"Should the Empire State Building need a place to hide, it could do so there." Mr. Bell steps back to unblock their view.

Ruth's never seen the Empire State Building. "What's down there?"

"Cars, no doubt. Backhoes. Wedding rings. Sneakers. Snakes. Bodies? Monsters? And all of it under a thousand feet of water and ice."

The kitchen is huge with open shelves covered in floral contact paper like a hotel. Ruth struggles to identify many of the culinary devices on the shelves. Old-fashioned tools, cousins to hand beaters, food mills, hot pots, fondues, apple corers, candy thermometers.

"There's a furnace in the basement. I'll get it going if you can spare me."

Ruth and Nat unpack their supplies.

"Looks like you've done well for yourself," Nat says.

Ruth nods.

"Maybe you should reconsider those plans for divorce."

"Maybe I already have."

Though it isn't much past three, the light is stretched and far away, heading to sunny California. The storm gains confidence. Ruth finds an odd light switch with two buttons, one ebony, one pearl. She pushes the pearl. An overhead fixture glows.

They put the dry goods in the pantry. The bins and shelves require a library ladder to access. She crams some of what's already there to make room. Capers, peanut butter, baking powder, shortening, caramels, popcorn, eighteen boxes of dried spaghetti, and jar after jar of pickled beets. There are six cases of red wine. There are two cans of lychee nuts, whatever those are. There are at least thirty-six cardboard boxes of toilet paper. And each box must contain at least two hundred rolls. SCOTTIES each box says. Someone really didn't want to run out of toilet paper. Inside the floor freezer Ruth finds venison steaks, bags of British peas, ice cream, meatballs, strawberries in syrup, bacon, and almonds. This is the life she dreamed of after Love of Christ! — ample food, quiet, Nat, and a fireplace. Ketchup, mustard, dill spears, and marmalade.

Mr. Bell builds a fire in the living room. Rubbing his hands over it, blowing air beneath the logs to spread the flames. He strips the piano of its dust cover.

"You play?"

"No." He tucks the cover under his arm.

"What?"

"I want to cover the car."

"Why?"

"To keep off the snow."

"You want to hide it," Nat says.

"Yes. In case."

"In case what?"

Mr. Bell shrugs. "I'll be back."

Ruth puts up the last of their food except butter, cheese, and onions. She cooks the onions in the butter. She fries three cheesy omelets in a pan. Ruth plates and serves the meal on TV trays printed with hunting scenes. The three of them dine in front of the living room fire. The lake ice turns blue then navy while they eat. Having slept very little last night, they are exhausted. At four-thirty the last light disappears from the sky. The storm has only just begun, but Nat and Ruth follow Mr. Bell up the center staircase. Its Persian runner leads down the second-story hallway. Antler sconces light the dark wood walls.

Mr. Bell opens one door. The room belongs to a boy. There are four bunk beds, room for eight children. There's a train set and a small bookshelf rising only as high as his hip. "I usually sleep in here if you don't mind." He leads them farther down the hall. "You're welcome to any of the other rooms, though best to keep the third story closed. The heat can't make it up there in winter."

Nat opens a door on a large suite. "How about in here?" he asks Ruth.

"Yes," Mr. Bell says. "That's the nicest. It has a view."

Ruth falls asleep in minutes, in her clothes, the only clothes she's got.

She wakes and she's alone. She hasn't any idea what time it is. She slips out of bed. The room is plain, cold. There's a bureau, a mirror, a rag rug, and a large black desk. In the bureau drawers: two unmatched socks, a keychain, two black buttons, and a beige pillowcase. The center desk drawer is empty except for a scrap of paper.

TO DO
fix hole in porch roof
energize people

And a list from a geography society.

Bethlehem	42°32'N	73°50'W
Burlington	42°45'N	75°11'W
Cambria	43°12'N	78°48'W
Lasher Creek	42°50'N	78°48'W
Mount Morris	42°42'N	77°53'W
Peekskill	41°17'N	73°55'W
Schenectady	42°51'39N	73°57'1W
Scriba	43°27'N	76°26'W
Seneca Falls	42°55'N	76°47'W
South Byron	43°2'N	78°2'W
Tomhannock Creek	42°53'N	73°36'W
Yorktown	41°17'N	73°49'W

The meteorites again. It must be a family thing.

She steps out into the hallway. She puts her hands on Mr. Bell's door as if checking for a fire. Outside the storm is wild, but she's not outside.

Downstairs someone's cooking.

"Morning, Mollypop."

"What time is it?"

"I don't know."

"Late?"

"Maybe. Breakfast is almost ready." He pours her juice and steers Ruth to a Dutch bench in the kitchen, where Nat drums his thumbs.

"One-eyed Jack? One-eyed Susan?" Mr. Bell asks.

Ruth looks confused.

"Toast with a Tummy?" No idea.

"Bull's-Eye? Egyptian Eye? Rocky Mountain Toast? Camel's Eye? Lighthouse Eggs? Hobo Eggs? Egg in a Hat? Egg in a Nest? Knotholes? Hocus-Pocus? Man in a Raft? Frog in a Pond? Bird in a Basket? Chick in a Well?"

She sips her juice suspiciously.

Mr. Bell drops his hands from his hips. He turns back to the stove, flips something in the fry pan, dishes it onto a plate, and presents it to Ruth.

She takes a bite and with mouth full says, "You mean Toad in a Hole." Mr. Bell slaps his forehead. "Exactly. Coffee?"

"Please."

He pulls out some Japanese contraption made of glass.

"What's that?"

"Coffeemaker. Belonged to one of my dads, I think."

"How many dads do you have?"

"Depends what year. Usually eight or nine."

"Pardon?" Nat asks.

Mr. Bell squares his gaze. "My family was not traditionally described."

Ruth sips. They chew. Nat lifts his gaze. They wait.

"I was an Etherist."

Ruth and Nat draw blanks.

"It was a religious organization."

"A charity?"

"A cult." Mr. Bell smiles. He shakes his head. "Etherists, though more properly the Eternal Ether House of Mardellion."

"What's Mardellion?"

"Our fearless prophet. He was the psychotic who introduced me to music and the solar system. He knew everything about rocks."

"What're Etherists?"

"Etherism. Meteors and multiple wives. A mashup of Mormons and Carl Sagan. You know Mormons?"

Ruth glances back to Father Arthur's lessons. "Not really."

"You know Sagan?"

"No."

"He was an astronomer."

"That's the meteorites?"

"Yeah. Yeah. Right. Mardellion thought one big meteor was going to land on this house and smash us into particles of free light."

"That's not very nice."

"No. He wasn't a nice man at all. Isn't."

"When was the last time you saw him?" Nat asks.

Mr. Bell sets his jaw at an uncomfortable angle. "He used to take me to mineral shows. He hated people who sold meteorites. He thought that was like selling slivers of the cross. So we'd go to gem shows, and Mardellion would set up a booth — this was years before IMCA —"

"What?"

"The International Meteorite Collectors Association. There were no regulations in place. He said he was an expert, so he was. He kept a picture of Sagan at the booth as if he was somehow endorsed by the man. People would line up to talk to Mardellion, show him their rocks. He didn't charge anything and sometimes even did a little recruiting at the shows. 'Chondrite,' he'd say or 'Stony iron. Looks like a desert landing.' Or 'Antarctica. Without a doubt.' Eventually, I'd file into the line, dressed like an urchin, hauling a huge rock with me, barely able to lift the thing. Most often it was some junk rock we'd pulled out of the motel's landscaping the night before. Schist or sandstone. Nothing special. I'd kick it, roll it, pitiful, making a scene, and then after waiting ten, fifteen minutes, I'd tell a guy in line, 'Mister, I really have to go the restroom. Do you mind watching this for me?' Never did the guy say no. I was a kid. But I wouldn't go to the john; I'd hide where I could spy. The closer the guy got to Mardellion, the more worried he'd look, wondering what happened to the kid who left behind the big rock. Finally, the guy would reach Mardellion, who'd look down. 'My wonder!' he'd shout out, starting to salivate. 'I've never seen such a perfect specimen of a pallasite! Do you realize how rare this is? I'll give you five thousand for it, right here—' 'It's not mine,' the guy would have to say. 'It's some kid's.' At which point Mardellion would say, 'Oh, I'm very sorry to hear that. When the kid returns, please give him my number as I have an appointment I cannot miss.' Mardellion would scratch some made-up phone number on a scrap of paper and quickly close up shop, apologizing to those in line. He'd pack it out of there in a jiffy. Once he was gone, I'd slink back over 'Darn,' I'd say, 'I missed him.' Ten times out of ten, the guy'd say, 'That's a cool rock. I don't know much, but I'll give you a thousand bucks for it.' 'In cash?' I'd ask.

"Mardellion would have the car waiting out front."

"Nice," Nat says.

"Yes. A handsome con and righteous according to Mardellion because the notion that one rock should be worth more than any other was cruel to him. He thought of rocks like people. Should dolomite be unloved? Should drug addicts? No, they should not." Mr. Bell thumbs his chin and nods. "We worked that gig for years until a show in Concord. Mardellion's doing his thing and I'm lugging my junk rock into place, making sure all the guys on line see me struggle, when we're recognized. The pool of New England mineral show enthusiasts is somewhat limited, and one of the guys we'd rolled a few years back saw me, saw Mardellion, and the whole con clicked. Boy, did he ever make a fuss. Hollering for security, calling for the cops. All the while he's got a viper grip around my arm. I saw Mardellion ducking out of the show and that was it. I don't know what happened to him after that. Prison, I heard."

"What about you?"

"I was arrested, taken straightaway, which was unfortunate. There were things I'd left behind here, things from my mom I really wanted to keep."

"You can get them now, yes?"

"If they're still here. Yes."

"So you went to jail?"

"I was only fourteen, under the sway of a con man. I had no birth certificate, no idea what my mother's real name was. I went to the state."

"Foster kid?" This makes Ruth smile.

"Yes, dear. Just like you." He doesn't look away from Ruth.

"So that was the last time you saw him?" Nat asks.

"Well," Mr. Bell says, and then nothing.

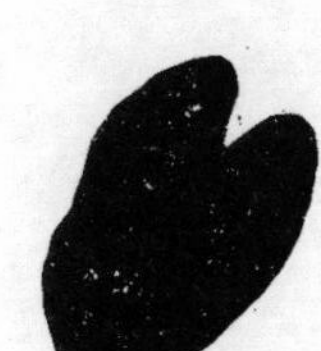

RUTH'S KNAPSACK DOES NOTHING. It sits between the beds without blinking. I unpack it like I'm cataloging evidence from a crime, like I've overlooked some essential clue. A flannel. Seven books of matches and some newspapers to start fires. A pair of socks, five pairs of plain underwear. *The Book of Ether.* Chocolate bars, nuts, pepperoni. The tarp. A compass. A flashlight. Two water bottles.

I turn on the TV. When the Wizard of Oz sends Dorothy off to get the witch's broomstick, he's sending Dorothy to her death in order to preserve his lie-based life. I lock the door from the inside. I think that's awful. I can't believe we're supposed to forgive the Wizard at the end.

There's a knock just after eight. The young woman from the office is wearing a mechanic's coat with the word *Mike* embroidered in red. "I'm Sheresa. Ready?"

I put Ruth's pack on my back. "I'm Cora. Yeah."

Sheresa drives a Crown Victoria with brown velvet seats. She's too short for such a car, so she has duct-taped hunks of two-by-fours to both the brake and gas pedals. She's even rigged an extension on the radio tuner, placing it within easy reach. On the dashboard there's a bumper sticker for an amusement park called House of Stairs and the odd slogan below, "It's Vertiginous!" The car turns over, and the radio announces the theft of a rare early American bill from the Museum of Coin and Currency.

"So. Where are you heading?" Sheresa asks.

"My aunt's trying to take me somewhere, a place she knows."

"Trying?"

"We're on foot."

"I noticed. No car. You're walking there? Aren't you pregnant?"

"Yeah."

"Are you religious or something?"

"No. Nothing against cars. We just don't have one anymore."

Sheresa's eyes get very wide. "Strange!" A compliment coming from her. "You must get tired."

"I did at first. But we take it easy. No more than five or six miles a day. Sometimes less. Not walking makes me more tired. I don't like to stop now that I've gotten used to it."

"Looks like you're going to have to stop pretty soon."

"I guess so. Maybe not." Maybe the baby will be a walker too. It's getting darker, but I can still see the landscape. St. Eugene is in a valley. The houses we pass are from a fairy tale. Deep in the woods, yellow lights in the windows. "Where are we going?"

"It's an event." Sheresa smiles.

"An event?"

"Yeah."

The air in the car is warm. The brown velvet seats of a big American sedan and someone else who doesn't want to tell me where we're going.

Sheresa parks. There are a number of other cars, odd rigs culled together from a post-apocalyptic junkyard. She checks her lipstick and hair in the rearview. "Ready?"

"For what?" There's a forest in front of us.

Her eyebrows lift twice, and she starts down a path into the woods. "Mind your step. Trees poison the ground so that nothing else can grow near them. Not even their own children."

"I'm not a tree."

"Right."

The other day a stranger in a grocery store told me that my baby has fingernails and, if it's a girl, the eggs that will be my grandchildren.

I have to move quickly to follow Sheresa. The path is amniotic, dark, humid, and inviting. I lose up and down, left and right. I navigate by listening to her feet. I break the back of a twig underfoot. Up ahead there's light. Safe haven. Sheresa's spreading a blanket beneath a weeping tree on the shore of a river. It's a wide stretch of the canal. Torches, lanterns, and candles glow, lights float on the water. It's a very quiet party. Everyone assembled keeps his voice low. I worry I've stumbled into some witches' coven.

"It's just begun."

Four vessels float on the Erie Canal, at the edge of the light. Each boat is more festive than the next. One has sails cut from a fur coat. One has sails made from a bridal gown. One is an assemblage of logs powered by paddle wheels. The last boat is two fiberglass tubs hinged into a pod. A periscope guides its small crew.

"What is it?"

Sheresa pulls a quart of malt liquor from her bag. "Captain Ahab and Huck Finn versus Lord Nelson and some sort of German U-boat." She takes a bite from a sandwich. "Last month Amerigo Vespucci beat the Rime of the Ancient Mariner in record time. A real upset since fiction always wins. Not to mention, I was the Mariner."

"You?"

"We're the Society for Confusing Literature and the Real Lies, aka TLA, History."

"TLA?"

"True Love Always. Dominic!" Dominic passes with a wave.

"What is it?"

"Oh," she says. "It's art. Sandwich?" She passes me a submarine of hummus, vegetables, and mustard. The crowd on the beach looks like a nomadic Ren Fair troupe from the year 2200. Every last part of the beast has been used for their dress. Sandals made of bald tires, lots of knickers and lacy thrift store blouses. Old leather, an aviator's cap and goggles, a hoop skirt, facial hair, suspenders, straw hats. Picnic hampers. Young people. Old people. Children and everyone so cool they must be freezing.

"Where'd you meet these people?"

"College."

"Not the college I went to."

The ships, rafts, and miniature frigates have made their way a bit closer to shore. A series of lanterns rigged on tall branches driven into the dirt reveal a crew of gypsies on the deck of each vessel. Sailors aboard the *Pequod* are already frantically bailing.

"They're not always seaworthy."

"I guess I don't know much about art."

Sheresa thinks that's funny. "Oh, that's funny," she says.

It doesn't take long for Huck Finn to win. The *Pequod* sinks of its own shoddiness while Huck's raft, simply constructed, goes on to triumph over history. Lord Nelson waves his one arm as his boat sinks. The Germans curse, *"Scheisse! Scheisse!"* Most of the people on the shore charge into the water to make sure history does not surface again. Huck Finn's raft is dragged onto the beach and added to a bonfire that the man Dominic starts with a canister of lighter fluid, shooting streams of flame high overhead. Fire falls and ignites the wood. Music begins to play. Three drummers, a trumpet, a trombone, tin whistles, and a violin. People dance. Sheresa takes my hand. Someone takes my other hand. We run up to the fire and back again, up to the fire and back again. There's singing, chanties loud and obscene. One made up on the spot: "Finn! Finn! The mightiest win! Down on your knees, Krauts, a blowjob for Jim!" The Jim from the raft, played by a young woman in overalls, accepts her pantomimed fellatio from one of the Germans dressed in a Boy Scout uniform.

My clothes stick to me on the ride home, sweat from dancing by the fire. I was a popular partner. Everyone wanted to dance with the pregnant lady, my belly a totem of good fortune. Sheresa is still making up songs that are vaguely about the ocean, vaguely about screwing. "So. What'd you think?"

"Fun."

"'Fun'? I say nuf to fun, Cora. People call some really messed-up shit 'fun.' Right?" She takes a deep breath. "I suppose it comes down, as it always does, to the question, Is it art? Right?"

That wasn't the question I had.

"Then, logically, what are the perimeters of art? And what purpose does this serve our lives?"

I confuse perimeter with protractor, which brings to mind my elementary school pencil box. Scissors, erasers, crayons, and pens. The pencil box smelled good. It smelled of beauty and art. It'd be nice to have friends like Sheresa.

"You need to remember artifice," she says. "Art isn't a hawk making lazy circles in the sky. Beauty doesn't equal art, and it can't just be the world in a package. It's got to take the world and mess it up some. Add the artifice as a lens, right?"

"It might seem like art to the hawk."

"True. True. But then everyone would be an artist, and I don't think that's right. Are you an artist?"

"I walk. A lot."

She misunderstands. "A walking artist. OK. I like that. That's good. Walking can definitely create things. Thoughts. Footsteps. Lines that intersect. Lines that connect us historically. Ley lines, right? You could connect every place in New York where daisies grow. Or the places where girls named Lisa live. Or sites where meteorites crash-landed. Right? What would that map look like and how would you read it? What message is that map trying to tell us?"

I like the idea that Ruth and I are walking artists, as if our tracks leave color behind. Blue and green. Orange painting the map we make each day. But if everybody in the world were a walking artist, the land would be so jammed with traces of everyone who ever came before. Haunted, polluted.

"And what about mothers? Mothers-to-be? Are they artists?"

I have no idea.

"Then there's the never-ending battle over what's real. Or realer. What does reality mean? True things that happen? What are those? My grandma says she saw a UFO. Is that more real? My uncle believes in angels. Whatever. Is fiction the real thing or is history?"

"History."

"Urr. Wrong. Want to guess again?"

I keep my mouth shut this time.

"If history's real, how come people can't stop making up lies when they try to write it down? Another fake memoir. Another fake memoir. The only truth is that fiction wins every time."

"So you're not real?"

"Oh, I'm real. I'm the story of Sheresa. I write a little bit of the fiction of me every day. You see what I'm talking about? Then once you have the boundaries of history and fiction secure, where does everything else fall? Somewhere in between the two. History holds up one side of our lives and fiction the other. Mother, father. Birth, death, and in between, that's where you find religion. That's where you find art, science, engineering. It's where things get made from belief and memory."

"I should have gone to college up here."

Sheresa thinks I'm being funny again. As we pull into the motel parking lot, she asks, "When's your baby due?"

"Soon?" I make a guess. Her headlights shine into my room. It's still dark.

"Here's something crazy to think about: You have two deaths inside your body right now. That's the only time that ever happens."

"That would make some Mother's Day card." I wonder why everyone I meet wants to tell me the bad parts of being a mom.

"Maybe that's why you're here at the motel."

"Maybe." I'm tired. I also have two births inside me. At least. "Thank you. I've never had an evening like this one."

"You're welcome." She bends to whisper something to my stomach, but I pull away. I'm the baby's mom, and while I like Sheresa, she talks about dead things a lot. My baby's not going to die. I'm not going to die. At least not for a while. She lifts her head. "OK. Good night. Good luck."

I get out of the car. "See you tomorrow?"

"I wouldn't miss tomorrow for all the world."

I wave. Sheresa backs out of the spot and puts her car into drive. As she's pulling away, she stops. The passenger-side window slides down, smooth old American. "Cora," she calls, though I'm standing right there.

"Yeah."

"I almost forgot. Ruth left a message."

"What?"

"She asked me to tell you."

"She talked to you?"

Sheresa glances for a moment to the asphalt illuminated by her headlights. She looks back to me. "She said don't leave him there alone. At the end."

"Leave her?"

"No. Him."

"Who?"

Sheresa shrugs. “I don’t know.”

“Ruth talked?”

Sheresa’s shoulders and nose scrunch up, as if saying, Isn’t that cute? She releases the brake and her car pulls away. She gives a floppily enthusiastic wave goodbye, like waving to a puppy. Her headlights swing back out onto the road.

Alone in the parking lot, I do not wish to be. Leave who? Where? I’m pooped.

The lack of light in the room doesn’t mean anything. Maybe Ruth is sleeping. Maybe she’s come back. I unlock our door. It’s not the room I left behind. Someone has trashed it. Thrown empty dresser drawers out of their bureaus, tossed the blankets on the ground. The TV is on the floor, face-down. Ruth and I don’t have anything except for the backpack I’m wearing, and even that doesn’t hold much. Someone was just angry. I think to flee, to catch Sheresa, but a shadow moves over me, and with the shadow comes a fantastic blow to my head, one that sends me all the way straight back into the dark, dark, dark.

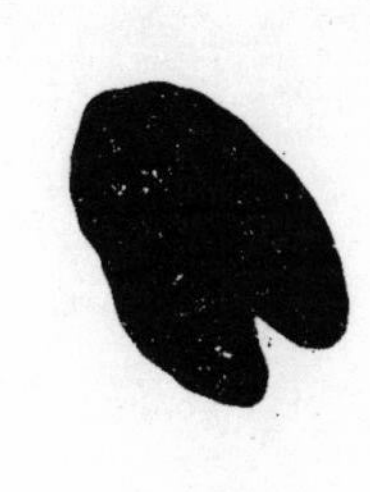

IT'S STILL SNOWING. Icicles smash off the roof in a rush. The wind's making weird sounds down the chimney. After breakfast Nat finds a wardrobe of winter garb in the mudroom—parkas, snowshoes, mufflers. He finds a compass. "Who wants to see the storm up close?"

Mr. Bell's playing solitaire. Ruth is distracted by a paperback mystery, *The Keening Wind* by Wanda La Fontaine. "No thanks."

"Not I."

So Nat fills the pocket of his coat with cereal and wanders out alone.

"Careful," Ruth calls after him, then, "Come back soon."

The door closes. A quiet hour passes. Mr. Bell repairs a broken chair. Ruth finds a collection of LPs. Cher, Electric Light Orchestra, Peaches and Herb, something called the Bevis Frond. Every record in the collection is old. No one has lived here for a while. No one buys records anymore. Whatever the reason, each album feels like a forgotten archive of the way life once was here on Earth. She chooses the Bee Gees, *Spirits Having Flown.* She likes the title. After figuring out the stereo, the needle begins to pop. The song opens with three-part, falsetto, brotherly harmony. "With you." A disco beat drops in loud and rolling. "Baby, I'm satisfied." It is inescapable. It is fantastic. Ruth and Mr. Bell eye each other. He rises from the couch and starts by swiveling his shoulders, lifting his arms overhead as if climbing up a beanstalk. He grooves slowly. Ruth is still seated. Mr. Bell clears a coffee table out of the way. He does the breaststroke, slides down the fire pole, sashays left, makes the pizza, sashays right. He drops to his knees, hops up to his toes. He turns up the volume, kazatskies and cabbage-patches. Mr. Bell moonwalks.

Ruth shuffles and straightens the cards he was playing. She sets the deck aside and stretches in preparation, shaking her hips gently, nearly by accident. Mr. Bell and Ruth dance wildly. He keeps the music coming or she does. Flipping the record, finding new ones. They boogie through Hall and Oates, Françoise Hardy, The Chi-Lites, Joan Jett, Doris Troy, the Orange Blossom Special, Harry Belafonte, and one record simply called *Wine, Women and Cha Cha.* The snow keeps falling. Mr. Bell cues up "Are You Lonesome Tonight?" Ruth blushes. He does not flinch. He takes her in his arms, leaving a tiny channel for mystery between them. They slow dance, spinning, sometimes close enough to feel the shapes beneath their clothes. Mr. Bell looks at her directly. "Shall?" the record asks, then skips. "Shall I? Shall I? Shall I?" It skips again. Without letting her out of his arms, without looking away, Mr. Bell delicately applies pressure to the stylus. "Come back?" Skip. "Come back? Come back?" He nudges the needle forward once more. "Again?"

When the song finishes, Ruth pats her brow dry. She's on fire. She tucks her chin and thanks Mr. Bell for the dance. "Cocoa?" She slips away from him.

"Thanks. I'm all set."

Ruth disappears into the kitchen, and the house falls silent again.

Nat finds many things outside, chief among his finds is the old mining town. A handful of buildings still stand. Others have been weathered so harshly that their private chambers — bedrooms, toilets, and attics — are twisted inside out. Windows and walls are filed parallel to the ceilings and floors. Electrical spiders dangle from the plaster. Exposed floral wallpaper. Snow is free to drift inside these half-homes. Some are in better shape than others. Nat snowshoes through.

Past the ghost town, he scrambles down an embankment, using tree trunks as anchors. He slides and falls just the same, landing at the base of the blast furnace. Its walls are like a castle's tower. The blocks of stone, anorthosite or sandstone, are as big as bears. Tie rods lash the old rocks in place, but the hole where hot iron once ran from the chamber into sand pigs has eroded into an entrance. Nat steps through into the gigantic chimney, and the storm disappears inside. Temperatures here once climbed as high as 2,500 degrees, even when ten feet away winters dipped to thirty below. A round light shines on him from the opening far above. He listens but hears nothing. He tosses a small stone up the chimney, then ducks. The rock falls back to earth as a good idea pushes up through the soil, not unlike the hand of a zombie reaching up to grab some brains.

Ruth is alone by the fireplace. Nat does not remove his winter clothes. "I want to show you something. Get suited up." The gear room is small and tangled with wooden water skis, jarts, snow pants, mittens, towlines, ice axes, snowshoes. Ruth chooses a pair made from guts.

They climb over drifts taller than their bodies. Though the snow is blowing in every direction, the path to the ghost town is a bit easier to tread now that Nat has stomped it down twice. He stops her in the woods. "There are a finite number of snowflakes here, which means you could count them."

She looks up into the storm. "No, you couldn't."

When they arrive at the broken-down village, Nat lifts his chin and smiles.

"What's this?"

"We could fix these houses up, make them homes for kids who are aging out."

Ruth dusts an armful of snow from the front window of one cottage. A gas stove, a rug. She removes her snowshoes at the door and steps inside carefully, as a person stepping out onto ice. In the kitchen there's a green citrus juicer the last tenants left behind, proof that life happened here before they arrived. Their living left a mark, maybe a small one, maybe not. Who built these homes? How long were they here? What words did they say as they worked? The shelves are wrapped with forget-me-not contact paper. Part of the floor is gone, and there's a pile of leaves where a rodent built its nest. There's a soap dish and a tin of vegetable shortening. There are bedrooms and a stove. Ruth enters one of the bedrooms, and the house creaks as if listing on a fulcrum. She steps back out. The old stove, the old linoleum, the old cabinet doors. It could be a home. "Yeah," she says. "That's good. That's really good."

"OK. First one for me. Second one for you. Then we'll keep going."

"One for Ceph?"

"Sure. Ceph, Colly, Raffaella. Everyone."

"Why do you get a home first?"

"It was my idea?" he suggests.

"To make a home for us? Please." Like children arguing over the shape of a dream.

"Fine. Yours can be first."

She spins around. "OK. I want this one. This one's mine."

Nat shrugs. "OK."

"OK. This one's mine."

Mr. Bell sits by the fire, pinching his face as if it is made from clay. "It's a very good idea, though maybe there are cabins a little closer to a town? A place where a person might purchase a hamburger or find a job?"

Nat and Ruth nod.

"How will you pay for the repairs?"

Nat shrugs.

"You'll need some money, a box full of money."

"Got one?"

"No, but I heard there might be one in an empty pool somewhere. Right?" Mr. Bell laughs. "Maybe there are homes that need fixing up a little farther away from here?"

Ruth's thawing out under a quilt. The squares of fabric are less than square, human-made. "Did it end badly?"

"The problem is I don't know that it has ended at all, though longevity certainly seems unlikely. Mardellion's followers were runaways, drug users, sick and bankrupt people. He gave them a home and helped people no one else was helping, which is really very close to taking advantage of desperate people."

Ruth pulls a thread off the quilt.

"Eventually Mardellion collected too many people, too many mouths to feed. Responsibility like that makes a person do reckless things."

"Like what?"

"First he found some lines in *The Book of Ether* that told him —"

"What's that?"

"*Book of Ether*? Mardellion's religious text. His greatest hits."

"He wrote a book?"

"It's prophecy, poetry of a sort. I'm sure there's a copy around here somewhere. Maybe up in the temple."

"The temple?"

Mr. Bell draws in his chin, smiles again.

"I thought this was some blue-blood Adirondack camp."

"Ah. No. Bring blankets. It's even colder up there."

One door in the upstairs hallway has a bronze latch shaped like a bird's beak. Mr. Bell lifts the latch. The staircase is unlit. "Watch yourself." They follow him up into the dark. Smells of mothballs. "One moment." Mr. Bell switches on a light. The room soars like an airport hangar, round as a chicken's egg, a perfectly white space-age chapel or sci-fi movie sound stage. They're inside the roof.

Ruth takes a seat on the floor. Nat plops down beside her, covering them with a blanket. Their breath is visible. She wraps up to her neck. Mr. Bell does the same, woolen blobs in a white room. Mr. Bell's silent a moment, looking around.

One side of the oval has been given over to a number of electronics, two television sets, an ancient computer, and another small record player, a lowly command central set in front of a swiveling captain's chair.

"What kind of name is Mardellion?"

"I don't know."

"That's his real name?"

Mr. Bell pulls his hair behind his ears. "Probably not."

"How'd he wind up here?"

"Drove out from Utah. The mine was shutting down, so he got it for a song. Moved his followers in, up here. Closer to God and outer space meant farther away from people's families and the law. Isolation set in. He starts chattering about being the messiah, about apocalypse. He starts in on underage girls."

"What?"

"People's daughters. He made them his wives." Mr. Bell sheds his blanket, standing. "There's a copy." He brings it back to them. "*Book of Ether.* All yours. My gift."

Ruth cracks it open, reads aloud:

95 The sky in multitude.
The face of the sky.
The Earth is a place.
The skies sent out a sound.
It is by no means the only place.
The sky, which is strong, and as a molten looking glass.
Let the skies pour down righteousness: let the earth open.
It is not even a typical place. The Cosmos is mostly empty.

Ruth stops. "What?"

"He took *The Book of Mormon,* a little *Cosmos,* a little Bible. Some Queen and Grace Jones. Neil Young. Cher. Bowie. Whatever moved him."

"It's plagiarized?"

Mr. Bell's smile shows his teeth. "Think of it more as a catalog, a collection of the words that made one man."

"Are you an Etherist, Mr. Bell?"

He shakes his head. "No. I am not an Etherist." He pulls the blanket over the back of his head. "Historically, culturally, yes. I've been dipped in the dye, raised by the hand, but I haven't believed a word Mardellion whispered since I was twelve."

"What happened then?"

"He made my mom disappear in the middle of the night."

"What?"

"She was mad about the girls. She was his actual wife, his legal wife."

"Mardellion's your father?"

"I suppose he is."

"Yikes."

"Indeed."

• • •

Nat's gone to bed. The sun set and it's still snowing, a supernatural snow, though probably the trees and rocks don't see it that way. Ruth stokes the living room fire, then draws a chair up before the records again. She thumbs her way through Rita Coolidge, Richard and Linda Thompson, Marianne Faithfull. She cues up the Thompsons' song "Wall of Death."

"You know the story behind this?" Mr. Bell asks.

"No. The Father didn't allow much music."

"It's the last record they made together before she lost her voice."

"Why'd she lose her voice?"

"Hysterical dysphonia. Broken heart. She and Richard were splitting up after a long marriage, three kids. He had a girlfriend, I think. Maybe Linda hit him over the head with a guitar, kicked him in the shins or something? He probably deserved it. They treated each other poorly, but they still had to sell the record, had to go on tour and sing together."

"She couldn't talk anymore?"

"It happens." Mr. Bell shrugs. "The second-to-last night of the tour, they were in LA, maybe the new girlfriend was in the audience, maybe there was a knife or a gun. Who knows. People say Linda sang more beautifully that night than ever before. Something beyond human abilities."

"Fury."

"Maybe. Grief. Shock. They've never released the tapes. Then she lost her voice."

"She ever get it back?"

"Yeah. But it took a long time. I'd imagine a person could get used to not talking. It would be hard to start again."

"If you grew up here, how'd you know about that?"

"My dear." Mr. Bell leans back; his T-shirt lifts, exposing a flash of stomach. "I've not lived among the Etherists since I was fourteen," he says, as if he's just a normal boy who grew to a man in America, someone who likes rock and roll.

Ruth makes a funny smile.

"What is it?"

"Nat and I used to think we invented you."

"Hmm."

"Like you were a dream we had. We made you up because we could never imagine where you came from."

"I'll try to take that as a compliment." He screws his eyes in mock puzzlement. "I might be strange, but I assure you" — his voice lowers — "I'm real." And to demonstrate his realness, Mr. Bell lifts Ruth's hand to his forehead like she's a cool towel on a fevered brow. He drags it across his cheek until Ruth is cupping his chin, his breath.

Ruth drops her hand back to her leg, breathing heavily, burned.

"The Thompsons spent some time in a religious sect themselves."

Ruth listens to Linda sing. "She did?" Linda Thompson's voice is power and submission, spirit without religion.

"Sure. Religions need women. Who else would do all the work?"

Ruth nods.

On the album cover, Richard sits on the floor in a yellow room. His legs are open, his arms are too. Bravado and confidence. Linda's trapped in a framed photograph on the wall above him. Just her head, no body. Richard doesn't look at Linda. Linda doesn't look at him.

"I often wonder who I'd be if my mother raised me. Maybe I'd be better."

"Maybe you'd be dead," he says.

"Yeah."

"And maybe you wouldn't be the wholly perfect Ruth you already are."

There's a closet in the living room. Ruth ducks into it, flushed. She digs through the board games and books there to calm the idea that Mr. Bell will, any minute now, devour her in a way that's not yet been confirmed in her life. In the closet she finds a Walkman and an old tape recorder that looks like a mini robot with a plug-in microphone and five lever buttons at one end. Beside it, a carton with three blank tapes. Ruth calms herself by pushing the buttons. She brings the device to him. "I want to record some of these songs."

"On that?" Mr. Bell lifts his top lip, like there's a bad odor. When Mr. Bell tries to act older than he is — as if he's full of knowledge and experience—it ends up making him seem even younger to Ruth.

"Yeah. So I can take it with me."

"That"—he points to the tape recorder—"is a Dictaphone. This," Mr. Bell says, flanking the stereo, his hands like a spokesmodel's, tilted to display, "is a hi-fi system. You know what that means?"

"No."

"High fidelity. Intense truthfulness. Painful purity. You cannot use an old Dictaphone to capture faithfulness."

Ruth thinks about this for a moment. I'll just record it when he's asleep. Hell with fidelity. She's not leaving the mountain without Linda Thompson. Ruth returns to the stacks. She thumbs past Mario Lanza and Kenny Loggins. "What's this?" She pulls out several copies of the same record. Each one wrapped in plain brown kraft paper like a porn mag. She removes one from its sleeve and is surprised to find that the vinyl is not black but a beautiful glowing yellow gold.

He clambers toward her on his knees. "The golden records. Man. I haven't seen these in a long time."

"What's on them?"

"Remember *Voyager*?"

"No."

"NASA sent up two satellites in '77, and on board both they packed golden records in case the satellite should ever encounter someone who might want to listen."

Ruth's eyes flash. "Aliens?"

"Yup."

"What's on the records?"

"Pictures of life on Earth. DNA sequences, babies, bugs. Music."

"A real catalog. How did they choose what got to go?"

"How do you make a record of everything in a finite space? Hard job."

"Yes. But what are these?"

"Mardellion thought the *Voyager* mission was perfection. Sagan and Ann Druyan produced the records, and for Mardellion it was faultless. See, Golden Records, Golden Tablets. The records made a link between Joseph Smith and Carl Sagan; religion and science. It was natural. So once someone had been with Mardellion long enough, he would 'reveal' his involvement with the *Voyager* missions. This was carefully guarded information, a secret, something a follower had to earn by proving their total faith. You'd have to have total faith to believe that bull. NASA hires a pharmacy clerk to represent Earth among the aliens? Not that Mardellion thought it was untrue. I think he really believed he was cosmically responsible for the Golden Records. It wouldn't be so hard. Belief just takes steady convincing. Mardellion had a studio in Massapequa press duplicates of the original songs sent to space. In reality, he had nothing to do with *Voyager*. Still, that doesn't mean the records aren't cool."

Mr. Bell removes the record from its sleeve. The center label says, *The Sounds of the Earth, To the Maker of Music—all worlds, all times.* He slips it onto the stereo and lies back on the thin and dusty rug. The record begins to pop.

An old man with a funny accent speaks.

"Is that Sagan?"

"Nah. Kurt Waldheim, Secretary-General of the UN and, sadly, a Nazi."

"They sent a Nazi into outer space?"

"They didn't know he was a Nazi in '77. Unfortunate though interesting choice, since it could almost convince you that some cosmic truth of our existence slips in no matter how much Sagan and Druyan tried to control it. Waldheim's dead now. Lots of the people on this record are dead now. We sent ghost stories up into space."

After Waldheim, many voices, speaking many languages. Ruth understands only one greeting: "Hello, from the children of Planet Earth." The record crackles. Then something frightening, shrieking and grunting.

"What's that?"

"Whales."

Raindrops, thunder, crickets and monkeys, footsteps, heartbeats, birdsong, trains. There's the sound of a mother kissing her child, saying, "Be a good boy," and all manner of songs: classical, drums, bagpipes, yelling, Pygmy girls chanting, Chuck Berry. The vinyl pops. The songs pile up. It keeps snowing. Mr. Bell announces each new track. Russian, Bulgarian, pan pipes, Mexican, Azerbaijani. Stravinsky. One song, just a man with a guitar. The man hums and moans. "Blind Willie Johnson. 'Dark Was the Night.'"

Ruth closes her eyes. Into Beethoven. Then a scratching, skipping, the sound of a zoom. Buzz and crackle trilling like a machine. "And what's that?"

"Ann Druyan's brainwaves."

"Are we supposed to be able to tell what she's thinking?"

"I don't know. Can you?"

Ruth listens. She opens her eyes. "No."

"She was thinking about falling in love."

"With who?"

"She and Carl got engaged after the first *Voyager* lifted off." Mr. Bell sits in front of Ruth. He shuts his lids for a minute. She watches him. When he opens his eyes, he asks, "Could you hear my brainwaves?"

She shakes her head no. "What were you thinking about?"

"Ruth Sykes."

She smiles at the ground. "Where are they?" She speaks quietly.

"Sagan's dead."

"No. Where are the *Voyagers*?"

"They left the solar system a while back. They're still going."

"Where?"

Mr. Bell leans back on his elbows. "Away from us. Away from each other."

The record reaches its end. She draws a circle on the rug with her finger. "Can we listen again?"

"Of course." Mr. Bell sets the needle at the start.

Ruth leans back on straight arms, makes two mountains of her legs. The record says, "I send greetings on behalf of the people of our planet." Mr. Bell, golden himself, kneels between Ruth's knees. "We step out of our solar system into the universe seeking only peace and friendship." He takes her chin in his hand. Her eyes lift. "We know full well that our planet and all its inhabitants are but a small part of the immense universe." Mr. Bell kisses her, his wife, for the first time, for real. "It is with humility and hope that we take this step." An orbit aligned, Ruth bends into him, returning his kiss, bouncing all she's got back to him across the soft darkness of deep and distant space.

THERE IN THE DARK, DARK, DARK, the road looks like a silver-and-blue fish. Its scales glitter with bits of glass and tar. The fish/road is as large as a semi. It has the face of a beautiful boy, a man. It lifts its head. "I need water," the fish says. "I'm dying." Me too, I think. Someone smashed my head and knocked me out.

When I turn to get the fish a glass of water, I'm no longer on the road but back in the motel room. "One moment," I tell the fish, stepping into the bathroom. I unseal the plastic off a fresh drinking glass, and I allow the water to run cool over my hand as an idea strikes. "Sir?" Is that how you address a fish? "There's a large tub in here where you'd be more comfortable. Or the canal. The Erie's right here. I could help you get back—" I peek my head into the bedroom. "Sir?" But the fish is gone.

"Hi." It's Ruth.

"Where've you been?"

"I needed to take care of something."

"I was so worried. What'd you take care of?"

"A friend."

"Who?"

"No one you know."

"The bad guy?"

Ruth looks shiny herself. She smiles. "There are no good guys or bad guys. Not really."

"Just don't leave me again. Or at least let me know if you're going to leave. OK? I didn't know what to do—whether to wait or what. I didn't know if you'd come back. Just tell me if you're going to leave again, OK?"

"How could I do that when I can't talk?"

She's got a point.

"You should lie down, Cora. Get some rest. We're leaving again in the morning." Ruth leads me over to one of the beds. She pulls back the covers. "Did you have fun with Sheresa tonight?"

"Yeah." I yawn and stretch. "She's great. I really like Sheresa."

"Me too. She told you about Nat, right?"

I lie down. "Yeah. Don't leave without him. Got it."

"Good, because that's why we're doing this."

"OK." I'm like a sleepwalker.

"Good night," Ruth says, and douses the light. She runs her fingers through my hair, combing through it. "Get some rest."

"Yeah. All right." My eyes shut for one minute. "You're not going to disappear again?"

"No."

"OK. Thanks. Don't leave where without him?"

"The End." Like she's finishing a bedtime story.

My eyes are closed and I feel peace like a coma, like a child being cared for by her mother. I'm so deep in sleep that I almost don't hear it when a man speaks.

"Sorry. I didn't mean to hit her," he says. "I thought it might be him."

I'd like to sit up and ask this man some questions, but moving my jaws and tongue would be extracting motion from a chunk of ice. It would take forever to melt the moving parts.

"She'll be OK," Ruth says.

Though my eyes are closed in the darkness, I can make out their bodies. The guy is sitting in a chair, tipping a bag of nuts into his hand, shelling them. They've cleaned up the room. "Pistachio?" He offers some to Ruth. It's the guy from the office earlier, the sexy bandito who speaks strangely and doesn't want to be called Carl.

She takes a few from his palm, and he pulls Ruth into his lap. She cracks a nut, pops one into her mouth. He wraps his arms around her. Ruth's Walkman's headphones are looped around her neck. A tiny bit of music leaks out. "Are You Lonesome Tonight?" He sings with Elvis, repeating the words. "'Shall I? Shall I? Shall I? Come back? Come back again? Again? Again?'" Ruth and the man and a quiet song.

"I'll miss you," he says. Beside the chair he's got an old water-damaged suitcase as if he's packed to go somewhere.

"We'll be together again soon. I promise."

He kisses her head. "My love," the man says.

"You need this."

The man opens his mouth, allowing Ruth to place a coin on his tongue. "My bell," she calls him. "My bell," and as she says it, the bell, so loud, starts to ring.

Ruth swats her hand on the motel's alarm clock.

It's still dark out. My brain hurts. Ruth comes to sit on the edge of my bed. She shakes my back.

"Where've you been?" I ask her.

She smiles.

"Hello?"

She smiles again because Ruth doesn't talk.

"Whoa." I hold my splitting head together. "I had a crazy dream."

She nods.

"You could talk."

She puts her hand on my forehead checking for fever. She puts another hand on my belly.

"Where's the fish? Where's your boyfriend? Bell?"

She lifts her eyebrows high, shrugs, and straps on her backpack. She nudges her chin toward the door.

I pull myself out of bed. "Hold on there, sister. Just slow down. You disappear for a day. Then you reappear and want me to just pop up, all ready like? Shit. I need a minute." I waddle my big way to the bathroom. I peek my head back out the door. "Maybe you didn't notice, but I'm about nine and a half months pregnant here." I wash slowly. I pee and collect my toothbrush and toothpaste. "You have a boyfriend, Ruth?" She kicks the carpet. Ruth blushes and shakes her head no. She's a solid wall again, but that doesn't stop my dream from slipping away, right through her.

In the light of the bathroom, I find my things. I check the bed, the desk. I take one last look and turn to follow her, but at the end of the bed, something crunches under my foot. Ruth grabs my shoulder. The light is bad, but it sounds like the shell of something hard — say, a nut; say, a pistachio nut. Ruth pulls me out the door. We walk quickly away from the motel's light. Ruth behind, pushing me on. One hundred yards into the darkness, she reaches for my wrist and leads me off the road, down the embankment. We cut through briars and into the black woods. Branches poke my face and belly. "Back off," I tell them. Ruth digs through her backpack. Her flashlight creates a narrow, overexposed swath on the low branches of hemlock trees. She takes my hand again like I'm a prisoner. We walk into the woods.

I should count our steps or leave a trail so we can find our way out, but it's already too late for me. Holding her hand, I shut my eyes, still half asleep. I stumble onto my ankle in a rut. I don't even care. I'm tired. I'm pregnant. I'm exhausted. We go so far into the woods, I wonder if we are now on our way out of the woods. Where is the middle of the woods? Where's the middle of this walk? Have we already passed that point? Do the woods ever end?

The sun hasn't risen. There's just a path made out of light, more trees, the back of my aunt's head and my belly making the smallest streak of color in the dark world, a walking artist. I accidently crush a fairy circle of mushrooms. This foot, that foot. I'm pretending I understand what's real and what's not. "Where are we going?" We duck under sharp branches. Time passes, bolts of long fabric. "Where are we going? Where are we going?" The light moves ahead of us, a small patch, seeing very little of the big woods.

Eventually I let go of her hand, lowering myself onto all fours. I sit back. "I have to rest." Ruth stands above me like the trees. She switches off the flashlight. She rubs my body everywhere, trying to warm me or scrubbing off my dirt. When's she done, she pulls me up to standing. We walk again. We walk so long, the sky blues. Green surrounds us, kelly and lime, pine trees and the other kind. Everything is alive in the woods. Except for the dead things. It's only scary if I am responsible for getting us out of here and I'm not. We might never get out. I don't even care.

We walk farther. The sun rises. We have walked straight into the woods for hours. The walking happens without me even noticing. Until again I tell her, "I have to stop." We're in a clearing of baby trees, soft grass, and orange needles. She folds an item of clothing for us both, pillows. She takes a drink of water and offers one to me. Ruth lies down. The quiet is so intense, it menaces from behind some of the larger trunks, but we're tired, hungry, nearly desperate. Not much can scare me anymore. The small of my back feels like bone rubbed against bone. I lie down beside Ruth and curl into her. The weight of the baby grinds my hip into the ground, curves my spine. The baby sits on my lungs and bladder, takes whatever it wants. I shut my eyes and I'm asleep.

Clouds move quickly overhead. Sleeping on the open ground, cold and hard, bones, stones. I half expect to find parts of our bodies disintegrating back to dirt, sprouting roots. Ruth unwraps a chocolate bar. She passes it to me. "Thank you." I'm starving and there's not a place on my body that doesn't hurt; maybe the tips of my earlobes have been spared.

These woods are where silence has come to lick its wounds.

I break off some more chocolate. "How long were we asleep?" A dumb question. I'm full of them. "Where are we going. Where'd you disappear to. Why'd you come back. Who was that guy in our room." I'm too tired for question marks.

Ruth raises her hands to her eyes. She looks soft, pretty. She packs our pillows. I sit on the forest floor. She starts walking again. She doesn't wait to see if I'm coming, and I'm too tired to follow her any farther. So this is how I'll die, rot like a log, turn to moss. She brought me all this way to abandon me in the woods where a sapling will one day spring from my navel. "I'm not coming, Ruth." She's gone twenty-five feet, zigzagging through the branches, snapping those that block her way. Ruth keeps walking. She's leaving me here. I'll be dead, but at least I won't have to get up. I look up through the branches. I am more lost from the world than anyone has ever been. More lost than people who lived here before here had a name. Those people understood stars. They still felt north in their bodies. I don't have any idea what happened to north. My life so far has made me stupid, helpless, dependent. I am not like the people who came before. They knew how to feed themselves, how to give birth by squatting in the roots of a tree. They were lost, but lost didn't matter back then, since there was no found. They could wander these woods before tribes, before people even. Following deer or bears or who knows what. The sort of lost that doesn't exist anymore anywhere.

Ruth doesn't stop walking away. This is how I'll die. That kind of lost. Until she does. I see the bumpers of her sneakers in front of me, her fingertips, chewed back to ragged nails, scratching on her jeans. I wait for her voice. She has to say something. Ruth looks into the woods from where we came. Her urgency surrounds me like skunk stink. Something is getting closer? Let it. I'm too tired. I'm done. So Ruth collects sticks to start a fire. A fire means we'll be here a while. I help her by collecting wood on my knees. It's easier than bending over. Ruth lights a tepee of sticks. I lie back down and the baby is a furnace beneath my navel, hot to the touch. Ruth curls up around me again, combs some leaves from my hair, straightens my part. The shriveled child — shaped like an ear or a gourd — keeps us warm with its fever.

When I wake, the woods are dark again. I have to pee and can see sufficiently to know that there's much I can't see. I hear leaves and I hear trees. I hear beetles walking, and their footfalls are as loud as a bogeyman with a machete coming through the woods. Ruth snores. One hand pinched between my legs helps me hold my pee until it can't be held back any longer. I force myself up, onto hands and knees and then to standing. Each footstep disturbs the night. I look for a spot away from our camp where I can hold on to a tree as I crouch. The rush of urine is loud. My nails dig into the tree's bark so the air smells of pitch and pee. When I am almost done, he starts to laugh.

Having spent years not believing in God, I call to him, her. God. God. God. There's a bad man in these woods. I fall back in the warm puddle, clutch up into a ball, try to stop breathing. God. God. God. There is a bad man in the woods. My shoulders creep up my neck, making a wall around the baby with my limbs. My head booms static in the silence. His steps come closer.

"I told you I'd follow wherever you went." He's mumbling, a greasy, deranged person.

God. God. God. I beg for God to exist.

"Wherever you went."

If I keep my head down, if I don't see him, he won't see me. God come. There are the man's shoes. He's standing just beside me. God. Help me. Save my child.

"You." He lifts his cane and, with it, gives my back a shove. "Looka me."

I can't move.

"Looka me." Angrier.

I turn my chin just slightly. With one feral animal eye, I see him, heavyset, raised wildly, still wearing his dark sunglasses. His sports jersey makes me loathe all sports, all teams. His mind is not right. "Where's Ruth?" His dirty pants and boots are male, foreign. His hair is clumpy with grease.

I shake my head no. My fear is toxic, stinking. I crouch in a ball. I don't want him to see the baby.

"Ruth." He gargles her thick name.

One eye up to the sky. God.

"She said she was mine."

His mind is not right. He crouches down next to me. I cannot lift my head off my chest. He smells of rotten raw things. I can't move. He lifts his hands as if to touch me but instead removes his sunglasses, and I'm sorry I see it. One eye is as stupid as a sheep's, blank. The other eye is not an eye but a hole carved out by a gunshot that traveled straight through this man's brain. He's so close to me.

"Ruth." His fat, wet lips stink of hard-boiled eggs. "You said you were mine."

God. God. Help my baby. Each moment I don't run is an exit I miss, shaving off the possibility I might not be chopped up. But I can't run.

"Stand up." He's furious. I do what he says. "Take me to Ruth." My damp hands shake at my sides so they won't draw attention to my belly. He follows behind. God, I call again. God. I keep walking, waiting for the blow to come, for him to kill me. I walk through the dark until I see Ruth. She's not sleeping anymore. She's a crazed warrior, furious in the forest. God.

"Leave her alone, Ceph. Go away." Ruth speaks again, but this time her words are slow. Her voice is an empty bucket kicked down a stone cellar staircase.

The man's head lists to one shoulder. "I tried to stop him," he says.

Ruth nods. "I know."

The man's glasses are off. I see the forest through the hole in his head. He staggers back as if shot again. I shut my eyes, and when I look, he's gone.

Ruth remains guarded. She pokes into the night with a stick, making sure he's gone. "You spoke," I tell her as she passes by me. "I heard you for real that time and I'm not dreaming, Ruth."

"Are you sure?" she asks. The thinnest string of a dream as it slips away, a snake across the ground. Even as I try to convince myself I heard her, I don't believe it. I hear a lot of things on the road that aren't really there. And what's a Ceph anyway?

Ruth packs our things. Dead and dark of night we walk, but I can still feel him behind every tree watching me. I'm filled with holes, night breezes inside chill me, all that fear and the impossible hole in his head. The baby turns and stretches inside, and a house I thought had many rooms turns out to have just one, where birth and death duke it out to decide whose turn it is this time.

The sun comes up. Ruth fingers the trunk of a bare tree. There's a pattern, a larvae fringe some creature tracked back and forth, drunk on whatever it ate, making writing no one can read. I want to get out of here. I want life to win, for now. I want to be a mother. We keep walking, trees and trees and sometimes a small clearing. I take no breaks. Dead leaves, dead needles, dead logs, but green everywhere. I can see the sky and I can see Ruth. Every now and again, a bird. We do not rest because now I know what we are running from, and it looks a lot like death. Still it is hard to understand when we step out of the forest and onto a road, stepping into Technicolor. Even Ruth laughs. What's a road doing in a place so lost?

We kick the dirt of it for a moment, testing its material.

"You know where this leads eventually?" I ask her. She raises her brow, and I'm about to say a McDonald's equipped with free Wi-Fi, but that seems mean. I look back into the forest. We both do, but the path we walked is already gone forever.

[illegible] I tried to stop him. Do

[illegible]

[illegible] through the hole in the
[illegible] I shut my eyes, and when

[illegible] into the night with a slight
[illegible] ter as she passed by me. I
[illegible] Grammy, high
[illegible] of a dream, as it now
[illegible] I have to confess myself
[illegible] things on the road that
[illegible]?
[illegible] the whole, but I can
[illegible] filled with holes
[illegible] the tunnel-like hole in
[illegible] house I thought
[illegible] where thumb and [illegible]
[illegible]

[illegible] There is
[illegible] and forth about
[illegible] I want to get out
[illegible] together. We have
[illegible] I take it
[illegible] because we were
[illegible] pass, and
[illegible] running from, and
[illegible] them, we are
[illegible] into Tatamy? How
[illegible]?
[illegible] in mind.
[illegible] I asked her this on
[illegible] equipped with tree [illegible]
[illegible] We both [illegible] but the
[illegible]

IN THE MORNING Ruth hears a rusty rhythmic duck squawk. Sounds like bedsprings or a trampoline. The sound's coming from outside, where, somehow, it is still snowing. Drifts have blown as high as the second story.

Dressed again in winter gear, moving through new snow, Ruth feels like a spaceman stumbling in anti-gravity. She circles the house, looking for the noise, and sees Mr. Bell's head clear a drift then disappear, clear a drift then disappear again. He's on a trampoline. Up and down, up and down goes his head. Ruth makes her slow way toward him. Mr. Bell is jumping on a diving board. Below him an empty pool is filling with snow.

"Hola." He's wearing only his combat boots and a trench coat against the storm.

"A pool," Ruth says.

"Bit cold for a swim."

She reaches the edge and looks down. The wind's cleared snow from one side of the pool, collected it in the other. Where it's clear, she sees rotting leaves and chunks of ice. The blue paint is chalky and chipped. Just below the diving board, as if it jumped, is something not pool-shaped, a snow-covered tumor in the deep end. "What's that?"

Mr. Bell keeps on jumping, shrugs.

Ruth pops out of her snowshoes and climbs an ancient, curved, and rattling ladder down into the pool. At the last rung, she drops into the snow, sinking up to her hips in the deep end, below the synchronized swims that once took place above, the underwater trysts. On her knees, Ruth shuffles to the lump and grabs hold of it, dusting new snow from its top. SCOTTIES it says. Ruth carries the box to the shelter of the diving board.

"Carl?" she says. The plank overhead shields her from the falling snow.

"Don't call me that."

"I can't call you Mister anymore."

"Then just Bell. OK?"

"What's wrong with Carl?" The board above continues to bounce close, ping back, close, and back again.

"It came from Mardellion."

"He was that bad?"

"Yes."

"OK. Bell." Ruth rips the weathered packing tape off the box. The flaps open, and there inside, safe from the storm, are many, many hundred-dollar bills bundled together, massed into a snug pile. Ruth would never imagine that a box this size could hold half a million dollars, but what has Ruth ever known about the shape of money before?

Mr. Bell stops jumping. He lies down on the board, dangling one ungloved hand over the side, a white bird out of reach, stretching, making slow signs. The hand tenses then calms, conducting the blizzard.

"Bell?"

The board creaks against the cold. "I'm here."

"There's a box of money in the bottom of the pool."

"Just like Nat said there'd be."

"I didn't believe him."

"What's the harm in believing?"

"You put this money here."

"Why would I do something like that?"

"I don't know. Why would you?"

With a box of money under one arm, Ruth climbs back out of the pool.

Nat is making his slow way toward them now through the deep snow, looking like an Arctic explorer. "What's up?" he asks.

"Well." Ruth has a seat on the diving board. Nat sits beside her. The box of money is between them like their messed-up newborn child.

"What's going on?" he asks.

She opens the flaps of the box. Both of them look inside, and it takes a moment for Nat to understand what he's looking at. They stare and wait for the box's contents to do something, to breathe or mew, sneeze or explode.

"Where'd that come from?"

"I found it in the pool."

Mr. Bell rolls onto his back, facing up into the falling snow.

"Why'd you say there was a box of money in an empty pool, and then there was a box of money in an empty pool?" Ruth asks.

"I was lying."

"That's what I thought. We saw that movie, and you made up a story to match it."

"Right."

"So then how'd you know the names of the kids' moms?"

"Jesus, Ruth. There was a list, a Xerox from the State, in the kitchen drawer every week. Everyone's mom, some dads, names, numbers. It was easy."

Ruth remembers the list now, can even picture her mom's name on it.

"They let me lie," Nat says.

"Paid you to lie."

"They paid you too."

"So just to be clear, there are no dead people?"

"There are dead people, but they don't talk to me. And they don't talk to you either." Nat opens the box flaps. "But this is real." Again they stare down into the box. "Mr. Bell?"

"Yes?"

"Is this yours?"

"You found it. It belongs to you now." He sits up. "But you better hide it somewhere. Not in the house."

"Why?"

"Besides kidnapping moms and raping underage girls, Mardellion wants a meteorite, big as an atomic bomb, to strike this house. He's been talking about it for years. He can't take care of his followers anymore, so a meteorite to blow the Etherists sky-high, a million bits of love and light."

"That's not going to happen."

"No, it's not, which is why he's making his own meteorite."

"How?"

"He's stockpiled a mining explosive called ANFO. The stuff that was left behind here. Says he's got enough to make a comet."

Ruth looks at Nat. "Comet?" she asks.

"Another kind of space rock. Bigger than a meteorite."

"That's how Zeke lost his nose."

"A comet hit his nose?"

"No. He was snorting the toilet bowl cleaner."

Just as Nat, the box, Ruth, and Mr. Bell are lined up on the diving board, ducks in a row, things that hadn't made sense before fall into order: a box of money, a comet, and a cult. Linked points on a map.

"We need to leave. Soon as this storm stops, we're out of here." Mr. Bell bangs his hands together.

"How? We're stuck," Ruth says.

"Why did you bring us here?" Nat asks.

"You don't want the money? It was here. I had to come get it before he destroys the place."

Nat and Ruth look back to the box.

"Calm down." Mr. Bell smiles. "There's no reason to panic. If we can't get out of here, no one can get in. Soon as the snow stops, we'll leave. We'll dig out tomorrow and be on our way. It's going to be fine."

They have no other choice, so they believe him.

Mr. Bell and Ruth make lunch. He chops. She opens cans. He puts his hand on Ruth's waist, sliding past her at the sink. They work together in the kitchen, rubbed smooth by friction. They make buttered rye toast, sardines, garbanzo beans, and beets. The three of them eat frozen blueberries with condensed milk in front of the living room fireplace.

Mr. Bell returns to the kitchen to clean up.

Ruth flicks a bit of hangnail off her tongue. "Remember the night the Mother came to a séance?"

"Yeah."

"I told her I was making it up, and she said that my being a liar didn't stop ghosts from talking. She said there were things in the world, not of the world."

"She's a drug addict."

"I'm just saying, unexplainable things happen even when you don't believe in them."

"Like what?"

"Eyeballs."

"I believe in eyeballs."

"But if you'd never seen them before, you'd think they were supernatural."

"How could I see them if I didn't have eyeballs?"

"Nat." She means, Fuck you. "What about tides? Goats? Yogurt?" She twists toward him.

"That's science."

"Snowflakes? Lungs? Premonitions?"

Nat nods. "I believe in snowflakes and lungs."

"But how do they happen? What makes ice form crystals?"

"I don't know. Go to college. Become a scientist. Use some of the money for that."

"What about people who know when they're being stared at? Things you can't explain. Phantom limbs. Pigeons finding their way home. What about a freaking box of money appearing in the bottom of the pool?" She slaps the side of the cardboard.

"Mr. Bell put it there."

"Why would he give us a half-million dollars? That's nuts."

"Maybe he owes us something."

"What?"

"I don't know. I'm just telling you what I can observe, an essential skill of scientists and con men alike."

"And you don't believe what you can't observe?"

"Hell nope." Nat's lips slice into an ungenerous line. "Humans are so good at imagining things, they invent gods who feel so real, they then betray us by not existing."

"God saved you when your own mom wouldn't." "If the Father is the best God can do, that's not good enough."

"So you don't believe anything you can't see?"

Nat thinks a moment. "Remember Miss Karen?"

"Barely." Miss Karen had been Nat's caseworker for seven years. She'd gone to grad school. She brought Nat to a tree museum once.

"Miss Karen took a vacation to Arizona, and when I saw her again at my next appointment, I told her the Father had been withholding dinner for three days because someone stuffed a sweatshirt down the toilet. Remember?"

"Ceph."

"Miss Karen said, 'When I was in the desert, a golden column of light appeared in front of me.' A UFO. She said, 'Don't worry about Arthur. The aliens are here, and they're going to take care of us.'" Nat squints. "Miss Karen wouldn't tell a lie, but I don't believe in UFOs."

"But you believe her so—"

"I did. I still do, but I can't get past thinking that if the aliens are here, how come they never rescued us, Ruth? Never. No aliens. And no God. And we could have used both."

Ruth sets her chin. "Forget God. Or don't call it that. I'm talking about mystery, unsolvable mystery. Maybe it's as simple as love. I say it exists, and here's how we're going to settle it. Ready?"

"Sure."

"OK. Whoever dies first, come back and tell the other."

"What if it doesn't work that way?"

"You're smart. Figure something out. Leave me a note. Dump a box of cereal on the floor. I'll know it's you."

"Or you'll convince yourself that the wind blowing through the house is me." Nat picks at his socks. "Don't do it, Ruth. You set yourself up for disappointment when you dabble with the supernatural. My mom used to sing, 'Fall on your knees, hear the angel voices,' and it was easy to believe that the universe made sense when my mom was kind and good, but then she left. So if you want to convince me that there's something bigger going on here, some sort of grand plan or map or order in the universe, you're going to have to first explain why God makes bad moms."

Ruth shrugs. "I don't know why."

"Well, I do and it's because he doesn't exist."

ONE HIGHWAY DEPARTMENT BUILDING, one gas station, one general store. The cashier is happy to see a pregnant woman, so is the man behind the deli counter. Ruth has a gallon of milk and some cereal in her basket. These are not our usual road supplies. These supplies suggest a place with bowls, spoons, refrigerators. "We're almost there?" I ask. Ruth smiles. She places the basket on the counter, adds two chocolate bars to the order.

"Today?"

Ruth says nothing.

"Yeah, today."

"Good luck," the cashier tells me.

"Good luck," says the woman pruning the shrubs outside.

"Thank you."

Ruth carries everything now, the groceries, her bag, my bag. I carry the baby. The end is coming, and having it in sight makes the walking a little easier. At every curve in the road, I expect something hidden to be revealed. Specifically, what the end looks like. Is the end good or bad? Then we gain the curve, and there's nothing around the bend except more road, some trees, and a farther curve up ahead I can't see past. We keep walking. Ruth seems even quieter than before, quieter than she's been since the car broke down back in another solar system. I can almost remember what color that car was.

We have a definitive number of steps remaining, a countable number, and then I don't know what. A bed or a couch. A bathtub. A baby. The end. Or else a new start. A house near the Falls for Ruth and El and me and the baby. That'd be nice, to live with them, to be near the Falls. It's important to live near water. I won't go back to what I was before I started walking. I don't want a lot of rubbish to smother things as quiet as Ruth, intelligent as this child, kind and complicated as El.

We head into another curve. Ruth twists the plastic grocery bag in her hand. The trees make a full canopy of shade with no power lines to cut them back. "Can we take a rest?" We sit on a rock covered with moss and British soldier lichen, little redcoats. Ruth is anxious to finish, but I'm a bit wary of the end as it's unknown. She stands, dusts her butt, reaches out a hand to help me up.

Each step we take chokes the width of the road, the possibility of retreat. This is not a road many people take, and to evidence this, around the next bend we're greeted with a sickening sight: a wooden trestle, rickety and ancient. It looks no sturdier than some jungle rope bridge. The river it crosses is so many hundreds of feet down that the boulders of the channel seem small and shadowy from here.

"We're crossing that?"

Ruth nods.

"It's not going to hold me." I'm only half joking. On one side of the bridge, the railing has been replaced as if a car making a speedy descent misjudged the curve and launched itself down onto the rocks below.

Ruth steps onto the bridge. She jumps up and down to demonstrate its sturdiness. This does little to assuage my fears. Ruth doesn't weigh anything. She's a feather of a woman compared to me and the baby. But Ruth crosses so I follow, and the bridge somehow holds us.

We pass the remains of an enormous blast furnace that looks like a terrifying castle. From there, around another bend, Ruth points and I see it up ahead. Through the trees, there's a lodge, strong and cold, built of stone on the shore of a lake. It could be the end. It looks magnificent enough. The wild beauty, pines and huge rocks, gives us pause. "Ruth," I say quietly, following her down an unkempt driveway. A stone portico covers the entrance. The house has a roof so peaked, it could contain a helicopter landing pad, opening up into the biggest lily in the world. A number of slates are missing.

"What is this place?"

But then Ruth doesn't stop at the house. This isn't the end. She leads me down to the lake. There's a small beach and a rotted dock. I stop at the water's edge. Ruth keeps going as if she could walk directly across the lake bottom and pop out the other side, as if she can't stop walking.

"Ruth!" My voice echoes back.

She's wet to her knees.

"What are you doing? Taking a swim?" So she stops, but she doesn't turn back to me. She stares into the water like she lost a ring under the surface and if she twists her face up just enough, she might be able to find it. "Ruth?"

When she finally turns, she's smiling. She points up to the house.

"Is this the place? Are we there?"

Yes, she nods.

"It's incredible. It's beautiful."

She agrees.

"Can we stay?"

She tilts her head to the left, shrugs.

"Can I see inside?"

She holds up a finger. One minute. She points back into the woods. Ruth tramps out of the lake.

"You want me to come?"

Plainly by now, clearly, Ruth doesn't answer. I follow her into the forest. She pushes pine boughs and briars with her bare hands, opening a path. She grabs prickers carefully, making a way for me through the woods. The trees are old. The trees are twisted by the unimaginable winter winds. Orange needles cover the ground. The mushroom El calls toad umbrella springs from the tree bark. Ruth's sneakers fart with lake water.

There are buildings in the woods. Small houses for a fairy population, an Adirondack summer camp. I count eight cottages each with window boxes and rhododendrons planted neatly out front. A number of goats graze nearby. Two women tend a vegetable garden where beans climb sunflower stalks. "Hi," I say as we pass. They both stand. One's hands are deformed. They look like claws. The other has the word "fukc" tattooed onto her cheek.

"Hi." They wave. Ruth keeps moving.

A man dressed in a pink prom gown, wearing bright blue cream eye shadow, has fallen asleep in the sun, comfortable in a chaise beside the garden. A cane and a pair of sunglasses have been left on another chair nearby. It's an Adirondack camp for circus freaks.

Among the cottages there's one singular home, a shell of the others. It's crusted with decay. Its wood is slipping back to humus and loam like it's the sacrificial unit that keeps the other cottages vital. Moss and mold bloom from what was once its roof, floors, walls. Ruth bypasses the restored cabins and heads directly for the abandoned one. Just outside its door, the rusted handle of a refrigerator lies on the ground underneath a sapling sprouted from the damp remains of a small rug. The house is ready to collapse, delicate as lacy leaf litter wintered over and over. Ruth pokes her head through one window. Slowly she nudges a foot through the door. I follow but crouch low, spreading my weight evenly as I can. We stand in what must have once been a living room. The workings of some gas fireplace have spilled out onto the floor, and there's a shred of wallpaper, a vine of green with purple violets clinging to one wall.

Ruth feels ahead with her foot before taking a step. She signals for me to stay put as she inches along, keeping to the joists, ducking through a collapsed jamb into the once kitchen. There are still a few human things here: a cast-iron sink and a small enamel stove, its name, *Magic Chef,* scripted in chrome. There's a hole in the kitchen floor big enough to lose a family through.

Dropping to her hands and knees, Ruth circumnavigates the hole, making her way to the Magic Chef. The oven screams when she pries open the hinged door. Ruth pokes her head inside the oven as if she could climb through to a different universe, as if pulling out a birthday cake. But it's not a cake. From the oven rack, Ruth removes a weathered cardboard box.

"What have you got there?"

The box flaps are closed. She jerks her chin back to where we came from, through the woods. Ruth and I keep on walking.

I thought the end would provide answers. "What's in the box?"

Nothing. We return to the big house, and on the front step she passes the box to me. I kink out one thigh and balance the box there on the side of my belly. The lid's not open enough to allow a peek inside, and, with both hands engaged in holding it, the contents remain a mystery.

Ruth rubs her hands on my cheeks, my ears, the baby. She hugs me despite the box. She's so happy to get here, smiling, laughing some. I've never seen her so happy. Beautiful, teenage Ruth dancing with Nat in El's kitchen all those years ago. The box smells of rot. Or else it's Ruth. She squeezes me tight, kisses my cheek, hand on the baby. She takes such good care of me.

Then Ruth lets me go.

She butts one shoulder against the front door, holding it open for me to enter first. The foyer tile has been ripped up in spots, and wood smoke has stained the hallway walls brown. There's sunlight and debris scattered on the floor, an ashtray, a clunky remote control, a Naugahyde jacket. The end.

I'm going to sit on a couch for two days, two weeks. I'm going to stare at the wall, take a bath, eat something I myself have cooked. I'm going to take a drive in one of the trucks parked in the driveway. I'm going to call El. We're here and it's over, and I can't even tell yet what that means because I'm empty. One last footstep shakes the sour, dried last bits of noise from my body. Empty but for the baby.

There's a stuffed moose head mounted to the wall. The rug in the foyer and the green curtains in the living room are worn reminders of the people who passed through here before. People like Ruth, others. People in bathing suits maybe or winter boots or grass skirts dressed for some skit night being held under lantern light down by the lakeside. All the masons and carpenters who built this place, working for years on a mountaintop far enough away from life that people forgot they were still alive. "What is this place?"

I turn back for Ruth's reaction, but she isn't there. "Hello?" I press my back against the living room wall, a moth on the bark of a mottled tree. The whites of my eyeballs beat left, right, left, right. My belly ruins my camouflage, and the box cuts into my hip. "Ruth?" I drop onto a dusty couch. I pry open the flaps.

Ruth's Walkman rests on top of more money than I have ever seen. The rotten stench intensifies and turns my stomach. I never thought all this walking would end with something as regular and disappointing as money.

Quickly, before she comes back, I put the headphones on my ears and push play. Nothing happens. Dead batteries.

I touch a stack of the bills. The money is soggy and limp, having given up any hope of being palmed into the hands of Mafioso bouncers at a discothèque. It's grown complacent, moldering in an abandoned house on a mountaintop.

Three windows look down to the lake. I don't see her outside, but I hear someone close the front door. A few blue jays screech. "Ruth?"

El keeps a photo from that New Year's Day so many years ago when Nat and Ruth came to visit. In the picture the four of us make a scraggly bunch, blurrier than memory. My mom has her arms around my neck. Ruth's head is turned to look at Nat. Nat stares into the camera.

For years I studied this photo, and my eye always went to him like mica. His hair. His muscle T-shirt, jeans, and a bandanna around his forehead. He looked kind in a spare, genuine way. He looked small but, even in the photo, mighty.

Ruth didn't come back for the money.

Nat squints as if I'll make more sense that way. I grip my belly and a sound like a snarl, *Invasion of the Body Snatchers,* comes from his throat. His hands are rough. His stubble is flecked with silver. "They said someone had come." He blinks, smiles. "You're Eleanor's daughter." His words land like pebbles on a pond, a satisfying sound to my unused eardrums. "Cora." He finds my name. "What are you doing here?"

"Ruth brought me."

"Ruth?" Then he says it again louder. "Ruth? She couldn't have." He shakes his head.

"Why not?"

His smile leaves. "Because Ruth is dead."

THE BOX IS NOT TOO HEAVY. Ruth carries it into the woods. Each branch of every tree is coated with snow. The sky is the same color white as the fathomless mountain below her. She stops halfway between Earth and the edge of the solar system, cold and warm, her mother and the end. *Voyager 1*? Check. *Voyager 2*? *Voyager 2*? Who is *Voyager 2*?

Ruth hides the money in a place no living soul would ever find it, and when she returns to the house, her toes have frozen to a pale larvae color. No one's in the living room. She drops the needle on Percy Sledge so that Mr. Bell, warming up a cup of tea, hears "Out of Left Field." He finds her. Her husband, legally, illegally.

"Mr. Bell," Ruth says, forgetting to leave off the *Mr.* And the formality of that name mixed with the informality of what she's imagining slows her breath.

"That didn't take you long," he says.

"No."

"Where's Nat?"

"He went out to start shoveling."

"But it's still snowing."

"I tried to tell him that." Mr. Bell takes her hand. "Are you busy, dear?" She follows him upstairs. The hallway's tall windows look down to the lake. Up here, far from the furnace, the rooms are chilly. Mr. Bell opens the door on another bedroom.

"It's freezing."

"All part of my plan."

There is a twin bed, a bureau, a window with a pink silk curtain.

What makes a home?

Take your hands in his. This plus this.

What makes the unsaid audible?

The distance between us.

Mr. Bell has power in his arms. Angles and tattoos she's never seen. He touches her face, the mess of it. He lifts her up. He lays her down, adoring her. Mr. Bell smells like the edge of a stream, and there, alone in a storm on a mountaintop, Ruth and Mr. Bell commit astonishing, if tiny, acts of gravity and attraction. They rest. They return to their fever. They rest and are troughed together in the sinkhole of the bed, swarmed by blankets, warmed by skin and how many long years it was before they knew each other, before it didn't have to hurt.

Ruth studies the bristles of his face and grows old with him, old as wood. Quiet and happy. On the ceiling above the bed, a leak has left behind a ripple of brown circles moving out from the center. His halo or the universe saying, I give this man just to you. I give you him wondrously, imperfectly made. Thunder and a night or a life by a fire with him in a warm home. The skin of his wrist. The leak's discoloration throbs and grows above them. Ruth considers her scar, her heart. He'll be inside her now forever. She counts the rings of the leak. Does each signify a year? A storm? And she's inside him. How long before love splits into two, cells dividing? *Voyager 1. Voyager 2.* Under the stain, Ruth holds tight to his back. The blob could beam them up to a waiting meteor. Her neck dips, infrared, ultraviolet, and when she rights her head, lifts this fog of love, *The Book of Ether* is sitting on top of the bureau no more than two feet away.

Ruth reaches for it. Her bare skin bristles outside the blankets.

Mr. Bell tucks his hair behind his ears. She brings the book back to the warm bed, legs in a diamond. The book opens in a bloom.

348 Dark unto you.
Dark over them.
Dark, dark, dark house where no one dares to go.
He hath set me in dark places, as they that be dead.

Ruth and Mr. Bell plow through bowls of ramen noodles in the kitchen. They speak in a hush. Nat still has not returned. "It has a strange way of making sense," Ruth whispers.

Mr. Bell nods. "The mis-arrangement of words suggests reincarnation. It suggests multiple, endless readings." He takes a bite, noodles dangling down his chin. "Not that I believe in that." He points to the last entry on the last page.

599 Shall
Shall I
Shall I come
Shall I come back
Shall I come back again?

"Elvis," he says. "We danced to it. Mardellion's forty-five had a skip that he interpreted as proof of his immortality."

"What do you think?"

"No way. Dirt to dirt. *One Life to Live.*"

Ruth winces.

"Why? What's wrong with that?" he asks. "Microbes. Bacteria. Worms underground that mingle our parts with everything. It's generous." He locks his fingers in hers. "And infinite." Mr. Bell squares his face to hers. "If you can get over the dreaded finite."

"Where's Nat?" she asks for the fifth time in one half-hour. "Is he clearing the whole road?" She pushes the remains of her meal across the table. "Maybe we'll be able to leave tonight. That would be good. Maybe we should go help him."

Mr. Bell checks the window again. Snow. Nothing else. "Yes, let's go help. Let's get out of here tonight if we can." Ruth carries her dish to the sink, and finally they hear footsteps in the living room. Ruth's so relieved. She lets out a long breath. "There he is." The kitchen door opens with certainty, pushed by a hand that knows it. "Nat," Ruth says, but she's wrong.

"No, dear. It's me." Holes far darker than a mountain lake. Ruth falls in. He opens his arms to her. "Welcome to my home," Zeke says. So Ruth knows for sure that there's nothing scary about dead people. It is the living who terrify.

Mr. Bell crumbles. "Mardellion." He names Zeke "Mardellion," which really somewhere some part of her brain already knew. "How did you get here?"

Zeke rubs his hands together. "That's a good story. A really good story. Care to hear it?"

They don't answer.

Zeke grabs the back of a chair but doesn't sit. He squeezes its top rung so tightly. He tells them anyway. "I met a friend of Ruth's down in Minerva. Ceph? He'd followed me all that way because he had it in his head, some crossed wire, that I was Ruth's husband and wouldn't believe me when I told him he had the wrong man." Zeke takes a seat, feeling very much at home. "Said he was coming to rescue Ruth. Take her away, take care of her. Poor guy."

Ruth's fingers jerk by her sides. "Ceph's here too?"

Zeke twitches his cheek as a horse's flank disturbs a fly. "No. Not anymore." An answer so vague, it's sinister. Darkness opens in the house.

Mr. Bell stands to shield Ruth, placing his body between theirs. "Ruth," Mr. Bell says as Zeke also stands, his awful head, Mardellion's terrible noseless face rises up, ripe, over Mr. Bell's. Moon leaves umbra.

"Run," Mr. Bell tells her. "Run. Run. Run."

Out the kitchen door into twilight. Ruth runs through the wet snow barefoot. She breathes air in leaden chunks. The snow has stopped. Ruth sees the Father's truck parked in the drive. There's no mistaking its huge, stupid tires, its flaming paint job. She takes off in the other direction, feeling her mind about to split. Things set in motion so many years ago. Ruth tramps though drifts so deep, her escape is in a dream, running without movement, making her slow-motion way down to the lake. The wind has swept its icy surface clear of snow, tracing paths across a surface that is solid in places, slurry in others. Ruth runs across the lake. Her bare feet flush with frozen pain.

132 Out of whose womb came the ice?

Ruth's flesh burns. The woods take little notice of her panic. Mr. Bell runs after her into the dusk light, out onto the lake, and Zeke follows behind both of them. He doesn't run but takes his righteous time in comfortable winter boots, rubber and fleece. The chase happens in silence as if one of them is imagining it.

Mr. Bell cuts off from Ruth's path, a decoy trail across the lake leading away from her. "Mardellion," he yells. "I'm over here."

A number of crows fly away and Ruth stops running. She's scared for Mr. Bell. The evening's quiet. Zeke's rolling gait looks like trouble, smiling in a proper snowsuit. The rough edge of his sinus cavity has caved in as though the hole will swallow his entire head. His face is collapsing.

"What happened to your nose?" Mr. Bell asks.

Zeke inserts a thumb into the crusted cavity, clearing dried sinus debris. Slowly as a television preacher, he smiles. "I let some light in." This makes Zeke laugh.

Pines click hoarfrosted branches. Ruth turns and flees again across the lake's slush and ice sharp as volcanic rock. Her bare feet are numb, the flesh raw. She swoops like an injured Sasquatch. As she nears the center of the lake, the surface jolts. The sound of the crack lashes deep into the woods and back again. A fault line lifts on the surface. Mr. Bell and Zeke brace themselves after the crack, arms out, knees bent low as surfers. Ruth runs for the other side.

"Whoa. Whoa," Zeke speaks like a cowboy, throwing up his hands in mock surrender. "You don't have to run from me. I don't want to hurt you."

She sloshes on. "Nat," she calls. "Nat?"

Zeke dislodges sputum from his bronchial tubes.

"Why are you doing this?" she asks.

"Why? The End's always coming. Right? You feel it?"

Ruth does feel something coming but can't say what. "No."

"Sure you do. Always have. Turning the last page, closing the book after a huge explosion destroys everything ever built. What do you think?"

"I think you're mentally ill," she manages.

"Some call it illness; I call it faith." He smiles broadly, strangely. "So after Carl here pointed out that your scar was a map of what's coming — comets, collisions — I thought you'd understand."

"No," Mr. Bell says. "No."

"Son, you're feeling bad about serving your wife up to me like a tasty piece of pie, but that doesn't mean you can just give her my money."

Sound travels so easily over the ice.

Ruth drops her chin. That's the weight. Once there were two spacecraft built and raised together. "What?"

"It hurts. I know." Zeke sounds pleased. "But Carl thought your scar could freshen up my followers. Rejuvenate the cause."

Mr. Bell takes his head in his hand. "I thought it might stop you from killing them all. Yes. I thought it might prevent mass murder."

"What?" she asks again.

"Your scar oddly resembles a map of all the meteorites we've got. Including Tahawus, mine, the great one to come. Kind of cosmic. Right?"

"My mother burned me with bleach," Ruth says.

Zeke snorts. He closes some of the distance between Ruth and himself. "Yeah. See, I know that now. Turns out there's nothing special about you."

"She's my wife." Mr. Bell looks up at her. "You are my wife, and I made a huge mistake when I told him about you. I didn't even know you yet. I'd seen you once, peeking through the curtain at the Father's house. I was desperate."

Zeke claps his hands. "He traded you for information about his mom. But he knew you weren't worth much, so he trumped up your value. Made up some BS about a map on your face, blah, blah. 'Gilding the granite' we call it."

Ruth watches Mr. Bell.

"A junk rock from a motel parking lot. Right, son?" Zeke laughs, nods. "I can't believe I fell for it, Carl. A moment of weakness. I forgot you're an expert con man."

Mr. Bell is squatting in the ice, ruined. "I didn't know you, Ruth, and I was desperate to find my mom. I didn't know he'd come for you the way he did. I should have never seen him again, but I'm trying to undo this mess. I'm trying to fix it."

"By bringing me to his house?"

Mr. Bell looks at her.

"You gave us the money to undo your betrayal?"

"Steady on," Zeke interrupts. "That's my money and I've come to get it."

"It's as much mine as it is yours," Mr. Bell says.

"'Cause your mother stole it from me?"

"You stole it from the Etherists. It's been in your house for years, and you were too thick to find it. All that time I was gone, it was sitting in the pantry with the toilet paper. I never came for it because I figured you'd found it years ago. I didn't even know it was still 'lost' until Ruth told me."

She walks away from both men. "Nat!" Her call bounces across the lake's surface.

"It's Ruth's money now," Mr. Bell adds.

"Afraid not, son." Zeke notices her flight. "I need you to come back, Ruth, and show me where you put it."

But she doesn't come back. She keeps heading to the far side.

Zeke snickers through a thin, diseased beard. "I really need you to stop now," and from the hollow of his back, as if scratching an itch, Zeke produces the tool of a coward and a cheat.

"What?" Mr. Bell greets the gun.

"Belonged to Ceph." Zeke holds it loosely, like it's a harmless tract he wants them to read, something to guide their steps in a brotherly gesture of friendship. "He"—Zeke coughs—"umm, gave it to me. In so many words." Zeke cracks a creepy smile.

"Don't," Mr. Bell says. "Don't—" But Zeke fires the gun into the trees past Ruth, forcing an unfair end to a slow race. Ruth stops, focused as a magnet now, rattling in the waves of that much sound. The three of them make an irregular triangle around a hot center. She bounces from bare foot to bare foot.

Zeke brushes hair from his cheek using the gun's barrel to do it, clipping his ear with the steel sight. He lifts his chin, trying to strike a less horrifying profile. "Hi." Zeke snickers, having captured her attention, gun still pointed in her general direction. "What'd you do with my money?"

"Why do you want the money?" Mr. Bell asks. "You can't take it with you wherever you're going." Mr. Bell waves his fingers up into the sky.

Zeke looks up, stroking his thin chin hairs, as if the stars are his cohorts. "I'm not going anywhere." His chin still lifted.

Ruth and Mr. Bell follow his gaze. Lots of frozen stars.

"You're just going to dispose of the others?" Mr. Bell asks. "Blow 'em up?"

"You chose an unfortunate time to return. They'll be here soon as this storm ends. And they're ready to go. Trust me. They don't even care that I'm not going with them. They want any excuse to get out of their miserable lives as soon as they can."

Ruth lifts her hands to her eyes, presses hard. "You killed Ceph?" she asks.

"About that," Zeke says. The gun barrel does a loop-de-loop, rolling, unraveling. "What can it mean? The whole thing based on a mistake? A mishearing or misunderstanding, right? He was trying to kill me. Really, he was trying to kill you, Carl. He just didn't know it." Zeke smiles. "You should be thanking me. I saved your life."

So Ruth turns and starts across the ice again, away from both of them. "OK. Stop now," Zeke says.

But she doesn't stop.

"Ruth. Stop." Zeke's voice is sharp, as if she's pulling blood from his body, tiny red threads dragged out of him across the white ice. The frozen lake crunches under her numb feet. She can't feel them anymore. Zeke's face goes blank. He points the gun and fires for the third time today, and even before the noise washes through Ruth's ears, she's turned back. Mr. Bell's blood strikes a pattern on the ice behind him, that of an exploding firework. His body canters, falling centered on the spectacle of red, redder still for the purity of the snow.

Zeke holds the gun at the end of his extended arm, a weak branch, a heavy rotted fruit.

The lake is silent. Pluto continues to exist, and Mr. Bell absorbs all that quiet through his open wound.

[illegible] hairs, as if the stars are his [illegible] still lifted.

[illegible] of frozen stars.

[illegible]' Mr Bell asks, 'How [illegible]

[illegible] They'll be here soon [illegible] Trusting. They don't [illegible] they want any exit, [illegible]

[illegible] [illegible]care. 'You killed [illegible]?'

[illegible] [illegible] does a loop-de-loop, [illegible] whole thing based on [illegible] thing right. He was trying [illegible] He just didn't know [illegible] I saved your life. [illegible] again, 'we, I mean' [illegible]

[illegible] putting blood back [illegible] across the white [illegible] She can't feel [illegible] his fingers and toes, for the [illegible] washes through, [illegible] a pattern on the [illegible] His body curls, [illegible] call for the pack of [illegible]

[illegible] extended arm, a [illegible]

[illegible] and Mr Bell [illegible]

[illegible]

NAT'S DRESSED AS the guilty caretaker in a mystery for kids, the guy at the end who's unmasked as the villain and you knew he was guilty the whole time. Then Nat moves and his body is golden wheat in a blue wind, disciplined and heroic as an oversaturated Western, an approximation of what America looked like when it was young. Not a villain at all.

The house is quiet, huge. There are dusty rugs, a chandelier of antlers and cobwebs overhead, throw blankets, and a case of books that's sat untouched for so long, the covers have grown together. I'm nervous as a jackrabbit. "Ruth isn't dead," I tell him.

"How'd you get here?"

"We walked."

"Who brought you? Who knew the way?"

To say it again is embarrassing. "Ruth brought me."

He squints into my left temple. "Ruth isn't dead?"

"No."

"What the fuck?" He's calm. "How?"

"How is she not dead?"

He fixes his gaze. "How'd you get here?"

"We walked from my mom's."

He points to my belly. "You walked?"

"Yeah."

"So you're not dead?" The absurdity of the question even makes Nat smile.

"What are you talking about?"

"Sorry." He hides his hands in his pockets. "You grew up, Cora."

I nod.

"You're pregnant."

"I am."

"So she's here and she's not dead?" He sets his jaw with anger. "Where is she?" He slams into the kitchen, getting angrier each time he moves.

"She's just out—"

"What did she tell you?" Nat turns back, postpones seeing her.

"— side. She didn't tell me anything. She doesn't talk. When was the last time you saw her?"

He thumbs his chin. "Last time I saw Ruth was here." Nat grabs the back of his neck and ducks into it. "Right before she and her husband stole all our money and left me alone up here in the dead of winter." Each of his words is hand-carved, sharp.

The muscles in my abdomen squeeze a moment before letting go. "She didn't tell me that. She doesn't talk."

He leans on a windowsill, back to the water. He resets his face. "The morning we were supposed to leave, I woke up early because we had to shovel our way out of the snow. They were already gone."

"Ruth has a husband?"

"Last time I saw her she did. I don't know now. It's been fourteen years."

"Long time."

"Yeah. A really long time. We'd taken care of each other since we were five years old, so I kept thinking she'll come back. She has to come back, but she never did. Eventually I convinced myself that she must be dead." Nat's teeth are set like pointed sticks around a fort. Five thousand one hundred and seven days behind his molars. "Now you're saying she's not."

"Well." I'm getting less sure every minute. "Why else would she leave you here alone?"

Nat lowers his hand with a fast swat. Dust swims in sunlight. "Maybe she was mad. We used to play a game, talk to dead people. She found out I was faking it, and to her that meant everything was fake. There was no God, no magic, and we could have used some magic. Except we found a big box of money and that *was* magic. Everything hard about our childhood was about to quit. We were going to be OK. Then she and Mr. Bell disappeared with the money."

"This money?" I jerk the cardboard box.

Nat looks from me to the box, from me to the box. He flips back the flaps and stares inside. Blocks of information get rearranged in his head until some of the blocks no longer fit. "Where'd you get this?" He drives his thumbs into his chin.

"In that old cottage. The one that's falling down." I point to the woods.

"Ruth's. I never fixed it up because she never came back."

"You never even looked for the money?"

"Why would I? If she wasn't cutting me out of the cash, why else would she leave without me?"

Nat and I meet eyes. It doesn't sound like something Ruth would do. Certain ideas creep in between us, a clock hand's ticking forward. I interrupt the ideas by talking. "Well. She's back now."

"But how is she back?" Nat taps his forehead, banging an old engine to make it start.

I don't have a good answer.

Nat sucks something, air, back into his mouth. "That first winter without her —" He's not sure how to describe it. "It's even lonely here when the trees have leaves and no snow blocks the road. Even with other people around." He grabs his wrist. "She said we were sisters, even closer. So I waited a year. I waited the next year and the next." He looks up. With his face like that, I can imagine the skull under his skin. "Eventually, I couldn't be angry at her anymore. It was killing me. I came to think she was dead."

"She's not." But the more times I tell him that, the less certain it seems. His logic follows better. He's thought about it longer. "I mean, I think she's not."

"So she just left me?" He pushes his pointer and thumb through his eyebrows, ironing a wrinkled sheet.

"No." I can't believe that either. "Maybe she can explain."

"I thought she didn't talk."

My body seizes again.

"Do you need anything? Some water? Tea?"

"That'd be good."

"Come." He pulls me off the couch with one hand. He smiles when he sees my belly upright. "Man," he says. "Man, oh, man."

The kitchen is enormous. Sliding brass cabinet latches, bead board, stained pine shelves. The kitchen's a mess. There's a heavy table covered with dishes and boxes of cold cereals. Juice containers, bean cans. Three sinks are filled with hardened dishes. Something's happening inside my body.

Nat uses an arm to clear two spots at the table for us, sweeping silverware, an empty cracker box, and a round paper canister of salt aside.

"Not much of a housekeeper?"

He rinses two mugs at the sink. Steam from the tap surrounds him. "Not my house. I stay out in the woods." He pulls a kettle off the floor. He finds tea bags in a tin canister, smells them, plops them into the mugs.

"Whose house is it?"

"Guy named Mardellion. I never met him."

"What kind of name is that?"

"Crazy name, crazy guy from what I understand. He was a cult leader who wanted a massive meteor to land on this house."

"Why?"

"Turn his followers back to stardust so they could fly off to outer space and he wouldn't have to take care of them anymore."

"What happened to him?"

"I don't know. I've been here a long time and he's never shown up." Nat pushes an empty box of rice onto the floor. "Neither did his meteor for that matter." The kettle rattles over the flame. Nat shuts the burner down.

I fold my hands across the baby. "Why are you here?"

"How can I leave without her? What if she came back?"

I tilt my head.

"Didn't she tell you anything?" He looks at me. "All right. All right. She doesn't talk." Nat pours the hot water, looks scalded. "I fixed up those old houses. I run a shelter for kids who age out."

"Nice." I think of El again. "That's really nice."

Nat rests elbows on the table. "Not always. Sometimes we're hungry. Sometimes there's fighting. Drugs. Not enough money. It's hard to escape where we came from. Even all the way up here." His eyes cross their sockets slowly, loaded tankers on a tight river. "Still it's better than a lot of other options. I'm sure your mom's told you."

"Yes."

"She did all right by you though, huh?"

"Yes. She did."

One of the boxes of cereal on the table tips itself over and pours its contents onto the floor like punctuation, a short symphony of grain meeting linoleum. Nat looks at the mess. The tea tastes like metal. Dust motes continue to hang in the late sunlight. Nat picks dirt from under a bitten nail. "You're here for me?"

"I think so."

"I'm glad to see you." He looks at me like no one ever told him not to stare. "What about you? What's your life been so far?"

My mouth makes a nervous click because all the easy answers to Nat's question read like an Internet search of my name and feel just as shallow: insurance adjuster, Daisy girl, honor student. I study the floor pattern, the grain of wood on the table. I think of other tables, other kitchens, and people who have sat across from me. "So far I've been a daughter. Not always a good one. And I'm a really good walker."

"And soon a mom."

"Yeah."

"How's El?"

"I need my mom," I tell him. "In fact, I really need her. Do you have a phone?"

"I do but the reception's horrible here. Sometimes it works up in the temple."

"The temple?" My stomach grips. The tightness steals my breath.

"Yup. Come on."

I follow Nat up a large center stair. It feels familiar, like following Ruth only now I'm on my way back to El. Velocity equals gravity at last. I had to gain some weight and distance before I could fall back to her. The upstairs hall is a long passage lined with closed doors and dark wood. My head itches with filth. My oily jeans and greasy socks are a carapace so worn, they'd hold their shape if I disrobed. They'd wait like a horse attending its rider, bucking and breathing, hoofing the ground. Good horse carried me so far. I grab the wall. The tightness passes through my middle again.

Nat turns to see if I'm all right. The shape of his shoulders, the cut of his uneven hair, applies more pressure on my lungs. I used to think Nat was so much older than me because we were kids. Now there's barely any difference. "How old are you?" I ask.

"Thirty-one."

"Funny a kid like me can catch up to you. I'm already twenty-five."

Nat stares at my belly. "I've never seen anything like that. It's weird."

"It's really weird."

"Can I?" He extends a hand.

"Everybody else does."

Nat steps up, puts his left hand on one side, his right hand on the other, making a closed circuit, a conduit for electricity so the baby can study its fingers by Nat's light. "I didn't think it would be so hard," he says. Having stepped into a form, dirt basic and fiery, we stay that way. Two bodies, three, in a shape older than geometry and all this blood between us.

I knew there was going to be something big at the end.

"I'm glad you're here," he says.

The temple is white, huge, smooth, rounded, and I've never seen anything like it. We're inside a tremendous egg. The ceiling soars high overhead. Below, tucked in a corner, is a sorry-looking command center: a small color television with coat hanger bunny ears and an ancient Coleco Adam Module #3 computer. "What is this place?"

Nat smiles. He tunes into his phone. "Let me see if I can get this to work."

I haven't seen a computer in a long time. Feels like running into an ex-boyfriend. I pull on the TV's knob, some daytime talk show in the static. Its hum sounds like a hive of yellow jackets, like everything I lost on the road is swarming, trying to flow back into me—Lord, Single Premium Immediate Annuity 1035 Exchange Request Forms, anti-aging creams, a movie starring John Travolta I once watched in a friend's basement rec room, the World Wide Web. I switch the set off quickly. I shift the mouse and am surprised when the old computer springs to life. A pale blue dot flashes, waiting. "This computer works."

Nat nods. He holds the phone in front of his waist as one might a flashlight. He paces the temple, searching for a connection.

My stomach muscles grab the baby and squeeze with everything they've got. Pale blue dot. I'm having a baby. The cursor blinks onscreen. I close my eyes, but it doesn't help. The computer's cursor blinks all the time now, wherever I go. The contraction releases, but the cursor's still waiting for me to ask something. What do you want to search for?

Nat's looking for a signal.

What do you want to search for?

Nat curses the phone.

My stomach grips hard. I really want my mom. The cursor's blink accelerates. Sweat forms on my brow. "Anything?" I ask Nat. I really want to find my mom. The contraction lets me go again.

"I can't even get one bar."

A portable record player, a high-design relic from the late '60s, is perched on a small white dais. A record waits to be spun. I drop the needle to the first track on an amber-colored album, a golden record. Chuck Berry's guitar, a switchblade, slices the air. Nat looks up and smiles. He closes the phone. "Never ever learned to read or write so well. Play the guitar. Ringing a bell. Go. Go. Go." The music is tinny and blaring through the small speaker. "Ringing a bell." Something inside me writhes. "Go, Johnny, go." The Jerk, the Pony, the Watusi. I angle my fingers as if lightning is streaming from their tips. A sound escapes from deep inside, a moan.

"You OK?" He puts a hand on the small of my back and one under my arm.

A contraction that stops the world again, this pale blue dot. What do you want to search for? My mom. I hold still. The record continues to spin. And Ruth. Where's Ruth? I look beyond the white ceiling wondering what did I hope for here at the end? Did I want the mystery solved? Or did I just want to know that the mystery has no end? And where, where, where is Ruth?

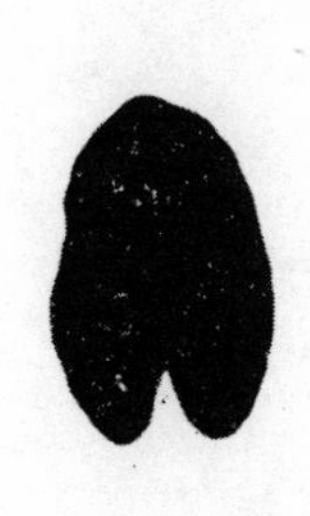

HE PUSHES UP TO SITTING. "Ouch." Mr. Bell grabs his arm. Blood darkens his sleeve. "That's a bit sore, Mardellion. And not entirely fair." The tiny bombs that parents bury under their child's skin take years to explode.

Zeke aims again.

"No!" Ruth screams. "No."

Mr. Bell breathes heavily. "Run, Ruth. Get out of here. What's he going to do? Shoot his own son?"

"I just did."

"Step onto the shore," Ruth tells Zeke. "Let me attend to him first, and then I'll get your money."

"What freaking tenderness." Zeke smiles. "You're lucky, Carl. '337 A solid house and wealth comes from your parents but a prudent wife comes from above.'" As if numbering the verses makes them unchangeable, unquestionable plotted points on a map, meteorites that land along the shores of a canal, instead of random rocks, mistakes, and drunken mothers, winding up wherever they choose. Zeke waves Ceph's gun up to the sky, one finger in the trigger guard. He lifts his empty palm with a crooked arm, a mockery of surrender. He backs his way onto the shore.

Ruth goes to Mr. Bell. She inspects the wound, imagining she'll look through his body straight into the lake and all the way down, one thousand feet in dark liquid. His blood makes a mist in the cold air. "Are you OK?"

"I'm so sorry." Mr. Bell breathes heavily. "Believe me. Please."

She ministers to him. Her mouth is open. "Shh." She swabs blood with her shirt and some spit, some of the freezing lake slush.

"Believe me," he says again.

She strokes his face. "I think I'm done believing." Ruth sits on the ice, cross-legged, freezing, wasted. She drops her arms open so Mr. Bell can rest in her lap. "Come," she pulls his head into the cradle of her legs, and there she curves her body over to protect him, looking to the darkness between them. She sees stars. She sees Nat. She sees Mr. Splitfoot. Help us, she asks them all, asks them hard. Help us, Nat. Her shoulders curl. She covers Mr. Bell with what she feels, grave love, a synapse. He is hers. He breathes into her damply, through her, as if they could fall into one another. The lake takes on the heat between them, between the distant planets. Steam and stew. You, it says, and you, activating a crack as swift as any gunshot, as swift as, say, a meteor that traveled across time and space to crash into this remote, accidental mountaintop lake in the Adirondacks. The ice opens up. The lake swallows two humans in love without knowing or caring, loathing judgment if the lake could loathe, if the lake could judge.

Underwater Ruth's lungs despise the cold. They spasm. She screams for Nat to help her, but something happens to sound underwater.

If Zeke, alone now, stunned far further than stupid, calls for them, pleads mercy, they don't hear it. If he drives the Father's absurd truck like a blind maniac down the twisted, snow-covered road, crossing the river chasm or maybe plunging into it, they don't hear because under the water the sky is ice, darkening with their descent blue to black and places beyond.

Mr. Bell holds her in his good arm, fighting for the surface using all the life he has inside to continue living. And Ruth holds Mr. Bell. They fall. The water is frigid and Ruth never could swim. Down, down, his boots, her hair tangled in his. The deepest lake in the Adirondacks is made by men and full of enough mystery to betray all humankind. There's water in their lungs. Mr. Bell holds her now and afterward. There's water in their ears and a voice warm as a mother's should be. They fall toward the voice, through the deepest lake in the Adirondacks. "When you were a baby," the voice says, "you used to point at birds." The gesture of their hands entwined, reaching up through their descent, clawing for the disappearing surface, could be misconstrued as fingers pointing out a goldfinch on a branch, a red cardinal nosing the grass for some seeds.

Later that night the lake freezes, sealing the scar under a dusting of snow.

Later still, days, maybe weeks, two crows fly past without even stopping. They were living. They are dead. We will change them into cedars. We know that this is impossible.

IT'S A SHORT SONG. Chuck Berry finishes and the contraction releases me.

"Time to go," Nat says.

"Where?"

"Whatever you want, Cora. A movie? A baby?" Nat helps me move slowly down the attic stairs, down the main stairs. He speaks softly in my ear. "It's going to be fine. A healthy, beautiful baby."

Nat is the first person to tell me that. He holds my hand. He grabs the box of money and car keys. He carries the box with us as if it were the suitcase he and I had carefully packed and planned for over nine months, nine years, ninety decades, and life, happy, happy life, is about to begin for us here on Earth.

Upstairs the golden record is still spinning, sending messages off to Mars, to M82, M87, and the Magellanic Bridge.

I readjust my grip on Nat, braiding our fingers. "Ready?" he asks again.

"Yeah."

We step outside and there she is. Standing by the edge of the lake, Ruth looks out across the water, her long dark hair.

"Ruth," he calls, and she turns. Nat sees her again, his sister. All the years he thought Ruth was dead. Now he knows she is because she lifts one hand to us, a wave hello, goodbye, gentle, like a window thrown open onto everything kind and good that Ruth always was.

Her other hand holds a box, the same box Nat is holding, weathered old cardboard. Her box is a twin, a sister, only hers is empty now. She smiles, so pleased to see Nat and me together at the end. She lifts the sun off the water, all of it. She gives Nat the things they once had to share, breath, life. She doesn't need those things anymore.

"Ruth," I call, as if I could stop her now, keep her here for myself. She smiles and her raised hand strikes a blinding flash, a brilliant light, bright enough to fool us into thinking it's a trick of the sun off the water. In that flash we lose sight of her for a moment, and when we see her again, Ruth is walking into the lake, returning to the water forever this time. She starts death again at the place where she died, this highest lake that runs down so many mountains into so many streams and rivers and seas, the great network, the water that brings her back to us. The box Ruth holds fills with the deepest lake in the Adirondacks.

"Ruth," Nat says again, but the flash clears and Ruth is gone back to Bell and the lovely depths, delighted by every star twinkling around her. Ruth was living. Ruth was gone. Ruth came back because she loved us. We make our way down to the shoreline. The hoodie Ruth borrowed from me so long ago, a world away, is on the sand of the bank, half buried, half in the water, because every story is a ghost story, even mine. Tiny waves rock the shore. We stare out at the place where Ruth disappeared, and in the lake I see the underwater path, the barely road of stones and bones the dead sometimes follow.

Something is happening inside. I kneel in the shallow water, splashing Ruth onto this child as if I might collect all of her, a book of everything. Twenty-six letters, twenty-three pairs of chromosomes, one hundred eighteen elements so far. I splash the water onto my baby. I collect this world. "Hello," the record says upstairs. "Hello from the children of planet Earth. Hello. Hello?" The beats and static, the clicks and clacks of a woman thinking hard about falling in love across space and time, across death. The way a mother whispers to her child. The way an old man sings, a record of lives lived. Nat holds on to me, kneels beside me. The Earth moves a thousand, a million miles per hour through space. "Cora," he says my name. We look out at the deep lake long enough for me to see what it took a journey to see. Ruth came back because the living need the dead. My belly squeezes. Nat tightens his fingers in mine, and for now I sweat human things, mysterious human things I don't understand. I feel her go. I feel what I don't even believe in: astonishing eyeballs, fearful symmetries, fingernails, ghosts, babies. I feel this life about to begin, this little girl, this little boy. Hello. Hello. Hello.

Acknowledgments

With grateful acknowledgement to the intelligent and loving women who helped take care of my children while I wrote this book: Virginia Mendez, Cindy Kubik, and Norma Borgen. Thank you, PJ Mark and Jenna Johnson for your encouragement and wisdom. Thank you to Bard College, Pratt Institute, the MacDowell Colony, and the Peter S. Reed Foundation. Thank you, all Hunts and Hagans. TLA, Rosa, Marie, Juliet, and Joe.